Scar of the
Bamboo Leaf

D1616974

SIENI A.M.

ISBN-10: 1500458384

ISBN-13: 978-1500458386

PROLOGUE

December 2002

Pain exploded in his jaw as his head snapped back from the force of the blow. Damn. He didn't see that left hook. Wiping blood from his lip with the back of his hand, Ry straightened and glared in the direction of his opponent. Dax breathed harshly as blood dripped from his nose, the sharp smell and metallic taste flooding his senses. He looked as bad as Ry felt. The side of his stomach was killing him but he pushed past it.

"Come on, you dirty Arab, what you got?" Dax spat on the ground, sneering. "Your dad one of those guys, huh? The ones that flew those planes?"

Ry felt the swell of anger at the demeaning slur, the insinuation that he had anything to do with what happened on 9/11 caused anger to swell inside him. The roaring sounds of students crowding the courtyard, pushing and shoving, encouraged them, and he knew it wouldn't be long before teachers were alerted to the fight. His head was dizzy but he shook it off. He wanted to finish this, and he wanted to be the one to throw the final punch.

"Where is he?" Dax taunted.

"Stop this, Ry! Dax, please!" a familiar voice pleaded from the perimeter of the crowd.

Ry ignored his stepsister and lunged for Dax, taking him by surprise and knocking him to the ground. For a big guy, he didn't go down easy, but Ry was leaner and quicker on his feet, and his mind was a red haze, clouded with rage. He straddled him, hurling punches into his face and gut. *Boom! Boom!* Dax grunted and strained and bucked underneath, throwing him off slightly, but Ry's fury kept him firmly rooted as he

1

landed blow after blow to Dax's face and chest. He mulled over each one of Dax's transgressions in his mind, fuelling his temper and powering his fists as a result. The slashed tires and racial slur spray painted on the windows of his truck was the final straw.

"Yo, yo teachers! Teachers!" The panicked murmurs warned Ry to stop, and his mind focused back on the semi-conscious body under his weight, the lust for violence seeping from his bones. Dax curled onto his side, groaning quietly, his face camouflaged in blood. Ry shook his head to clear the furor and took a few shaky breaths before he was yanked from behind, his hoodie stretching against his neck almost choking him until he landed on the concrete ground.

"Enough! Get off him!" Mr. Tanner's voice bellowed from above.

The crowd thickened with a frenzy of noise while Dax remained unmoving on the ground. Mr. Tanner yelled for the school nurse and an ambulance was called. Ry's heart raced as he turned away from the blood. His head spun and he wanted to throw up. *Run! Escape!* his mind screamed, but his movements were jerky and sluggish. He didn't see the security guard pick him up from behind and shove him toward the school office. Grimacing from the pain in his stomach, he hoped it wasn't a cracked rib. His head throbbed with the echoes of the ambulance siren.

"You really did it this time, Ryler," the guard mumbled behind him. Shoving him down onto a bench, he growled, "Wait here."

His mother arrived soon after with worry lines marring her pretty face, and his stepfather followed closely behind, concern etched around his mouth. Anna and Tom Montgomery were a well-known and respected couple in their small community. Anna was a homeopathist working from a room she'd converted into an office in their three-story home, and she had been trying for months to shove remedies at Ry. In the beginning, he had obliged her preparations—everything from aconite for restlessness to arnica for aches and pains—but now he was exasperated with her trying to "fix him" and dodged her ministrations. His stepfather was a corporate attorney and a partner in a firm in New Haven, and the long journey to and from work afforded him little time at home. Ry slouched a little lower on the bench outside of the school office and dreaded his punishment.

Ten minutes passed. Twenty. While his parents met with the principal behind closed doors, Ry willed away the image of Dax's lifeless body on the ground and preoccupied himself instead with thoughts of his punishment. Grounded for a month? His truck keys confiscated? At worst, he suspected another suspension from school. A few days away from this hell wouldn't be so bad, he concluded.

His stepfather strode out first, his face strained with tension. He shook hands with the principal and they exchanged a few words, and Ry caught some in between … "badly broken" … "won't be pressing charges"… "won't happen again." He caught his mother's eyes, the corners of her mouth tilted into a dismal smile, and wondered what had been said.

They drove home in thick silence, the quiet unsettling and keeping Ry on edge. While he braced himself to be reprimanded as soon as they were tucked in the safe confines of the car, he didn't expect for them to not speak a word, not to each other, not to him. Reaching the house, he waited until they were inside for the brutal lecture to begin, but nothing came.

"Get yourself cleaned up and then we'll talk," his stepfather ordered in the same voice Ry imagined him using in court.

Ry climbed the stairs to his room and locked the door. Shrugging out of his leather jacket and toeing off his boots, he slumped down on his bed and closed his eyes. Now that he was still, he was more keenly aware that every inch of his torso ached, as if he had just been thrown into a meat grinder. He didn't want to imagine how Dax was feeling.

Reaching for the Discman on his bedside table, Ry put on the headphones and cranked up a song about being a question to the world and how it could expect him to change when it remained the same. He felt the lyrics sink down into his bones, the thrum of the melody thumping in his ears and spreading through his bloodstream, spurring on some of the leftover adrenaline from the fight. His heart raced in tandem to the beat while his mind drifted to the past twelve months. He didn't fit in. He never had. They didn't understand. Every circle he seemed to move around in attracted trouble. Or trouble attracted him. He was half Arab, living in a town where he was in the minority, and the townsfolk never let him forget it. There were the typical labels and racial slurs disguised as jokes that were expected to be laughed off, but once in a while it went too far and he fought it. His fists made him feel like he was in control when he felt like he had none, and girls seemed to dig that. Not that he gave them any particular attention, but he saw the way they looked at him, their eyes roving him up and down before they rested on the tattoo inked on the inside of his forearm.

He didn't know how long he was asleep when the pounding on his door woke him up. His CD player tinkered away with a song, and the headphones had loosened and were lying on his pillow. He noticed soft light from the street lamps pouring through the slits in the curtains.

"Ryler!" His stepfather's voice bellowed on the other end. "Open the door!"

Groaning, he slid off his bed and opened the door a crack. Tom perused his son's swollen lip and disheveled hair with disapproval.

"Get cleaned up and come downstairs. Your mother's waiting." He turned and stormed away in his business attire.

Ry lowered his eyes and hauled himself to the bathroom at the end of the hallway. Skye, his stepsister, braced herself against her bedroom door, worrying her bottom lip, eyes soft, as he walked past ignoring her.

"I heard what Dax said to you, Ry," she said lightly. "That wasn't right."

Ry faltered a step but continued down the hall, shutting his stepsister out with the close of the bathroom door.

Cold water stung the cracks on his hands and face. He looked up at his reflection in the mirror and frowned. God, he looked like crap. There was a cut above his eyebrow and left cheek, and his bottom lip was swollen to twice its size. At least Dax didn't get the nose or eyes. A broken nose hurt like a mother, and a black eye was just damn ugly.

He squinted at his reflection.

He didn't look like any of them ... not his mother, his stepfather, or stepsister. Not the whole damn town. The differences ran deeper than blood, and Dax's taunts came back to him and flooded his head. He pushed them away and fled the bathroom.

He smelled his mother's cooking when he descended the stairs. The open living plan unfortunately didn't afford him privacy to sneak down without notice. His stepfather lounged in his usual leather arm chair, and he flicked his eyes up from a business magazine, meeting Ry's dark eyes for a heartbeat before continuing reading.

They ate mostly in silence. Ry sat back and stole glances at his parents, but they seemed to be focused intently on their food. The atmosphere was thick with something Ry couldn't work out. So far, there had been no word about the fight, and he was starting to get a little suspicious. Between pushing pasta around on his plate, he watched his mother bite her bottom lip and avoid his eyes. What was going on?

When the table was cleared and the whir of the dishwasher sounded, Ry started for the stairs when Tom stopped him.

"Ryler." Ry half turned and looked at him as his stepfather gestured to the sofa. "Sit."

He slumped down on the leather chair and tried not to wince from the ache in his abdomen. His stepfather remained standing, his mother sitting opposite him. Skye had long ago disappeared to her room. Silent

4

contemplation hung in the air for several minutes before Ry raised his eyebrows at them.

"You almost killed that kid today," Tom started. "This is the third fight you've gotten into in a month, not to mention the other ones outside of school hours." His gray eyes bore down on him. "You're not going back to school."

Ry's heart started to race as he leaned back a little unsteadily on the sofa. "How long is my suspension for this time?"

"It's indefinite." Ignoring the pain in his gut, Ry sat up slowly in alarm as Tom continued, "We talked to the principal and came to an agreement. You won't be graduating this summer, at least not from this school. You've been expelled, Ryler."

Ry's head began to spin. "What are you talking about?"

His stepfather tossed down a stack of printed papers on the coffee table, and Ry's eyes followed the movement. "What's that?"

His mother spoke up. "Tom, maybe we should have this talk in the morning when we've had time—"

"No, Anna," he cut in. "This intervention will take place right now. This has gone on for too long."

"What are you talking about?" Ry demanded again. He pointed to the stack of papers. "What is that?"

Tom looked at his stepson, unblinking. "That's information on the new school you'll be attending … in Samoa."

Ry's brows slashed downwards. "Sa-what? Where the hell is that?" He looked at his stepfather's hardened face, the muscle in his jaw locked in tension.

"It's a country in the South Pacific."

Ry felt as if he'd been punched again. *"What?"* He ignored the burn in his torso and leaned over, snatching the papers off the table. The title at the top of the page screamed at him in bold. **Toa Boys' Academy: A Quality Life for Your Teenage Son**. What the hell? Was this some kind of twisted joke? Ry caught glimpses of other words typed neatly on the document: *treatment, difficult son, cusp of adulthood, lost his way, therapy*. His hands shook and anger started low in his chest and spread up his neck to his eyes until they narrowed into slits.

His voice was quiet, menacing. "You're sending me away? To some rehabilitation center in a far-off, God knows where the hell it is place?" He slammed his fist into the armchair. "You can't make me go!" Ry threw the papers down on the carpeted floor.

Tom's voice was eerily calm. "We can and we will. If you don't go, Dax's parents will have no problem pressing charges. The choice is

Samoa or an assault charge hanging over your head for the rest of your life." Ry's fists clenched until his fingernails dug into his palms. "It's already been taken care of. You leave next week for ten months."

"What?" His breath came out in choppy bursts, his heart thundering in his chest. He looked between his stepfather and mother before settling his eyes on her. His voice lowered, "Mom, you can't do this. Don't let him do this."

"Ryler," she started calmly, "we believe a change in scenery will be good for you. We think it's best for you to get away from here for a little while. I know it's been hard for you lately, but I won't sit back and watch you destroy your life. Think of this as an opportunity. You need to be surrounded by people who can help you. The people we've been in touch with at the school are wonderful and capable, and you'll be able to complete your senior year there."

Ry's hands shot up to encircle his head. "No, no, no."

His mother continued over his muttering. "It's not a detention center … think of it as a kind of boarding school."

"Boarding school? What—for messed-up kids like me?" He cursed under his breath and ran a hand over his face. "Is that what you're saying? That I'm unstable and crazy enough to be sent away? Mom, I know I messed up, but this … this is like a prison sentence."

"It's not a prison," Tom said evenly. "This place is for teenage boys, like you, who need direction in their lives. Your mother and I have done all we can to help you, discipline you, to set you straight, but it's not working, Son." He cleared his throat. "Look, I get it. Things have been tough for you especially in the past year, but no matter what we say or do, you go back out there and you fight again and again. You're spiraling out of control, Ry, and one of these days we won't be able to save you. It could get so bad that there won't be anything your mother or I can do to help you. That kid you fought today, you beat him up real bad." He reached down for the papers and picked one off the floor. "We assured his parents and the principal that we'll take care of it, and we will … with this new school. It's all set."

Ry lowered his eyes. "You had this all planned out, didn't you?"

"We found out about this place a few months ago," his mother said.

Ry snapped his head to her. Foreign feelings filled his chest and he tried to push them away. If he had to label them, he was confused, pissed off, and a little hurt. Maybe something was wrong with him, he thought. Fear swelled predominantly in his gut, overriding the physical pain that was there, and he tried to quash it with anger. "And you were just waiting for the perfect moment to tell me. Three strikes and you're out, is that it?"

His stepfather spoke with finality. "It's done, Ryler. You will get on that plane next week or risk assault charges and the danger of winding up in jail. You're only seventeen years old and believe me when I say a life with that kind of track record is not a road you want to head down." He turned to leave, and Ry sucked in an unsteady breath, feeling as if everything was pressing down on him all at once, his control slipping away.

"So that's it, then? Ship me off and then what?"

Tom turned only his head and spoke calmly, "You come back a changed man, Ryler."

CHAPTER ONE

Samoa, January 2003

Before Kiva ever heard about the tragic tale of Romeo and Juliet, the forbidden love between Tristan and Isolde, and the heartbreaking loss Dante felt over his muse Beatrice, there was Sina and the eel from the South Pacific.

Like these epic couples, the legend of young Sina and her pet eel ended in tragedy. A tale told from infancy of an unlikely friendship that develops into adulthood until it becomes a one-sided love story. As Sina grew into a maiden, the eel became enraptured by her grace and beauty. She was exquisite both within and without, and to her obvious horror, she fled from the eel when his love became unnatural. But this did not deter the eel, and he pursued her over the land and mountains. Sina was terrified and called out for help. Aided by her family and the people of her village, they captured the eel to eat. As it lay dying, its final words to Sina were a declaration of love and a mission. He asked her to take his head and bury it in the ground. After some time, a tree would grow and bear a cluster of fruit. The fruit would become a coconut and when Sina drank from one of its three pores, it would be as if she were kissing the eel. He told her if she ever loved him, she would do this one last favor for him. As her people feasted on the body of the eel, Sina was struck by the violence of his death and overtaken by sorrow. She reclaimed the head and buried it, and the coconut tree came to be.

The image of Sina tearfully drinking from the coconut flashed in Kiva's mind as she began to sketch. Smooth lines and dark curves became visible beneath her hand as inky charcoal filled the shadows, soft shading bordered the contours, and a figure took shape with a bowed spine and hair flowing over a pool of water. Kiva imagined Sina's broken heart, mourning the loss of her friend until her tears merged with that of the still water, the salty pearls dripping from her cheeks doing little to cause significant ripples in the pool. The scene played out like a film before Kiva. The moon was full and high in the sky, partially obscured by cotton candy clouds; the villagers had long gone to bed, their quiet snores drifting away with the sea breeze, and Sina would creep away from her house and approach the one place she and the eel would play when she was a child.

"Interesting interpretation," Miss Lene's voice came from over Kiva's shoulder and stilled her hand.

Kiva smiled shyly at her drawing without turning around. "Thank you, Miss Lene."

"Why is Sina crying?" her teacher asked.

Kiva straightened in her chair and wiped the moisture from her upper lip. The classroom was stifling with the midday's heat, and with art being the last class of the day, the back of her shirt was drenched in sweat. The under pits of her arms were moist, and she looked forward to getting home to the rural hills of Tiavi where it was much cooler. But for now Kiva wanted time to slow. To say she loved art class would be an understatement according to her good friend, Silei.

Kiva lived and breathed for it. It was the anchor that grounded her as much as it was the spool of a kite, unraveling and catching in the wind, soaring higher and higher. No sooner than when her pencil met paper, she was soaring like that kite, ascending through unchartered worlds of her own creation, where characters filled up the lonely spaces that had occupied her life for far too long. From her sketches she could live vicariously through her subject, traverse time and place, experience an adventurous journey firsthand, and take a legend and interpret it in a way that spoke and connected to her. If Kiva had to put up with the single overhanging fan and the occasional breeze that streamed through the missing louvers, then it was enough for her.

"Because she misses her friend," she started. "Because she feels responsible for causing his death."

Miss Lene circled around her desk. "Then why did she run away in the first place?"

Kiva glanced down at her sketch, as if seeing it for the first time through her teacher's eyes. "She was afraid. She and the eel were good as friends, only friends, until he wanted more. And what he wanted, she couldn't give him because there was no possible way. How could there be? They were from two different environments, two different worlds—

he, the water, and she, the land."

"So, she was prejudiced?"

"No—" Kiva lifted her slim shoulder in a half shrug. "Yes. Maybe. I don't like to think that she was, but maybe out of fear she didn't understand the consequences of what would happen. I don't see it ending any other way though. This isn't a typical fairy tale where the princess kisses the frog and he turns into a handsome prince. In fact, this isn't a fairy tale at all. There was never going to be a happily ever after for Sina and the eel. Did she fail him? As a friend, yes. But could there have been romance between them? No. Never. But his death was not for nothing. His sacrifice caused growth, brought prosperity and food to the people. But for Sina, the physical reminder of the coconut will always bring her sorrow. While she's grateful for her country's wealth, she can't help but miss him. Like her, I would have felt that loss of losing a friend."

Miss Lene smiled down at her. "Excellent work, Kiva. I like that you're portraying an emotional side of Sina." She tapped her finger on her desk before turning away to another student.

A sarcastic voice came from the desk at her left. "That's great. Now can you draw mine? I suck at this." Kiva looked over at Silei and grinned. She was met with a frown instead, her dark brown brows dipped to form a crease. "It looks like my eel's doing a pole dance."

Kiva peered over at Silei's rough sketch of an eel wrapped seductively around a coconut tree.

"It's not that bad. But ... doesn't the tree grow after he's dead?"

Silei half shrugged. "Yeah, so? Maybe he was resurrected or"—she snapped her fingers— "maybe this is him in his spirit form. You know, to come back and haunt Sina."

Kiva grinned. "That's a little twisted, but I like it. You should go for it."

Silei groaned and dropped her head onto her desk. "I'm not good at this. Give me a puzzle, a mathematical equation, anything but this." Resting on her forearms, she turned and faced Kiva. "You're so much better at this creative stuff than I am."

Kiva smiled at her. "There's no better or worse way about it, Si. You've got a great story going, so just see where it takes you."

"A pole-dancing eel? Right."

"Well then, just think of it as a puzzle that needs to fit together. The balance between shadows and lines, vision and story."

"Easy for you to say," she grumbled.

The bell chimed noisily, bringing an end to the school week. With a collective sigh, students scrambled to pack up their pencils and books into their bags. Kiva stood at the same time Silei tore off her drawing and scrunched it into a ball.

"Are we still on for the movies tomorrow?" she asked as Kiva slung her heavy backpack over her shoulder.

"Sorry, can't. I have to teach an art class. My aunt fell and broke her wrist the other day."

"Oh no, do you need help?" Silei's eyes suddenly widened with excitement. "I know! I can stay the night. We can have a sleepover!"

Kiva laughed at her enthusiasm. "Yeah, okay. We can grab a movie and pizza on the way home."

"Done. I'll call my mom. You can catch a ride with me."

Kiva didn't argue with that. While taking the village bus after school was a daily feat, she wasn't going to pass up on Silei's father's personal driver picking them up in his air-conditioned Land Cruiser. Being the daughter of a high-ranking government official certainly had its perks, and since neither one of them could drive yet, this one came in the form of a stout middle-aged man with a penchant for perfuming the car with pineapple essence and blaring Bonnie M songs.

Silei snapped her phone shut and smiled. "We're all set. Sefa should already be outside waiting." She hooked her arm around Kiva's elbow and made their way to the parking lot.

With *The Wedding Singer* DVD and a large BBQ chicken pizza in the backseat, Sefa pulled up to Kiva's house, leaving the engine running and "Rasputin" blasting through the speakers. Silei thanked him, and they cut across the driveway.

A colonial-style building rose atop a small crest, complete with peeling blue paint and moss-covered screen windows on the second floor. Kiva's aunt called it her tropical castle on the hill, and despite its unkempt, crumbling exterior, Kiva loved it. It had been home to her, her entire fifteen years. It once held the appeal and charm of new, wealthy settlers, hosting large parties among Samoa's finest expatriates with their dreams of new money and opportunity, but was now reduced to rickety floors and faulty pipelines. It had been in Aunt Naomi's family for decades, since before the country's independence in 1962, her roots dating back to some of the earliest German colonists. Kiva loved to think about the countless feet that came and went over the years, the myriad of stories, and the pulse of life that remained.

The garden, if you could call it one, had more tropical trees, weeds, and wild shrubbery than vibrant flowers. Commitment and attention was devoted to the art center situated further down the hill behind the house. Humble in both size and accomplishment, Kiva wished she could say it was a thriving business, but besides a few visitors from time to time—and some classes held now and then—they barely scraped by.

They passed an unfamiliar white van parked beside the house. Kiva gave it little thought as she bent to take off her sandals at the back door and her long hair fell out from its bun. The pencil she used to keep it together clacked on the floor. She picked it up, wound her hair around, and stabbed it through. The screen door banged shut behind them as they sauntered into the spacious kitchen, the cool lapis tiles under her soles a welcome reprieve on her aching feet. A fresh scent drifted to her nose as she took in the scene of jaggedly-cut lemons on the kitchen counter.

Her aunt stood in front of the sink and half turned her body at the noise. "Hi, girls! It's so good to see you, Silei," she greeted her with a kiss on the cheek.

Silei dropped her bag on the floor. "Thanks, Naomi. Is it okay if I stay the night? I thought I'd help Kiva out tomorrow."

Naomi waved her good hand in the air, "Of course it's fine, honey. You can stay here any weekend you like as long as it's alright with your parents."

Kiva bit into a slice of pizza. "How's the wrist?" she gestured to the one covered in a thick blue cast that ran the length of her arm from her elbow to her knuckles. It looked out of place for a woman who was always on the go and whose strong brown hands had been dipped in dye, smoothed out clay, and pounded the u'a cloth. Kiva wanted to draw swirls and patterns on it to represent the artsy woman she was.

Her aunt gave a ladylike chuckle. "The wrist? The wrist is taking its grand ol' time healing. It's me that's deprived. I can't do anything! And anything I can do takes longer to accomplish, which reminds me. Mau is down there giving a class, and he needs these extra carving tools. Can you take them to him? He's had the boys from Toa Academy here all afternoon and I'm trying to organize drinks for them. Look at these depraved lemons. I can't even cut one open." She sighed. "They'll just have to settle for Tang instead."

Silei almost choked on her slice of pizza. "Those American bad boys are here?" She immediately untied her French braid until her thick brown hair hung alluringly over one shoulder. Naomi shot her an exasperated look. "What?" Silei asked innocently when she was satisfied with her primping. "My braid was too tight and starting to give me a headache anyway."

Smothering a smile, Kiva picked up the box of tools and started toward the door. "Come on Mistress Casanova, chores await."

The path to the art center was an uneven grassy slope lined with fern trees. Kiva struggled to grip onto the sides of the box as she made her way down barefoot, her limp pronounced with each step, her right shoulder rising and falling to make up for her uneven height. Low mutterings and the distinct sound of a chisel scraping wood reached her ears before the building came into view.

Kiva's uncle hailed from the Bay of Fagaloa where woodcarving was prominent among the village men. As a natural consequence, he made it his life's work to encourage this ancient form of art. Next to creating traditional display weapons, *tanoa* bowls for kava ceremonies, and decorative artifacts for the home, he was the most patient and competent teacher on the subject, visiting the local art school from time to time and giving workshops to tourists. He usually traveled to high schools teaching students, so it was news to Kiva that he was conducting a class here. For one, the space was small, and for another they were too far from most schools that probably struggled with finances and would have to hire transportation on a regular basis to reach them.

The art building was simple in design, a basic tin roof over four walls and wooden posts. Steps led toward a wraparound balcony where wide French doors swung open to a single room. The doors were the one indulgence Mau afforded the place, having fitted the glass and carved the wood frames himself. Along one wall hung sketches and textural portraits, while on the other stood shelves lined with locally made artifacts for sale. The back of the room was reserved for art classes and had cupboards stocked with supplies and paper, glue and clay. A large rectangular table stained with paint and dye usually stood prominently in the middle of the room but was pushed against the back wall to accommodate for the class today. Sitting on the ground in a semicircle were the boys from the Academy with slabs of wood in front of them near their feet.

Kiva had heard about this school, everyone in Samoa had, but she had never been in the same space as them until now. All she knew about the Academy was that it had been established to cater for troubled teenage boys sent from America to reform their challenging ways before they returned to their families. Kiva had heard that the program was a strict one, combined with US standard academia, therapy sessions, and immersion into the Samoan culture.

Intrigued, she examined the students sitting closely on the floor with their backs to her and Silei listening to her uncle's instructions. Mau held up a slab of wood partly carved with designs and talked about the tree it came from and the process in which it was extracted. She and Silei remained silent, not wanting to interrupt the quiet stillness in the room that her uncle commanded.

Kiva counted eleven students altogether and observed the way they were all dressed in the same light gray T-shirts and cargo shorts. She didn't know what she was expecting, but they certainly didn't look like troublemakers from where she stood. They looked … normal, whatever that meant. They were a diverse group, a mix between African American and Caucasian, with some sporting short haircuts that reminded her of the ones typical in the army. Their superiors sat a short distance away, holding firm expressions, and Kiva didn't want to think about crossing one of them.

Her eyes darted back to the group on the floor. What had they done to land them here? It must have been a strange adjustment for them, a cultural shock no less. She couldn't imagine being abruptly uprooted from her family and home, shipped off thousands of miles away to transform within a period of time in a foreign country she'd probably never heard of before. The expectation to return a metamorphosed person and the pressure to become one would be a challenging feat. Her eyes took in each boy and she wondered what each of their stories was. What had they done? What kinds of families did they come from? Did they like it here? Did they have a choice?

She noticed his tattoo first.

A black script of indecipherable symbols stamped on the inside of his right forearm.

From this distance, she couldn't interpret the pattern, the font small and merging closely together. Her eyes trailed along his arms before she paused and drew in a shaky breath. Scars and jagged lines crisscrossed over each other near his left wrist and appeared as if they had once been serious, deep wounds before they healed to puckered and bulging skin. Did he cut? The idea shocked her, but then another emotion swelled in her chest and took her over by complete surprise. Raw compassion filled the spaces in her heart. She didn't know this boy, but she couldn't help but feel hurt inside for him.

Kiva's uncle stopped talking, jerking her out of her thoughts, and gestured for the box of tools in her hands. She snapped her eyes forward while the boys' heads swung their way. Everyone's but his. Kiva shifted uncomfortably while Silei smiled brilliantly on cue.

"Thank you, Kiva." Mau pointed to a place on the ground to set the box down. She did so gladly and then wanted to turn around and retreat back to the house as quickly as she could. He continued on with the lesson, and their center-stage moment was over. Kiva grabbed Silei's hand, tugging her out. When they descended the steps and were at a safe distance away, Silei burst into giggles.

"Well, that was fun," she laughed. "Did you see the look on some of their faces? It was as if they hadn't seen a girl in months!" Kiva suspected that they probably hadn't. "Some of them were kind of cute." Silei gathered her curls and twisted them into a high bun.

"What happened to your headache?" Kiva asked.

"Ugh, it's too hot. Mission's complete anyway."

When they entered the kitchen, Naomi was pouring artificially bright juice into cups. "Did you see Hana after school today?" she asked, turning only her head. "She should have been home by now."

Silei shot her a tentative look while Kiva replayed the image of her older cousin sliding into Junior's convertible after school—a boy notorious for his unruly reputation. She didn't want to hurt her aunt, but she didn't want to lie to her either. God knew Naomi got wounded enough by the actions of her only child. After all, Kiva knew what that felt like firsthand.

"No one wanted you, Kiva," Hana had sneered quietly to her so her parents couldn't hear. "Not your mother, not your father, no one. And you know what? I don't want you either. Not as a cousin, not as a so-called sister, nothing. You are nobody to me, and you are nobody to my parents. The only reason they took you in is because they had no choice. Not because they loved you—no, never because of that. You're just here taking up unwanted space until you're old enough to leave. Don't ever forget that, *Makiva*." Scathing words that had been spoken a year ago often replayed in her mind. Like black ink blotting onto ivory paper, they seeped into Kiva's young heart and threatened to remain a permanent stain. She refused to believe them though, despite the pain caused, because if she did it would break what little sense of belonging she had carved out for herself in a place that harbored and nurtured her first love: art. Kiva buried herself in her sketches, as a result, layering images and lines and patterns over a stain that sometimes wouldn't go away.

Hana wasn't easy to live with, and her parents had been struggling for years to maintain authority over her since she hit adolescence. Her attempts to assert independence were met with dictatorship parenting that pushed her further away from the home and into the world of tight clothes and boys. When Hana realized her parents never seemed to have the same issues with Kiva, her hatred zeroed in on her younger cousin.

It didn't help matters either that she was repeating her final year in high school, seeing all her friends moving on and making grandiose plans for their future without her.

Kiva swallowed hard at the memory and answered her aunt honestly. "I think she may have got a ride home with Junior."

A pulse jumped on Naomi's forehead, the only visible sign that she was upset. Shifting the tray on the counter, she spoke in a tight voice. "Girls, I need you take these drinks out, please."

Kiva quietly arranged the glasses and balanced them on the tray down the green slope. Representative of her entire life, it was a balancing act—not to tip the scales, not to rock the boat within her family. As much as Kiva loved her aunt and uncle, she reminded herself that this was a temporary arrangement until she finished school and moved overseas to pursue a fine arts degree. She hadn't once traveled abroad, except to take the overnight ferry to Pago Pago for her grandfather's funeral a year ago, but that didn't count in her eyes. Wellington. Melbourne. *Paris*. These were the vibrant cities Kiva wanted to explore—to walk their pavements in anonymity and immerse herself in their museums in awe. She knew it was a far-fetched dream, one she would have to work very, very hard to reel in, but she was determined to achieve it.

When Kiva and Silei entered the art center again, her uncle was demonstrating the proper way of holding a chisel and mallet. With skilled hands he deftly carved the shape of a turtle.

"When this design board is complete, it will contain patterns and animals typical to our environment—the trochus shell, starfish, breadfruit leaf," he said. "Like a stamp, it will then be pressed onto the *siapo*, cloth made from the bark of the paper mulberry tree or *u'a*, and then covered in brown ink made from local plants. You will find these designs everywhere. It is a visual story of the environment fabricated from natural products. But more than that, it is the story of myself and many Samoans imprinted onto the *siapo*. It speaks to us about our land, our food, our home. Some of you may even recognize patterns from the *tatau* or tattoo." Mau exposed the inky black tattoo on his knees and thighs, the *pe'a*, and then pointed to a similar pattern on the cloth he held in his hands. Kiva recognized it immediately as one she had designed years ago. "Each one of you will have the chance to tell your own story through your piece of wood and *siapo* cloth. I want you to carve the pattern of your life that will serve as a representation for the remainder of your time here in Samoa and hopefully for the rest of your lives."

Kiva's interest piqued. She set the tray down and listened intently to her uncle's lesson. His voice was baritone rich and had always commanded the attention of people.

"This pattern can be anything that speaks to you as an individual, something significant to you either from back home or even something you have picked up from being here. Each step of the process that will bring your story to life will be created by you—the wood carving, the *u'a* cloth, the dye, and finally the printing. I will be teaching you to carve, and Kiva"—he gestured toward her—"will teach you the art of *siapo* and dye making."

Kiva blanched at the mention of her name. Stunned in her spot, she fidgeted and pulled on the hem of her shirt sleeve. It shouldn't have bothered her that he'd just volunteered her for the task—she knew the intricate process inside out from years of observing and practicing—but an unsettling feeling bobbed in her stomach nevertheless, and sweat pricked along the back of her neck. *Why am I apprehensive to teach these students?* Her eyes dashed over to the boy with the tattoo, and he stared back. Taking a slow, steady breath, Kiva averted her gaze, but not before she noticed trimmed mahogany hair, a sculpted jaw line, and cocoa-hued eyes. Her pulse raced. Those brown eyes were hard and indifferent; his eyebrows dipped in challenge, and she swallowed hard at their intensity. There was a story behind that tattoo, those scars, that fierce stare, and she wondered briefly what he would carve, what representation of his life he would stamp onto the *siapo*. She realized then with a sickening dread that she would soon learn every single life story in that room … a story too personal for a stranger like her to coax onto the bark cloth. It was one thing wondering about it in her head, but having to work closely with them now was another reality.

Kiva's nervousness roared to life like the surging tide. If it wasn't for Silei's arm looped through her own, she would have slipped quietly from the room and sought her place of solitude to gather her thoughts. How was she going teach these students? The art of *siapo* making was Naomi's specialty, not hers, but since her aunt's injury, Kiva knew she had no choice but to step in and fill her shoes. Behavioral challenges aside, she felt it was going to be awkward with the age difference; most of these boys looked older than her by a couple of years, and she had never taught anyone beyond seven-year-olds—kids who hung onto her every word, eager to learn. Give them a lump of brown clay and they went crazy over it.

Mau's voice broke through her thoughts. "The purpose of this task is to carve your identity onto something tangible. In this case, the slab of wood. Who are you as an individual? It's difficult to reflect on that when it's stuck in here." He tapped his head with his thick forefinger. "Your mind is a busy place with lots of heavy emotions, lots of questions. Why am I here? What am I doing in Samoa? Why did my parents send me? Everything is battling together to be heard. Let it go. Bring it out. I want to see it come to life here." He swept his hand across the *siapo*. "You may not know what that is right away, but through this process it is my hope that it will become clearer to you. Firstly, ask yourself what it means to become a man. For young men such as yourselves, it is not easy in this day and age to navigate through everything that gets thrown your way to find the answer. What defines a man? For a man in Samoa, this may come in the form of getting the *pe'a* tattoo. There is pain, blood, and the grinding of teeth to bite back the agony to achieve the end result. It is a sacred process that takes days, and when it is finally done, there is a tremendous show of pride on the part of the individual who completed it. But let me tell you something, boys. It will mean nothing if a man does not carry the responsibility that comes with it. Like the *pe'a* on my body, it is a symbol, but it doesn't hold much significance if I don't live up to my duty as a man to my wife, my family, and my village. If and only when that occurs, it will always remain nothing more than a nice combination of patterns and little else. In saying that, this project won't mean anything if you don't put your heart into it. I want there to be purpose behind what you carve."

Kiva admired her uncle's lesson from where she stood rooted to the floor. He taught with precision, heart, and genuine honesty. Mau swept the towel across his forehead to gather the sweat that pooled there. Beneath thick, brows he scanned the group of boys expectantly.

When Kiva stole a glance at the boy with the tattoo to gauge his reaction, his gaze was locked on the floor, the tension in his jaw visible from where she stood. Returning her eyes to the front of the room, she let out another shaky breath.

CHAPTER TWO

Kiva heated the pizza they'd bought that afternoon for dinner. She and Silei joined her aunt and uncle around the circular dining table situated under a low hanging light decorated with local seashells—something Naomi made and was particularly proud of. Earlier Kiva had whipped together a vegetable stir fry and was passing it to Silei when Mau cleared his throat.

"Kiva, will it be alright with you to teach those Academy boys? I know I put you on the spot today, but I had no choice since your aunt's wrist is still healing."

Naomi gaped at her husband from the end of the table. "Mau! You're putting her out there among those rowdy boys?"

"They were not rowdy, Naomi. In fact, today they were very attentive," Mau responded patiently.

"I know, but that's not the point," Naomi snapped.

Kiva placed a slice of pizza on her plate. "It's alright, Naomi. I've watched the way you make *siapo*. I can replicate the same process." And since they were literally short a hand, she knew Mau's request didn't come lightly. Much to Naomi's disappointment, the doctor had told her it would take at least six weeks for her wrist to heal, longer if she applied any unnecessary movement to it.

"We know you are fully capable, Kiva," Mau replied. "But these students are different. Some of them will be a challenge. It won't be like the young kids that come for art class."

Kiva's heart raced when she thought about the boy with the fierce glare and mysterious tattoo. "I can handle it."

Silei masked a smile behind a cough.

Naomi's fork clattered onto her plate. "No, Mau. I don't like this. Why didn't you speak to me about this first?"

"I didn't want you to worry, Naomi. Besides, she won't be alone," Mau reasoned calmly. "I will be there, and so will some of the chaperones from the Academy. The classes will be held twice a week, and Kiva's part of the lessons won't start for some time until after they've completed their carvings—maybe in a few weeks. By then they will be completely committed to this project."

Naomi's eyebrows furrowed together and she muttered under her breath which was still loud enough to hear around the table. "I don't understand why you can't just do the lessons at their school, and then Kiva doesn't have to get involved. We can hire someone else to take her place."

"The school requested that it be held in an authentic environment, to see firsthand how things are done the natural way. Besides, it's easier if it's conducted here. All the materials needed are here, and the process is a long one and will take some time. Plus, you know we can't afford to hire anyone right now, not with the way our finances are at the moment."

Kiva pinched the inside of her cheek with her teeth. It made her worry when her uncle spoke about the financial difficulties of the art center. While she was touched by her aunt's concern, and she knew she was just trying to protect her, Kiva wanted to do whatever she could to help alleviate their stress. This reason alone helped quell any reservations she had about teaching the Academy students. "I'll do it," she said. "It's going to be okay."

Naomi's look battled between fierce protectiveness and tenderness as the pinch between her brows matched her pursed lips. "I'm just worried for you, Kiva." Her gaze shifted to her husband. "You put a pretty girl in front of those boys and, yes, I'm going to naturally worry."

Silei poked Kiva under the table and grinned on the sly. Lowering her head, Kiva shook it slightly. Now was definitely not the time for one of Silei's innuendos about the situation, and it was best not to say anything to further provoke an argument between her aunt and uncle.

"It'll be fine, Naomi," Mau said. "I have a feeling this project will be good for those boys. For all of us." Mau's thick brows suddenly dipped into a frown. "Why isn't Hana home yet? It's seven-thirty!" Distorting his greasy mouth into a grim line, his anger was palpable in the way he suddenly curled his fingers around his cup. "She should have been home hours ago to help with the chores. Where is she?"

"We will talk with her when she comes home," Naomi promised in a stern voice. "Let's finish dinner first."

Kiva and Silei cleared the table, washing and drying the dishes while Naomi retired to the living room to watch the evening news before Mau ventured outside to lock up the center.

Upstairs in her bedroom, Kiva slumped down on her bed. Her back and shoulders ached from lugging around a school bag laden with heavy text books, and she closed her eyes under the cocoon of her arm and let her mind wander to her sketches. Particularly proud of one she had been working on for weeks, her hands itched to get blackened with charcoal to complete it.

Silei pulled Kiva away from her thoughts when she switched on the portable radio to the local FM station. Friday Dedication Night was the most popular air time when the DJ encouraged listeners to call in with song requests and messages for friends. Silei hummed to an upbeat jam, the smell of nail polish assaulting Kiva's nose, the electric blue and purple camouflaging her nails perfectly.

"Going for peacock fingers?"

Silei grinned. "It's the only time I can wear this stuff."

She was right. Their school's strict uniform policy dictated no nail polish, no makeup, no dangly earrings, and definitely no more than one piercing in each ear. Silei was lucky she could hide her belly piercing under the folds of her school shirt. Forced to use a cauterized needle and an ice cube to numb the skin, Kiva would never forget the precise moment the needle she held in her shaky hand had punctured skin and blood ruptured, digging out flesh to create a big enough hole for her belly ring, a gift Silei got from a cousin in New Zealand, and something she never wanted to repeat again after her friend almost passed out from the pain.

Kiva picked a coral pink, changed her mind, and went for dusky lavender. She scraped away the charcoal from beneath her nails. Her fingers were long and knuckle-less, her nails naturally French-tipped when they weren't caked in paint or dye. She blew on them to help dry the polish.

"So … are we going to talk about your new job with those *palagi* boys?" she asked.

Kiva shrugged noncommittally. "What's to talk about?"

"Just how jittery you got when that hot guy with the tattoo stared at you. Talk about intense."

So she'd noticed that too. Kiva shifted on her bed.

"He doesn't look like any of the others. He looks *afakasi*."

Kiva agreed with her. He did look half-caste, like an exotic blend of

Caucasian and Middle Eastern, his features dark and skin a natural bronze complexion. She pondered briefly what his striking face with its harsh angles and lines would look like if he smiled.

"Too bad we can't just rock up to their school and hang out with them," Silei sighed.

Curious, Kiva peered at her. "What do you know about their school?"

She shrugged. "Nothing much. My house girl's boyfriend works as a security guard over there and he sometimes tells us things. Their CD players and cell phones are taken away when they arrive. They go straight into learning about the Samoan language and customs. You know, about respect and obedience and all that. It's pretty strict. They can't hang out in town or go wherever they want. Only when they've passed certain levels, like if they behave really well, the rules are loosened and they get more freedom."

"How?"

"I don't know. All I know is that you're one lucky girl, Kiva, getting to spend time with them every week."

Kiva certainly didn't feel lucky and shrugged away the comment. In truth, she was still a little apprehensive about the whole idea.

"Time for a bit of fun," Silei said mischievously. She picked up her cell phone and dialed a number, and the DJ answered.

"Hello, caller, you're on the air. Who would you like to give a shout out to?"

Silei cleared her throat and put on an accent—one that reminded Kiva of their Samoan teacher at school when she attempted English. "Yes, my name is Liliana Rosa and I want to say hi to my boyfriend, Junior Teva." Kiva's eyes rounded in surprise, and Silei winked at her. Purring into the receiver she said, "I want to tell him that I love him oh so very much and that I've been waiting for him to come visit me, but I have no idea what's taking so long. I've even made him his favorite chocolate cake." She gave a little pout for dramatic effect.

The DJ chuckled. "Alright. There you have it. Junior, if you're hearing this, your girl is waiting for you. What song would you like to dedicate to him, Liliana Rosa?"

"*One Minute Man* by Missy Elliot."

Before the song trilled over the air, they heard a car pull up in the driveway. A car door shut at the same time Mau's heavy footsteps could be heard crossing the living room. Silei and Kiva peered through the open louvers and caught him stepping outside.

"You're late!" he bellowed. "Where have you been? Who's this?"

Junior's car sat idly behind Mau's pickup truck, its headlights outlining Hana's curves. She had changed out of her school uniform and was dressed in shorts and a tight camisole. Kiva and Silei didn't hear her response as she flung her arms dramatically in the air. Mau stormed past her until he reached the driver's side. By the looks of his overbearing, stiff posture, menacing words were exchanged before Junior reversed and peeled out of the driveway.

Mau's voice boomed across the yard. "Hana, you are never seeing that boy again. Do you hear me? No more of this nonsense!"

Hana's retort came from within the house. "Dad, relax. You're so embarrassing!"

"Don't talk back to your father like that," Naomi snapped. "Have some respect, young lady."

"Embarrassing?" Mau retorted over her. "That doesn't even come close to how I'm feeling right now. The next time I see that boy's face around here, I will use it as a chisel to carve one of my pieces."

Silei let lose a giggle.

"We did not raise you to go off and do whatever you want with boys around the island. Look at the time!" he continued.

"We were just doing our homework—"

"No. You should have been here doing your homework and doing some chores. From now on, you will not accept rides from that boy. You will catch the bus after school with Kiva."

"What? No!"

Hana's protests were muffled by her mother's voice. "No complaints, Hana. This is for your own good."

Silei snorted beside her. "So the princess is going to catch the bus with you? Let's see how long that lasts."

Kiva sighed and leaned back on her bed. She looked forward to this new arrangement probably as much as Hana did, and Hana loathed it.

It was a tiring wait between transfers from school to the main depot and then an hour's journey from town to home. The actual ride was overcrowded and stuffy, jostling within a rickety, wooden bus painted lemon green on the outside. Velvet drapes hung within, a scene from the Last Supper proudly displayed on the interior. Tinsel decorations from a few Christmases ago dangled and jiggled to the bumps and pot holes on the tar-sealed road. Kiva was convinced the cushion-less seats were manufactured from the hardest wood found in the rainforest, uncomfortable and bum numbing when forty people were squeezed inside like a tight coil. Children and young people were forced to sit on the laps of adults. With no air-conditioning, the windows opened to a breeze that carried with it the mixture of sweaty armpits, sour breath, and perfume spray of public servants, farmers, and school children alike after a long day in town. Babies cried, music blared once out of earshot of the policemen patrolling the urban areas, and the laughter of a few old ladies combined into a cacophony of chaos and harmony. The bus driver was a middle-aged man with bushy eyebrows and a sagging mouth, a lit cigarette hanging from the corner of it. He knew everyone's destination before they got the chance to pull on the fishing line that alerted him to slow down and pull over.

Kiva often sat next to the same two people: Ester, an old lady—Kiva guessed at her age—from a village two stops before hers, and Tui, their ten-year-old neighbor who went to school near town. He and Kiva got off at the same place and walked the dusty, rural road together that led to their homes two miles apart, his further inland than Kiva's. It was always a case of musical chairs when it came to bus seating with Tui sitting on Kiva's lap once it reached capacity and Ester next to them. Kiva liked Ester for the honest way she voiced her eccentric opinions, nothing held her back, but once in a while, she said something that reminded her of the little notes you'd find inside a fortune cookie. "The secret to life is to laugh. Even when you want to cry, laugh it out. Turn the serious into something ridiculously comical that you won't remember why you wanted to cry in the first place," she had said more than once.

Kiva shut out Hana and Naomi's arguing and made her way to the bathroom down the hall, locking the door behind her. She stripped and stepped into the shower. Cold water squirted overhead and raised goose bumps along her skin. After a quick lather and rinse, she wrapped a scratchy towel around her body and padded her way back to her room.

Later in the night when the house was silent and it was clear that her aunt and uncle had retired to bed, Kiva and Silei crept downstairs to the living room, DVD in hand. Flicking on a side lamp, Silei popped the disc into the player while Kiva retrieved a couple packets of banana chips from the cupboard. Settling on the couch, a noise from her right drew her attention to where Hana trampled down the steps, the contours of her face masked in shadow but not darkened enough to hide her pursed lips.

Kiva smiled warily in her direction. "Hey, Hana, want to join us? We're about to watch a movie."

Ignoring her, she headed to the kitchen where Kiva could hear the refrigerator door open and close with a clunk. She proceeded to stomp noisily up the steps without consideration for her sleeping parents.

Silei scoffed with annoyance and mumbled under her breath, "That girl has a serious attitude problem."

Kiva pretended to watch Adam Sandler's character serenade a wedding crowd while her mind hovered to her cousin, who more often than not behaved like a frosty princess. Ironic, since her name meant everything but. *Mahana.* Tahitian for sun and light. It exuded the physical beauty her cousin was aware she had—lush brown curls, full lips, and eyes that rivaled with amber honey. She was named after Naomi's best friend. When Naomi was a child, her parents uprooted the family and traveled to the Cook Islands to teach English at a secondary school. She soon met her best friend, Mahana, who had also moved from French Polynesia, and they became inseparable soon after. Naomi always liked to share the story.

Kiva's full name on the other hand, *Mativa,* was representative of how she came to be, the result of a passionate rendezvous, unwanted then given away. Her name was the only parting gift her mother gave her, if one could call it that, besides the decision to deliver her to her older sister to raise. They had been estranged ever since.

Diagnosed as an infant with a limb length discrepancy, Kiva was used to the curious stares from strangers and fierce whispers behind her back when they thought she wasn't listening. She had a seven centimeter leg length inequality, and her heavy gait was obvious. The last to leave a classroom to avoid the impatient *tsking* sounds from some of the students, having to sit out on the sidelines during sporting events, and the inability to master the Samoan *siva* elegantly because she couldn't glide gracefully across the floor, she was no stranger to the challenges it brought to her young life, her limp a free pass to feeling oddly different and secluded. Despite the back pain that resulted, she had long ago accepted her limp and refused to let it mentally debilitate her. She knew there were various treatment methods out there—shoe lifts, which wouldn't work for her anyway, and surgical limb lengthening techniques, which weren't available in Samoa—but her family couldn't afford the costs anyway if they flew overseas for treatment. So she learned at an early age to simply take the good with the bad. It had empowered her as a result, a feeling that sparked from the inside that she held onto with every fiber of her being. Some days took more effort than others, but she'd found solitude in her sketches and in teaching art classes to kids.

Her name had been abbreviated to *Kiva* by the time she attended preschool, out of pity or compassion she wasn't sure. She was simply grateful for the guardians she was lucky to have, who treated her with unparalleled love and the art that occupied her heart. Her aunt and uncle never spoke about her disability through words, encouraging her instead through their actions to work hard and strive for excellence. They also never raised the sensitive topic of her biological parents, and Kiva didn't give much thought to the woman who gave birth to her. She didn't like to dwell on it. But once in a while, and particularly during the bleakest moments when Hana gave her a hard time, the usual questions trickled in and remained. *Did she wonder about me? Did she ever call her sister to check up on me?* Kiva didn't have the courage to ask Naomi yet. She didn't want to upset her or her uncle. She didn't know who her father was, and what little she knew of her mother was brief: her name was Viola and she lived somewhere in Europe with a Scandinavian boyfriend. Hana seemed to have more knowledge about her. She made Kiva aware on countless occasions that she had been unwanted as a child, and while they had been raised together as sisters, Hana had always been distant and hurtful toward her. Kiva could never understand why.

Silei's laughter brought Kiva's focus to a scene inside an eighties dance club. She blinked away her tiredness and tried to shove her thoughts away to enjoy the movie. A concoction of neon colors and music blurred together as she stretched out on the couch. But before long, her eyes drooped shut and she was caught in a dark, fathomless net.

CHAPTER THREE

"Kiva! Kiva! Look! My tooth fell out!"

Kiva peered over her shoulder at one of her art students and smiled. A little boy with ivory-hued hair sporting a now toothless gap beamed proudly up at her as she shut the door to the art closet and turned around to give him her full attention.

"Iakopo! That's fantastic! Do you know what that means now?" She crouched down to his level.

"What?" His light brown eyes widened in excitement against his pale Albino skin.

"That means you're growing up real fast and before you know it"— Kiva tousled his hair— "you'll be bigger and taller than me one day."

Jacob's smile grew wide as he pumped a fist in the air. "Yes!"

More children filtered into the art center. Tavita. Lanuola. Cristina. Kiva counted nine kids in total. Excitement filled the atmosphere as the kids made their way around the large rectangular table.

"Are we starting on water paints today?"

"I want to draw a dinosaur."

"Miss Kiva, why do you always have a pencil stuck in your hair?"

Kiva couldn't help her smile as she raised one arm in the air to gain their attention. "Alright everyone, settle down."

The children sat around the table, elbows propped along the smooth edge. Their little heads and shoulders barely towered over the flat surface. Silei seated herself on a stool and yawned silently.

"Good morning, everyone," Kiva said enthusiastically. "It's so great to see you all here, bright and early. This is my friend, Silei." She pointed in her direction as Silei gave a little wave. "She's going to be helping us today. To answer your question, Lanuola, yes, we will be starting on water colors." Several enthusiastic "yeses" rippled around the table. "Before we begin the painting process, I'm going to hand out pieces of paper and pencils for you to sketch your drawing onto first. While I do that, think of some ideas of what you would like to draw. Think of something you can add a lot of color to."

"I want to draw a dinosaur," Tavita repeated.

"That's great, Tavita. Go for it."

"How do I draw it?"

"Maybe Silei can help you outline one."

Silei shot Kiva a slightly panicked look and spoke through thinned lips so the children couldn't hear. "A dinosaur? Really? You know I suck at this."

Kiva grinned. "You wanted to help."

"Hand out pieces of paper, pencils, that kind of stuff. Not *actual* drawing."

They walked around taping pieces of paper down in front of each student, and they got busy sketching and erasing. A fish formed. A princess and castle. Something that resembled Spiderman and a web of insects.

"These are looking amazing," Kiva encouraged.

Silei pinched her lips when Tavita erased the dinosaur's tail she'd outlined for him.

"Not like that, Silei. It has to have spikes."

"Why don't you show me then, Tavita," she responded dryly.

The children applied a wet sponge onto the tops of their papers until they were lightly damp. Taking brushes and paint, they mixed and experimented until clear water turned murky and an array of liquid colors exploded onto the surface of the table.

Kiva made her way from child to child praising their work. She came around to the side of Cristina and observed that she had combined hues of green and blue into what looked like a bird's eye view of the ocean.

Curious, she squatted down next to her chair. "Tell me about your picture, Cristina."

Cristina spoke shyly, "This is the *lavalava* my grandma wraps around me when my mommy is away at work. My grandma says it is special because it will keep me safe until she gets back."

Kiva's throat tightened briefly, and she couldn't help but think about this little girl's family. She was an only child with separated parents and a mother who traveled overseas frequently for work.

"Your grandma is absolutely right, Cristina. I love these colors, too."

28

"Tila from school thinks I'm a baby though."

"Because you have a special *lavalava*?"

Cristina nodded.

Kiva placed a hand over her arm. "Well, I don't know about Tila, but when I want to feel safe, you know what I do?"

"What?"

Kiva pointed to the *pulu* tree just down the hill from the center. "I climb inside that tree over there."

It wasn't large in comparison to the *pulu* trees Kiva had seen in and around town. Roots jutted out randomly near the base and led up to a squat, thick trunk and sturdy branches, perfect for climbing and holding her weight. Leaves hung heavily from a distance, but inside the core Kiva looked up and peered through the spaces and blue sky wavered and danced. Thin vines dangled, some touching the ground, which she thought looked pretty.

Cristina giggled beside her. "It's like a big leafy blanket."

Kiva smiled. "That's exactly what it is. A big leafy blanket." Her own security blanket, she thought.

She straightened and gave instructions for tidying up. Silei collected the paint brushes while the children washed their hands. Their parents picked them up shortly after, and Kiva was left to scrub the table down, sweep the floor from pencil shavings, and clean out the paints. Sefa arrived soon after to take Silei home. She lived forty-five minutes away from Kiva, closer to Apia on the north side of the island. Naomi and Mau had left by now to run last minute errands in town, and Kiva make an educated guess that Hana was still asleep in her room. The house was quiet save for the creak and pop of the roofing iron heating up from the sun, Naomi's cat, Masi, purring under the plastic table outside, and the distant sound of gears changing as a bus crested over the hill of Afiamalu and raced toward Siumu village. An abundance of dense bushes and trees separated their home from their closest neighbors who were half a mile away. The Pacific Ocean glittered and stretched in the distance, but the nearest beach was too far away for Kiva to walk to.

Kiva grabbed her sketchbook from her room and limped barefoot to the *pulu* tree. As she climbed the familiar rough bark, anticipation gave way to vivid images in her mind. She recalled a line from her favorite poet as she inhaled and exhaled from the climb. A foot here. Brushing aside tangled vines there. Cling onto a branch. And lift. Her arms trembled as she hoisted herself upwards, taking all the weight away from her legs. Higher and higher she went, until she arrived at her perch. Kiva sat against a V created by two limbs and leaned back. No one could see her, unless they were directly under the *pulu* looking up. The *ma'oma'o* bird whistled a few branches above her, its sound welcoming.

Flipping through the frayed edges of her book, they were almost filled with black sketches, layers of pages as precious to her as the nineteenth century-old *siapo* hanging in the musée du quay Branly. They fell away beneath her fingertips until she found her latest project. Kiva took the pencil from out of her hair and she was lost. Lost in a world of vision and imagery, lines and curves.

The female warrior stood atop a precipice of rock overlooking a torrent of water, its waves rushing in and around her, meeting resistance and protesting in a bellow of violent waves. Despite its force, her body didn't shift from the push and pull of the wind, her bare feet planted solidly on prickly lava. Her calves were strong and pronounced, the *siapo* wrapped around her torso stiff and starchy, the imprints on it bearing her life's purpose. Her hands fisted at her sides, as if anticipating an invisible threat. Whatever obstacle unfolded itself before her, she was ready and willing to fight. The sharp edge of the weapon sat idly beside her, carved from the sturdiest wood. In still form it looked nothing more than a decorative artifact, but in her hands it was unyielding and tenacious, slicing through air and flesh without mercy.

Shading with her fingertip, Kiva's fingers appeared gloved in soot. The weight of her straight, brown hair trailed down her back, and lose tendrils whipped around her face from the breeze. Brushing a few strands from her mouth, Kiva wouldn't be surprised if her face had a few smudges here and there as well.

She heard her uncle's truck pull into the driveway—a red, rusty old thing that stuttered and choked when placed in park and cars gladly passed it on the road to avoid suffocating from the black fumes it emitted. Mau called it his Lady in Red, while Kiva secretly named it The Beast.

"Kiva!" Naomi called. "Come help carry in the shopping, please."

She quickly climbed down the tree to greet them and lifted bags of fresh watercress, their green leaves still sprinkling with water, a bundle of semi-red tomatoes, and a sack of rice out of the backseat. Depositing them on the kitchen table, Mau walked in behind her and wiped the sweat from his brow with the hand towel he usually had draped over his shoulder.

"Kiva, how was class today?" He rested on the sofa while Naomi busied herself putting things away in the cupboard.

"It went well. Everyone showed up. We started on water colors and the kids enjoyed it."

"Very good." He nodded absently. "I will need your help later on to collect the *u'a*. I want it ready for your lessons."

U'a or the paper mulberry tree was a long, slender tree stripped and used for *siapo*. A friend of Mau's grew it on his property in a low-lying area near the coast and allowed them to venture into his grove when needed. After a price was agreed upon between Mau and the family, they searched for the perfect height to chop down. While these trees grew tall with little foliage at the top, Kiva's hands could encircle the diameter perfectly. With a few swift blows of the machete, the trunk fell easily, and every time she cut one down she was reminded of a childhood story about a giving tree, a tree that loved a little boy and gave ceaselessly until the end of its stumped life.

"I'm ready to go now," Kiva answered her uncle.

He nodded and stood. "Let's go then before it gets dark. I want to get back in time to watch the rugby match."

***

The grove of *u'a* stood apart from the wild banana growing around the property of the family home. No fence line separated the land, but residents seemed to know where one plantation ended and another began.

Thick foliage surrounded Kiva, making it difficult to avoid the scratch of long, leafy bush on her arms and legs. The air was thick and humid, the ground moist and pliant under her feet. She followed her uncle and his friend Pili along a windy path that led to the familiar trees with leaves that reminded her of the Canadian maple leaf. Or a Sultan's palace. Pili's son went ahead of them, chopping down the longest leaves that obscured the path, and was assigned the job of collecting the stalks and carrying them back to their truck once they were done.

Mau and Kiva surveyed the heights of the mulberry trees, calculating the exact number they would need to cut down. Gripping the machete firmly in her hand, she began chopping, and imagined she was the vehement warrior in her sketchbook, wielding a weapon carved with intricate patterns.

After the stalks had been bundled and placed in the back of Mau's truck, they rode home to old-school Samoan music, and Kiva stuck her arm out the window, cutting the wind with her hand.

"I finally have an idea for Teuila Festival," she said.

"You've decided to enter the art competition?"

She nodded. "I haven't started on it yet, but I think I want to sketch on canvas. The theme this year is 'True Self.'" The posters displayed around town were effective in their simplicity: against a white background was an enlarged fingerprint in black and the title in bold below it.

"I've been asked to be a judge for it."

Kiva's eyebrows rose and she swung her head toward him. "Is that so?" This could be good for her, she thought a little cheekily.

The corner of his mouth lifted. "Don't even think about it."

"I just did."

"Well, don't ask it, then."

Kiva laughed. "I don't even know why it has to be a competition. Why can't it just be an open gallery to celebrate creativity instead of subjecting art pieces to judgment?"

"I agree. But whether it's a competition or not, the viewer will always judge it for what it is. Besides, there are guidelines for a reason and as long as you follow them, there shouldn't be a problem. We assess each piece based on that criteria."

Kiva ticked them off her fingers because she'd memorized each one. "Number one, your piece must be able to interpret with clarity the theme to the viewer. Number two, the piece must be creative and original. Number three, the composition and overall design must reflect the theme, and number four, it should be impressionable to the viewer. Is it outstanding in other words? I sure hope it will be."

"I've never known you to let a few rules get in the way of your creativity, Kiva. You'll be fine."

Kiva was pleased with his praise and confidence in her. Teuila Festival, a once a year event and the biggest in the country, was a celebration of culture and a fusion of everything: color, food, dance, and song. Where prides swelled and talents were flaunted. With the festival several months away, Kiva had enough time to polish her ideas before she set paint to canvas. The prize money, should she win, would be sufficient enough to restock some of the art supplies they were low on in the center and then perhaps purchase a new sketchbook and pencils for herself.

Reaching home, Kiva placed the bundle inside the center, locked up, and dashed up to the house. She fetched her school bag and did her homework on the dining room table. Her head swirled from completing mathematic equations, writing several paragraphs on the themes from *To Kill a Mockingbird*, and a research paper on a study of China's one-child policy. She stretched her arms above her head and popped her neck from side to side.

Naomi sat opposite her and handed her a steaming cup of *koko*. "Thought you might like a sugar boost."

Kiva thanked her and sipped the hot brew. Granules of grated cocoa rolled around her tongue. Delicious.

The rest of the weekend passed quickly—church, a simple Sunday feast they shared with Tui and his family, and a restful nap. Hana sequestered herself in her room for most of it and only ventured out to eat and shower. Kiva guessed she was still sour over the idea of catching the village bus with her.

Kiva spent Sunday afternoon concealed in her tree, adding finishing touches to her female warrior. She hesitated when it came to her face, which she had left unconventionally last on purpose. Her first instinct was to sketch beautiful physical features … whatever the definition of beauty was. Thickly-shaped eyebrows? Full lips? A delicate nose? Perhaps. But Kiva decided to invent her own idea. She gave her round cheeks contoured by a strong jawline, determined eyes that could also be tender, a confident mouth with the hint of a smile. It was a face that did not emulate her own, but her aunt's. Kiva smiled to herself as she shaded in her black hair rippling through the breeze like an emblem. There was a fierce story behind this woman's eyes, her eyebrows dipped in concentration, eyes shimmering with purpose, and she wanted to tell it. She was strong. Capable. Exquisite. And she could withstand whatever tempest was thrown her way.

Initialing her signature at the bottom, Kiva gave it one final glance before she took a deep breath filled with the air of contentment and turned the page.

CHAPTER FOUR

Kiva was relieved when school came to an end on Monday, but it was short lived when she met Hana to catch the bus home. They had been waiting just a few minutes at the main depot before the exasperated sighs began.

"It's so damn hot!" her cousin complained.

Everyone was hot. She didn't have to voice it aloud. Sweat trickled down Kiva's forehead, and she wiped it away with the back of her hand. Her hair coming undone, she released it briefly before coiling it into a bun and stabbing a pencil through it to hold it in place.

"Where is this bloody bus?" Hana bit out, irritation in her voice.

"It'll be here soon," Kiva answered calmly. "Just be patient."

Hana huffed and stalked away to stand underneath the shade of a tree and took out her cell phone, a gift no doubt from Junior since they were a rare luxury and she knew they couldn't afford one.

Kiva retrieved her sketchbook from her bag and flicked through to a blank page. Digging out a spare pencil, she began drawing the cracks in the cement, where tiny vegetation sprung to life, large tire marks left from a heavy skid of a vehicle, and moss creeping up the side of a bench.

Ten minutes passed when Kiva peered up to see that Tui had joined them, but not Ester. She chased away the flies that had migrated from a nearby rubbish bin from her legs, the sickly rotten smell drifting to them making her want to gag.

When the bus finally arrived, they clambered aboard, relieved to be out of the sun, and located a seat near the back. Hana shut the world out by plugging her earphones into a CD player and leaned against the window frame.

The bus quickly filled and with a start and rumble, it careened out of the depot and maneuvered its way through town, past *pulu* trees and government offices, embassies and cafes. It stopped on its ascent to pick up a few more people, and Tui was forced to sit on Kiva's lap. For a ten-year-old kid, he was gangly but not exactly light, his height almost matching her own. Kiva's legs soon became numb, trapping humidity and sweat under her thighs.

Villages zipped by in a blur—Papauta with its strict girl's boarding school and agricultural center, Vaoala with its Western-style homes for foreign expats. They passed private market stalls, stray dogs, and children walking home from school. Kiva took it all in through the spaces between people's heads and shoulders shuffling and bouncing side to side. The air shifted and became cooler. Fog shrouded the road, and the bus driver flicked on the headlights. They had reached the highest point in the road, passing cow pastures and impenetrable bush when the bus evened out and started its descent. Homes were scarce here, separated from each other by tall grass and trees. A dip in the road and they were moving downwards, toward Tiavi. Almost home. Kiva held her breath at the sharp decline, a steep drop in the road that sent her stomach to her throat. Greenery whizzed by with a few small homes and huts scattered in between and a river leading to a thunderous waterfall. The Pacific Ocean glistened in the far distance, its various shades of blue slivered by ivory waves.

The bus slowed and pulled to a stop opposite a metal scaffold that held garbage, and they descended the steps onto the hot tar road.

"Well, that wasn't so bad," Kiva coughed as the bus departed, leaving a plume of black smoke behind.

Hana fanned her hands in front of her face. "Wasn't bad? I hated it!" She picked up her bag and crossed the road to the dirt path that led home. "I'm not doing it again." A mumble, then a curse.

Tui raised his eyebrows at Kiva and whispered, "Maybe tomorrow I'll try sitting on *her* lap. I can even fart on it to make it extra comfortable."

Kiva couldn't help but laugh. "Come on. Let's catch up with her."

The path home was a dusty one, camouflaged by pot holes and tripping rocks. The late afternoon sun beat relentlessly down on Kiva's face making her squint against its harsh rays.

She was slightly taken aback by the white van parked in the driveway when she reached the house, the boys from the Academy present for their second lesson. She could barely hear their chisels at work when she entered through the kitchen door. Noticing the pile of dishes left in the sink from lunch, she changed into a comfortable cotton shirt and sarong and headed there first to clean up. Since her aunt's fall, the responsibility of kitchen duty and laundry had been delegated to Kiva, in addition to her regular chores of tidying and ironing, while Hana was responsible for sweeping, mopping the floors, and feeding Masi. Although, Kiva had to double check to make sure Masi's bowl hadn't gone empty for too long. After the dishes had been washed and dried, she gathered the bucket of dirty clothes, reached for the box of detergent, and headed outside to the water tank.

A pipe jutted out from its mossy exterior while tea leaf plants grew wildly nearby. It was where Kiva sat on a little plastic stool and hand washed clothes stained from food, paint, and sweat. Hitching and tucking her sarong over and under her knees, she scrubbed and scrubbed until her hands were scoured. Cold water splashed over her legs and arms causing goose bumps to prickle along her neck while her loose hair floated around her face. Kiva's arms were heavy from the rhythm: scrub, fold, scrub again, rinse, wring. She was hot and cold, then hot and cold again from the exertion.

The art center was invisible from where she sat in the tank's shadow, the gushing of water masking the sounds of carving. Behind her grew a tiny vegetable garden of cucumbers and lettuce, and beyond that a cluster of bamboo that had been thriving on the property for decades. That cluster lined the perimeter of the yard until it stopped abruptly behind the art center. No one knew exactly how it came to be planted there since it wasn't native to Samoa, but Kiva liked that its leaves rustled and whistled in the breeze like a flute's song. Banana and papaya trees were interspersed around the property and attracted birds.

She sniffed and brushed the hair from her eyes, straightened her back, and let out a heavy breath through her mouth. Gathering the clean clothes into the bucket, she hitched it to her hip and crossed over to the line that draped from one end of the tilted yard to the other. Kiva slowed her pace when she saw the boys from the Academy emerging from the art center, descending the steps to the awaiting white van. Some of their faces were sweaty from the heat, their movements sluggish and tired. The boy with the tattoo was among the last to appear, and while the rest had mostly ignored her presence, he glanced up and his steps slowed as he held her gaze. Kiva noticed that his gray shirt was disheveled from sweat and exertion. His thick eyebrows dipped to form a crease, and his hard face was lined with fatigue. Her pulse tripped but she forced herself to match him eye to eye before he turned the corner and was swallowed by the ferns.

She heard the van start and leave, its engine drifting further and further away. Kiva scanned the yard and found her uncle's presence lacking. Abandoning the bucket of clothes, she crossed over to the steps of the center and ascended them.

Peering over carved pieces on the rectangular table, Mau had a pensive look on his face when she entered.

"How did it go today?" Kiva asked as she moved closer to join him.

In front of her laid eleven slabs of dark wood, not smooth like a dining room table's but jutted and ragged in places. She recognized the shapes of incomplete patterns, some more defined than others.

"It was interesting," he said almost to himself. "Some of the students took to it like they'd been carving most of their lives. Others had a harder time grasping an idea for themselves."

Kiva scanned each slab carefully, some impressing her with their arcs and straight lines, and attempted to guess the work of the boy with the mysterious tattoo. Her instincts led her to one and she paused.

She stared unblinking. And read. And reread the sentence again.

This is stupid.

Her eyes narrowed at the words, a slashing of letters that looked almost like graffiti, the lack of care and respect evident in the way he had deliberately scarred the wood. She couldn't help but feel a burn igniting on the inside. *Why didn't her uncle stop this?* She wondered briefly what he would do, how he would handle this at the next class.

Mau shook his head and chuckled beside her, taking her by surprise. She swung her head to him.

"How is this funny?" she asked, concerned for the challenge ahead of him.

Her uncle wiped the sweat from his brow. "He has guts, I'll give him that."

"What are you going to do? You can't accept this." Kiva waved a hand in its direction as if to make it disappear off the table.

"Don't be upset, Kiva. I asked these students to tell a story, their story. It can be a very personal thing to do. If this boy, Ryler, has a hard time telling it, then he just needs time. Anger usually veils itself as fear. He will come around. He just needs a little time. A little direction."

Kiva's mind tried to process her uncle's words, but it lingered on his name. Ryler. So his name was Ryler. "How are you not upset about this? He's disrespected you," she retorted.

Mau's mouth twisted to the side like a shrug. "It could have been worse."

"How?"

"He could have carved, 'This is effing stupid.'"

She gaped at him.

"Kiva, don't look so shocked. I was once a young man, too. I know how they think … that's why I'm so hard on Hana and her attachment to that boy, Junior. Anyway, that's beside the point. The purpose of this whole project is to help channel these boys' challenges, to tap into the heart of their issues and let it out. Think of the wood as a punching bag. As long as they don't hurt themselves or anyone else in the process, they can pound out their frustrations onto it."

Kiva furrowed her brows at his conviction. How could he be so certain that this project would work? That these boys could change?

As if interpreting her silent thoughts, Mau answered, "Young people are like sponges, soaking everything up as they go. They can be both brilliant and foolish, but if we seize the part that makes them brilliant, then there can only be positive things that come out of it, hmm?" He gave her a pointed look that smoothed out into tired empathy. "These boys are like the bamboo … foreign and unknown in this environment. But like the bamboo, if you plant and nurture it in the right soil, it has the potential to grow vibrant and strong. When the harshest wind blows, it will bend and not break. They just need a little help straightening themselves. Wherever these kids have come from, whatever they've experienced and seen, it is a part of who they are. We need to respect that, too."

He turned away and started collecting the carving tools inside a box. Kiva reached for the broom and started sweeping the chips of wood from off the floor, mulling her uncle's words in her head. She stole a few glances over her shoulder at the carving.

This is stupid.

The words were mocking, teasing, and she couldn't help the swell of anger that grew inside her at the insult to her uncle. She felt the sting of shame on his behalf and wanted to protect him from it. "How will he fix this?" she asked.

"He won't get a new slab of wood. He'll just have to work over this one, build on the carvings that are already there."

Mau gathered a few tools and started toward the door, leaving her alone in the art center with her scattered thoughts.

She was still contemplating his words later, perched in the *pulu* tree, pencil poised over a blank page. Through the spaces in the leaves, the dusky sky blushed pink and orange, the combination of colors like a rendering of a water painting. Closing her eyes, she could hear the whisper of nature, the buzz of a mosquito nearby, the creak of the bamboo stalks as they bowed to the wind. The words Ryler carved echoed in her head over and over until Kiva couldn't help but replicate it down on the paper.

This is stupid.

The script was similar to his, imperfect and harsh, lines that resembled the zigzag of lightning when it hit the ground, and just like lightning, it stirred unease inside of her anticipating the thunderous boom that would soon follow, making her want to cower for cover. Is that the message he was trying to convey? Did he want to frighten people away?

Frowning at her facsimile, Kiva took each letter and altered it … first into a stem, strong with diameter lines encircling the culm … and then into foliage, leaves tipped and sharp like a blade. She repeated the same process with the next letter and the next and the next, until the words disappeared and were replaced by a collection of bamboo stalks and leaves.

Gazing down at the transformation, she initialed her name at the bottom of the page, tucked the book under her arm and climbed carefully down the branches before jumping barefoot to the ground. Straightening, Kiva headed toward the house and glanced once at the art center, wondering how the boy with the mysterious tattoo—Ryler—would transform his.

CHAPTER FIVE

The rest of the week passed slowly with the same uneventful routine: school, bus, chores, homework.

On Friday afternoon, Kiva took a seat in art class, her stomach hitching with excitement. She fanned herself with a notepad to chase away the stifling humidity, the air choking with it, heavy and looming. Her eyes darted around and noticed a boy restlessly whipping a pencil between his fingers, another almost lulled to sleep by the heat. Silei sat at a desk to her right, blowing air down her shirt.

"What is your definition of beauty?" Miss Lene asked the class before writing the words "Beauty and Art" on the blackboard. She turned and leaned against the imposing wooden desk at the front of the room, her two-piece dress wrinkled from the humidity. Kiva pricked at the question, remembering her female warrior.

"When you look at an art piece for the first time, what makes it beautiful and appealing to you?"

A boy by the name of Trey raised his hand, his voice slick and suggestive. "Are we talking about people here? Because if that's the case, I really think Silei is a beautiful piece of art. We should sketch her. In the nude."

A ripple of laughter erupted, and Silei balled a piece of paper and threw it at his head. Ducking, he winked at her cockily and straightened when Miss Lene snapped at him, calling everyone to attention.

"Beauty is subjective," Silei responded coolly when the class calmed. She pursed her lips before locking gazes with Trey. "What I find *ugly* won't necessarily mean others will. Unfortunately."

A few snorts and snickers resounded while Trey clutched his heart in mock pretense. Kiva caught Silei rolling her eyes then fighting back a smile.

Miss Lene called for silence. "Thank you, Silei, for your insight. You're right. Art and beauty are subjective. There is a fine line between the two, and fortunately for us there are guidelines in the world of art."

She lifted a poster off her desk and held it up for us to see. Two native women sat together on the ground, one more idly than the other, leaning forward with her legs outstretched under a red sarong, arm extended and elbow locked to support her weight. The other sat cross-legged, her eyes almost darting and suspicious. Kiva recognized it immediately as Paul Gauguin's from a post card Naomi received from her best friend years ago. The women were fully clothed, one more so than the other, covered from neck to toe in a dress that reflected colonial influence.

"This canvas piece was created in 1891 and is entitled *Tahitian Women on a Beach*," Miss Lene explained. "The artist, a Frenchman by the name of Gauguin, left Europe and traveled the world in pursuit of artistic purity and beauty. Do you think he captured it here?"

Kiva studied the painting closely before raising her hand. "I think he did."

"How so, Kiva?"

"I think in the simple way that he depicted women carrying out their daily tasks … one looks like she's weaving a basket of some sort while the other is keeping her company."

Miss Lene nodded. "You've nailed a key word here—simplicity. Simplicity in this particular painting manifests itself through two primary subjects, these women. The artist draws your eye to them immediately through vivid color and balance. Gauguin was ahead of his time because of his use of bright color in his paintings. In this case, it adds beauty to the women and not the other way around.

"There are other qualities that make art beautiful: nature, overall visual unity, balance and harmony, surprise, and spontaneity. Unfortunately, the way we view art today has become somewhat judgmental and distant. We remove ourselves from an art piece, assessing it from afar, but there is much to be said about beauty in art when it has the ability to transform."

Miss Lene lifted another poster depicting a simple cave painting where a couple of bulls were charging forward, their horns sharp and pronounced.

"What's so beautiful about that? It looks like a child's drawing," one student claimed.

Miss Lene smiled patiently. "This drawing is over fifty thousand years old. The cavemen who created it instilled in these animals symbols of power and strength—qualities they wished they could have. If you look carefully, there are always messages contained in art, no matter how simple they may appear to be."

Miss Lene lifted a stack of paper from her desk and asked a student to help distribute them. When Kiva was handed one, she glanced down at a pattern of Aboriginal art that contained swirls and colorful dots.

"For Australian Aborigines, art was traditionally used as a means for communication. This came in various forms: rock engravings, cave paintings, designs carved into trees, and wooden articles such as boomerangs. The symbols used on these surfaces were expressions of their beliefs and stories. Everything held significant meaning—their lands and skies, trees and animals.

"For the Aborigines, their belief in the 'Dreamtime' or creation story is of most significance. It's a story that transcends the physical and describes the balance between the spiritual, natural, and moral elements of the world.

"Take a look at the symbols on your page. Each swirl and line represents an icon: women and children, men with boomerangs or sitting around camp fires, water holes, animal tracks. The colors of the dots are each significant—yellow for the sun, brown for the soil, red for the desert sand, and white for the clouds in the sky. When combined together, the paintings are used for teaching a story, one that could have both an educational purpose and a higher level of meaning. Look at the back of the page," Miss Lene instructed.

Kiva flipped over the paper. A hand print that was distinguished by the paint surrounding it was imprinted on a rock.

"There is a story in the north of Australia about a young Aborigine boy being carried on his father's shoulders to a rock wall. His father sprayed his hand with red ochre against the rock, imprinting a stencil of his hand. Traditionally, the purpose of this was to record a person's presence with a site. The stamp connected a person to a particular place as a result. It associated a person to the land, and the hand print became a symbol of power and identity."

"Kind of like writing 'Trey was here' all over this desk?" Trey interrupted.

Miss Lene suppressed the urge to roll her eyes in exasperation. "No, Trey," she answered patiently. "That would be called graffiti, which as you know is against school policy. The Aborigines maintained a spiritual connection to the earth through symbols and stories. They didn't disrupt nature but became almost one with it." She returned to the blackboard. "This brings us to our next art project." Next to *Beauty and Art* she added *Identity*.

"In this country, how do most people identify themselves?" she asked when she faced the classroom.

One girl by the name of Cora raised her hand. "By *faa*-Samoa, the Samoan way of life, which is through culture, family, and God. These elements dictate to us how we're supposed to behave at all times, with respect and obedience."

"Yes, that's the most common explanation. Let's look closely at the element of culture and the idea of behavior and identity. Take the *matai* or chiefly system, for example. To have a *matai* title is to take on the responsibility of caring for one's extended family and serving their interests. This dictates to them how they should behave toward their family and others and is a clear, defining example of identifying themselves in the culture. Another example is by undergoing the process of the *tatau* or tattoo. As you know for men it is the *pe'a*, for women, the *malu*. These cultural tattoos have long been associated with one's identity and the courage and respect that go with receiving one."

Miss Lene held up black and white photographs of said tattoos. The man had his bare back turned to the photographer. The dark ink marks of his tattoo covered his back, bottom, and thighs, the horizontal and vertical patterns so bold there appeared to be thick black lines in some places. "The *pe'a* is a symbol of manhood and identity and the responsibility that comes with it. Both men and women are respected for their courage when they receive these tattoos because the process is not an easy one." The woman's *malu* beheld etchings from her upper thighs to knees, its design more evenly spaced and delicate. "Each mark on the woman represents something in nature," Miss Lene explained. "See this crisscross on her legs? That is the *aveau*, the starfish. There are many patterns like this that can be used in the tattoo—the *fetu* (star), *gogo* (seagull), *alualu* (jellyfish)." Miss Lene turned to the blackboard and drew several of these designs. When she turned around she clapped her hands together to rid herself of the chalk dust. "Some of you may decide to get the *pe'a* or *malu* done when you're older and that's a wonderful journey for you and your family to embark on. It is a form of artistic beauty as much as it is a sign of courage and responsibility. Some of you will not, and that's okay, too. The decision is yours to make for whatever personal or cultural reasons you may have.

"For this next project, I want you to create motifs and symbols that will communicate something about yourself, your identity, and your character. What makes you unique? What makes you beautiful? What gives you empowerment? Look at the three elements of culture, family, and God for guidance. With these symbols, I want you to sketch them on the inside of your handprint, like the Aboriginal one on the page that was handed out. Alternatively, you could choose to sketch a three-dimensional hand instead and draw symbols inside of that."

Miss Lene came around distributing paper, and Kiva sat contemplating her project. She had always been fascinated with sketching hands, particularly the inside of the palm, with its life lines and checkerboard marks, hands poised and unfurling with knobby knuckles and wrinkled fingers. They had always been a beautiful part of the human body, possessing the capacity to be both gentle and nurturing as well as cause physical and mental pain. They were a vessel for communication. To create. Hold. Care for. And in some cases destroy, hit, and punch. You could always tell a lot about a person's life simply by observing their hands. Was there dirt underneath the nails like that of a farmer's? Were their nails chipped or nervously bitten? Calloused and sun exposed? Perfectly manicured? Bore a tan ring? Layers of pages in her sketchbook were devoted to hands—her aunt's with her graceful, long fingers, and her uncle's larger ones with their scars from years of accidental slips with the carving knife. She sketched stranger's hands at the bus stop and market place, one lady's in particular fascinating Kiva with a tattoo on the inside of her forefinger in swirly calligraphy that spelled "No fear." When Kiva checked her other forefinger it read, "No regrets."

What did her own hands tell her about her life? Kiva peered down at her left hand with its distinct blue veins and oval fingerprint swirls. A light dusking of hair grew at the base of each ring-less finger, the lavender nail polish from a week ago scraped off.

"Kiva," Miss Lene paused when she slipped a piece of paper on her desk. "I heard that you're submitting work for the Teuila Festival's art competition. Have you decided what you'll be doing?"

"I have a few ideas but haven't started on it yet."

"Well, this project could be a good jump start for you, since the theme for the competition is 'True Self.' It's definitely something to think about. Let me know if I can help in any way."

Kiva nodded and Miss Lene breezed away.

She sat unmoving while her mind churned over with ideas until the bell rang and she packed her things and rushed to meet Hana at the bus stop. She found her scowling near the benches when the bus pulled up. Besides the bumping of legs as they sat side by side, Hana largely ignored her, the silent distance growing thick between them until Kiva's thoughts took her miles away.

What symbols were representations of her identity? Her art was her first love, she knew that, but was that enough? Something nagged at her consciousness, and she came to the realization that before she could identify herself to something, she needed to belong somewhere. Where did she fit? She certainly didn't fit in the *matai* system—she didn't have a chiefly title and she probably never would receive one. She wasn't a man with the gift of oral speech or bore the tattoo markings of the daughter of a high-ranking chief. In fact she was no one's daughter. She didn't live in a traditional village surrounded by nothing but bush and cattle since Mau and Naomi moved away from their own, nor did she live in a traditional family. She didn't know who her biological parents were; her aunt and uncle had no choice but to take her in when she was born out of wedlock. Who was she then? If a significant part of the equation for being a Samoan was culture and family, then she felt as if she were sitting out on the fringes looking in. That left her with God—the final piece in the equation. While she attended church diligently with her aunt and uncle every Sunday, it was the moments of solitude when she was in the *pulu* tree where she felt the most drawn to Him. The whisper of wind rustling the leaves. The stained sunset through the branches. The song of the *ma'oma'o* bird. The chiming of crickets in the bushes. Dusk had a distinct sound, and it was in this pocket of time where she didn't feel so alone.

The bus's sudden screech of tires jarred through Kiva's thoughts. She peered outside to see that it had stopped beside the garbage load. Descending quickly, she and Hana swiftly crossed the road and walked home in silence.

The white van's presence in the driveway made   Kiva's heart thud against her ribs, and a mysterious anticipation settled over her. Hobbling into the house, she carried out her chores with efficiency, hanging the laundry on the line and checking on Masi's bowl while stealing curious glances at the art center.

After a long pause, she decided to enter it.

Poised along the far wall to avoid distraction, Kiva perused the students scattered around the room, heads and shoulders bent over their wood carvings, the clink and thud of the chisel and mallet competing over each other. Mau paced his time with each student evenly, making his way around, offering guidance when needed. Kiva couldn't make out his words from where she sat, only a few low mutterings accompanied by the shake or nod of his head.

Her eyes strayed until they settled on the boy with the mysterious tattoo. Ryler. Her suspicions were correct about his work when she noticed the slab of wood with the sliced words in front of him. He hadn't spoken a word to any of the other boys, didn't acknowledge them, and they avoided him too, as if he'd erected an invisible wall and they were aware of it.

Her uncle had no problem stepping through it though. He was with him now, speaking in low tones and gesturing to his work. What was he saying? Kiva strained to hear, but nothing came to her over the cacophony of sounds in the room. A muscle in Ryler's jaw ticked as he sat, head bent, listening to him. Mau remained with him for some time, talking and listening, acknowledging the need to spend more time. Finally, he gave him a tap on the shoulder and a satisfied nod before moving away.

Kiva noticed when Ryler picked up a carving knife, pausing in concentration, his face tentative and contemplative, before he met it with wood, the muscles in his broad back contorting and flexing from the grip and release of the tool. What had he decided to carve? Kiva wanted to inch her way forward to find out but kept herself firmly planted. An hour passed and still she sat riveted to her spot.

A couple sharp drops on the roof were the only warning to the torrential downpour that followed.

"*Makiva!*" Hana's voice shouted from across the yard and made her jump. "It's raining! Get the laundry!"

Kiva scrambled off the floor, the noise drawing attention, and limped as quickly as she could to the line. The knifelike raindrops hit her on the back, stinging, and soaked through her shirt. Ignoring the pricks, she rushed to unpeg each piece of clothing, throwing it in the bucket and returning for more. The rain came down harder and faster, blurring her eyesight, the sound of a thunderclap roaring in her ears. Tea towels, Mau's shirt, Hana's school skirt. Breathless, her quick movements had long ago uncoiled her hair, wild and swirling in the wind; the pencil slipped out, lost somewhere. She was nearing the end of the line, grappling with a sheet, when she glanced up and noticed the boys running from the center to the van, their lesson over.

Ryler appeared last through the door, his brown eyes trained on her, and descended the stairs with heavy, deliberate steps. Kiva stared wide eyed as he stepped into the rain and came toward her with unhurried, even strides. She watched as raindrops pelted his gray shirt, soaking through to his shoulders until the wet dots spread and connected.

When he was a foot away, he lifted his hand.

"You dropped this," he said, his voice low and hoarse, as if he was just getting over a cold. He smelled of wood dust and sweat.

She glanced down at his hand and saw the pencil she used to pin up her hair. It must have fallen in the art center in her haste to get to the laundry. Reaching for it, she noticed the deep scars on his left wrist and paused. From this close they looked even worse.

"It's not what you think," he answered, interpreting her thoughts.

Kiva snapped her eyes to his face. His brown eyes penetrated hers, thick lashes dripping from the rain, a line formed between his eyebrows. She tried not to fidget under his gaze and glanced to the right of his face. She saw a scar near his eye, something she hadn't noticed before.

She calmly returned her gaze to him. "And what do I think?"

"You think that I did this to myself on purpose."

"Did you?" She breathed.

He shook his head. "It was from a fight. The other guy had a broken bottle and I tried to block him."

Kiva hissed as if she had been the one cut open and bleeding. Her eyes found the scar again and her stomach plummeted at the thought of the pain it must have caused. She felt suddenly light-headed and blinked to clear the blur clouding her mind. When she glanced at his face again, he was studying her with a hardened air of indifference.

The sound of the van's horn blared from the drive way.

"Ryler! Hurry up, we're going!" A superior impatiently gestured for him in the rain.

"You better go," Kiva said hastily. "Thanks for returning this." She took the pencil from his hand and curled her fingers around it.

Ryler remained unmoving. Why wasn't he going? Did he want to get into trouble? He finally stepped away and turned, jogging over to the waiting van, his shirt now drenched through and stuck to his retreating back.

Kiva watched him go before letting out a shaky breath. She gathered her long hair in a bun, wrapped it once, twice, before stabbing the pencil through. Hoisting the bucket to her waist she shuffled to the house, her wet *lavalava* swaddled tightly around her legs making it difficult to walk.

"My uniform better not be wet!" Hana snapped when she entered through the door.

"Hana, calm down," came her mother's reply from the kitchen. "You can always iron it out until it's dry."

Hana snatched the bucket from Kiva's grip and rifled through it. "It's soaked through!" she complained when she found it near the bottom.

Kiva studied the clothes and saw that they were a little more than damp. "Hana, there was no time. I got there as fast as I could but the rain came quickly." Loud and heavy raindrops accompanied her words, the room darkening from the gathering gray clouds overhead.

Ignoring her, Hana marched off to the bedrooms to look for the iron. Kiva followed her upstairs to change out of her wet clothes. Returning to the lounge in a clean white shirt and sarong, she picked up a towel from the bucket to cover her head, ducked outside, and limped down to the art center.

There was a particular carving she was anxious to see.

CHAPTER SIX

Kiva studied the slab of wood, the words that had tarnished it a week ago barely vanished. They were replaced now by an awkward vein of lines, the letters transformed into a myriad of streaks, like spindly fingers stretching vertically in search of something. Kiva studied their path that led to a foreign script she couldn't decipher. While it looked obvious that it was a rushed job, the cursive letters were a combination of mesmerizing twists and elegant curls, and she couldn't help reaching out with her fingers to trace each one.

"It's Arabic."

She jumped from Mau's voice. She hadn't seen him in the center when she'd arrived out of the rain leaving wet footprints on the concrete floor. Glancing over her shoulder, she saw him standing in the doorway, wiping raindrops from his face.

She shifted hesitatingly before asking, "What does it mean?" She thought about the lengthy time he had spent with Ryler, the exchange that he seemed to soak in, and the carving that now resulted.

"He told me it translates to 'Meet violence with violence.'"

Kiva frowned in confusion. It seemed like a crime that beautiful script could be translated into such harsh words. "But when you were with him, what did you tell him?"

"I asked him to think about the most important thing there was in the world to him. I asked him if something were to threaten it, what he would do to protect it."

"And what did he say?"

Mau shrugged. "He said there was nothing he cared about."

Kiva turned back to the slab of wood and studied its calligraphy.

"That boy scares me," she barely whispered.

Mau stiffened. "How? Has he hurt you? Threatened you?"

She shook her head. "No, nothing like that. He scares me because he's so … indifferent … complacent. It's as if he doesn't take any of this seriously and has already given up."

"Don't mistake indifference for a cry for help, Kiva. That boy is hurting and probably hasn't found something positive to be passionate about. If we find that we are stuck in life, the greatest obstacle that stands in the way of our progress is usually ourselves—our shortcomings, our insecurities, even our ego. In order to move forward, we must firstly conquer ourselves—our thoughts, our words, and actions, and most often it takes us hitting our lowest point before we can bounce back. You wait and see. One day that boy will care enough about something to fight for it, and then there will be no stopping him. Like the vines that wrap around that tree you like to climb so much, it will occupy every space in his life, and then he will never let it go because he will know what it means to be without."

He started to close the windows while Kiva mulled over his words. How did one go about conquering themselves? How did her uncle expect these students to triumph over whatever issues they were dealing with?

"Come on, let's go help Naomi in the kitchen," he said tiredly.

Kiva nodded and crossed the room, flicking off the lights as she went, before following her uncle out of the center into the drizzling rain.

***

She later lay restless in bed.

Since the power had switched off from the storm, everyone had gone to sleep early except for her. She couldn't shut down. At night the old house came alive with creaks and groans from the wind pushing through the cracks and louvers, and she stayed awake listening to their eerie conversation. She also couldn't get the words on the carving out of her head.

Meet violence with violence.

Her eyebrows creased in thought as her overactive imagination conjured violent images of Ryler fighting, resulting in the scars that peppered his wrist and face. Is that why he had been sent to Samoa? Kiva sat up and crossed her legs under the cool sheets. Reaching for her art book, she flicked on the small flashlight she had propped on her bedside table and withdrew the pencil from her hair. Expelling a deep breath, she began to sketch.

A forearm was outlined. A crisscross of scarred tissue on the left wrist was formed. Large fingers poised as if they were about to clench. The space between his thumb and forefinger angular, the thick pad of his thumb almost double the size of her own.

The room was silent save for the scratching of pencil against paper, the slide and shift of her hand as it shaded and highlighted, the underside of her palm collecting pencil dust. The rain eased into a soft tapping against the tin roof overhead and small shadows pranced across the page, spilling onto the sheets. Sitting back to admire her sketch, Kiva imagined those same hands fisted, connecting bone to flesh, the cause of someone else's pain. What kind of pain did he harbor to lash out in this way?

Initialing her name at the bottom, Kiva slid under the sheet now warm from her body. She kept the flash light on as her eyes blinked slowly, once, twice, until they drifted closed.

She dreamed of an endless turquoise lagoon, the paddle she dipped into the water sending gentle ripples across a once calm surface, the wooden canoe skimming silently across a liquid mirror reflecting a perfect, cloudless sky. She pulled the paddle out and rested it at her feet, choosing instead to plunge her hands in the Pacific's warmth. The seawater trickled into the spaces between her fingers until it reached the bones in her wrists.

This must be the spot, she decided.

Her body followed in a graceful launch.

She felt the contrast immediately—a heavy weight and darkness, a liquid cage. Opening her eyes underwater, she squinted against the sting of salt and blinked to adjust her eyesight. It felt as if she was peering through a plastic bag. Kiva kicked her legs and dove deeper into the bottomless ocean, mystery just a few feet away. An undercurrent welcomed her, pulling her into its vortex, and without fear, Kiva allowed it to coax her in, knowing somehow that it would lead her to where she needed to go.

The oysters lay disorderly on the ocean floor, spread around from the force of the current and half buried under the ocean's dust. Kiva plucked one, her hands scratching rough sand under her fingernails. The texture was rough and slimy, the corners sharp in some places.

Her chest tightened, protesting for air, and Kiva kicked her way to the surface, the clam pressed safely inside her fist. Breaking the surface, she located the canoe several feet away and reached it with unhurried strokes. She swung her leg over the side until she could hoist herself aboard. Sniffing, she brushed the moisture from out of her eyes and face. The clam lay cradled in the palms of her hands.

Positioning her thumbs at the lips, she attempted to pry it open. Slipping, the curved edge cut her skin, blood dripping and mingling with the salt on her bare legs. Hissing from the stinging pain, she tried again, digging her nails deeper into the small mouth. She pushed past the burn in her hands, the space growing wider until it cracked open a little, and she forced it apart. Prodding a bloody finger into the clammy core, she felt around for the pearl she knew was buried inside.

It slipped out, the color a blend of indigo black, the shape an imperfect oval.

Smiling softly to herself, Kiva held it firmly between her thumb and forefinger and raised it to eye level.

"Found you," she whispered triumphantly.

Kiva flung her eyes open to shadows dancing across the walls from the light of the flashlight. Something wet fell across her face. The rain was in full force now, pummeling against the roof and coming in through the open louvers. The curtains blew wildly, sending chills over her body. Kiva stood unsteadily and shut them, returning to bed a little sober than when she woke up.

Blinking down at her sketchbook, which was open at the page of his hand, Kiva traced it gently, smearing the pencil markings. *What had that dream been about?* Pulling the sheet to her chin, she stared at the shadows playing across the ceiling and had a distinct feeling her dream had something to do with Ryler.

***

"I love what you've done to your piece of clay," Kiva commented to Lanuola as she paused beside her at the art table. The children smashed their little fingers into their brown molds, shaping turtles and geckos. Outside the heat permeated the atmosphere, and Kiva left the French doors and windows open to the art center to welcome the breeze.

"Thank you. I'm making a fish, like the fish my big brother caught the other night for dinner."

"That's very interesting," Kiva responded. "Did you go with him?"

"Yup! I helped pull the net in."

"I'm making a dinosaur!" Tavita blared above the noise in the room.

"I can see that." Kiva shifted around to him. "I like the wings on it."

"It's a pterodactyl. I learned about it in a book my uncle got me," he added excitedly.

Kiva shot him a wide smile when he struggled with the pronunciation.

"I'm making you, Miss Kiva," Iakopo spoke up.

Surprised, Kiva glanced at a clay figure lying across the surface of the table, one leg significantly shorter than the other. When Kiva didn't respond, the other children peered over at it. Touched, she swallowed the hard knot in her throat.

"It does look like me, Iakopo."

She limped around the table.

"Is that why you walk like that, Miss Kiva?" asked Cristina.

Kiva paused and faced her. It didn't bother her that they were giving attention to her leg. She couldn't hide the limp and she knew they were curious. "Yes. Since I was a baby, I've always walked like this."

"Why? Everyone else has the same size legs."

Kiva gave her a soft smile. "Because I was made this way."

Cristina nodded slowly in understanding. "Like the same way God made Iakopo's hair and skin white?"

"Yes. That's exactly it."

"Why would God do that? Make people different? My baby cousin can't see because he was born blind. Did God make a mistake, then?"

Kiva swallowed hard, recognizing this as a teachable moment, and tried to gather her thoughts together. "God is a mystery, but I don't think He makes mistakes. We've all been given challenges—some you can see on the outside, while others can be found on the inside. This doesn't mean that the ones on the inside are any easier though. Challenges are hard, but they can also teach us things like patience, courage, and strength—qualities that help us to grow spiritually. They also teach us to be grateful for what we *can* do … for your cousin, it can be the ability to listen to beautiful, uplifting music or to hear the soothing sound of his mother's voice."

Cristina was sticking her thumbs in the clay leaving little imprints, and Kiva thought she had moved on from the conversation. "I think you're pretty strong," she finally said.

Kiva was taken aback. "Thanks, Cristina."

She looked up, blinking away the bangs that irritated her eyes. "Does it hurt? To walk like that?"

Kiva shook her head. "Only if it stops me from doing the things that I love to do."

"Like what?"

"Well"—a small smile spread across her lips as she tapped her finger against her chin—"like climb trees and draw and teach art and"—her smile turned playful and she started tickling Cristina on her stomach—"tickle little kids!" Cristina's shriek of laughter filled the room until the children jumped out of their seats.

"Tickle me, too!"

Kiva laughed and started attacking as many stomachs and underarms as her two hands could move, but there were too many of them and she soon found herself overtaken and pinned on the floor with nine pairs of hands tickling her. Kiva squirmed and peeled with laughter. Their little hands were relentless.

"Okay, okay, I surrender!" She gasped for air, feeling the little hole in her heart swell with joy. She peered up at their beaming faces and felt like nothing in the world could compare to the feeling that expanded in her chest. "Who's ready for a snack?"

"Me!" they all chorused.

"Alright, let's wash up first."

Kiva maneuvered herself off the floor and retrieved bags of taro chips for everyone. As they happily munched away, Kiva started cleaning the table and packing up the art supplies. They could keep the clay work and take it home to their parents.

After the last child was picked up, she locked up the art center and made her way to the house. The grassy pathway was damp from the previous day's storm, the fern leaves drooping heavily with moisture. They brushed along Kiva's arms, leaving tear stains on her sleeves.

She stopped when she noticed her uncle's truck missing in the driveway and in its place was Junior's old-school GM convertible. She knew Mau and Naomi had left to run errands in town and wouldn't be back for at least a couple of hours. Kiva sucked her bottom lip into her mouth and bit it. She didn't want to go inside the house, afraid of what she might find. Hana's defiance against her parents was something she also didn't want to deal with. Gazing down at the *pulu* tree, it beckoned her to climb inside the safety of its limbs, but she had to firstly retrieve her sketchbook from her room.

She limped into the living room, shutting the door quietly behind her. Climbing the stairs, she noticed the door to her cousin's room wide open with no one inside. Relief flooded her, and Kiva expelled the breath she was holding in her chest. Reaching her room, she searched for the sketchbook on her bed when she heard the unmistakable sound of a thump followed by a muffled voice emanating from down the hall. Finding the book tucked under her pillow, Kiva retraced her steps back into the hallway and gazed down the corridor at the closed door to her aunt and uncle's room.

Anger and panic surged inside her.

How could Hana use their room like this? Her parents could be arriving at any moment. Torn between ripping the door open and just leaving them to be discovered, Kiva clenched her fists and pounded them against the wall, rattling the framed pictures. The noises from the room stopped abruptly and after a moment the door swung open. Hana stepped out tying a sarong around her body, her usually impeccable hair tousled around her shoulders.

Her eyes narrowed when she saw Kiva. "You," she said with deadly calm, but Kiva didn't miss the shimmer of fear in her cousin's eyes or the way her lips were pressed tightly together as she sauntered down the hall. "You better not say anything. To anyone." Her voice wobbled.

Junior brushed up behind her, shirtless, and kissed Hana on the head. She relaxed a little in his embrace. "She won't, baby. Cripple here will keep her mouth shut, won't you?"

"Oh, that's original. Did you come up with that all by yourself?" Kiva answered, her voice a little shaky, fists still clenched at her side.

His eyes flicked to hers and flashed a warning. "What did you just say?"

"Just get out," she said a little more steadily, her heart pounding like the racket she had just caused on the walls.

Kiva looked away when he pulled her cousin's head back by the hair at her nape and devoured her mouth in a rough kiss. She continued to study the peeling paint on the wall when he whispered filthy promises and smacked her on the bottom before ambling down the stairs. They listened in tense silence as Junior opened and slammed the car door, revving the engine, and spinning away.

Hana whirled around so fast Kiva took a step back. Pointing a menacing finger in her face she barked out, "Don't breathe a word of this to my parents, you hear me?" Kiva stared back. She hadn't planned to utter a word.

"Say it!" Hana shouted.

Kiva shuffled and looked away. There were a hundred things she wanted to say to her older cousin, but she hated confrontation, especially when it came to her. Hana's tone made her feel as if she'd been slapped. Her mind whirred under the pressure and the words were lost. Hana snickered, interpreting her silence as submission, sparking anger and disappointment low in her gut. For her cousin, but mostly for herself.

Hana folded her arms across her chest and popped out a hip. "Poor little Kiva. You're so naïve. Never had a boyfriend. Never been kissed." She arched a perfect brow when Kiva didn't say anything. "Are you even normal? That's what every girl wants." And then she leaned closer, whispering, "That's what your own mother was like."

Kiva willed herself to remain calm when hurt speared her from the inside. Her cousin had no idea what she wanted—that she had dreams of traveling abroad and sketching along the Seine, of sitting in a lecture theater and absorbing its energy into her fingertips. That she indeed looked forward to being with someone who made her heart race and whose heart raced because of her. Someone who acknowledged her weaknesses, her flaws, and imperfections and not only looked beyond them but embraced them as a part of her reality. While she was inexperienced, she imagined love to be gentle smiles and sweet bear hugs, acts of kindness and uplifting conversations, openness and safety—and within that safety, a love so easy that she could be free to be herself. Her best self.

One day.

"He's not right for you, Hana. This sneaking around and disrespect, you'll only get hurt in the end."

Hana lowered her eyes and hissed menacingly, "Don't judge me with your goody little two-shoes."

"I'm not judging you—I'm looking out for you. Junior has defied Mau. You shouldn't be with a guy who disrespects your father."

Taken aback, her cousin recovered quickly by sneering, her lip curling in distaste. "I don't need you, *Makiva*, to look out for me, okay? What could a girl with a dull leg do for me, anyway?"

Kiva swallowed the tightness in her throat. "Why are you like this toward me? What have I ever done to you?"

"Don't pretend that you don't know!" Her voice teetered with emotion.

Kiva froze, feeling as if she was getting to the heart of Hana's outrage. She spoke softly, hoping her tone would encourage her to open up. "Know what, Hana?"

"I overheard them talking. About you. About me." She emphasized the last two words with bitterness.

"Who?"

Hana sniffed and looked away. "Just go climb that stupid tree of yours and stay out of my life."

"Hana, please talk to me—"

But her cousin had turned away and marched to her room, slamming the door behind her.

Kiva stared after her in puzzlement, tugging on her bottom lip, her emotions in turmoil, before spinning around and fleeing to her tree. While she sought refuge in its large leafy canopy, the leaves pressed down on her, suffocating her instead. It was always the same story when someone wanted to hurt her; they attacked her physical weakness first, the most noticeable target. She couldn't help feeling the familiar pain flare up from within, but more than that she couldn't help but be rattled by Hana's accusations. What had she been referring to? What had Kiva done?

She tried to remember the tickles and laughter from the children at art class, and sweet Iakopo with his clay mold of her, but as her arms and legs shook from the climb, clinging onto branches as if they could save her, the joy she felt a little less than an hour ago was crushed and withered away in its roots.

CHAPTER SEVEN

Contrary to the art class Kiva taught the children on Saturday, their curiosity and excitement translating into enthusiastic chatter and ending with tickles, eleven brooding students sat silent before her, their bored expressions dashing what little confidence she had when she entered the art center.

Her heavy gait had drawn a few curious stares, and she overheard one boy whisper in an American accent, "Why does she walk like that?"

Kiva glanced nervously at her uncle who sat to the side and nodded to her in encouragement. Now that the carvings were complete, she was finally charged with the task of teaching the art of *siapo* making. The time couldn't come any sooner, the anxiety she felt over the previous weeks giving her stomach cramps. She admitted to herself that part of that anxiety was related to the little incident she'd had with Hana. They'd largely ignored each other ever since, but it didn't help the gnawing feeling in her gut. She pushed it down and surveyed the carvings before her. She admitted she was impressed with some of them. Ryler's carving hadn't changed much except for the lines that were now carved deeper, the words more defined.

Clearing her throat, she picked a stalk off the ground, choosing to forgo the rectangular table to sit on the floor. She had worn her *lavalava* modestly long to her ankles today, covering as much of her uneven legs as possible.

"The *siapo* cloth is created through the process of stripping the stalk of the paper mulberry tree," she began, "and then rolling the strips to help straighten the bark." Kiva demonstrated these steps by firstly tearing a little section at the bottom of the stalk with a small knife, then using her teeth to pull the bark until she reached a section where she could grip it with her hands. She placed the end of the stalk under her left foot to ground it in place and began to tear the bark off the wood.

"Do we have to use our teeth?" interrupted a student.

Kiva glanced at a boy with cheeks tinged pink from the heat and offered a small smile. "Yes. It's easier to strip the stalk this way." He reacted with a bewildered look.

Once stripped, Kiva rolled the material with the outer bark facing the roll. Kiva immediately unfolded it and sat with the thick end in her hands. "Once the bark is unrolled, we take a knife and carefully cut a straight line across it, but not so far to cut into the bast, which is the inner bark." Kiva carefully peeled this with the help of her knife until she had enough material to grab with her hands. She then skillfully peeled the bark away from the bast, pausing now and again to use her knife to cut at a sticky part where the bark threatened to tear up the inner bark. "Once the bark is ready for *siapo* making, it is scraped with shells we call *sisi*. After it's scraped, the bark is then beaten with a wooden mallet on a *tutua* or wooden anvil. After this, it is laid out to dry, and the corners are pulled tight and held down with stones. It can take up to a couple of hours to dry. After the material is dry, the first sheet is laid on the printing block, in this case your carvings, and glue made from the arrowroot plant is dabbed to patch up any small holes."

Kiva lifted a wood block carved with traditional designs and placed it in front of her. "The dye that is used to imprint the bark cloth is made from natural products. Black is obtained from burning the candlenut seed and scraping the soot that catches on stones when placed near smoke; red is acquired by scraping *'ele*, red ochre, a stone found in some parts in Samoa. For this lesson, we will be using brown dye extracted from the *o'a* tree and red ochre."

Kiva picked up a dried sheet of bark she had prepared earlier for the lesson and laid it on the printing block. She dabbed on arrowroot glue before placing a second layer on top. Dipping a cloth into the bowl of the *o'a* dye, she rubbed this over the bark liberally, pressing the two layers together. "The cloth that I'm using for dyeing is made from a cutting of the same tree that we use for the *siapo*. It's tied at the end to make a type of padded brush." Next, Kiva shredded ochre with a grater Mau had made from cutting off the bottom of an old fish tin and drilling holes on it. The red substance filtered through, and Kiva repeated the process—glue, layering, dyeing.

Designs started to appear—the coconut leaf, pandanus blooms, a starfish—as the ink seeped through, staining the wood block underneath. Heart racing, Kiva smiled to herself as the patterns emerged sharper, the colors darker, the tips of her fingers stained from the amber and crimson dye. "This type of dyeing is called the '*elei*' or rubbing method."

When it was complete, she tilted it up carefully for everyone to see. "And there you have it, the *siapo* cloth."

Kiva peered out to the room to see some of the students studying the cloth; one scratching a mosquito bite on his leg, another stifling a yawn with his arm. She flicked her eyes briefly to Ryler, who sat toward the back, head cocked to the side, rubbing a hand over his mouth and jaw. A flutter erupted in her stomach and Kiva turned her head away. Now that she had so intimately sketched his hand in the safety of her room, she felt uncomfortable sitting a few feet away from him, as if she harbored some secret connection to him he wasn't aware of.

She focused her mind on the next stage of the lesson instead. "Today we will begin the process by stripping and preparing the bark for drying. By the next class it will already be dried and ready for dyeing."

Stalks were distributed around, and the boys examined them with curiosity before getting to work. Kiva stood and limped over to offer her assistance where needed.

She drew nearer to Ryler and noticed him thumbing the end of his stalk.

"Here," she said patiently, sitting down beside him. She took the small knife she carried and sliced a cut at the end of it. "Now you can use your hands and teeth to take it off."

"You think peeling bark and waiting for it to dry will help me?" he asked in a low, menacing voice.

Kiva stilled when she realized what he was asking her. He had his doubts, and she knew he had been skeptical about this whole assignment from the beginning. Turning so she was facing his profile, she responded gently, "When you say it like that, I can see how this project might seem trivial. But Mau feels it's important enough, that you are all important enough. I'm just here to help."

Ryler ran a hand through his thick brown hair, exposing the ink on his forearm. Kiva's eyes snapped to it, and she studied the swirls that were imprinted with beautiful penmanship, the calligraphy exquisite to her artist's eye, and recognized it immediately as a similar script to his carving. "What does your tattoo say?" she asked with undisguised interest.

Ryler picked up the stalk and started peeling back the bark with his hands, the muscles in his forearms contracting. His eyebrows crinkled at her curiosity. "It's my name in Arabic."

"That says Ryler?"

He looked over at her. "How do you know my name?"

Caught off guard, Kiva tried to suppress a sheepish smile. "Mau mentioned it …" She half shrugged.

After a pause he finally said, "It's actually my first name, Taaraz. Ryler is my second name."

Surprised by this new information, she rolled his first name around in her head in the way he pronounced it: *Tah-rahz.* "Why do you go by Ryler?" she asked.

He ripped off the bark, his movements quick and assured. No need for teeth, she noticed. "It's what I've been called since I was a kid. When my mother and I moved in with her parents, they didn't want anything to do with my father or his ethnicity, so the name went."

Kiva noticed by the hard set of his jaw that he didn't want to be probed further. But something also told her that even though his family had tried to banish traces of his Middle Eastern side, he wasn't letting it go. "What does it mean? Taaraz?" His name was a tentative pronouncement on her lips.

Ryler peered over at her. "It means strong, powerful. What I carved on the wood here? That about sums it up. It's who I am, Kiva. It's all you or anyone needs to know about me. I've acknowledged it, carved it out, but there's no changing it."

His words stung, smothering the surprise she had that he'd remembered her name. "Maybe," she said, the word slipping out with added conviction.

Ryler raised an eyebrow, and his hands tightened at the end of the bark, ripping it off with a little too much force. "You don't believe me?"

She chose her next words with care, unsure of how he would react. "I'm not trying to disrespect you, Ryler. I don't know what you've been through or where you come from, but I can't help it. Your name, Taaraz, means strength. Strength doesn't have to be manifested in a violent way." He glared at her as she continued. "The name of your school—Toa Academy—is also forged with strength. It has a very powerful meaning. Toa means 'warrior,' and a Samoan warrior is someone who respects, protects, and takes care of his people."

His eyebrows dipped into a crease. "You're right," he bit out. "You don't know me, and you don't know where I've come from. I'm here but I'm not changing. Not for you, the whole damn school, or anyone else." *Ouch.* She flinched at his defiance and harsh tone, which commanded an end to their conversation. What did she expect? That a few words of encouragement might change his perspective? He wasn't her responsibility nor was she his mentor. But however defeated she was, she couldn't help feeling a little invested in him and his life story. Something pulled at her, even if she couldn't put a name to it.

"I dare you," she said a little shakier than she hoped.

"What?"

"I dare you to challenge yourself. To make the effort to step out of your angry little bubble. To do it for yourself, if not for your family. You've come here with your glass completely full with your issues and challenges and everything else that has gone wrong in your life. All Mau asks is that you empty yourself of some of that hatred so you can allow for something else to enter inside. You might be surprised at what that might be."

He glared at her while she swallowed hard. She started to notice the other boys growing restless around her while they waited for the next step in the process. Her uncle gestured for her attention and she nodded her understanding. "I'll leave you to it then," she said as she started to rise. She stood a little too quickly and felt her left leg give way awkwardly, threatening to topple her over. Her stomach clenched in horror as she sucked in a breath and flung an arm out to balance herself.

Ryler watched her wobble and shot his hand out to steady her. His fingers wrapped around her arm above her elbow to help steady her. He held her firmly yet gently, she observed, as she found her footing. She felt his strength radiating through her skin with a hand she was all too familiar sketching. A hand that now had calluses under the fingers and palms from days of carving.

"Thanks, I'm … I'm okay now," she stammered. When she stood as upright as she could, her back and shoulder bent at an angle, he let her go. Knowing how mortified she would have been if she had fallen over, Kiva straightened her sarong and gave him a shaky smile. "You're not so bad after all, Taaraz Ryler."

He hung his head and shook it, and Kiva didn't miss the slight twitch of his mouth. When he looked up through hooded eyes, her heart lurched.

"Call me Ry," he said in his deep voice, and she got the distinct feeling he was offering an apology.

She smiled softly in return. "Okay … Ry."

It was a start, albeit a small one, but her face immediately sobered when she remembered his earlier tone and disposition. She suddenly swelled with the need to do something more, to say something monumental that might touch the recesses of his mind and spirit, and hoped she didn't come across sounding completely random or stupid or cliché in the process. Inhaling unsteadily, she proceeded to quote a line from one of her favorite poets about listening to the messages embedded in adversities and to not let them get you down. When she was done, she held a breath and watched for his reaction.

Ry simply arched a brow. "You read Rumi."

Kiva's lips curved into a smile when he recognized the source, and was it just her imagination that he sounded a little impressed? "Yes." She breathed. "He's my favorite poet."

The thirteenth century Persian poet meant more to her than any other writer she had come across. After discovering a book of poems at the public library, she copied word for word the enlightening words that spilled out from each page until she resorted to almost photocopying the entire book and slipping pieces of scrap paper in between old art books in her room. She had arranged a collage of her favorite excerpts, dispersed among sketches of what she imagined the galaxy to look like. His poems made her view the world in a different light, as if every cell and atom contributed to something greater. Was he as affected like her by his words? Had it tipped his axis and moved him in an astronomic way?

"So tell me, Rumi-enthusiast," Ry probed dryly, "what might that message look like?"

Kiva licked her lips. "I like to believe that there is hope in pain, that there is a purpose behind whatever life throws at us. That if we close our mind to the hurt and open our heart instead, we may find a way out."

He measured her in silence before asking, "Open our heart to what, Kiva?"

"That's a mystery I'm still trying to work out, but I imagine it has something to do with a shift in perspective. To being open to the possibility of change if it promises to help us grow. To step out of our comfort zone and take a risk without the fear of failure holding us back. And if we fail, then that's okay, too. Every opportunity contributes to learning—whether it's something new that we gain or something valuable that needs to be emphasized. We often guard our hearts, but we are capable of so much if we could connect with it in an honest and spiritual way. In saying that though, I don't think we can ever let go of our pain. Just that if we acknowledge it without allowing it to overtake and rule our lives, we're making a monumental step forward." She offered him a crooked smile. "Easier said than done?" Ry huffed out his laughter. Her next words were spoken softly, "You used those hands to fight ... now use them to create. You've been given this chance, Ry."

She didn't elaborate further, and he was quiet in a contemplative way. She turned to leave and could feel him watching her as she limped to the front of the room where Mau was distributing shells and wooden mallets.

There wasn't enough to go around so smaller groups were formed where each student could take turns. After cleaning the bark with the shells, the room soon filled with the sounds of harsh poundings, the bark being battered down until it was flattened out like limp pancakes. Finding an area for them to dry was going to be a challenge given the lack of available space in the center, but Kiva planned for mats to be brought down from the house so they could be placed outside on the grass. The weather report indicated fine weather with an occasional shower or two so she was on high alert for the slightest sprinkle of rain.

The time passed without incident until Kiva was surprised to find that she was enjoying herself. Where she was tense when she first entered the art center, she now eased comfortably in her role and found the students to be pliant and cooperative. Whatever lessons on respect and obedience the Academy drilled into them was working to the class's favor as far as she could see. Of course she was aware that their chaperones were always present together with her uncle. Thankful for his quiet support, she helped place rocks along the corners of the stretched bark and glimpsed up at the clouds hovering above blocking the sun. Judging by the puffy white mushroom shape, she didn't think it was going to pour anytime soon, but that didn't mean there couldn't be a spontaneous rain shower at any moment.

When she lowered her eyes, she noticed Ry watching her from the verandah with an unreadable expression on his face. They hadn't spoken since her little near-fall, and she wished now that she could. She wanted to hear more about where he came from, about his family, his tattoo and what it meant to him. She glanced away instead and resumed placing the bark across the mat, arranging, with the help of a few students, rocks to hold them down.

A shadow passed close by and she glanced up to see Ry crouched down a few feet away. She couldn't help but smile a little on the inside. They worked together in silence until Mau called everyone to gather around near the steps.

He wiped his brow of the sweat pooling on his forehead. "Well done, boys. You worked hard today. On Friday you'll be taught how to mix your own dye, and then you will see your carvings come to life on the *siapo*. Let's pack up and then you can go."

They made their way inside the center, and Kiva helped pick up the left over bark strewn across the floor and then observed as the students bounded down the stairs to the van after they were done tidying up.

She watched Ry's retreating back and sighed inwardly. One more class and then it was over. She would never see him again after the coming Friday.

Turning away, she didn't notice him looking back over his shoulder.

CHAPTER EIGHT

Frowning down at her project, Kiva wasn't sure she had adequately portrayed the symbols that most represented her as a person. Miss Lene had asked the class to create motifs that communicated something about their identity and uniqueness, and Kiva had so far sketched her hand but little else. Palm facing, her fingers were spread delicately as if they were tuning an invisible guitar. The pads of her thumb and index finger were smudged with ink to symbolize the sketch artist that she was. But something was missing. She needed more.

Glancing over at Silei's work, she noticed that she had filled the entire space on her paper with doodles of shoes, jewelry, the Cross, and something that resembled patterns of the *malu* tattoo. Kiva knew Silei wanted to get her thighs and legs inked in the traditional way when she graduated from university, and since it was a process that would bring about unbearable pain, Kiva secretly commended her bravery. Never one to take enthusiastically to art projects, she was also happy to see that her best friend embraced this one with keen interest.

Blowing air out through her mouth, she peered around the classroom to notice that she wasn't the only one restless with the assignment. One kid was scratching his ear while another was shaking her head and sighing audibly. Returning her gaze to her paper, she pulled a favorite poem from memory in which Rumi asked the question, *"Do you know what you are?"* She inscribed his answer along the length of her index finger on the piece of paper: *"You are a manuscript of a divine letter. You are a mirror reflecting a noble face."*

Kiva had a unique face. Her dark brown eyes were large for her oval face and her nose was flat. Her upper lip was thicker than the bottom one, giving her an inverted pout. She had non-existent eyebrows, not because she over plucked them, but because they were so light you could barely see them from a distance. When left unbound, her light brown hair laid dull and lifeless across her back. It was more straight than curly, and she wasn't very creative when it came to hairstyles, choosing to pin it up with a pencil when the heat became unbearable. Her features were a dichotomy of sorts—while her hair was light, her skin tone was darker than her extended family's, and she had sometimes been called *meauli*—black—by some of them. In the safety of her bedroom, she sometimes stood in front of the full-length mirror and curiously perused her growing body and curves, her awkward limbs and bent shoulders. Her eyes took in her tilted body and trailed downwards until they stopped at her uneven legs, one bent at the knee to accommodate for the other's length. Her shorter leg was leaner in the thigh and significantly smaller in the calf area, her foot size naturally different from the other. She didn't have special shoes to match her feet, and as a result one would always slap her heel, like a toddler prancing around in her mother's sandals.

When she came across this particular verse in the library, she felt comforted to be reminded that she belonged to something greater than her physical body and the physical world around her. She knew it bespoke of a mystical connection to the divine, that she was more than just a living, breathing being. She had a soul. Everyone did. Her philosophy of life was simple: be honest, be kind and just. She acknowledged that every living being had the capacity to connect to something celestial if they tapped into the core of their existence. That, in itself, was pretty amazing.

Those periods of solitude in her favorite tree were the moments she felt the most connected.

Kiva picked up her pencil and began to draw the *pulu* tree near her wrist, its branches spreading and surrounding her hand protectively like an embrace.

Thoughts of Ry and their conversation about poetry and his tattoo came unbidden. She called to mind the dream of the lagoon and pearl, its dark hue shimmering brilliantly and nestled delicately in her bloody hands, and she began to sketch its round texture in the center of her palm, shading in the soft curve and filling in the spaces where shadows played. The dream was still so vivid in her mind. She believed in signs, both physical and instinctual, and she trusted her gut feeling to guide her. What Ry had shared with her gave Kiva a small glimpse into his life, and she was intrigued to learn more. Despite the hardness he pulled off,

SIENI A.M.

the distance he put between himself and the others that screamed *stay away*, her instinct told her otherwise. She felt a thrill surge in her gut that she would be seeing him that afternoon for the final *siapo* class.

Checking the time on the dust-coated clock above the black board, Kiva added finishing touches to her sketch before the end of the period. She started to gather her belongings together when Silei snatched her paper.

"Oh, nice. I like," she said.

Kiva gave her a tight smile. "Thanks." Best friend or not, she felt vulnerability start to spread inside—a response that always accompanied the artist inside of her when bearing her heart to the world, especially with a project like the one they were currently working on. She couldn't help but feel she was being judged on it, and she didn't think she would ever overcome that feeling. Silei had never even seen the inside of her sketchbooks. No one had.

"You don't have any *malu* markings here. You don't want to get one?"

Kiva felt the knot in her belly tighten. No. She didn't want to undergo one. She would have to be lying down and the idea of stretching out in an unguarded position frightened her. She didn't want any part of her uneven legs exposed to the gawking eyes and hands of the several tattoo artists pulling and stretching her skin taut, from her inner thighs to her knees, while others sang songs of encouragement, her discomfort both within and outside her body on display for the village to see. She had witnessed her older cousins receive theirs in their grandmother's village. Traditionally done in pairs, one by one the women were called, and the entire process took several hours.

It was the small details that Kiva remembered. The blood stained cloth that was used to wipe their legs. The balled fist on the corner of the pillow near her cousin's head. The tooth indents on her lower lip from biting down hard. The tense crease on her brow. And the excruciating silence punctuated by the tap-tap-tapping of the tools. The women never uttered a sound. The only sounds came from the lilting songs and the drumming of the chisel as it drove into delicate skin. She heard the knees were the worst—when that chisel met bone, the pain was a torment made visible by the harrowing expressions on her cousins' faces. They were daughters of a high-ranking chief, Mau's older brother. Kiva had been responsible for fanning away the flies near their strewn bodies. If she could offer comfort in some small way, she did it for them wholeheartedly to ease away the lines of strain on their faces while her aunt applied damp cloths over their heads and led the songs.

68

No. Kiva didn't want to undergo pain on that scale, even if the tradeoff was a significant one.

She felt faint just thinking about vaccinations, and that was only one needle at a time—the tattoo chisel had several blade-like points of penetration that extended agony over hours. She had silently cried all the way to the hospital to get a tetanus shot when she stepped on a rusty nail near the water tank. She was eleven and had been running barefoot in the yard. Her aunt had to coerce her into the truck, threatening to take away her sketchbook if she refused.

Kiva shook her head. "It's not for me."

There had been a resurgence in recent years of young women from both within Samoa and abroad that underwent the traditional process, resulting in a sisterhood that bridged families and extended beyond villages, cities, and international lines. Her best friend would become a part of that community.

She studied her now in silence before nodding slowly. "Okay, that's cool. Respect if you do, respect if you don't, right?"

Kiva smiled. "Right … but I'll be there for you when it's your time, Si."

Silei flashed her a grin. "You better be."

Miss Lene called for the sketches to be handed in just as the bell rang shrilly.

***

Kiva sniffed tobacco smoke drifting through the open sill as she climbed the narrow steps of the bus and passed the driver whose arm was stretched outside, dangling a cigarette. Her face split into a grin when she saw Ester sitting in their usual seat a couple rows from the back. Hana had plopped herself at the rear and was already plugged into her music.

Ester tapped her knee when she settled down next to her, the veins in her old hands protruding from the humidity. "Look at the mountains." She pointed out through the window toward the direction the bus would take. Kiva noticed dark clouds gathering in the distance. "Looks like another rainfall."

The bus started with a sputter and lurched fitfully before the engine roared to life. The driver shook his head at his blunder and they exited the bus terminal, taking the corner a little too sharply.

They whizzed through town and headed uphill, stopping now and then to pick up school children along the road. Tui sat on Kiva's lap as the bus reached capacity. She glanced behind her to see Hana blushing on the lap of a guy similar in age dressed in his school uniform, the colors indicating he went to an all-boys school near town.

Kiva listened patiently as Ester spoke of the fine mats she was weaving and the neighbor's pigs that annoyingly dug up her garden. She ignored the uncomfortable weight on her lap and the jostling head two inches from her face. Someone nearby was eating a pork bun, the savory aroma reaching her nose, and Kiva swallowed the saliva that pooled in her mouth. Her stomach had been cramping since noon, and judging by the mammoth-sized pimple that had sprouted on her forehead when she awoke in the morning, her period was expected to begin soon. They passed several villages and many cars passed them on the narrow rural road. The bus swayed around corners and struggled over steep slopes.

It was a couple stops after she said goodbye to the old lady that the bus came to a jerky stop at the crest of a hill. The engine spluttered and died in what sounded to Kiva as metal grinding, her teeth clacking around in her jaw from the sudden tremble. The driver shook his head, flung his cigarette away, and worked the gears, turning the key in the ignition to flare it to life. Several attempts to start the engine yielded little progress, and Kiva could hear impatient groans and *tsks* growing around her as the reality of their situation dawned on them.

"Alright, everyone off," the driver finally announced before he jumped out and motioned for a young man from his village to help him. They disappeared around the front of the bus.

Kiva grabbed her bag and followed Tui down the steps.

Passengers gathered in the shade of the bushes and trees lining the road, darting hopeful glances toward the driver and his young assistant. Surrounded by cattle and uncultivated land, they hadn't yet reached the crown of the mountain, the midway point of their journey. Most of their homes were miles away, and in this terrain would take hours to reach by foot.

Some of the younger crowd had already set out and Kiva got an idea.

"Come on," she called to Tui and Hana. "We might as well start walking and then hopefully get a lift up."

As expected Hana narrowed her eyes and scowled.

***

They had been walking uphill for thirty minutes when Kiva's shoe broke. A flimsy plastic sandal that was school uniform protocol, she kicked it off and stayed close to the grass, avoiding the sweltering fever rising from the tar-sealed road. Despite cloud cover, the sultry heat penetrated the atmosphere, creating invisible bubbles heavy with humidity that Kiva sucked in with each inhale, and she exhaled with difficulty. She wasn't the fittest person around, and she was definitely feeling it in her thighs. Sweat pooled on her upper lip and gathered and dripped down between her shoulder blades. Her cramps had intensified, and her lower back protested with discomfort. Her steps felt sluggish, and she hissed when her bare foot came in contact with prickles. She paused and looked ahead where Tui and Hana were twenty paces ahead of her.

Tui turned and acknowledged her. "Are you okay?" he yelled.

Kiva squinted against the severe ache in her stomach and waved him on.

They had been unsuccessful in flagging down a car; the vehicles that had passed them so far were already occupied with passengers they'd left behind near the bus.

She peered over her shoulder but couldn't see the promise of an approaching truck or van—anything they could scramble in the back of—that would get them over the steep incline.

Come on, I'm late, Kiva thought with rising concern.

She attempted to limp faster. She didn't have a watch to check the time, but she knew the *siapo* class would have started by now. She didn't think her uncle would postpone the final lesson because she wasn't there. The instructions for dyeing were simple; they had all the ingredients to mix the colors ready to go in the art center. The students simply had to rub them over their bark cloths and wait for them to dry. She wanted to be there for that more than anything, and if she was really being honest with herself she admitted there was someone in particular she wanted to see for the last time.

She heard a car approach from behind and instead of gaining speed on the hill, it slowed down and purred alongside her.

"Hey cripple," Junior called out. "You don't look so good." His tone didn't relay compassion.

Kiva stopped, took in a shallow breath, and her heart sank. She knew how this was going to play out before Hana screamed in delight.

"Baby!" She ran back down the slope, her pretty face a mask of relief. "You got my message, thank God. What took you so long?" Clambering over his lap, she slapped a heavy kiss on the side of his neck.

Kiva heard Tui's embarrassed grunt as he joined them. Public displays of affection were a rare occurrence. In fact, they didn't exist. In a country where the national television station blacked out romantic scenes in movies, skipping to ads about laundry detergent and local coffee instead, said something of the level of tolerance on such matters.

"Let's get out of here," Hana said when she'd settled in her seat.

"Wait—what about us?" Tui raised his voice.

Kiva held her cousin's gaze and sent vibes that she hoped would appeal to some semblance of her humanity wedged deep inside. Hana pursed her lips instead and turned away.

"Sorry, kid. There's no space," Junior answered nonchalantly.

That wasn't true. Both Tui and Kiva glanced at the back seat of his convertible. They could easily fit three people back there.

Tui shook his head in disbelief. "Are you kidding me? At least take Kiva. You know she has a bad leg."

"I'm sure another car will come soon," Hana said hastily, flicking her hand in dismissal, avoiding eye contact. "Come on, baby, let's go, I'm hungry."

Kiva's stomach protested with a groan, but it didn't help her case when they pulled away leaving a plume of smoke behind. Tui picked up a stone and threw it in their direction, barely missing the bumper where it bounced off the road into a ditch.

"Unbelievable," he mumbled under his breath as they watched the silver car grow smaller.

Kiva dug her nails in her palms leaving little half-moon indents in her skin and expelled a breath. "Don't worry about it, Tui. I didn't expect anything less."

Thunder boomed ominously in the distance and they exchanged looks.

"Well, I hope the rain ruins his leather interior," he bit out.

Kiva cracked a smile as rain hammered over them, making her gasp. It was a reprieve from the heat, a welcome relief from this whole ridiculous ordeal. She dropped her school bag, stretched her arms out, and lifted her face to the sky. "Woo-hoo!" she screamed without hesitation. It felt incredible. Closing her eyes, she ignored the sting against her eyelids, cheeks, and lips.

"Don't know what you're so happy about," she heard Tui grumble. "We still have an hour to go. At least."

Kiva laughed then. Belly clutching, on-the-brink of lunacy laughter. She bent over and gripped her knees and couldn't stop the shakes that rolled off her. Wow. She needed this.

"Are you alright?" Tui sounded annoyed.

"Yes. No. Yes." She managed to gasp between peals of laughter. "I don't know."

Tui shook his head and then set out ahead of her.

Kiva let out a long sigh and wiped the tears that slipped and mingled with the rain. Who knew a rain storm coupled with laughter could be so therapeutic? Kiva bent to retrieve her bag from the ground. When she straightened, she hissed audibly and clutched her abdomen. The cramp lacerated her stomach and spread to her lower back. *Oh God,* she groaned inwardly. *Not again, not now.* When it smoothed out, she quickly sobered and followed Tui's footsteps.

The rain beat against them, cutting the atmosphere diagonally, the flood that now gathered and spilled from out of the ditch sliding across the road and pressing against Kiva's ankles, making it difficult to walk.

Minutes stretched and became an enemy.

Kiva pushed through the exhaustion that threatened to buckle at her knees, the pain pulsing in her stomach now an unrelenting ache. She wished now more than ever she had little red shoes she could tap that would magically transport her to the warmth of her bed, a hot water bottle pressed to her abdomen. Why had she been laughing hysterically earlier? She couldn't remember what was so funny.

It was the blast of a horn that alerted her to an oncoming vehicle driving from the direction of home, its headlights on high beam in the storm. Kiva squinted against the rain and recognized the white van immediately, and her pulse tripped.

It was over.

The faces of the Academy students blurred together as the van whizzed by, sending a spray of water on her school skirt. Kiva turned and watched it disappear around the bend in the road, its break lights visible from the growing distance. Well, that was the end of that, she thought dejectedly. Disappointment formed a lump in her throat and was a hard pill to swallow.

Another horn blared and Kiva whipped her head round at the familiar noise. Her uncle pulled up beside her and stretched over to roll down the passenger side window. "Get in!" he called over the pounding of the rain.

CHAPTER NINE

Kiva burrowed under the covers of her bed, tucking her legs into a fetal position, pressing the hot water bottle close to her stomach to lock in the warmth. Her back pain returned and her head hurt from the argument Naomi and Hana had gotten into when they'd arrived home after dropping off Tui. Her aunt had caught onto Hana's little car stunt with Junior when they abandoned Kiva on the side of the road, and they'd argued as a result.

Now she just wanted to close her eyes, forget everything, and succumb to sleep.

Mau had filled her in on the class on the drive back. When he realized she was going to be late, Naomi had taken over, giving verbal instructions without bringing harm to her wrist. The students were able to complete their projects—her uncle commented on how well they turned out—and they took their *siapo* away with them. Kiva was sorry she hadn't seen their visual stories stamped onto the bark cloth. It was akin to watching a brilliant film and then having the power suddenly turn off at the penultimate moment. She had been looking forward to seeing this assignment to the end, to observe for herself whether it helped these students reflect in some small way their path and choices. As an art teacher, there was something gratifying about seeing magic come alive under the tips of her students' fingers and the effect it had on their lives. Granted, the Academy students weren't always enthusiastic about the whole idea—*she* hadn't been too thrilled either in the beginning—but she had come to witness some powerful messages embedded in their carvings. Now there was no closure for her, and the artist inside was more than a little disheartened.

She awoke at dusk when the sky was stained orange and the curtains whirled softly above her bed, blowing chilly remnants of the rain. Disoriented, Kiva rose and blinked away her drowsiness. She stretched, testing her muscles, and winced against the humming ache that settled over her body. Her lower back was stiff and her legs throbbed, but at least her cramps were gone.

Kiva retrieved her sketchbook from under her pillow, withdrew the pencil from her hair, and lost herself in lines and shadows, imagery and emotion. After she purged herself onto the page, she limped downstairs and found it abandoned. A note stuck to the refrigerator informed her that her aunt and uncle had gone to visit extended family in the village and that they'd taken Hana with them.

Kiva welcomed the solitude of an empty house, the creaks and groans of a century-old home accompanying her as she made herself a sandwich to eat.

Masi's incessant meows drew her outside where she saw that it'd killed a mouse and was poised, ready to devour it. "Good kitty." Kiva squeaked and tried to keep the contents in her stomach down. She retreated from the bloody sight and headed toward her tree.

The sky was almost pitch-black, the smoky wisps of orange fading away. The post-storm breeze tousled her hair and ruffled her sarong. Kiva remained at the base of the trunk, having little energy to climb its clammy branches, and allowed its leaves to trickle droplets over her instead. Her thoughts drifted to her cousin and their strained relationship. How could she fix it? How could she get her to communicate whatever was bothering her? According to Hana, she was to blame for something. But what? Sighing, she locked eyes with the art center and crossed the yard to it.

Mau had closed the French doors but left it unlocked. Kiva let herself in, flicking on the lights. She inhaled the distant scent of mixed dye and papery bark. Running her hand over the stained table in the center of the room she glanced at the portraits for sale hanging on the far wall. She had often felt like the figures in the paintings: surrounded by vibrant color but stuck in one position. Heading over to them, she straightened one and started tidying around it. Wetting a cloth, she wiped away the dust on the shelves where artifacts were placed gingerly for customers despite the fact that they hadn't had many of those come through in the past few months.

Kiva continued to bristle around the center, sweeping and wiping and dusting. She was arranging paint brushes in containers when she noticed something wedged in the shadows between the sink and supplies cupboard. She bent and pulled the rolled parchment out, spread it between her fingers, and her eyes widened.

He'd forgotten to take his project.

The familiar jagged lines and script appeared now not from a carving but through the *siapo*, seeped in brown dye that was still damp. The calligraphy was smeared, as if he'd rolled it up before it was completely dry. *Meet violence with violence.* He'd been so adamant that this verse characterizes the person he is.

Kiva studied the patterns and then squinted at something in the corner. Raising it closer, she tried to make out the words scrawled vertically in black ink along the border, the handwriting scraggly and camouflaged at first glance. She angled the *siapo* to read the verse, and her heart raced when she recognized the quote. It was one she had inscribed years ago, tucked away in one of her many scrap books. At the time she had been afflicted by sadness and wanted a way out, an escape from her everyday life.

Ry hadn't forgotten his project after all but hidden it on purpose for her to find. Kiva shook her head and reread the words.

In the poem, Rumi bespoke of the strains he felt from his everyday life, the misperceptions and difficulties that tired him, which created in him an ardent desire to distance himself from everything and everyone, including his own self.

What are you trying to tell me, Ry?

She looked up from the *siapo*, but the room was empty, devoid of students, and she had no way of finding out.

CHAPTER TEN

Six months later

Two days before Kiva turned sixteen, Silei and her driver showed up at the house blasting the horn and causing a racket in the front yard. Kiva peered through her bedroom window to see her leaning out the door of the white Land Cruiser, Sefa frowning and shaking his head beside her. "Kiva!" she shouted. "Get your butt down here! Let's go!"

Kiva pulled a brush through her hair, checked her appearance in the mirror, and limped hurriedly down the steps. Today she had chosen a summer dress, the outfit an early birthday present from Silei. She loved the floral print that hugged her curves and flared at the waist, stopping just below her knees.

"What's with all the excitement?" Naomi called from across her herb garden, a smile playing across her lips. The cast had come off months ago giving her the mobility she missed when tending her vegetables. Fresh cherry tomatoes, cucumbers, and parsley graced the dinner table almost every night since. Hana's presence at the table had increased since she'd left Kiva on the side of the road, and her attitude had tempered toward everyone, but Kiva knew that she was still seeing Junior now and then, only more on the sly.

Between school and chores, Kiva spent her afternoons in the art center where she explored ideas for the upcoming art competition. Expanding on the concept of the hand sketch she'd created for school, Kiva experimented with somber colors and textures. She found it challenging to define and pinpoint a particular message she wanted to convey, and consequently ripped apart and discarded several papers, littering the floor of the art center. Her uncle had arched one brow and left her alone. She was back to square one now with nothing but a blank canvas to show for her befuddled thoughts.

"Hi, Naomi!" Silei responded. "Is it okay if I take Kiva to the movies for her birthday?"

Naomi raised her arm and wiped her brow on her sleeve. "A bit early to celebrate isn't it?" she teased. "Of course it's fine. I've already arranged to take over the kids' art class today; we're going to be doing tie-dyeing. Kiva, take a twenty from my purse on the kitchen table. You look beautiful, by the way. Now go have fun!" She shooed them away with her soiled hands.

Kiva had never been to the movies before, and the excitement she had harbored all week bubbled inside. She didn't care that they were watching an action adventure flick, a choice Trey and his buddies made. Silei had started seeing him shortly after the art class he'd teased her in, and their relationship became a dichotomy of sorts—they laughed, they argued, they broke up then made up. During the term break, her parents had flown her to Auckland where she spent the time eating KFC and shopping for herself and Trey. She returned with music CDs for him and the floral dress for Kiva.

"You look amazing!" she gushed when Kiva buckled her seat belt.

"Thanks to you." Kiva smiled, smoothing the folds of her dress over her lap. "You have great taste and it fits perfectly."

They pulled up at the crowded cinema thirty minutes later where people could be seen milling around outside blocking flashy posters that boasted the latest releases. It was a small theater with only two big screens and a box office that opened to the street, but the place always seemed to be busy. On this Saturday morning it was even more so with the *Pirates of the Caribbean* release.

"Thanks, Sefa. I'll call you when we're done?" Silei asked.

He grunted in reply and drove away.

Silei grabbed Kiva's hand and they weaved their way through the crowd. "There they are!" she said when she spotted Trey and his friends. Three imposing boys stood apart with their arms crossed over their chests, looking very much like the threatening rugby players they wanted to convey. Granted their high school team hadn't won a single game yet, but that didn't seem to deter their stance.

"Hey, Si." Trey sauntered over to them. "Happy early birthday, Kiva." He smiled in her direction. Afa and Leti stood back and nodded once. Kiva didn't know them very well but recognized them from her English class. Trey handed them their tickets. "Ready to go in?"

Kiva smelled popcorn when they stepped into the main

amphitheater. Glancing around she noticed red leather benches situated around the room, illuminated posters mounted on the walls, and the restrooms in the far corner. To her right was a confectionary counter where Silei and Trey lined up to purchase snacks. The room was congested and dimly lit, the crowd that had been standing outside now materializing around her, shoving and pushing their way toward the stairs that led inside the theater.

Silei handed her a soda and popcorn. "Let's line up."

The line in question felt like a rugby scrum. Or what Kiva imagined a scrum would be like. She was pressed on all sides by people who were taller and broader than her, invading her space and breathing down her back.

When the crowd shuffled forward, parting slightly to give her room to move, she glimpsed a familiar group of students in gray T-shirts off to the side and her pulse jumped.

What were they doing here?

Her eyes immediately darted from face to face assessing each one for harsh angles and a locked jawline. She found him, leaning against the wall, looking directly at her. His eyebrows were dipped in a frown, his mouth thinned in a straight line. He had found her first before she'd realized he was there. The crowd shifted and Kiva felt one of the guys pressing their palm on her lower back urging her forward. The space was swallowed by people again, and Ry and the Academy students disappeared from view. Were they here to watch the same movie? She climbed the steps, handed her movie ticket to the guy manning the door, and then hustled inside an expansive room lined with leather chairs.

The theater could easily seat a hundred people, and Trey led them to the middle rows where Kiva found herself wedged between Silei and Trey's friends.

As movie goers filed in, Kiva glanced over her shoulder and noticed the students from the Academy occupying seats a couple rows back. She swung her head round and focused on the blank screen in front of her.

"Are you alright?" Silei asked between mouthfuls of popcorn.

"Yeah, I'm fine. I just saw some of the guys from the Academy school back there."

Silei's eyes widened a fraction and she grinned mischievously.

"Don't you start," Kiva said with mock warning. Her lips wobbled a little at the corners while her stomach buzzed in a slow building frenzy.

The lights dimmed and an action-packed trailer flashed across the screen, the noise rumbling through Kiva's bones. She relaxed in her chair, determined to enjoy the experience, and sipped her drink.

About midway through the movie, Kiva hadn't anticipated an excessive amount of soda would result in her desperate need for the restroom. Torn between missing scenes and waiting it out until the end, she finally whispered into Silei's ear that she was heading out and then slipped as stealthily as she could past Afa and Leti. Using the light from the screen behind her to ignite the way, she limped toward the exit at the rear. The screen illuminated faces, but she focused on the swinging doors that led outside.

After she washed her hands, Kiva checked herself briefly in the bathroom mirror, tucking a few loose strands of hair behind her ear and smoothed down her dress. She opened the door and collided into a broad chest. Strong hands reached out and steadied her.

"Kiva," a familiar voice said.

"Ry?" Blinking, she peered up at him and blurted, "What are you doing here?"

He gave her an amused look. "Uh, going to the bathroom?"

With a tight-lipped smile, she shook her head. "No, I mean at the movies."

He shrugged. "Been rewarded for good behavior, I guess. We get to go out and do a few fun things now and then."

Kiva looked at his face, which had deepened in color since the last time she saw him. He seemed leaner, healthier, his build more athletic. "It's so nice to see you again. You look great," she complimented with a sincere smile.

The corner of his mouth twitched. "Thanks … They've been working us hard in the classroom and the plantations, if you believe that. We've been out rowing in those wooden canoes, fishing, hiking through the bush." He paused and shook his head. "It's been a hell of a few months."

"Not your typical high school experience?" Kiva couldn't help but grin.

Ry exhaled on a laugh and her heart swelled at the sound of it. "Far from it." His face subdued before he confessed in a low tone, "I'll admit it's been tough … being here in this place—" He rubbed the back of his neck. "It's been hard to say the least."

Kiva's heart moved with his admission, and she couldn't help but ask, "In what way?"

His brows dipped to form a crease. "More mentally challenging than anything else … This knowing, this awareness … this whole freaking ordeal. Let's just say I've had to face a few demons of my own and it hasn't been a pretty reunion." He expelled a loud breath. "I don't know why I'm telling you any of this crap. It's not your problem."

She shook her head. "No, it's fine. I don't mind. You're an interesting person, Ry."

He almost laughed. "Well, that's definitely a first." Shifting on his feet, he jutted his chin toward the theater. "You should get back before your boyfriend wonders where you are."

Kiva shook her head again. "I don't have a boyfriend. Those are friends from school. Well, Silei is my best friend and Trey is her boyfriend. I barely know the other two."

He furrowed his brows before nodding once. She moved to side step him then halted. There was something she wanted to ask first. Shoulder to shoulder, she gazed up at his face. "Why did you leave it behind?"

The muscle in his jaw jumped as he interpreted her question. "I don't know. I felt like you'd want to see it."

"I did, thank you. I was disappointed I didn't get the chance to teach the last class."

"Yeah, where were you?"

She sighed and waved her hand dismissively. "I got held up. It's a long story." She didn't want to rehash the details of Hana and Junior and their convertible. "That quote you wrote on the *siapo* … I've felt that way before." She suddenly looked away wondering why she was opening up about something painful she'd never explored with anyone else before. Perhaps she felt there was safety in these fleeting moments with Ry, where there was no promise of another encounter, as if her words would be carried away with him when they parted, never to be reflected back at her again.

"Like you wish you could have a do-over of your life?" he asked.

"Yes," She breathed and looked back up at him.

"I get it."

She shrugged in resignation. "But, I know I can't. The only thing I can do over is my approach to things. To have the faith that whatever hardship gets thrown my way is in some way supposed to mold me to be a better, stronger person."

"Yeah? And how's that approach working out for you?"

She laughed at his dry tone. "I'm not going to pretend that it's easy … I'm not extraordinary. I have my faults. I can push and fight, but sometimes there are more powerful forces out there than my own will. That's where my faith comes in. I have to trust that these forces have a message and that the only way to understand them is to endure them."

His mouth tilted a little in the corner. "Now you're the interesting one, Kiva."

Someone shouted from across the hall, startling her. "Ryler! What's taking so long?"

Ry sighed. "I better get going. Don't want them thinking I've run away."

Kiva cocked her head and couldn't help the spread of a grin. "And where would you go?"

"I don't know." He smirked. "Maybe I'd head down to the wharf and put my paddling skills to the test, see how far I get."

"You'd be lucky if you reached the reef."

"You dissing my agility?" he teased.

Kiva smiled, the apples of her cheeks pronounced, and he measured her quietly, his brown eyes relaxing around the corners, pinning hers until she shuffled awkwardly on her feet.

"Well, it was good to see you again." She didn't want to leave, but she knew their time was up.

"You too, Kiva."

"Take care, okay?" She smiled softly then turned with difficulty, as if there was an invisible tug pulling at her, and limped away.

CHAPTER ELEVEN

On the way home, Silei made Sefa pull over so she could drive. The country road was deserted of pedestrians and there was little traffic on either lane. He reluctantly swapped seats with her and gave her a few initial driving instructions.

"You're lucky this is an automatic. It's easier to learn," he said as he secured his seat belt. "Now don't crash into the bushes or your father will fire me."

"Relax, Sefa. I've got this."

Silei adjusted the seat and revved the engine to life. She drove several meters before laughing with glee. "This is awesome! I'm actually driving!"

The car jerked forward as she pressed her foot a little too hard on the accelerator.

"Alright, slow down," Sefa warned.

"Kiva, you want to try?" Silei swung her head round to her in the backseat.

"Watch the road!" Sefa barked.

Kiva smiled and shook her head.

The Land Cruiser pulled up behind a village bus swaying with people and slowed right down. Kiva noticed elbows sticking out the sides of the windows, and the hatch at the rear was lowered where legs and feet could be seen dangling through the port hole. A basket of coconuts and raw pieces of meat were tied securely at the back.

Silei pressed the pedal and swerved to overtake it.

"Don't even think about it," Sefa cautioned. "We're on a steep hill, and I don't want you to lose control."

A car passed them heading the opposite direction, and Silei slowed to a stop before pulling under a tree.

"I want Kiva to have a go," she said when she turned off the engine. "She'll be sixteen soon," she offered as explanation.

Sefa frowned. "How can she drive?"

Kiva's cheeks burned a little. "Silei, it's okay—"

"It's an automatic, like you said. Her right leg is perfectly fine to push the accelerator and to use the break," Silei cut in.

Sefa shook his head and mumbled something under his breath. "You ask for too much sometimes, Silei. If something happens—"

"Nothing will happen. Kiva is the most careful person I know." She turned and winked at her then opened the driver's side door.

"Silei, I don't feel comfortable putting Sefa in this position," Kiva whispered as they passed each other outside the vehicle.

"Don't worry, it's fine." Silei smiled reassuringly. "Sefa will survive with a few more gray hairs on his head."

Kiva laughed to hide her nerves. "That'll be because of you, not me."

Her heart pounded as she climbed into the driver's seat. The view from the driver's side seemed higher and just a little bit intimidating, the steering wheel under her hands solid.

"Are you sure you can do this?" Sefa asked beside her.

Kiva gave him her most convincing smile. With shaking hands, she turned the ignition and the engine rumbled powerfully.

"Firstly, check to see if there are any cars passing before you move onto the road. Now turn the steering wheel, put the gear in drive, and ease your foot off the break."

Kiva followed his instructions with precision. She didn't want anything to happen to this government vehicle, with scratches and all, and she definitely didn't want to get into trouble with the country's Minister of Health. Silei's father was a serious man, both on national television and in person.

She guided the four-wheel drive onto the tar seal and straightened it in her lane. They traveled steadily on the narrow road, and Kiva was grateful there were no sudden bends and turns. Gripping onto the wheel with two hands, she breathed a loud sigh and flashed Silei a bright smile in the rearview mirror. So far so good.

She chanced a glance at Sefa and noticed his hand wrapped tightly on the arm rest.

"Are you okay there, Sefa?"

"I'll be okay once I'm driving again," he murmured.

They approached a steep drop in the road, and the waterfall to the left masked the thundering of Kiva's heart. The dip was known locally as "the rollercoaster" because your stomach lurched from the sharp decline. It was a common occurrence that the faster you drove, the more your body felt airborne and your insides went haywire.

"Slow down, Kiva," Sefa advised.

"Speed up!" Silei demanded.

Kiva gripped the steering wheel tighter and sat up a little straighter. Feeling confident, she took her foot off the accelerator and let it hover near the break, allowing gravity to pull them forward. The Land Cruiser tilted down and picked up speed on its own.

"Chooohooo!" Silei screamed.

"Slow down!" Sefa shouted at the same time.

The vehicle barreled down the steep slope, and Kiva's pulse pounded from the adrenaline rush. When the road evened out, she placed her foot carefully on the break to slow it down. The Land Cruiser obeyed until she pulled it over to the side of the road.

Her mouth broke into a brilliant smile. "That was amazing!"

"That was incredible." Silei laughed from the backseat.

"And that almost gave me a heart attack. Now get out," Sefa demanded furiously. "No more driving lessons for you girls." He stormed around the vehicle as Kiva and Silei broke into giggles.

"Thank you, Sefa," Kiva acknowledged when they'd traded seats.

He grunted in irritation and pulled out onto the road.

After they dropped her off at home, Kiva wove her way through the ferns and headed toward the art center. A deadline and blank canvas called to her. Even if she had to stare at it until inspiration came to her, she would do just that. She felt rejuvenated from her outing and from her little driving stunt, and her hands tingled to devise, sketch, mix colors—whatever it took to get her creativity flowing. She was smiling to herself when she stepped into the room, the familiar smell wrapping warmth around her. She found her uncle bent over a slab of wood on the floor, his carving tools spread around him.

He looked up when she neared. "Ah, you're back. How was the movie?"

Kiva didn't remember much of the second half after her little bathroom break. "It was fun. It was an adventure fantasy about pirates. You might enjoy it." She gestured to the table. "Starting something new?"

Mau nodded. "I've been commissioned to carve a few pieces for a diplomatic group visiting from Japan."

Kiva's mouth popped open. "That's great news!" The exposure was going to be good for the art center. For her uncle. For all of them. "How did that happen?"

"Someone from the tourism bureau called a few days ago. They want to gift my carvings to the visitors when they arrive for a conference."

"That's amazing, Mau. When do you have to do this by?"

"About three weeks. I have to carve ten pieces, so I don't have a lot of time."

Kiva immediately offered her assistance. "What can I do?"

He looked up at her. "Don't you have that project to work on for Teuila? It's only a few weeks away."

Kiva shrugged. "Yes ... but that can wait." The expectation she'd placed on herself for the last few months had been pressuring her to the point that she had felt numb, her creativity stunted.

"Everything okay?" he asked with concern.

Kiva sighed. "The original idea I had? I keep going back and forth, changing my mind."

"'True Self' is a very personal theme. What are you having a hard time with?"

Kiva picked up one of the carving tools and flicked the end of it with her thumb. "I'm having a hard time reflecting on the idea of what my *true self* is. I have a few jumbled ideas, but I can't seem to separate them into anything coherent."

"The idea of 'self' is rarely clear cut. There are many, many layers."

"I believe it," she mumbled. "Miss Lene assigned the class to do this art project about identity. It raised a lot of questions in my mind about myself, about what I've been doing in my life, about what I want to do later." *About where she truly belonged,* she added internally.

Mau nodded thoughtfully. "To find one's place in the world is a journey that can take some people their whole lives to figure out, for others it comes more naturally. I believe that no one will ever really find that answer until they start to look outward. Ask yourself this question: how can I make my life less about myself and more about others? Once you set yourself on a path that can be of service to other people, then one will feel truly fulfilled. You find yourself in the process. Your identity or purpose in life becomes not about yourself but about living for those with whom you come into contact with."

"Is that why you teach art?"

"Art is like a language. It's the language of the soul. If there's an opportunity to connect with one's soul, to guide others to tap into their core, their spirit, then my answer is yes."

He started to chip away at the wood. When she didn't move he added encouragingly, "Get to work, Kiva. No more delay."

Kiva retrieved a blank canvas from the cupboard and set it on the table. Her pencil hovered over the untouched space as her head filled with images of motifs and ornaments she had been raised around. Everything she cared about was on this very acre, from the tree outside that was imprinted with her foot prints to the art center and all of the contents contained inside that were a result of tireless hard work. She belonged here. From the cell of dust that settled on her fingertips to the pulse of life represented on the faces on the hanging canvases. Her spirit had been nurtured, received nourishment and replenished. Every inch of space had carved a place inside her heart.

She lowered her hand and began to sketch.

They worked in silence, the light tapping of the chisel the only sound filling the room. Kiva found it soothing. Distinct sounds conjured up memories, and her thoughts wavered to a time when she could barely see over the table she was now working on.

Mau broke through her reverie. "The Academy called today."

Kiva raised her head slowly. "What did they want?"

"They're looking around for businesses who'd be interested in hiring some of their students as temps for a couple weeks. Work experience is part of their program. I told them I can take one of them to assist me with these carvings. He starts on Monday."

Kiva stared at her uncle's dark head and coaxed her heartbeat to slow. "Who?"

Mau didn't look up from the piece of wood he was working on. "I asked for that Ryler kid. Do you remember him?"

CHAPTER TWELVE

Come Monday afternoon, Kiva found herself quickening her pace from the main road to the house. She ignored the questioning looks on Tui and Hana's faces and climbed the stairs to her room where she slid her backpack to the floor and took out her sketchbook. Changing into a comfortable shirt and sarong, she limped toward the art center, the voice of her uncle reaching her ears before she crossed the threshold. Mau and Ry looked up from wooden blocks when she entered the room.

"Ah, you're home. How was school?" her uncle asked.

Kiva ignored the stitch in her stomach and offered a tight-lipped smile. She could feel Ry's gaze lingering on her face when she answered. Mau gestured between them, making introductions, and Kiva noticed Ry shift awkwardly on his feet, his hands shoved inside his pockets. He was dressed in the standard gray T-shirt and khaki shorts, and his thick brown hair was buzzed short since she saw him at the movies. The change was unexpected and made him look even more ominous, and Kiva's eyes widened as she offered him a smile, hoping it didn't come across wobbly. The corner of his mouth curved faintly, as if interpreting her surprise.

"I was just telling Ryler about the carvings that need to be done for the diplomats," Mau said.

"What have you decided?" Kiva turned her attention to him.

"We'll make the *tanoa* bowl—ten of them for each visitor." He clapped Ryler on the shoulder. "You ready for this?"

Ry responded formally, "Yes, sir."

Kiva's smile broadened. The idea that her uncle was entrusting him with an important task made her swell with warmth. "I'll be over here working on my project. Let me know if you need anything." She fetched her canvas and set it up in the farthest corner of the table, her profile to them. It took her a moment for her racing heart to calm but as their voices faded in the background, she became absorbed in dark contours and arcs.

The silhouette of a girl's slender neck and chin appeared in the center of the page. The protruding bun. A few escaped tendrils. Her upper lip jutting out. Eyelash flicks. Kiva planned to fill the woman's profile in black. A trail of little black birds rose from the back of her shoulder and flew upwards until they became larger imprints of the *ma'oma'o*, a bird known only to exist in Samoa. It wasn't the most beautiful bird around, but its music was unparalleled to anything Kiva had ever heard. *What is your heart's desire, little bird?* She imagined the *ma'oma'o* answering her in lilting tones. She imagined the girl's aspirations tethered to each wing beat, soaring to great heights until there was only an incandescent blue sky.

She later got up to begin her chores and watched from the laundry line as Ry and Mau descended the steps after they were done for the day and strode toward the truck. Unaware of her presence, she listened as they chatted to each other, their voices drowning away as the engine stuttered to life and they drove away.

This occurred several more days before Ry spoke to her.

"What are you working on?"

Kiva raised her head above the horizontal edge of the canvas and peered at him before sweeping her gaze around the room. She hadn't realized her uncle had left.

"Mau stepped out to find a few tools," he offered as explanation.

She returned her gaze to him and nodded in acknowledgment. "I'm working on something for an art competition."

"You're concentrating really hard," he appraised her. "Your eyebrows are doing this funny little dip."

Kiva pressed her forefinger between her eyes and smoothed out the crease. He was right. She was probably sticking out her tongue in the corner of her mouth as well. She half shrugged and smiled tentatively at him. "Are you happy to be back?" she asked.

He nodded slowly. "The change in scenery is good. I like Mau. He doesn't mince words, and he doesn't put up with crap."

She chuckled quietly. "No, he doesn't."

He returned his attention to the wood in his hands. "He treats me like a normal person."

Kiva licked her lips before asking, "How are you usually treated?"

"Like I'm someone to be feared or subdued. People have either avoided me or fought me."

"Should I fear you?"

"No, Kiva," he said softly and shook his head. "Besides, Mau said he'd kick my ass if I laid a hand on you."

"He didn't!"

"Not in those exact words, but I got the idea." He gave her a lopsided grin and she smiled warmly in return, settling more comfortably on the stool. "Your father's a good man," he added.

"He's not my father. Mau's my uncle. His wife, Naomi, is my mother's sister."

Ry's brows rose. "Those labels don't seem to matter."

"You're right. They don't," she said in a soft tone. "This is my home." She gestured around the room before returning her gaze to him. "What's your story, Ry? Why are you here in Samoa?"

He blew out an audible breath and scrubbed his jaw. "You're forward."

She smiled lightly. "If you don't want to talk about it, that's okay," she allayed.

"No ... I want to tell you." He looked away, focusing on the slab of wood in front of him. "I went too far and almost beat a kid to death." Kiva's fingers curled tightly around the pencil. "I should have been arrested, but I was sent here instead. It wasn't the first fight I'd gotten into, but it was the one that had the most harmful effects."

She sat unmoving, unsure of what to say. Her eyes roved the angles of his face as he picked at something on the wood. His thick eyebrows gathered together into a troubled expression, his mouth downturned. She remained still, willing him with her silence to go on.

"I was starting to spiral out of control," he continued. "And that guy ... he set me off. He did and said some things, and my anger clouded my mind. I just saw red. I wanted to hurt him, and it felt good at the time." He shook his head as if in regret.

"Is he okay?" she barely whispered.

"He was hospitalized."

"Why?" That single word was asking him why he would carry out such an act.

Ry gazed at her thoughtfully, his eyes grim. "Have you ever felt that your world was crushing down on you to the point that you just wanted to give up? That the people around you saw the darkness and the filth and decided you were worthless? That not only could they not stand the way you looked but placed labels on you that you had no control over?

90

That the only power you had was to violently fight back?" His questions were rhetorical, but Kiva didn't miss the suppressed pain behind them. "My parents met at college. She was a freshman and he was much older. He had come over from Egypt on a student visa. When it expired and he was preparing to return home, he asked my mother to leave with him. Her parents opposed their relationship and they called immigration and had my dad taken away. They hated him, wanted nothing to do with him, and he was sent back to Egypt. When my mother found out she was pregnant, he was long gone, and she had to quit school to take care of me. As you can guess, that didn't go down well with my grandparents."

Kiva let out a breath, taking all of this in. "Does he know about you? Your father?"

Ry shook his head. "No. My grandparents cut off all communication."

"Why would they do that? Not let him know at least?"

He shrugged. "Maybe they didn't want him to have any more incentive to try and come back. They're upper-class folk with a daughter whose promising future was ruined. They blamed him. They blamed me. This tattoo on my arm is the only semblance I have of him. It's his name also. After I was born, we moved to live with my grandparents because my mother couldn't afford to be on her own and she needed help. I remember there were arguments all the time, suppressed anger, and I think my first word was actually a cuss word. We finally moved out when I was two and it was tough. She went back to school when I started kindergarten and worked hard to build a home for us, but I knew she wasn't happy. She tried to hide it, but kids can always tell that kind of thing, you know? I was four when she got married for the first time. He was a staff sergeant in the army and when he got deployed to the Gulf War, the distance became too difficult for my mom, so they got divorced. She had a string of boyfriends after that, and sometimes they were good to me, sometimes they weren't. When I turned fifteen she met my stepdad, and he treated her like a queen, saved her from loneliness. He has a daughter and when we moved into their house, we were supposed to become this one big happy family." He grimaced. "At first I was happy to move, to get away and start something new. My stepdad is a great guy; he makes my mom happy and that's good enough for me. He accepted me, but not everyone in that town did. When I started at my new school, it was hard to make friends and I was bullied for being different. It was a new place, new family, new everything, so I fought back the only way I knew how." He blew out a rough breath. "I feel like I've been fighting my whole life, Kiva—with my grandparents, with my old school, with the whole damn town. I come from a small place of seven thousand people, the majority of them white. I'm half Arab. For a lot of people that's become a dirty word, especially after 9/11. When I'd walk down the halls at school, people would part for me as if they were afraid, but then when I'd reach my locker, it would have 'terrorist' written all over it in black marker. So when people believed me to be a violent monster, I gave them what they expected. I fought back and made some stupid mistakes." He shook his head. "When I was checking in for my flight to come here, they took one look at my face, saw the name in my passport, then pulled me aside to be strip searched. What I'm sharing with you is not for pity or to excuse my actions, especially toward that guy I beat up. It's just been my life." He shoved a hand atop his shaved head. "It's hard to explain, but I knew I hit rock bottom when I was sent here."

Kiva nodded in understanding. While she didn't condone violence of any kind, she appreciated that he was being open and honest with her. It took courage to sift through the past, and humility to talk about one's mistakes. A part of her also came to realize that he had been gravely misunderstood most of his life.

"Your scars …"

Ry rubbed the scar near his eye absentmindedly. "I got it from a fight with a guy at a party. He was drunk and said some stupid things and I got mad and fought him. He smashed his drink and attacked me."

"This was from a broken bottle?"

"The same one." He held up his left hand where scars were slashed across his wrist.

At that moment Mau stepped into the room with a few tools in his right hand and a couple bottles of cola in the other. He gave one drink to Ry and the other to Kiva.

"How's it going?" he asked Ry.

While Ry filled him in on the progress of his work, Kiva took the glass bottle and popped the lid off with her teeth.

"Whoa," she heard Ry say. "That didn't look painful at all."

Her teeth pinged and numbed. "It wasn't," she said, trying to keep a straight face. "This is the local way of opening a soda bottle. Do you want me to teach you?"

"I wouldn't recommend it if you want to keep your teeth intact," Mau said with a reproachful tone.

Kiva slid off the stool and approached Ry. "Here," she said, taking the bottle from him. Tilting it against the edge of the table, she hooked the cap in place and pounded it down with the palm of her hand. The momentum popped the lid open, releasing it with a sharp fizz. "There you go," she handed it back to him.

"Thanks," he said, amusement in his voice, before lifting it to his mouth. Kiva tried not to notice the way his Adam's apple bobbed when he swallowed. Her cheeks warmed and she turned, retracing her steps back to the canvas. Lifting her pencil, she started shading in a wing.

They continued working into the late afternoon when Kiva packed up her things and returned to the house to begin her chores. The noises from the art center followed her around as she swept dead leaves from the ground and took down the laundry. Her thoughts lingered on Ry and what he had divulged. A part of her empathized with him and his childhood. The knowledge that his father had no idea Ry existed left her feeling empty inside for him, and while she didn't beget her own biological father, Mau had filled that void and continued to remain a strong presence in her life. A larger part of her wanted to help Ry, but she knew she wasn't a specialist. She didn't have the education to make informed decisions or judgments about his rehabilitation. She couldn't fix him, and she knew that real change—the kind where conscious effort was made, where words transformed into actions—could only come from within. She replayed their conversation in her head, stopping at the point he made about labels. He'd said people placed labels on him that he had little control over. She could relate to that.

Cripple.

Dull.

Ungraceful.

She'd heard it all. Kiva tamped them down as an idea came to her. With a little innovation on her part and willing participation on his, she realized there was something she could do.

Carrying the clothes bucket to the house, she found Naomi cutting strips of dyed cloth on the couch. Kiva kicked off her sandals and joined her. Lifting a shirt out of the bucket, she began to fold back the sleeves.

"How's it going out there?" her aunt asked.

"Mau's happy to have an apprentice." Kiva placed the folded shirt aside, creating a pile. "Also ... Ry opened up to me and told me about his family, about why he was sent here."

Naomi raised a brow. "Oh, really?"

"I want to help him, Naomi."

"I know you do, honey. There's healing in carving, in art in general. Mau recognizes that and that's why Ryler is here."

Kiva picked up a tea towel, flicking it out in front of her.

"I have to admit, I'm a little uneasy about having him around," Naomi added, picking up a skirt to fold.

"Ry's nice," Kiva said.

"You call him Ry?"

Kiva shrugged. "He said to." She peered over at her aunt who wore a concerned expression on her face. "What?"

"Nicknames are usually reserved for close friends. He clearly considers you a friend. I'm not sure how I feel about that."

"Naomi, I'm not going to do anything stupid. Besides, he could probably use a friend right now. A family."

Naomi returned her attention to the skirt she was folding.

"Okay," she finally said after a contemplative silence.

"Okay, what?"

"I'll be nice to him."

Before Kiva could formulate a response, Mau and Ry entered through the kitchen door, stamping their dusty feet on the rug. Standing beside her stout uncle, Ry towered over him, placing him at almost six feet. His eyes explored the room with uncertainty before they came to rest on her. Kiva wondered what he thought of the life-size paintings on the walls interspersed by bookshelves with literature on art history and gardening. The *elei* material she was sitting on had been hand printed by Naomi, the azure blue now faded with time. They complimented the canary walls, which were spotted with mildew in some places. It was an artist's room and her aunt's personality permeated the details, from the stitch of fabric on the pillows that cushioned her back to the partial fingerprint fired on the decorative teapot on the coffee table. Ry stood in the rainforest-hued kitchen and looked out of place. Kiva approached him, hoping her proximity would help ease his apprehension. She wanted to reach out to him but placed her hands on the counter instead, stretching her fingers in his direction. Locking eyes with him, she offered a warm smile which he acknowledged with a slight nod. It was one thing to be in the safe confines of the art center where he was a student or an assistant, but now he was in their home, a step closer to her family, to her.

Naomi stood from her folding. "Ryler, I'm Naomi," she introduced with a polite smile.

Ry clasped her outstretched hand and shook it.

"Have you seen my keys?" her uncle asked while he washed his hands in the sink. "I'm going to drop off Ryler."

"They should be on the counter, but do you have to go now?" she asked Mau before turning to Ry. "Would you like to stay for dinner,

Ryler? It's Kiva's birthday today and I made lemon curry chicken and chocolate cake for dessert."

Ry's eyes shot to Kiva, his expression one of surprise. "It's your birthday?" She smiled shyly in response. "Happy birthday," he added, the hardness in his face softening.

"Will you stay?" her aunt probed. Her voice was like honey, encouraging, and Kiva silently thanked her for her natural ability to be welcoming.

Ry shifted slightly on his feet. "I'd like to, but I have to get back to the school. Curfew and all."

Naomi smiled warmly without the hint of judgment. "Of course. Another time then."

Ry looked over the counter that separated him from Kiva and held her gaze for a beat before tipping his chin down in farewell.

CHAPTER THIRTEEN

"Why didn't you tell me it was your birthday yesterday?"

Kiva raised her head above her canvas and met Ry's questioning gaze. He sat across from her on the table, sanding down wood.

Unlike some people, Kiva didn't like the attention elaborate birthday celebrations prompted, especially if she was the recipient of that attention. She much preferred intimate settings to embellished parties. The evening before had been sweet in its simplicity. Her aunt had lit candles on the chocolate cake, and Kiva silently wished for success to come to the art center before she blew them out, for Hana to treat her kindly for once, and for the hurt in her heart to go away.

"It's not a big deal," she answered casually.

"Yeah?" He arched a brow. "Chocolate cake would have beaten runny custard any day."

Kiva scrunched up her nose at the thought. "You're probably right."

"What I wouldn't give for a hot apple pie and scoop of ice cream. Or hot fudge. I'm still trying to get used to the gray gunk they serve us with the little slime balls that look like fish eyes." He made a face and Kiva suppressed a smile.

"You mean *suafa'i*?"

"Yeah, that's it—slimy banana soup."

She smothered a laugh, returning her attention to the girl's silhouette and birds spread before her. Her fingers, now blackened to the first knuckle, worked to fill in the image of the girl with charcoal she collected from the ground. "What else do you miss from home?" she asked curiously.

Ry stilled. "Not very much … except my music—putting on

96

headphones and just escaping."

"What do you listen to?"

"A variety—alternative, techno, rap, some R&B."

"Have you heard of PM Dawn?"

He nodded. "Sure, I've heard of them."

"Their music is like lyrical poetry. So much emotion." Kiva remembered listening to her aunt's mixed cassette of nineties music blaring in the house. Sadly, it hadn't lasted long when the tape tangled and snapped, and she hadn't been able to replace it since. "'Looking Through Patient Eyes' is a song about remorse and angst, regret and sadness. It's like the singer knows there's no hope, but hangs onto it anyway."

She looked up to see Ry studying her. "You're a bit of a romantic, huh?" he asked.

"Yes." She sighed without shame. "I like to believe there's hope, even for those who feel there's none." She half shrugged. "I like happily ever afters."

"Don't kid yourself, Kiva," he said in a low tone. "There's only work and disappointment and someone who eventually bows out. Not everything is Disney."

Kiva furrowed her brows at his subtext. Was he speaking about his parents? His grandparents' prejudice? Did he blame his dad somehow for leaving? For not fighting harder to be with his mother? "You're right. I imagine there is work. A lot of it. But I'm not talking about the fairy tale endings you read about in children's stories. I'm talking about the love after you've seen the flaws and blemishes and still choose to stay. Love is hard, but it's also patient and kind and intentional. It's about witnessing how that other person responds to hardship when they've been through pain and sacrifice, but it's also about shouldering some of the burden that makes that person want to give up …" She swallowed thickly. "I'd like to believe everyone is worthy of that kind of love." Even her birth parents, once upon a time ago, she added internally but chose not to say aloud. They'd never got that chance with each other.

Something flickered in his expression but he didn't say anything and they quietly reverted to their respective projects, the trail of their conversation hanging thickly in the air. Kiva wondered about the complexities of relationships. Having never been in a relationship before, she only knew of love from observing her aunt and uncle. Their union was akin to a fortress: protected, cherished, respected. She hadn't missed the small acts of kindness they carried out for each other, the private, gentle smiles, but what she admired most was that through the stress of running a business together, the unpredictability of customers and financial strain over the years, they'd kept it together. It hadn't always been easy. They'd argued behind closed doors, their raised muffled voices carrying down the hall and alarming even her, but when it had stopped and they crossed over the threshold, they'd somehow worked it out. As inexperienced as she was, she wasn't so naïve to believe that it was always going to be hearts and flowers.

She shook her head of her thoughts and changed the subject. "I was surprised to read the quote from Rumi on the *siapo*—the one you left behind."

"Why's that?"

"Well ... you don't exactly come across as the reading-poetry type."

A ghost of a smile flitted across his lips. "You judged me?"

Kiva would have felt chagrined that he called her out so easily, but his relaxed tone eased her to be upfront. "I did," she admitted. "I'm sorry."

"Don't be. You're not the first." His matter-of-fact statement made her flinch on the inside. He reached for another slab of wood and began sanding it down, and her eyes were drawn to the tension in his forearms. They were browned from sun exposure, the dusting of hair catching fire from the afternoon light slanting through the windows. "I started reading everything I could get my hands on by Persian and Arab writers about the same time I got this tattoo," he said. "I've been trying to learn Arabic as well, but it hasn't been easy."

This news took her by complete surprise and something that felt like admiration bloomed inside her chest. Kiva approved of someone who read—especially if they read Rumi—as much as she revered a person who took the time to study another language. Arabic. Wow. It was as foreign to her as that distant part of the world.

"Share something with me?" she asked.

His brow raised. "What do you want to know?"

"One of the stories you've read."

Ry regarded her silently before shifting his eyes to a distant point, conjuring one from memory. "Alright," he said slowly. "But be warned, this doesn't have a happily ever after. Not in the sense that you'd want, anyway."

"Okay." Kiva placed her hands in her lap, intent on listening.

Ry cleared his throat and began. His voice was low and gravelly, and Kiva soon found herself being carried away to a sprawling city with clay buildings camouflaged against desert mountains. "There's a legend that

98

has been told for thousands of years in the Middle East—the story of Layla and Majnun. Some say it is based on a true story about a poet named Qays ibn al-Mulawwah ibn Muzahim and a young woman called Layla, who he meets at *maktab*, a traditional school. When Qays and Layla see each other for the first time, they fall in love instantly. He writes poetry about her, saying it out loud on the streets for everyone to hear. Because this is not normal, especially in those days, Qays becomes known as *Majnun,* a madman.

"People begin to gossip and when Layla's father hears about this, he gets very angry. He thinks his daughter is ruined. He bans Layla from leaving the house, stopping her from seeing Majnun. When Majnun hears this, he goes and asks for permission to marry Layla, but he is instantly rejected by her father. The father tells Majnun that he doesn't want his daughter to be with a madman. He also tells him that he has arranged for Layla to be married to another man from a different village.

"Majnun is filled with so much anguish. Heartbroken, he decides to leave the city. He travels to a temple where his own father begs him to pray to God for help. Majnun begins to pray but not for himself. He prays for Layla, for the love he has for her. His poetry becomes his salvation, his only link to her.

"Meanwhile, Layla obeys her father's wishes and marries the man from the other village. But she never forgets Majnun.

"Majnun's parents miss their son and begin to leave food for him at the bottom of the mountains, hoping he will come home to them. But Majnun never goes back. He lives in the wilderness. Many people traveling to the city see him along the roadside speaking aloud poetry and writing it down in the hot sand. They believe the stories that he has indeed become a madman.

"Many years go by and Majnun's parents pass away. When Layla hears about this, she begs an old traveler to take the news to Majnun, and he sets out in search of the madman. When he finds Majnun and tells him about his parents' deaths, Majnun is filled with grief and goes further away.

"Time goes by and Layla's husband dies. Layla has hope that she will be reunited with Majnun, but this is not to be because traditionally she must mourn the death of her husband for two whole years before she can remarry. As a result, Layla dies of a broken heart alone in her home."

"She never got to see him?" Leva asked.

"No. When Majnun learns of Layla's death, he travels to her graveside where he cries in agony over her resting place and then finally passes away."

When he stopped speaking, Kiva noticed the charcoal she clung onto had disintegrated in her hands. "That's such a sad story. What does it mean?" she wondered aloud.

Ry returned his focus to the piece of wood in his hands. "It's a tale about having a spiritual experience—an earthly love story with a heavenly message. Majnun and Layla's love was pure, their connection beyond the physical, their story a representation of the soul's search for meaning. Majnun's love for Layla, the poetry he recited for her, is a symbol of his search for God and his union with Him, at death."

They were quiet for a moment before Kiva spoke.

"Do you believe in God, Ry?" she asked with gentleness in her voice.

"Do you?" He looked over at her.

She smiled softly and answered simply, "I do."

He shook his head, his voice charred between resignation and defeat when he spoke. "I read these stories, but it's hard to believe in them when you've seen the things I've seen, heard the things I've heard, done the things I've done—words and actions that make me lose faith in people, but mostly in myself."

Sometimes it took one small act of compassion to affect another person's heart, and Kiva wanted that for Ry. He had gone long without it. She explored the details of his face, the angular shape of his whiskered jaw, thick eyebrows that framed his eyes, and dark lashes. When she met his eyes with her own—eyes that reminded her of the blackest dye from the *siapo* cloth—something in her heart stirred ... a subtle shift blossomed inside her chest that occurred during the infinitesimal moment it took for her to inhale and exhale. The act itself was so simple but the feeling that now resided was of such a magnitude that she didn't think she'd ever forget it.

She decided then to put her idea into motion.

Kiva had spent the evening before enlisting the help of Tui from next door. He'd chopped down a sturdy bamboo stalk and drilled holes along the top while Mau and Naomi stood aside with concerned amusement on their faces.

"Are you sure about this?" Naomi had asked. "I don't want anyone getting hurt."

"It'll be fine," Mau reassured her. "Kiva knows what she's doing."

Kiva was pleased to have her uncle's support; it had helped boost her courage, but now in the blaring light of the afternoon sun with Ry sitting across from her, she wasn't so sure anymore.

Having a little premonition of how he would react—with

apprehension she assumed—Kiva inhaled a shuddering breath and gathered her courage from the air particles surrounding her, as if its presence in her lungs could comfort her.

"Ry?" He raised his head and she let the breath go. "What did people call you back home? The labels you spoke of before. What were they?"

His brows pinched into a frown. "Why do you want to know?"

"I'm just ... curious."

His face hardened as she expected. Scraping the charcoal from beneath her fingernails, she rushed to speak. "My full name is Mativa. In my case it means poor, not in the impoverished sense but more in the pitiful sense." Ry's expression became steely, and she found it easier to avert her gaze and focus on his hands. "It's a typical practice to call children in this country names that will serve to humble them. You will not believe some of them. Pig, dog, papaya ... It sounds funny in retrospect but it really isn't. My birth mother named me because I was born with a leg length deficiency. She pitied me—this poor abnormal child—and I have been called every one of its synonyms since." She took another deep breath. "If you don't want to talk about the labels you've been called, I understand. I won't make you say them out loud. But ... will you write them down instead?" She retrieved a piece of paper and pencil and slid it toward him. "I won't read it."

Ry eyed the contents on the table with suspicion as Kiva's heart raced, and whatever doubts she had about this whole plan roared to life as she watched him battle with her request. Lines formed between his brows and his mouth pressed together.

Before she could berate herself for this whole stupid idea, he spoke, his voice low, "Kiva ... what are you trying to do?"

She fidgeted a little on her stool. "There's something I want to show you afterward. Please"—she twisted her fingers together—"trust me."

His chest broadened then dropped heavily when he let go of a deep breath. He reached with his fingers toward the paper and pencil, and Kiva watched silently as he scribbled down a list. When he was done, she gave him a closed-lipped smile, the excitement she felt building inside her crinkling around her eyes.

"Follow me," she said softly, slipping off the stool and heading toward the French doors. Retrieving a canister of kerosene and some matches, she heard him shuffle behind her, his long strides catching up easily to her as she hobbled down the steps toward the back of the yard, past her aunt's vegetable garden, the water tank, and banyan tree.

The bamboo stalk lay on the ground, one end propped up by a piece of timber wood so it was raised off the grass. It had been drying in the sun all day, and Kiva hoped it was ready for what she was about to do. She crouched beside it and set the kerosene and matches down next to her. Ry was frowning against the sun's rays when she glanced up at him.

"This is called *faga'ofe* or bamboo gun," she started. "The way it works is that kerosene is poured into the small hole over here, and when you apply a little oxygen and fire, a blast will come out through there." She pointed toward the end of the stalk. "The longer the buildup, the louder the bang."

"Okay ..." he said, his forehead wrinkling.

Kiva smiled gently up at him before her eyes shifted to his hands. "I want you to take that piece of paper you're holding and rip it into tiny pieces."

Ry's gaze sharpened before the corner of his lips curved upwards. "Are you really going to do what I think you're going to do?"

She returned a broad smile. "What *we're* going to do, yes. Now shred it."

Ry complied until he had white confetti in his hands.

Kiva stood and slowly approached him. She felt him watch her as she gathered the pieces from the palm of his hands into her quivering ones. Turning away, she stooped over the end of the bamboo stalk and stuffed them inside. She had no idea if this was going to work, if the pieces of paper would remain inside from the moisture or scatter out once she started to blow.

"Come," she said when she was done, taking his elbow and leading him away. "You don't want to be near this end when it goes off."

Kiva squatted at the opposite end and blew into the hole before lighting a match over the opening. Smoke started to billow from the other end. When nothing happened, she blew again and lit another match. She repeated the process until she started to hear sharp flicks that promised the onset of an outburst. When she blew and lit the match once more, pressure built until the rear of the bamboo exploded with a deafening boom.

"Holy crap!" Ry blurted as the eruption shook the ground they stood on. Even though Kiva was expecting it, the noise still startled her, the sound ringing in her ears. She was sure it could be heard at least a mile away.

"What the hell was that?"

Her mouth spread into a broad smile. "It's a local version of fireworks."

"Is it legal?"

She nodded. "It's mostly used around the island during celebrations.

New Year's, Independence Day, that sort of thing."

Some of the pieces of paper had burst out during the blast and were now dispersed haphazardly on the grass. Kiva and Ry watched them flutter to the ground before he turned to her and said, "My turn."

They spent the next twenty minutes creating explosions in the back yard, effectively scattering the birds from the trees and other little critters Kiva wasn't too fond of, and she felt exhilarated, heady, like the free fall she experienced when she drove for the first time over the rollercoaster hill. When Ry laughed, the sound deep and full, she couldn't help noticing the hard lines around his eyes ease and the dip in the corner of his mouth deepen. When he caught her watching, Kiva looked away self-consciously.

"You have some charcoal on your face," he said, his voice throaty. She was beginning to love the sound of his voice, a little rough and smoky, like he was getting over the flu. He stepped closer as if he was going to reach for her and then stopped himself.

Kiva remembered that her fingertips were smudged in black. Using the clean part of her palm, she scrubbed her skin until it felt raw. "Is it gone?" He pointed to her chin and she cleaned it there, sensing her cheeks grow warm because he was observing her so closely.

"It's gone now," he said softly.

She glanced toward the art building, feeling like a hundred birds had taken off in her stomach. They started in the direction of the center in silence, the pieces of paper abandoned and forgotten, the labels scrawled across them now torn and trimmed with fire.

Kiva hoped it helped Ry forget, too.

"Thanks, bamboo girl," he said behind her, his thick voice raising the hairs on the back of her nape, and her eyes lit up with an overjoyed smile. Now there was a name she didn't mind being called.

CHAPTER FOURTEEN

Kiva loved what she had created so far for the art competition. The images started to come together to form a coherent balance between striking and simplicity, and she decided it was the best piece of work she'd produced so far. It was so close to her heart that she didn't know how she was going to detach herself enough to allow it to be displayed for public viewing and judgment. For a moment she'd contemplated handing in the sketch she'd made in Miss Lene's art class of her hand, the pearl and banyan tree, but later abandoned the idea. She'd started this project and knew she would be disappointed in herself if a little fear stopped her now.

She began to sketch symbols on the inside of each bird to represent the girl's ambitions and dreams … her desire to earn a fine arts degree, travel the globe, to one day open her own art studio and offer classes to children. Embedded in each wing was hope and the faith that she could achieve it all. The birds themselves took on an ethereal shape, like that of fluttering bamboo leaves. She remembered her uncle's words about the bamboo … that it grew to be a resilient tree, bending easily with the wind. She liked that a lot.

The theme of the competition was centered on the idea of self and identity, and Kiva hoped one's future aspirations could be tied in. After all, they hadn't taken place yet, but if one was actively striving toward those goals, then she figured it was okay. Life was made up of little moments in the present, stitched and secured and tethered to some invisible thread in the future.

She hadn't yet decided on the background of the canvas. Perhaps she would paint it with a solid color, maybe a shade of blue to emulate the sky, a place fit for birds to be free, and then write verses across it in a black curly script—words to encourage the girl in the canvas to keep striving.

It was getting late in the evening and the sun was starting to dip into the ocean in the distance, the colors mirroring that of the heavens. Ry had been working hard that afternoon, and Kiva left him alone with his project while she concentrated on her own. His face was lined with exhaustion by the time he was preparing to return to the school, so she'd rushed to the house, sliced a generous piece of leftover birthday cake, wrapped it in tinfoil, and hurried back to the center.

"What's this?" he asked when she handed it to him.

"It's not runny custard," she answered jovially.

A slow smile spread transforming his tired face. "Thanks, Kiva."

She was alone now in the room, and the remnants of Mau and Ry's carvings stretched around her on the floor. Kiva inhaled the fresh scent of wood carvings as her eyes roved their unfinished work.

They still had a long way to go.

She smiled to herself when she thought about how far Ry had come since the first day she'd laid eyes on him several months ago. He was respectful and attentive to her uncle's instructions and vigilant and disciplined when following them through. Mau had likewise been patient in return. When they weren't paying attention to her, she liked to watch their interactions, particularly when Ry made a mistake, his hand slipping with the carving knife and holding back a curse, and Mau had simply said, "Try again."

Naomi had several times made an appearance in the center that day, offering cold drinks and snacks, and Ry's demeanor started to change as he became more relaxed. Her aunt had always said that the way to a man's heart was to feed his belly, and by the size of her uncle's protruding one, she'd been doing precisely that for years.

Ry saw her art piece earlier that day. Kiva hadn't planned on it, but she also hadn't planned to hide it forever. Her nerves flared when he stood inches from her back, silently absorbing the girl's black silhouette and birds while his warmth and scent surrounded her. Her hands turned clammy when she thought about exposing a personal side of herself to Ry, more so than the hundreds of people who'd be flocking to the gallery during the festival, because at least then she could steer clear of her art work and avoid the judgments of strangers by immersing herself in the other displays. But left alone now in this setting felt more intimate than anything she'd ever experienced before, and with Ry standing so close and her dreams laid bare, Kiva had nowhere to escape to.

Mau had briefly left the art center to retrieve a few things from the house, and Ry was moving some carvings to a corner of the room when he'd come around the table where she was working and paused. Aware that he had stopped behind her, Kiva drew in a silent breath and held it. He was so much taller than her, and it became even more evident when she was sitting. She urged her heart to slow as she tried to look at the canvas through his eyes. Could he see her heart through the arcs and curves? Her loneliness through the slight downwards tilt of the girl's head? Could he see through the patterns and decipher their inner meanings? She didn't have the courage to turn around and interpret for herself through his eyes. Her own were too vulnerable.

The room was quiet save for their breathing—his calm and steady while hers was rapid—and the atmosphere charged with something potent. Her anxiety grew and grew into an invisible bubble until she felt like the drum beats of her own heart could pop it.

Several minutes of intense silence passed, and just when she thought she couldn't take anymore, he finally spoke in a low voice, "What does this bird represent, Kiva?"

Releasing the breath she'd been holding, Kiva followed the direction of his finger when he raised it inches from her shoulder.

"Hope," she said quietly.

A heavy pause resulted before he asked, "And this one?"

She licked her lips. "A home."

"Haven't you found one here?" His tone was puzzled.

"In this art center? Yes. But there are many spaces that can be considered a home. It's not always about a physical location. It's also in the people you surround yourself with and the interactions you have with them … I guess I haven't found peace with all of them."

She imagined him furrowing his brows in contemplation. He pointed again and she gazed at the little bird. This one was smaller than the others, the images contained inside delicate like lace. Her voice tapered off when she answered, "Longing …"

"For what?"

Kiva looked down at her blackened hands and shook her head. She wasn't ready to divulge something so personal. It would pull him in a little too close, and she admitted feeling a little unsure of her emotions at the moment.

He was quiet then, and she could tell he was no longer looking at the canvas. Very slowly she turned around and peered up at him. His expression was pensive, the deep lines between his eyebrows drawn together making him appear older than his teenage years. Kiva swallowed hard and waited for him to say something.

Ry surprised her with his response, his voice rough and almost reverent. "Thank you, Kiva." There was so much weight behind those three little words that nothing else needed to be spoken. He held her gaze for a moment, and she felt something pass between them before he stepped away and returned to his work.

Now in the dim light of dusk, Kiva knew something had changed. She'd felt it, as surely as if she'd felt the early morning sun on her face, and a tiny smile flitted across her lips.

She was bent over her canvas when a noise emanating from outside pulled her out of her thoughts. A muffled sob erupted and her ears pricked in alarm. The sound wavered as if whoever it was tried to stop, but it was unmistakable to Kiva that someone was crying.

The stool scraped across the floor as she rose and limped to the window and peered through the dusty screen. Dusk had fallen, casting shadows across the bamboo trees that clustered near the center. When she didn't see anyone, she walked to the door and descended the steps to investigate.

As she drew nearer to the bamboo, she noticed someone concealed behind the stalks, crouched down on the ground. Kiva approached slowly in an attempt not to startle the person. The grass was cool under her bare feet, the leaves from the bamboo a little slippery to walk on.

She immediately recognized her cousin's dark outline.

"Hana?" she called.

Hana stiffened and whipped her head around, her puffy eyes and tear streaked face making her look vulnerable. Her eyes flashed with fear before she bit out in anger, "Leave me alone, Kiva."

Kiva remained where she was. "Are you alright?" she asked tentatively.

Hana turned away, cutting her off. She shuddered with a cry and buried her face in her hands. Kiva didn't know what to do. Should she stay or go? While she internally battled this over in her mind, her feet unconsciously shuffled closer—close enough to offer support but far enough so she didn't crowd her cousin. Hana continued to sob violently into her hands, her shoulders shaking from the force. Her unguarded position exposed a side of her Kiva had never seen before, and despite everything her cousin had done and said to hurt her, she couldn't bring herself to walk away.

"Hey," she said softly and moved closer, touching her arm.

Hana recoiled as if she'd been scalded. "Don't touch me!"

"I'm just trying—"

"No!" Her voice cracked. "Just go, okay?"

"I can help ... if you'd let me," Kiva offered and Hana snickered derisively.

"There's no point ... I already tried."

Kiva furrowed her brows. "What do you mean?"

Hana sniffed and turned her head away from her cousin. "I'm pregnant, and I tried to get rid of it."

Kiva sucked in a ragged breath. Her cousin's easy admission, delivered without remorse, without care, made her light-headed. "Oh, Hana ... what ..." she barely whispered, afraid to ask the next question for fear of her answer, "... did you ... did you do it?"

Hana stood up so quickly she almost toppled her over. "Wouldn't *you* like to know?" Her voice was charred between anger and defeat as she swiped at her tears. "So you can go ahead and judge me."

"Hana, please," Kiva pleaded. Between the cracks in her cousin's furor, a girl who masked herself with sensuality and dark eyeliner and who was wading around in the same muck as everybody else, Kiva saw the pain and confusion, the loss of control and hopelessness, and she sincerely felt sorry for her.

"I couldn't do it, okay?" Fresh tears sprung from her eyes and she wiped them away roughly. "I tried"—she shook her head—"I did everything I could think of. I drank some stuff. I tried to fall down the stairs."

Kiva couldn't help when her own eyes welled with tears. "Why, Hana?" Her voice was a tremor, "Why ... why try?"

"Don't you get it?" her cousin cried. "My life is ruined! I won't be able to go back to school and face my classmates. I won't be able to leave this place, this goddamned island. I won't be able to do anything. My parents are going to be hysterical when they find out, and it'll just be one more reason for them to be disappointed in me." She twisted away and was quiet for a moment, and the small reprieve allowed Kiva to think. What were they going to do? What were Naomi and Mau going to say? She anticipated their angry reaction, her uncle's temper flaring, and couldn't blame Hana for the way she felt.

She swallowed the hard lump in her throat. "Does Junior know?"

Hana turned back around and a pained expression crossed her face. "He dumped me when I told him."

Kiva looked at her cousin's unkempt hair and state of dress, the way her long shirt hid her curves and the crooked sarong tied high around her waist. How long had she known? How long had she been alone with this knowledge?

"I'm here, Hana," she said in a broken voice. "What can I do?"

Hana huffed out a scornful laugh. "You just don't give up, do you?" She shook her head and her tone changed and took on a cold, detached quality. "Do you want to know the real reason why I wanted to get rid of it?" She swallowed hard as Hana took a step closer. "I wanted to do what your own mother failed to do sixteen years ago."

Kiva stared at her numbly. Her mind temporarily fazed in and out before she shook her head and said faintly, "What did you say?"

"I said your mother tried to abort you."

Kiva's throat constricted and an intense ache started low in her chest, squeezing and compressing, as if someone had kicked her there in slow motion and left her to fight for air. She dragged in a breath and with it the staggering pain as she shuffled back, her body telling her to retreat, to protect herself. But Hana continued her barrage.

"You didn't know? Your father was a married man who came to Samoa on a business trip and your mother seduced him. He gave her empty promises that he'd return for her, but he never did. She got pissed off when she realized she was pregnant and alone and then tried to get rid of you."

Hana hurtled stones with her words, cracking her limbs and bones, her very self-worth, until Kiva couldn't take anymore. There was too much. Too much pain, too much information to digest. She turned away to block it out, swaying on her feet, but Hana wouldn't let it go and talked to her retreating back.

"It's about time someone told you—everyone in the family knows except for you. They all think of you as this fragile little child in need of protection. My parents have always favored you more, loved you more, because they took pity on you. I heard them speaking … saying how wonderful you are, how blessed they are to have you in their lives. And you! You just had to go and love art and this place and be this perfect little angel." Her voice wobbled with emotion. "You were just easier to love than me." Kiva found it hard to breathe—to think—as she took an unsteady step toward the art center. Hana's voice rose. "But now I will have someone who will love me more!"

Darkness pressed down on her. The sounds Kiva found so soothing at this time of the day, the slow buildup of crickets, the creak of the bamboo as it bent to the evening breeze, were reduced to white noise against the thunderous beat of her heart thumping in her ears.

"Kiva? Hana!" Naomi's voice called from the house. "Where are you two? I need help with dinner."

Kiva picked up her pace, stumbled and righted herself, and rounded the back of the center meeting her aunt midway down the slanted lawn. Without looking directly at her face, she gestured with her hand to where Hana was left standing near the bamboo. "She ... she needs you," she said, her chin quivering. Her eyes became watery, and she rushed on, praying that her aunt couldn't tell how she was feeling by the tremor in her voice, because Kiva was feeling like her heart was shredding into pieces that no amount of compassion from Naomi or Mau could put back together.

Keep it together, she chanted to herself as she fought the tears that pooled in her eyes. She ascended the steps to the art center and without turning on the lights shuffled to where the table was in the middle of the room. She didn't need the light. She knew every corner of this space as if it were another one of her limbs. Her heart was breaking and she longed to climb her tree but didn't think she had the strength to.

Her gaze lingered on the shadows that played across her canvas where dark symbols and patterns now mocked her.

All of these years. She was so naïve. She was so stupid.

She had tried to keep it away, to keep the doubt out, to create something beautiful for herself to hold onto, but with just a few words—the apparent truth of her parentage—Hana had managed to destroy any semblance of that.

She always knew she had been sheltered, that her aunt and uncle had kept the specific details about her birth parents away from her, and in a way she had accepted it. Their love had been enough, but hearing what her own mother had tried to do, that she attempted to rid herself of her baby—of *her*—broke a part of Kiva. She couldn't help when desperate questions flooded her head. Is that why she was born with a leg length deficiency? Was it a physical result of her mother trying to rid her body of her fetus? Could she not overcome the hurt caused by her father's actions enough to want her? Was she so unworthy of her love?

Apparently so.

Touching its edge, she trailed the length of her canvas with her fingertip. It hurt to look at it now—this girl with her hopes and dreams. With the back of her palm Kiva swept it off the table and heard it clatter to the floor. Trembling, she slid down to the cold concrete floor and braced her arms over her uneven legs. She'd never felt so utterly alone and bare, her emotions raw and desolate.

She hadn't planned to find out like this. She'd pictured a moment with Naomi over a cup of hot *koko* and a conversation that started along the lines of, "Your mother loved you and wanted the best for you ..." and Kiva would have listened and accepted and continued on with the beautiful life she had surrounded herself with.

Pain engulfed her. Consumed her. Sorrow. Despair. Emotions battled for control in her body and without any fight left, she closed her eyes and surrendered to the tears that slipped under her lashes in the dark.

CHAPTER FIFTEEN

Kiva avoided everyone as much as she could in the days that followed.

She went to school, returned home, and busied herself with renewed intensity in her chores. Her body went through the motions while her mind was a turmoil of feelings—grief, fury, and confusion clamoring over each other, fighting for some form of release. And the pain. The pain was a dead weight around her heart. She scrubbed the laundry until her fingers were raw and bleeding, stirred the pot of chop suey until it sloshed over the sides, and then withdrew to her tree in the late afternoons until she couldn't see the pages of her sketchbook anymore.

There were moments she felt as if a black cloud hovered over her head, just waiting to rain down on her, and any slight shift in the atmosphere would set her off into a quivering, crying mess.

Mau had called a family meeting that night, and while the dinner turned cold on the dining room table, Hana knotted her fingers nervously and informed her parents about her pregnancy. Stunned disbelief permeated the atmosphere, which quickly evolved into shouting until it dissolved into angry tears and apologies.

Kiva suffered her own internal battle in silence. After all, it wasn't about her and what she was going through. She kept quiet throughout the entire incident, flinching now and then when Mau raised his voice.

When they'd calmed and Hana was wrapped in her mother's arms, Kiva retreated to her bedroom for the rest of the night. With the door to her room ajar, she heard Naomi take her daughter to bed, whispering soothing words to calm her, assuring her that together they would look after the baby. That she needed to start eating healthily. That she could take a few days off from school until she felt strong enough to attend. That she was still loved.

Kiva sketched and sketched and sketched.

Her art book became her source of solace—the only outlet she could purge her emotions onto.

Pinched eyebrows.

Pained eyes.

Moist lashes.

Mingled with her own tears.

Sometimes it helped. Sometimes it didn't. Sometimes she felt as if she was going to implode on the inside.

When Silei called concerned, Kiva told her she hadn't been feeling well lately. Her best friend informed her that she was traveling to Sydney for the school holidays and that she was sad she'd miss out on seeing her artwork at the Teuila Festival, but that she would promise to bring back a present to make up for it.

Kiva hadn't given a second thought to the canvas she'd discarded in the art center because she hadn't set foot inside its four walls since. With the festival a week away, she didn't think she would submit anything in after all. Her heart just wasn't in it anymore.

She knew Ry continued to arrive and work in the afternoons but she hadn't seen or talked to him. She would forgo venturing outside and instead stayed in her room to do her homework. One afternoon she'd heard them walking toward Mau's pickup truck, and she moved the curtain to get a glimpse of him. Ry was poised at the passenger side door, one hand propped at the ledge of the window, glancing toward the house with an unreadable expression on his face.

The last day of school before term break always seemed like the first day of holidays. Teachers meandered casually to the classrooms, doling out work that required little effort. Her English teacher simply distributed a crossword puzzle, while in her history class they were made to sand down the penned graffiti on their desks. When the last bell rang, Kiva packed up her belongings and made her way to the bus stop. She didn't need to wait for her cousin. Hana had taken the week off from school, and Kiva surmised she was relieved for the respite the upcoming break would afford her.

She met Ester and Tui at the bench and together chased away the flies that landed near their feet. The bus was running late as usual, and Ester opened her purse and shared the hot, greasy pancakes she'd purchased from the market. Kiva swallowed her last bite when the familiar green bus pulled up, stirring dust around them. Wiping the oil from her hands on her school skirt, she clambered on and made her way to the back. Ester sat beside her and began to immediately regale her with stories about her grandkids. Kiva listened politely as they pulled out of the lot, the sharp turn making her grip onto the seat in front of her. As the bus reached capacity, Tui sat heavily on her lap, and she turned her head to the right where the window was to feel the cool breeze on her face.

A single, normal moment in her life. Nothing extraordinary about it.

A minute, an hour, a whole day was made up of these unremarkable junctures in time where people carried on with their normal routine … and the unfairness and powerlessness of it all was that there would be no sufficient warning when something drastic was about to occur, that the routine would become severed, divorced from the regular pattern, changed from one mundane moment to another. No time to pause and reflect, to say, "Wait! Please, I'm not ready. We're not ready." Just a mysterious pull from a will stronger than yours toward something you'd never expect to happen to you.

The first time Kiva felt something was wrong was when she heard a grinding noise originating from the back of the bus. It was loud enough to jar her out of her thoughts and swing her head toward the driver who was gripping onto the steering wheel and pumping the brake. As the noise increased in volume, the passengers became eerily quiet as their attention was drawn to the front, the tension rising thickly and causing her heart to accelerate.

They had long ago crested the main ridge and were tipped downwards, racing toward the rollercoaster hill, surging past several stops including Ester's. She dug her nails into Kiva's arm and said anxiously, "What's happening? What's going on?" The bus swerved from one side to the other, eliciting a few gasps and yelps from the passengers until someone exclaimed desperately, "*Fia ola!*" *I want to live!*

And then it all happened in one moment.

Chaos broke out inside the bus as some of the young men from the village scrambled to reach the door in a dire attempt to escape. The aisle became a battleground of people shoving, pushing, and shouting while children cried and women screamed. The bus driver yelled profanities—ordering them to sit down, to be calm, to shut up—and Kiva didn't miss the lick of fear in his voice. She gripped onto Ester's hand and tightened her arm around Tui's waist, her eyes round with fear as she saw the bodies jumping, falling into the ditch. Up ahead she recognized the dip in the road indicating the beginning of the rollercoaster hill, and the bus advanced toward it without slowing. Why wasn't the driver braking?

Terror squeezed her lungs as the severity of their situation ambushed her, causing her to shake uncontrollably. If they went over, there was no way they'd survive the inevitable crash at the end of the strip. Kiva's breaths came out in choppy bursts. Her heart raced erratically, the blood pumping hard and fast, injecting her veins with dread. The wind snapped at her face, cutting into her skin. She'd never felt so completely helpless, eyes darting back and forth, her body tremoring, legs and arms clutched tightly and clamming up with perspiration. They were trapped, boxed inside a wooden coffin made for forty, Ester to her left and the barred window to her right. She wanted to scream but couldn't muster enough air as terrible thoughts about how much it was going to hurt penetrated her mind. Would they even survive?

The driver struggled for control over the steering wheel as the bus veered dangerously close to the ditch. A wall of mountain terrain rushed toward them on the left side, and before Kiva could analyze his intent, the driver careened sharply toward it, crossing the middle barrier, the tail end of the bus swinging uncontrollably like a pendulum clock.

Her stomach tensed.

Her heart pounded and the sound of it thrashed in her ears.

A shriek pierced through the roar.

And then impact.

The sound hit her first—the crunching noise of metal and rock and wood—before she was flung forward, cracking her nose against Tui's back.

And just as quickly and without mercy, without any chance to recover, the bus lurched sideways, tipping toward the right, the encroaching tar-sealed road rushing toward her.

Kiva gasped and found her voice, her throat working even when other parts of her were broken, and this time the person who screamed was her.

CHAPTER SIXTEEN

She was trapped in oblivion, in complete darkness, but she wasn't alone.

Someone was touching her, moving her.

Strong, gentle arms enveloped her limp body and lifted it with little effort.

"Come on, Kiva, stay with me," an anguished voice said close to her ear.

Adrenaline quickened the muscle struggling to beat in her chest.

Was it …? How could he be here?

She wanted to believe it was him, to see for herself, but a rational part of her knew she hadn't reached home yet, that they'd never made it that far, that he should have been in the art center cradling a piece of wood, not her.

A dark veil blanketed her, obscuring her vision, and she didn't have the strength to open her eyes. She hurt everywhere—her face, her chest, her right thigh and arm, and ragged breathing set in as she tried to account for her injuries. How badly wounded was she? She shivered. It was so cold. Why was she trembling? She tasted blood and groaned when she was shifted onto a corrugated, steel surface and heard her uncle's voice bellow out a command and her aunt's panicked reply. She wanted to cry out from the movement, but mostly from relief. They had come for her! They were here. Where were Ester and Tui? She hoped they were being tended to as well.

The familiar rumble of Mau's pickup truck started, and she was jostled to the side as it bumped onto the road. A deep, guttural sound emerged from her throat and she immediately felt his calloused hands on her face, smoothing away her hair, touching her eyebrows, her jawline.

"Shh, it's alright, Kiva," Ry soothed. "We're on the way to the hospital, and you're going to be okay. You're going to make it and then we're going to explode the crap out of those bamboo guns. Just hang on …"

She wanted to smile, to believe him, to cling onto the desperate hope in his voice, but she had difficulty breathing and felt herself drifting. Is this what it felt like to die? If it was, she hoped to be delivered from it soon because the pain was an unforgiving companion. It was all-consuming and marring, leaving no cell unscathed, and she just wanted to give in to the torment so it would go away. The wind was everywhere, aggressive and unrelenting, as if it was a ventilator goading life back into her, and she realized she was stretched out in the back of the truck, exposed to the elements. Ry continued to talk to her in reassuring tones, pulling at the fringes of her consciousness, telling her to hold on, to fight, and Kiva promised herself that if she ever pulled through this, if she recovered, or even if she didn't, she would be forever grateful to him for saying all the right things, for allaying a little of her anxiety, for just being *there*.

When the truck stopped, loud, urgent voices replaced Ry's, and she was being lifted again and placed on a firm mattress. A blur of movement, the scrape of a curtain being drawn, different hands on her, gloved and purposeful, holding her steady, checking her airway, intubating her, and she wanted to gag and choke and fight them off. She felt several pricks on the outside of her left wrist and climbing further up on her forearm, and Kiva wondered briefly why she was ever afraid of needles because it was nothing compared to the agony that overwhelmed her body. An inferno blazed on her right arm—her artist's hand—and she couldn't move it. What was happening? Why did it feel like her skin was burning and clawing at her from the inside out? She wished she could open her eyes to investigate for herself, but she was trapped in an opaque web and felt utterly vulnerable, her life entrusted to a few people.

Kiva found herself bargaining with God, pleading with Him to spare her life, to give her another chance, and in return she promised to try harder to become a stronger person, to be more honest and less afraid, but then movement rattled her thoughts and she was brought back to the present. She was pricked and prodded and jostled. What was happening? Where were they wheeling her to?

She didn't have the answers, but before she slipped deeper into the

darkness, she caught a few words that put the terror back in her …
    "We're taking her into surgery."
    "Can her arm be saved?"
    A tired sigh. "I'm going to try."

CHAPTER SEVENTEEN

The inside of her mouth was like a lava field, parched and in desperate need of water.

She swallowed thickly and blinked the drowsiness away from her vision.

"Good, she's coming around," a feminine voice said close by. Kiva blinked a couple more times before a young woman in her thirties came into view. She was dressed in blue scrubs and had the kind of gentle, round face and soft eyes that would immediately instill calm. "Mativa, can you hear me?" she asked.

Kiva moved her head slightly to the side and spoke hoarsely. "Thirsty …" The top of her tongue was dry like sand and her throat ached at the effort to speak.

"Yes, you must be," the woman smiled warmly. "You lost a lot of blood and your body is dehydrated. We've hooked you up to IV fluids, but you can take small sips of water until your throat feels well enough to drink more."

"Thank you, doctor," Naomi breathed and laid a hand over Kiva's head, smoothing the hair away from her face. She felt so drowsy.

A nurse stood near the door and cleared her throat. "Excuse me, Dr. Tala, you're needed in room four."

The young woman smiled at Kiva and stood to leave, "Please excuse me. I'll return later to check up on you. In the meantime get plenty of rest." Kiva watched her exit the room before she relaxed at her aunt's touch. She wanted to drift to sleep when the magnitude of her plight slammed into her. Like a movie reel in fast motion, fragments of the crash replayed in her mind. She relived the horror. The excruciating pain. *Ry.* And the final words spoken before she slipped under.

Her arm. She'd lost her arm—the very limb that carried her dreams.

*Oh God, please **no**!*

Her heart hammered wildly against her ribs as she glanced anxiously down at her body. She was tucked under a starched white sheet, and both arms rested above it. Relief crashed over her like a thunderous waterfall, and her breaths came out in short, tight gasps, as if she'd been thrashing under water and her head just broke the surface. Her left arm was bruised and had every shade of purple slashed across it, but her eyes were drawn to the one on the right where it was wrapped in white gauze and supported in a sling.

Naomi pressed her hand more firmly against her forehead and said tenderly, "Hush, it's okay, Kiva."

"What ... what happened?" she rasped.

"There was a piece of wood lodged in your arm and the doctors had to surgically remove it."

Kiva swallowed hard and her aunt stood from her seat, clearing her throat, "Here. Let me get you some water." She fetched a bottle of water and straw and pressed it to her niece's cracked lips. Kiva took a few tentative sips and relaxed into the pillow.

"How long have I been here?" She peered through the space in the curtain and noticed the grass and trees awash with fresh light.

"It's almost seven in the morning. You've been here overnight." Her aunt's face was lined with exhaustion and worry, and Kiva noticed she was wearing the same clothes from the morning before.

"You've stayed ... the whole time?" she asked.

Naomi looked at her strangely. "Well of course I have. Where else would I be? You are my daughter, Kiva."

Kiva's chin quivered at that simple statement spoken so matter-of-factly, words that validated what she'd known all along but when spoken now caressed her soul. She turned her head away, swallowing the hard knot in her throat. "What ... what happened to the bus? Is everyone okay?" She wanted to know where Ester and Tui were. Were they at home or recovering in another part of the hospital?

Naomi sighed heavily. She paused, as if unsure of the extent of information to divulge, whether it was too soon to share the news that would no doubt be on the front page news that day. "You were one of the lucky ones, Kiva. Eleven people didn't make it, including the driver."

"What about Tui?" she asked anxiously.

"He's going to be okay. I spoke to his parents earlier. He broke a few bones, but he's going to be alright."

Kiva let out a relieved breath. "And Ester? The old lady? She was sitting next to me."

Naomi shook her head. "I don't know, Kiva. There are a few people in critical condition while some others have already been discharged. The hospital's been busy all night." She spoke of the couple of motorists who'd been trailing the bus and witnessed the whole thing. How several villagers arrived and found two young men in the ditch, dead from their injuries.

The bus had toppled on its side, the roof separated and broken apart. Green wood had disintegrated and scattered debris alongside the road.

When word about the crash reached the art center, they believed the worst, and she, Mau, and Ry wasted no time piling into the truck and rushed to the scene. Naomi spoke of the horror she saw when they'd arrived. "I knew you were on that bus, and I felt sick to my stomach." Her voice wavered. "There were people everywhere, some lying on the ground, some crying on the side of the road, but we couldn't see you." She inhaled unsteadily. "Ryler found you first, trapped between two seats. We were worried to move you, but you were losing a lot of blood and we had to get you to the hospital." Kiva's pulse started to quicken when she remembered being carefully lifted. "Ry carried you out and tied a tourniquet around your arm to stop the bleeding. When we arrived and the nurses were asking for people to donate blood, he was the first person to volunteer. He didn't want to leave, but Mau had to take him back to the school."

Kiva's throat tightened with emotion. "Where ... where's Mau now?"

"He's on his way. He went home to get Hana and to collect a few things for us."

Kiva exhaled a shuddering breath. She didn't know how she was going to react to seeing her cousin again after what she'd said under the bamboo. Her words still cut deep.

"The doctor said you'll be staying here for a few days. You hit your head and suffered a concussion so Dr. Tala wants to keep you to be safe."

Kiva glanced down at her right arm and tried to wriggle her fingers. "How long will my arm take to heal?"

Naomi sighed. "It's going to take some time, Kiva. You won't be sketching for a while, that's for sure. But you were very lucky ... The doctor said the piece of wood they removed almost pierced the nerve to your muscles."

Kiva stared at her aunt for a long moment. "So ..." she started, her voice trembling, "… will I … will it be okay?"

Naomi nodded. "The doctor believes so. They'll have to remove the stitches later and there will most likely be a scar, but that's a small price to pay."

Kiva exhaled an audible breath and sunk deeply into the pillow, staring up at the ceiling.

Mau and Hana stepped into the room, his face alight with relief while hers was a mask of cool indifference. Kiva experienced opposing emotions at seeing them. She smiled at her uncle as he reached her bedside. Hana dropped their overnight bags and bedding on the floor and lingered near the door.

"Kiva, how are you feeling?"

Kiva's eyes pricked with tears. It was too much—the torment from the past few days, the overwhelming relief now. "I'm okay, Mau," she answered in a wobbly tone.

He patted her left hand, careful not to touch the IV line, and sighed heavily. "It's good to see you're awake."

She gestured to her bandaged arm. "I don't think I'll be submitting my art piece for the festival now."

Mau shook his head, "Don't worry about that. Just concentrate on resting and getting back home."

Kiva swallowed the tightness in her throat and looked over at Hana. Her thick hair was pulled up into a messy bun and her expression was troubled, the lines around her eyes hollowed out and dark. Hana pressed her lips together and looked uncomfortably away.

Naomi busied herself with retrieving her belongings from the bag and excused herself to take a quick shower.

When she returned later, a nurse was in the room.

"Think you can get up and take a shower?" she asked Kiva, and she nodded in acquiescence.

After her IV line and catheter were unhooked and removed, Naomi helped her to the bathroom. Kiva felt dizzy and her right thigh ached when she applied pressure on it. She leaned against her aunt as she attempted to brush her teeth with her left hand. Gazing into the mirror, she winced at her appearance where her eyes were ringed in black and her nose was tainted dark brown with a bruise. Naomi undressed her carefully and used a small bucket to pour water over her body, avoiding the sling on her right arm. The water was deathly cold, causing goose bumps to prickle across her skin. Kiva shuddered and groaned from the movement, and by the time she returned to her bed dressed in an oversized T-shirt and sarong, she was exhausted from the exertion.

Breakfast was a simple meal, some tropical fruit and toast, but Kiva couldn't finish it. She didn't have much of an appetite and preferred to drink water instead. Hana was sent to purchase juice, and Kiva was grateful for the sweetness that coated her taste buds and helped rid the bitterness in her mouth that was a result of the pain meds.

Later in the morning journalists arrived hoping to interview the passengers on the bus, but she was asleep and Naomi turned them away.

She awoke at noon and managed to swallow a few spoonfuls of chicken soup. Mau and Hana left shortly after to return to the art center, and Naomi stretched out on the mat with simple bedding Hana had brought from home. Kiva listened to her soft breathing as she slept on the ground parallel to her bed. Her eyes wandered outside while her mind floated to the events that had transpired in the past week. She recalled the hurt caused by Hana's revelation and felt her throat squeeze. Her head ached and she shook it to quash the memory away. She was so tired. Emotionally. Mentally. Physically. She missed Silei and wished she was nearby and not traveling abroad for the holidays. She worried for Ester and hoped she was okay. She wanted to see Ry and thank him. She was disappointed she wouldn't be able to complete her artwork for the festival. Her fingers twitched with an overwhelming urge to sketch. She wanted the healing process to quicken so she could return to teaching art to her kids and climbing her tree. Kiva sighed and closed her eyes in an attempt to still her muddled thoughts.

When she awoke later, she learned that Ester had died. She was informed by a nurse who had come to give her more pain medication when Kiva asked for information about the other passengers. Ester's daughters arrived from New Zealand and were planning the funeral in a couple of days. Ester died instantly, she was told, and Kiva found it in her mourning heart to be thankful she hadn't suffered. She didn't think she'd be discharged in time to attend the funeral but made a point to ask Naomi if they could arrange for flowers to be delivered on their behalf. She had a sketch of Ester's veined, wrinkly hands in her art book—beautiful, hardworking hands that tended her garden and weaved fine mats. Kiva planned to frame and gift it to her family when she was well enough to move.

Tui and his parents visited her later that afternoon. She welcomed the distraction which gave her a mental reprieve, and observed the oversized cast on Tui's scrawny body. His right forearm had fractured from the impact, including a couple of fingers, and he had a gash under his ear which required a few stitches. He beamed when he told her he was being released that evening.

The bridge of Kiva's nose was bruised and swollen, and she had a deep cut on her forehead which was stitched and patched under white gauze. She didn't need a mirror to tell her that she looked frightening. Her hair hadn't been washed in a couple of days and was probably tangled with dried blood. Her right arm was starting to ache, her bruises were sore to the touch, and she desperately needed to use the bathroom but cringed at the thought of hobbling the distance. Mau and Hana hadn't returned and Naomi left briefly to purchase food for herself. By the time dusk crept in, Kiva felt alone, depleted of energy, and wanted to go home.

CHAPTER EIGHTEEN

Kiva was determined to return to her regular routine as soon as possible, or as much as her recovering arm and bruises would allow. She'd been discharged the day before with instructions from a nurse to keep it elevated and avoid getting it wet at the risk of infection. She didn't know how that was going to be possible since the gauze and sling had been removed. Her arm was now painted with a mustard-hued betadine and resembled a butchered sausage. The stitches trailed from her shoulder to the inside of her forearm and reminded her of miniature train tracks. A train of pain destined to leave her with a grotesque scar, she concluded. She'd winced the first time she saw it unwrapped, and was provided with antibiotics and informed to return to the surgical clinic in three days to remove the stitches. Kiva admitted feeling nauseous about going back. She was told the process would be painless—"Like plucking eyebrows," the nurse said without emotion— but this did little to allay her worries.

She soon learned that the simple acts of hooking on a bra and tying her hair up and securing it with a pencil were almost impossible to do. She wore her hair down today as a result, dressed herself in a black top and a carelessly-tied sarong, and decided she needed to get out of the house before she became cooped up listening to Hana throw up in the bathroom. Although she was past her first trimester, the morning sickness hadn't eased. Despite their initial reactions, Mau and Naomi were beginning to get used to the idea of becoming grandparents. While they weren't exactly jovial about Hana's situation, Kiva understood that they wouldn't push her to marry Junior since he clearly didn't show any interest in her or their child.

She stepped out into the backyard and a cool mist touched her face, sending shivers along her skin. She limped toward the art center, her steps careful and deliberate on the downwards slope, and avoided brushing up against the drooping ferns.

She crossed over the threshold and was immediately enveloped with the room's familiar woodsy scent. It was cool and dim despite the mid-afternoon sun, and she wanted to keep it that way. Without turning on the lights, she limped to the center of the room where a wave of nostalgia hit her and she couldn't help it when tears stung her eyes. Nothing had changed. The portraits on the wall were coated with the same filmy dust, paint brushes cluttered near the sink, and Mau and Ry's half-finished carvings were spread on the ground as if there had been nothing to upset its work flow. And of course nothing had, she thought sadly. They still had a deadline to meet.

Kiva shuffled further into the room when an object caught her attention. Her canvas was placed purposely in the center of the table, as if whoever picked it up didn't want her to miss its presence.

She moved closer and lifted her left hand to trace the edge. Her fingers trembled as she touched a frayed corner. At careful inspection she discovered that nothing else was damaged. The black girl and birds were still there with their delicate arcs and patterns, hidden connotations and aspiring dreams. Except now it was a dissolved dream to have it hang in the festival's gallery. She gave herself a mental kick for ever feeling afraid to display her art work. Now that it was too late, she couldn't help being disappointed that she wouldn't be taking part in the competition. Since the accident, her sense of clarity had been heightened where fear gave way to courage and she realized time was a fleeting element. If there was something Ester's fulfilled life and sudden death taught her, it was that while you couldn't control the end, you could control everything leading to it.

"What am I going to do with you?" she whispered at the canvas.

"You're going to finish it."

Kiva whipped her head around and saw Ry framing the doorway. Her head and heart reacted differently; her head hurt at the abrupt movement, while her heart leaped with elation at seeing him. Suppressing a groan, she pivoted slowly to face him.

Ry stood with his legs apart, his hands fisted at the sides. His face was shadowed in the dim light, and she couldn't make out his features until he stepped inside and closed the distance between them. Kiva counted five long strides before he was a foot away. She peered up at him and her lips curved into a gentle smile.

"Hi," she said softly.

Ry blew out a heavy breath before he closed his eyes briefly in anguish. When he opened them, his expression was tortured, eyes stormy. He inspected her face, lingering on the sutures near her eyebrow and the brown bruise across her nose before traveling down her right arm, quietly counting each stitch as he went.

"Does it hurt?"

"Only a little."

He clenched and unclenched his jaw.

She tucked a strand of hair behind her ear. "It looks worse than it feels ... Why do you look so angry?"

His brows deepened into a harsh line. "Kiva, there was blood everywhere, and you looked ..." He blew out a rough breath. "I had no idea if you were going to be okay or not. That night they prepped you for surgery, Mau had to take me back to the school and I had no way of knowing whether you'd survived or not until the next day when he picked me up and brought me here." He shook his head before adding, "And then I just had to go on carving like nothing happened."

Kiva's eyes softened at his concern. "I heard you donated blood."

"I did," he answered gruffly and her throat tightened. "But they had to double check everything first because of my damn tattoos. It was the first time I started to regret having them."

"You have more than one tattoo?"

His lips were set in a grim line as he nodded. "But in the end I think the nurses were as desperate as I was and just let me donate."

"There's island medicine for you." She added more gently, "Thank you ... for everything that you did."

A weighty pause resulted where he seemed to calm. He blew out another rough breath and glanced over her head at the canvas on the table. "The competition is two days away. You still have time to submit this."

Kiva half turned toward her art work. "I don't know ... It's not complete, but I can't move my arm, and I have to keep it elevated." She'd been cradling it against her stomach since she left the hospital, and her muscles were starting to feel sore, the stitches taut and uncomfortable, making her a little light-headed.

"It hurts, doesn't it? To hold it up like that?"

When she didn't say anything, Ry bit back a curse and glanced around the center. He strode to the cupboard and opened it, rifling through the drawers.

"What are you looking for?"

He spun around and gestured toward her arm. "You need a sling for your arm, Kiva," he said a little too forcefully. "Why don't you have one?"

"Well, they weren't exactly handing them out at the hospital."

His eyes settled on her sarong. "Are you wearing anything under that *lavalava?*"

Her eyes rounded. "Excuse me?" she squeaked out.

"Shorts. Are you wearing them?"

She gulped and shook her head, "No." That wasn't true. She always wore shorts underneath everything—sarongs, her school skirt, even to church, but there was no way she was taking her *lavalava* off and exposing her uneven legs to him. Her cheeks burned.

"Liar." He drew closer and his face gentled. "Kiva, you need something to support your arm. You look like you're about to pass out. I can turn your *lavalava* into a sling."

She jerked her head and replied hastily, "No, its fine—I'm fine."

The corner of his mouth twitched into a smile. "Your nose just grew a few more inches."

"I don't know how that's possible when it's all smashed up and ugly looking," she retorted. Biting her lip, she turned her head away.

"Hey." Touching her chin, he turned her toward him. "You don't have to do anything you're not comfortable doing, alright? I'm just trying to help. In fact, I can help you complete your project. Whatever you can't accomplish with your good hand, I'll step in and do the rest."

She studied him in silence as her mind mulled over his offer. She hadn't thought about asking for help from anyone, and his sincerity made her heart bloom. She admitted deep down that she really wanted to see her canvas completed, and even if she didn't win, it would be enough for her to have it displayed. "You'd really do that?"

"Absolutely. I'll just have to let Mau know, but I don't think it'll be a problem."

Kiva nodded reluctantly. "Okay ... but he's one of the judges for the competition. I don't know if he'll support the idea."

"You've just been in an accident, Kiva. I'm sure the judges, particularly Mau, will understand. Besides, you've done the majority of the work. It's all your idea, planned and executed by you. I'm just here to help with the finishing touches, or if you're happy with the way it is, you could submit it right away. Either way, I don't think you should give up."

Kiva let out a puff of breath. He was right. She was so close to completion. What she had left to do was paint the background, which she could accomplish with her left hand, and then scrawl a verse across it, which she would need Ry to do. Excitement started to stir inside her.

"Okay, we can do this." She smiled tenderly up at him.

"Good. But before we start, I'm going up to the house to ask your aunt for another *lavalava.*"

Kiva half laughed as he backed up a few steps, flashing her a crooked grin before spinning toward the door.

***

With her right arm in a makeshift sling, Kiva mixed watercolors until she was satisfied with a hue of sky blue. Positioning the brush against the canvas, she started with light, even strokes until her left hand was steady enough to pick up the pace. She had settled in her usual stool with a view of the room and occasionally glanced up to watch Mau and Ry hard at work. When they proposed the idea to him, Mau approved of Ry helping her with the finishing touches and even suggested stopping their carving early so he could begin right away.

Kiva planned to coat the canvas with a thin layer of paint and then place it out in the sun so it could dry faster. She had already chosen the verse Ry would scrawl down. It was one she'd revisited over and over again, memorizing the lines until they were embedded in her soul.

When she inspected her canvas an hour later, it was dry and ready.

"That's looking good, Kiva," Mau complimented when she brought it in. "I'm really proud of you."

"Should you be seeing this now?" she asked as they crowded around her art piece on the table.

Mau waved a hand in dismissal. "It's fine. You have my vote, anyway." She laughed and he clapped a hand over Ry's shoulder. "Alright kids, I'm heading up to the house. I'm beat and I need a drink." He dragged a towel over his sweaty forehead. "Let me know when you're done here, and I'll drive you back."

"Yes, sir," Ry responded seriously.

They watched him leave before they turned and locked gazes across the table. Silence stretched between them, pregnant with the kind of tension that set off butterflies in her stomach. Three feet of rainforest wood separated them. Dust motes rose visibly where the late afternoon sun beamed through the windows.

"Thanks for doing this again," Kiva finally said, breaking the spell. Emotions ricocheted inside of her. She wanted to reach out and touch him, to show with her hands how grateful she was, to fill the spaces in between his fingers with her own.

Ry's chest expanded as he inhaled a breath and let it go. "Tell me what you want me to do."

She retrieved a black marker. "I need your best handwriting skills. I have a quote which I'd like you to inscribe over the paint. I want the words to outline the girl's face so it'll curve from one end to the other, starting from her neck and ending at the top of her head. The verse is not very long so it should be able to fit in one continuous arch."

He peered contemplatively at the canvas and nodded once. "Which quote?" he asked without looking at her. She recited it from memory, and his lip tugged upward in a half smile when he recognized the source. "Alright. Let's get started then."

His handwriting slanted to the right and didn't curl like her own, the letters blocky and a little spaced out. She stood back and watched in silence while he handled her canvas carefully, as if it were a priceless ornament. His writing was neat and comprehensible and would do well to enhance the portrait, she thought contentedly. When he was done, he put the pen down and quietly stepped away to make room for her to approach.

Do you know what you are?
You are a manuscript of a divine letter.
You are a mirror reflecting a noble face.
This universe is not outside of you.
Look inside yourself;
everything that you want,
you are already that.
Rumi

She read it twice over, three times, absorbing each word and syllable, until she felt as if the galaxy and its stars were swelling inside of her.

She took it all in—the black girl with the eyelashes and hair in a bun, the birds that resembled fluttering bamboo leaves amidst soft blue—and suddenly everything she had been harboring over the years from the questions about her birth mother to her own sense of identity and belonging overwhelmed her to the point where the canvas appeared watery behind her eyes.

"What's the theme of the competition?" Ry murmured beside her.

Kiva blinked away the wetness in her eyes. "True Self." She swallowed the tightness in her throat and gazed intently at her art work. "When my mother was pregnant with me, she tried to have me aborted." His brows pulled together. "To imagine that I may not have existed ... that I wouldn't have been standing here today ..." A tear slid down her cheek. "When she didn't succeed, she gave me up anyway." She blew out an unsteady sigh, her shoulders shuddering as a result.

She was so tired.

She was ready to be done with self-pity and doubt. She was ready to do away with the hurt.

She was ready to detach, to not be enslaved by her emotions anymore, to let it all go.

Everything she had experienced from the buried pain and exposed truth, to the accident and its epiphanies, brought her to this moment. She was a girl with a limp. She was a girl with dark brown skin. She was a girl with dreams, and while she couldn't glide gracefully across a stage or win a relay race, she could just as likely sketch the girls who could. It didn't matter what legs God gave her because if she could walk, crawl, or limp toward her dreams, it was enough. She had flaws and insecurities, but she wasn't without her strengths. She could mold, paint, and create *siapo* from scratch, and she could teach others how to do it, too. And oh, how she loved the children who walked through the center's doors every Saturday morning with their enthusiasm and honesty. She could drive now, even if it was only with an automatic vehicle, and she had a best friend who treated her as an equal and accepted her for her physical awkwardness. She had loving guardians, who she acknowledged were doing their best, and she had a cousin who was going to be a mother, and despite the pangs caused by Hana's revelation, Kiva knew underneath her hard shell she was hurting inside. Reflecting on her actions, she realized now that those who hurt others hurt the most internally themselves. She had witnessed it behind Hana's wounded eyes and knew that her lashing out near the bamboos was a cry for help.

Kiva's little universe wasn't perfect, but it wasn't without hope either. Each participant in her life struggled and pawed and wrestled with their own challenges, sometimes failing, other times soaring, but it was through those difficult and rough times when one's character was shaped and molded. Like a piece of raw wood chiseled and cut by the carving knife until it resembled something of beauty. Like the pearl in her dream, she thought, where its extraction didn't come without pain, without blood, without struggle.

Like Ry and his purpose for coming to Samoa and to the art center, to her little universe in the Pacific.

She loved him.

She loved this misunderstood, beautiful, dark-featured boy with his scars, demons, and disheartenment. She didn't know when it started, couldn't remember the exact moment, but falling for him was like the quiet drop of ink on ivory parchment ... gradual at first until it seeped, spread, and swirled. Like exquisite Arabic calligraphy. She loved him now as surely as the dye permeated onto *siapo* or the ink tattooed onto skin. She loved this boy who had been pushed and bullied and fought back in his own misguided way, but who was not without human nobility. Beneath his tough exterior, he was intelligent and passionate. He cared, even if he didn't realize it, and he had a tender heart that she hoped would encompass hers. He was like the bamboo, bent but not broken. She wanted to emulate that.

She wanted to be that strong warrior woman from her sketchbook.

She was going to strive to be that metaphorical warrior woman in real life.

She just had to keep reminding herself that she could.

Ry moved in front of her, blocking her view of the canvas.

"Kiva." His voice was a hoarse whisper. He trailed the pad of his thumb across her cheek and gently tilted her head upwards. His brown eyes were pained before they smoothed into determination. "I won't try to understand what was going through your mother's mind or what led to her decisions ... but I want you to believe that this place is infinitely better with you in it. Since I've come to know you, you've shown more resilience than anyone I've ever met. You have a quiet strength that is more powerful than both of my fists combined. You are more than the name your mother gave you, more than how you were conceived, and this art piece and everything that it represents is evidence of all that and more."

Her pulse raced at his words. Smiling softly, she circled her fingers around his wrist. "I know ... I'm trying. I'm starting to believe that for myself now."

He held her gaze and her heart blossomed at the imploring look in his eyes before he released his hand from her face. Swallowing thickly, his eyes toiled with an inner turmoil that made her brows dip into a slight frown. Taking a step back, his face closed off just as quickly.

"Will you come to the gallery tomorrow evening?" she asked, not wanting to break the connection.

He smiled sadly. "I don't know, Kiva." Rubbing the back of his neck, he shifted uncomfortably on his feet. "The Academy is competing against a few other high schools in the *sasa* competition earlier in the day."

"Seriously?" Her eyes widened in surprise. "I had no idea you were doing that. I'd love to see your performance."

He laughed softly. "I don't know about that—making a fool of myself is more like it. I just hope my *lavalava* doesn't fall off."

She grinned at his attempt to ease the mood and felt a wash of relief flow through her. He was still here, present with her. That was good. "I'd love to be there," she added.

He gave her a faint smile, one that didn't reach his eyes, and her heart started to sink. "Look, I better go," he said hastily. "Mau's waiting." He backed up a few steps. "Good luck with tomorrow night. You're gonna do great."

She nibbled her bottom lip as her heart tugged in his direction. "Okay … thanks again for everything you did."

"No problem. Glad I could help."

Kiva watched helplessly as he turned and walked toward the door, sensing with remorse that he was pulling away.

CHAPTER NINETEEN

Kiva flapped her hand in front of her face in an attempt to fan herself. The heat in the hall was stifling, the humidity sticking to her back and pooling beneath her knees. Mechanical fans hung low from the ceiling but did little to whip sufficient air around the expansive room.

Glancing over her shoulder at the hundreds of people crammed in the arena, she wished they were closer to the front. The seats she had procured were edged near the grubby wall and offered a limited view of the stage. She decided she would slip to the side and stand if she had to when the Academy students came out. Wedged between her aunt and uncle, Mau grunted and cleared his throat impatiently as they waited for the next school to perform. Naomi wiped the sweat from her brow with a delicate handkerchief and engaged in lively conversation with the lady next to her. When Kiva told them about Ry's performance, Mau had already known and insisted they attend the competition to support him. She was touched by that, moved by the fact that they were here together for Ry. Peering through the spaces in the crowd, she couldn't see him or any of the other students and wondered if he was okay. She sensed something had transcended when he exited the art center the day before, and the feeling left her with an anxious clawing in her stomach. In her haste to get ready, she had forgotten to fold a *lavalava* into a sling, and she was left swatting flies away from her stitches. Her hair was in a messy braid and her feet were dirty from walking across the dusty car park. Sighing unevenly, she fidgeted in her seat and winced from the pain in her arm.

"Got ants in your pants?" Mau asked beside her, his eyebrow raised, and she let out a breathless laugh.

She had no idea what to expect from a group of foreign students and was nervous, fearing the mocking laughter the crowd would no doubt deliver if they messed up. So far she had been impressed with the performances from the other schools, and it was apparent that months of practice were paying off. The colorful costumes were a visual feast of bright feathers, oil-slicked torsos, and tropical prints. The timely beat of the drum accompanied by the swift slaps sent her heart thrumming in tandem to the rhythm. The actions of the *sasa* dance had to be sharp and polished, delivered with skilled proficiency that took time to master, and if one move was out of sync, it would disrupt the flow of the group and deduct points from the judges.

Kiva wrung her clammy fingers together in her lap and bounced her leg up and down. Earlier that day she received a call from Silei in Sydney who had been frenetic over the phone after she'd learned of the accident from her parents.

"I heard you almost died!" she sobbed, and Kiva smiled sympathetically on the receiving end.

"I'm fine, Si. Just a few scratches here and there. Nothing I can't bounce back from."

"You were so lucky," Silei hiccupped. "I'm sorry I wasn't there with you at the hospital. I bought you a present. Several in fact. Do you want to know what they are? I was going to keep it a surprise, but I want to tell you now. It'll make me feel better."

As she rambled on, Kiva missed her friend even more.

The squeal of the mic broke through her thoughts as a middle-aged woman dressed in a stiff floral outfit held it close to her rouge-painted lips and introduced the next school. When she announced the Academy's name, the crowd clapped with enthusiasm and Kiva's heart thundered against her ribs. Straightening in her seat, she craned her neck and focused on the empty stage where tropical foliage decorated the back wall.

Drum beats reverberated across the arena as the students entered in an explosion of noise and movement and quickly formed two straight lines. Kiva's eyes darted from face to face until she finally found him at the rear. His hands were on his hips as he stood, legs braced apart, head held high, giving nothing away of the nerves she expected he'd be feeling. They wore their *lavalavas* high above their knees, as most Samoan boys did for this dance, showcasing their thighs and calves, which were wrapped with stripped banana leaves. Chests bare, their tanned skin slick with coconut oil, and Kiva couldn't help but stare at Ry's wide shoulders and tapered waist. She'd never seen him without a shirt on, and while he wasn't the biggest guy there, he was certainly the tallest and fittest. His muscles were lean and defined and shifted with each step of the dance. Her eyes widened slightly when she noticed another tattoo along the ridge of his ribs. From this distance she couldn't make out the design but she was curious to know. Holding her breath, her gaze never wavered from him as he moved into a cross-legged stance and delivered the actions with ease and confidence. Easing back into the chair, she exhaled and started to enjoy the performance. He was good. They were all very good. Their accompanied shouts and yelps caused the crowd to stir with excitement, and when the *sasa* finally came to an end, the hall erupted with incredulous applause. Kiva stood, as most people did around her, and beamed with pride.

She watched expectantly as Ry strode across the stage and hoped he would turn around and catch her gaze. She felt the urge to go to him and praise him for his spectacular performance, but the lady with the mic came on and diverted her attention.

They sat through three more performances before the judges deliberated on the winner. While they waited for the results to be announced, Kiva's gaze swept the packed hall searching for Ry. She didn't spot him until the schools were called to the front of the arena. Heads bent, the students listened intently as a judge listed the winners. When she announced that Toa Academy came in second overall, the boys shouted and slapped each other gleefully on the backs. Cheers resonated around them, and Mau let out a wolf whistle. "*Malo* boys! Well done!" he shouted.

After the trophies and cash prizes were handed out, the throng of people started to dissipate, and Mau jerked his head toward the front of the hall. "Come on," he said to Kiva and Naomi. "Let's go congratulate our boys."

Weaving their way toward the Academy students, Kiva's stomach plummeted from nerves, and she tucked a strand of hair behind her ear and hoped she didn't appear too sweaty. As they neared, Ry caught her eye and surprise flickered across his face.

"Ryler!" Mau's voice boomed with delight, drawing Ry's attention toward him. "You did very well."

"Thank you, Mau," he responded politely.

"You looked like a warrior out there," Mau patted him on the shoulder. "*Malo*."

Ry hadn't yet changed out of his costume—or put a shirt on—and Kiva's heart raced at his proximity. He smelled of coconut oil and sweat, and she was able now to see the tattoo clearly on the side of his stomach. Another intricate script in Arabic, but it was longer. Gnawing on her bottom lip, she wanted to ask him what it meant, but somehow this one felt more intimate because he'd chosen a place that was typically covered up with clothing.

While her aunt and uncle left to greet the other boys, she hung back and waited for them to make the rounds.

"Thanks for coming," Ry rasped beside her. "Means a lot."

With her profile to him, she smiled softly. "I wouldn't have missed it for anything, Ry. You were incredible out there."

From the corner of her eye, she noticed him glancing away and shuffling on his feet.

Heart banging, she peered over at him. "Are we okay?" When he didn't say anything, she licked her lips and continued, "I felt something change yesterday when you left. I just hope—" Her brows knitted together. "I hope that whatever you're going through at the moment, you can talk to me if you want. I'll listen."

Ry let go of a rough breath. Rubbing the back of his neck, he started to speak, then shook his head as if he'd changed his mind. Through the crowd, Mau gestured toward her that it was time to leave. Ducking her head, she said, "I have to go, but I hope you'll be able to come tonight." Without a word from him, she turned with a heavy heart and limped away, knowing instinctively that he was watching.

She was quiet on the drive home while her mind churned over and over. What was wrong? Did she do or say something to push him away? It was difficult to walk away from the person you loved when they wouldn't communicate any of their thoughts with you. That resulted with Kiva drawing her own conclusions and conjuring scenarios in her mind, making her feel restless and apprehensive. What if he realized that she had fallen in love with him and he didn't feel the same way in return? Naomi had always said that she displayed her emotions so clearly on her face. What if by withdrawing himself he was subtly turning her down? That thought left a slash across her heart. She always imagined the act of falling in love involved a catch—the catching of each other before the doubts and second guessing and risk of crashing occurred. She was in a vulnerable position, dangling off a precipice with no idea where she'd land.

Wrapped in a damp towel, Kiva stood at the edge of her bed and peered down at the couple of formal dress choices she had for the art gala. They'd been in her closet for a number of years and didn't appear special anymore. For such a fancy event at the Robert Louis Stevenson museum, she wished she'd had something new to wear. Sighing, she grabbed the navy blue maxi and slipped it over her head with her good hand. The soft material whispered over her skin and fell to her ankles. Panting from the ache in her arm, she stood in front of the full-length mirror and assessed her appearance. Elegantly accentuated curves filled out in parts of the dress that previously swallowed her. Her brown hair was wet and bedraggled and needed to be combed but her eyes were round and bright with anticipation. Adjusting her bra straps, she slipped the cap sleeves down a little off her shoulders and twirled from left to right to get a better glimpse of herself.

"Kiva?" Naomi called from the hallway. Pushing the door open, she stepped in wearing a vibrant outfit. "My, look at you!" She gasped when she saw her niece. "You look absolutely beautiful. So grown-up." Kiva beamed at the compliment. "I came to ask if you'd like me to fix your hair."

"Yes, please." She breathed.

She sat unmoving on the bed and watched through the mirror as her aunt brushed out the tangles and pinned strands up into a classic updo. When Naomi pushed the last of the pins in, she spoke in a serious voice. "Kiva, I want you to know that whatever happens tonight … whether you win or not, receive a prize or walk away empty-handed, Mau and I are incredibly proud of you and your hard work. You are a winner in my eyes, and if you ask me, I personally don't like all of the competitive nature surrounding this festival, but if winning is what it takes to motivate people, then so be it." She leaned back. "There. You're all set." Smiling at her through the mirror, she added more softly, "My beautiful girl … you look just like your—" she stopped, sucked in a breath, and reeled in her emotions. "Never mind." She waved a dismissive hand in the air and got up to leave.

"Wait—" Kiva caught her arm. "I don't mind … you talking about her. About your sister, my …" *Mother*, she was about to say, but stopped herself. That wasn't true. Her mother was the very woman standing in front of her. Now that Kiva was aware of the darkest parts concerning her birth parents, she was curious to learn the rest of their story. "One of these days I would like to hear about her from you. But not now, not today. Someday though. Over a cup of *koko*."

Naomi gazed down at her for a cautious moment before she offered a tremulous smile. "Okay, Kiva. Okay."

"Come on ladies, let's go!" Mau bellowed from downstairs. "We don't want to be late!"

Naomi rolled her eyes. "Let's go before he misses out on the pupus."

They hustled into the truck and arrived at the brightly lit museum twenty minutes later. Kiva took in the colonial-style building, the restored home of the author himself, with its wooden balustrades and wrap around porch that leveled two stories high. Soft music reached her ears as they crossed the grassy lot and climbed the steps toward the gallery where Mau started chatting to a group of people he recognized. Kiva was immediately drawn to the art pieces displayed throughout the large balcony cordoned off for the event. Surrounded by a flourishing tropical garden, carved pieces and portraits boasted their artists' creativity and flair. People dressed in vivid colors and alluring styles wove around artifacts, holding champagne flutes and programs embossed in silver script. Kiva plucked one from a table nearby and scanned the list for her name. She spotted it near the bottom and her stomach did a somersault: *Mativa Mau. "Scar of the Bamboo Leaf." Charcoal and water paint on canvas. Item# 34.*

She blew out an unsteady breath and looked up. All of this was suddenly becoming real.

"Kiva, there's someone I'd like you to meet," Naomi said. Taking her elbow, she led her to a corner of the room where a life-sized canvas was displayed. A middle-aged woman dressed in a simple red dress broke away from a group of people and smiled at them.

"Naomi," she said, bracing her arms, "it's so lovely to see you again after so many years. How have you been?"

Kiva examined her unlined face, which was as smooth as brown clay, before her eyes traveled to her thick white hair wrapped elegantly in a bun. She had an elegant air about her as she carried an elaborate fan adorned with shells and peacock feathers and waved it gently in front of her face. Kiva got a whiff of her pleasant perfume which smelled like orange blossoms.

"I'm very well, Dr. Vanu," Naomi smiled in return. "I'd like you to meet Mativa. She's my artist prodigy. She's submitted an art piece for tonight," she added proudly.

"Mativa Mau?" she asked and Kiva nodded. Dr. Vanu extended her French manicured hand to her. "I was just admiring your artwork. It's always wonderful to meet young artists."

"Dr. Vanu and I have known each other for many years. She's an art history professor from the University of Hawaii," Naomi explained. "She specializes in lapita pottery and how its discovery has led historians to theorize pre-historic Pacific peoples."

Kiva's eyes widened with fascination. She'd briefly heard about this form of pottery before but didn't know much about its origins. "Has lapita been found in Samoa?"

"It has been discovered in one site, dating back to 800 BC," Dr. Vanu answered. "Of course there were only fragments found, but what was clearly evident were the intricate patterns resembling a similar likeness to the Samoan tattoo."

Kiva's mind deliberated over an idea. "Would it be possible to recreate this form of pottery today?"

Dr. Vanu cocked her head slightly and studied her. "It would be possible, yes. All you will need is clay soils and temper ranged from crushed basalt rocks or sand mixed with shells. After you mold a vessel together and create patterns around it, you then fire it over an open fire, like they still do in some parts of Fiji and the Solomon Islands."

Naomi turned to Kiva and asked, "Why? What do you have in mind?"

"I just think it'll be a neat idea to do this with the kids one day. We could revive this ancient form of pottery and open it to the public for display." She turned to Dr. Vanu and explained, "I teach art class to a bunch of seven-year-olds every Saturday morning."

"Why, that's a splendid idea," she praised. Smiling, Dr. Vanu added, "You know, we have an excellent art program at the university, and we are always looking for a diversity of students. A talented woman such as yourself could do very well there."

Kiva's heart raced at the thought of attending university in Hawaii as Naomi clucked excitedly beside her. "Oh, wouldn't that be wonderful, Kiva!"

Dr. Vanu smiled. "If you're interested, there are a number of international scholarships available to promising students. When do you graduate from high school?"

"Uh …" Kiva was at a loss for words, and Naomi nudged her to speak. "In two years."

"You should seriously consider it, then." Bending near her ear, she added, "I can put in a good word for you, too."

Kiva nodded jerkily. "I'll think about it. Thank you, Dr. Vanu." Her mind reeled over the idea of studying in Hawaii. She would give anything to attend university there. It wasn't too far either, just one flight away from home. She could do it. She just had to work really hard until then.

Dr. Vanu angled her head. "You know … I knew your mother, Viola. She and I were friends a long time ago. You look just like her."

Both Kiva and Naomi tensed.

"Where is she these days?" the doctor asked, unaware of the discomfort she was causing.

"She lives in London now," Naomi answered politely. Kiva tried to smile but it came out a little wobbly.

"Oh, London!" Dr. Vanu exclaimed. "A wonderful city. I have many professor friends there. Many of them art historians." Turning to Kiva, she added, "Think about what I've said. You have time now to plan for your future studies. Who knows, you could become a professor yourself." She faced Naomi and exchanged pleasantries with her, asking her about the art center, how it was going. As their voices blended in the background, Kiva thought about Dr. Vanu's connection to Viola. How long had she known her mother? When Dr. Vanu excused herself to talk to a group of people that had joined them, Kiva and Noami politely stepped away.

When they were at a safe distance away, Kiva looked over at her questioningly. "So … she knew Viola?"

Naomi nodded. "Yes, they went to school together. They weren't particularly close, but everyone seemed to know Viola. When Dr. Vanu left to study overseas, I don't believe they kept in touch." She reached for a cocktail shrimp from a passing waiter and popped it in her mouth. "Did you find your artwork yet?"

Kiva shook her head. "Not yet, but I'm going to roam the room."

"Alright, you do that. I'm going to say hello to a friend I see from my tie-dye class. I'll find you later, okay?"

"Okay," Kiva answered.

Naomi breezed away and disappeared into the crowd. Kiva couldn't see Mau and guessed he was probably deliberating with the other judges. She took in a deep breath, ready for her senses to take in the visual beauty surrounding her. Despite the little reminder about her mother, she was in artists' heaven.

Moving from piece to piece, she got glimpses into the hearts and minds of the talented people behind each piece of artwork as they interpreted themselves onto wood, canvas, the *siapo*. She didn't know any of them personally, but it was clear to her that they were all very dedicated to their craft.

When she finally found the girl with the fluttering birds and slanted script, nothing could have prepared her for seeing it. Standing away at a distance, it was surreal having her canvas displayed among other amazing artwork in such a setting. Humbled, she suddenly found it difficult to breathe. Curling her hand tightly around the program, she willed her heart to slow.

"It looks great," came a familiar voice from behind her.

Spinning around, Ry stood with his hands shoved in his pockets watching her. He was dressed in a white button-down which set off his olive skin and wore a grin that disarmed her for a moment.

Kiva's lips broke out into a smile. "You're here! How ...?"

He jutted his chin to the right. "Mau asked the Academy for special permission for me to attend after the performance this afternoon. The driver just dropped me off."

Kiva couldn't believe it. "Mau did that?" she whispered. Why would he do that? She didn't stop to mull over the answer. Overwhelmed with joy, she reached out and surprised them both by drawing her arms around his waist and resting her head against his chest. She heard his sharp intake of breath, felt his body tense, before he exhaled and slid his hands over her arms gently, careful not to touch her stitches. She didn't know where his feelings lie, what he was thinking, but she knew her own heart and knew that at that very moment everything felt right. They fit perfectly, and she wanted to be buried just like this in his arms for as long as she could. Inhaling, he smelled of fresh soap and clean linen. She listened to the staccato of his heartbeat before it slowed into a steady rhythm, and welcomed the love that built and swelled within her own. She loved him. All of him. Just the way he was. Right here. Right now.

A loud cough sounded nearby, and she immediately withdrew and peered around Ry's shoulder at a woman's disapproved glare. The woman shook her head and clicked away in her heels.

Stepping back, Kiva looked up at Ry and let out a breathless laugh. She'd forgotten momentarily that they were surrounded by people. Smiling crookedly, he reached out and tucked a lose strand of hair behind her ear. Her eyes softened at the gesture.

Glancing over her head he asked, "Why this title? *Scar of the Bamboo Leaf*?"

"I named it yesterday. Behind the art center, there's a cluster of bamboo trees that have been growing on the property for years. No one knows where they came from or how they ended up there in the first place because they're not local flora, and yet they thrive. I've done some reading, and the bamboo is known to be a resilient plant because its culms are strong and can bend easily with the wind. The only delicate part is its leaves. You can always tell the health of the bamboo by observing its leaves. If they haven't received enough water, they will curl within themselves to preserve moisture. But if the bamboo becomes dehydrated, the leaves will gradually discolor, break off, and flutter away. The interesting part though is that they don't go far. They'll usually fall to the immediate ground surrounding the shoots and stems, creating soft mulch that recycles the nutrients necessary for the bamboo to flourish."

"Let me guess … you're like the bamboo leaf. Delicate but also rooted in strength."

She smiled and turned to the canvas. "This is me, scars and all. For the longest time, I had become that shriveled, dried leaf in desperate need of nourishment. Sometimes I withdrew within myself, turning to my sketches as a salve for my pain. Other times I broke off completely, and these dreams were all I had to hold on to. That, and my love for Rumi, of course." His mouth tugged upwards into a half smile. "But now I've learned that even when you're broken, there's still hope, because our true self embodies so much more than the cracks in our lives … so long as you have a part of yourself that you can give away to someone else—even for just a moment—it can make a difference in your life and theirs." Clearing her throat, she added, "The first time Mau talked about you, he said you were like the bamboo. Foreign to this land but when planted in the right soil has the capacity to grow into a lustrous tree. I believe it … I believe in you."

Ry was quiet for a moment, and Kiva counted ten heartbeats before he finally spoke in a hoarse voice. "Are you my little leaf, Kiva?"

Her heart raced. *Yes*, she wanted to say. *If you want me to be*. But when she peered up at him, searching his face, his expression was troubled. Swallowing her answer, she glanced away. This was so much harder than she thought it would be, and she was suddenly out there on the ledge again, her heart dangling from a precipice. "I think it's okay to be a leaf to somebody you care about," she finally said. "I believe we can all use one at least once in our lives." If she couldn't be someone more to him, then she would have to settle for that. Her heart breaking, she plastered on a smile and changed the subject. "Have you had the chance to see the other displays?" When he shook his head, Kiva guided him to another part of the room.

They spent the next hour admiring the other pieces and eating mini quiches and sausage rolls. Sipping orange juice, they engaged in conversation with several of Naomi and Mau's acquaintances until the same prominent professor she'd met earlier walked to the podium and gave the keynote address. Thanking the artists for their participation, Dr. Vanu was handed an envelope and read off the names of the winners. When Kiva received third place, she almost choked on the juice from shock.

Naomi nudged her forward and whispered, "Go on, Kiva. They called you. Go get your prize."

With shaky knees, she walked to the podium, shook hands with the professor, and accepted flowers and an envelope she guessed contained a check.

"Congratulations, Mativa," Dr. Vanu commented with a smile.

Raising the envelope to her forehead in a gesture of gratitude, Kiva's heart pounded from the attention she received, and she quickly limped back to Ry and Naomi.

Ry grinned that crooked grin of his when she joined him in the crowd. Bending to her ear he rasped, "Proud of you, Kiva." His voice chased shivers down her spine.

"Thank you, Ry." She smiled and felt warmth curl around her heart.

CHAPTER TWENTY

Kiva slid into the back seat of the pickup truck and Ry followed her in. Rolling down the window, the evening's breeze tickled her skin and cooled her face. As Mau cranked the engine, Naomi shifted in the passenger seat and stretched her arm to touch her knee. "Well done, Kiva." She beamed. "Your canvas was a beautiful sight to see among all those other displays." She turned around and spoke to Mau, "We should seriously consider having an art show of our own at the center. It would certainly attract potential customers. We could advertise around town and make some of those delicious shrimp dishes to serve. What do you think?"

Mau grunted in response. "I think Kiva can be in charge of organizing it, right, Kiva?"

"Kiva had a wonderful idea about making lapita pottery with the kids. I think they'd really enjoy that. They'd also learn a bit about their ancestors in the process."

Kiva could imagine it already: clearing the space in the middle of the room for people to walk around and peruse their art work and creating family friendly snacks for refreshments. She could even learn how to bake some of the delicious mini cupcakes they served tonight.

The truck reached the main road and turned toward town where the Academy school was located. Darkness fell over the backseat interspersed by the dim street lamps overhead, casting shadows over Kiva's lap.

"How's school going, Ryler?" Mau asked.

"It's going well," he answered. "I'm actually graduating in a couple of weeks."

Kiva swung her head to him. "You are?" she asked, surprised.

She saw his dark profile nod, and her heart plummeted. Before she could ask the next question, Naomi took the words right out of her mouth.

"What are your plans afterward?"

Ry braced his hands in his lap and gazed out the window. "I'll head back home. I've decided to apply to college, see where it takes me."

"Oh, that's wonderful," Naomi said. "What do you plan to study?"

"Architecture. I want to do something with my hands—design and create things from the bottom up."

Kiva's throat tightened as she remembered their conversation months ago about using his hands to create. Her chest filled with pressure at the thought of his departure. He was leaving. No wonder he had been distant.

"How has it been here for you here?" Naomi asked.

Ry blew out a breath and his tone turned serious, "It's been … a life-changing experience."

"In what ways?"

"Well, for starters it took me away from the trouble I was getting into back home. Samoa is a place where you simultaneously lose yourself and then find yourself again. After being exposed to the culture here, to the meaning of family and respect, my perspective on life has changed. But it hasn't always been like this. When I first arrived, I was really angry, and I fought everyone with my attitude."

Mau chuckled. "I remember your first carving."

Ry shook his head and said bashfully, "Yeah, sorry about that." He cleared his throat. "Things started to shift afterward. The Academy pushed me to seriously think about my choices and actions. They accepted me even when I was difficult to get along with, and the people I've met along the way have shown me how to aspire to something greater … to look ahead to my future and formulate dreams that I never would have imagined for myself. So that's what I'm going to do … go back and apply to college."

Kiva swallowed hard and turned toward her window. As happy as she tried to be for him and his plans, she couldn't believe he was leaving. She guessed a part of her always knew that he would ultimately graduate, but not right now, not right away, and not so soon after she had fallen for him.

"That's a wonderful plan, Ryler," Naomi said. "I'm sure your parents will be very proud to hear that and to have you back, too. We wish you all the best in your endeavors."

"Time to celebrate!" Mau added. "For Kiva's success tonight and for Ryler's future. Let's go and get some milkshakes before we drop you off."

They pulled into the MacDonald's drive-thru a few minutes later and placed their order.

"I can't remember the last time I had one of these," Ry said as he accepted a chocolate shake. He sipped through the straw and leaned back. "So good."

Naomi flicked on the radio, infusing the cab with a song about missing gentle hands and shadows gliding across a girl's face. The singer's voice was rough and strong, the lyrics and guitar strums filling Kiva with a yearning so strong she didn't think she could keep it enclosed within her heart. Her eyes burned with shimmering tears and she turned toward the window, thankful that it was dark and Ry couldn't see her face. But very quietly, his long fingers threaded through her own making her gasp silently and causing a tear to slip down her cheek. The pulse on the inside of her wrist accelerated, and she was sure he could feel it, too. The pad of his thumb stroked the raised veins on the back of her hand and she remained still, unable to look at him, exposing her pained expression to the breeze and darkness outside instead, taking in the sensation of his warmth and gentle comfort beside her. Despite the fact that he was sitting next to her, his tall frame taking up much of the backseat, she missed him already and held on as if she was imprinting herself onto him.

When they reached the school, a security guard stepped out of a little shack and rounded the driver's side to greet her uncle. They laughed and joked and Kiva got the distinct feeling that they'd become good buddies since Mau dropped Ry off every day.

Ry let go of her hand before he opened the door and stepped out. "Thanks for the lift," he called out to Mau.

"Good night, Ryler," Naomi said. "We'll see you soon."

Without a backwards glance to her, Kiva watched through the chain-linked fence as he moved further away in the dim light, turned a corner, and disappeared from view. Her heart sank as she made out the building of the school, a single-story structure painted in white with potted plants on the balcony. Outdoor lights illuminated the surrounding area where several smaller huts were clustered around and tropical shrubs and a garden bordered the pathways that connected each building. It was pleasant-looking, Kiva thought, and reminded her of a quaint tropical resort.

Mau reversed out of the driveway and blew the horn a couple times in farewell.

Later that night when Kiva slipped out of the dress and into her pajamas, Naomi came into her room and perched on the edge of the bed. Patting it, Kiva went to sit beside her and turned her back to her so she could take out the pins from her hair. She listened to the calm shift of pins as they were removed and placed on the bedside table.

After a quiet moment, Naomi spoke softly. "I know you love him."

Kiva stilled as her heart took off racing. Apprehension penetrated her mind as she contemplated her aunt's spot-on observation and her feelings about her falling for a boy, and not just any local boy, but a boy who came from overseas and had a troubled past. Would she be upset if she answered truthfully? Swallowing thickly, she decided that whatever Naomi's reaction, she couldn't deny her heart.

"Yes … I do."

She heard her sigh, take a deep breath, then ask, "Have you acted on that attraction?"

Kiva's cheeks flamed as she understood her aunt's meaning and shook her head.

"I only ask because I want you to think very clearly about all of this … besides the fact that I don't want what happened to Hana to happen to you, he's leaving, Kiva, and you'll probably never see him again."

"I know …" she whispered. "But it doesn't change my feelings, and right now I love and I hurt and I'm so confused and I don't know if he feels the same way."

"I can see that he cares for you, but he probably doesn't want to hurt you by becoming involved in something that will make it difficult for you both when it comes time for him to leave."

Kiva shifted around so she was face to face with her. "So, that's it then? We just say goodbye?"

Naomi reached out and brushed a strand off her shoulder. "I think it's for the best, Kiva. You both come from two different places and you're heading in two different directions. You're going to have to let him go eventually, move on, concentrate on finishing school, and then fulfill those big dreams of yours."

"Then what would have been the purpose of all of this? I see him, Naomi. I see the truth in him."

Naomi sighed and compassion crinkled around her eyes. "Sometimes, a person will come into your life and leave an imprint in your heart … but it doesn't always have to lead to something romantic. Sometimes, it's just a passing moment where your lives diverge and connect for a brief period of time, a gift for one instant, and nothing more."

Kiva's brows dipped into a crease. "But I want more."

"I know you do." She leaned back a little. "I remember when I first fell for a boy in my last year of high school. My whole world revolved around him and when I was going to see him next. He wasn't loud or obnoxious like the other boys but was mysterious and a bit of a recluse, which made him more interesting to me." She smiled softly reminiscing. "One day after school we happened to be walking together in the same direction and we started talking. Or I did most of the talking, and he just listened silently. It was like that for several days—me babbling away, while he was quiet. He sure taught me patience." She laughed. "I had to pry information out of him like pulling teeth. But then when he finally opened up, I found out that he had quite a sense of humor. He made me laugh every day after that."

"What happened next?"

She sighed. "He left for New Zealand for a family emergency and never came back. I never saw him again. I remember feeling heartbroken and upset, but then life went on. I grew up and met Mau and that kind of love is something else. If you can love someone even after your heart has stopped pounding every time he walks into the room, then it's real." Her eyes shifted to Kiva. "What I'm trying to say is that you're young, and there'll be another. My grandmother used to tell me to make space in my heart for others because it's always big enough. You have a big heart, Kiva, and you'll love again."

Again? How could Kiva fathom looking beyond what she felt now? How could she suppress her heart? What she felt for Ry settled into her very bones and couldn't be ground into powder and flicked away with the current of the wind.

Naomi got up from the bed. "Think about what I've said. I'm going to go check on Hana, see how she's feeling." She squeezed her shoulder and left the room.

Kiva blinked and stared down at her hands. Reaching for her art book, she never wanted to sketch more in her life than in that moment.

CHAPTER TWENTY-ONE

Over the next couple days, Ry returned to the art center in the afternoons to work on the carvings with Mau, and Kiva only saw him when she took drinks and refreshments out to them. Head down, he worked tirelessly to have the *tanoa* bowls completed before the week's end when they had to be presented to the diplomats. She noticed he was still keeping his distance, only looking up to accept a drink or sandwich from her, but when she'd had her stitches taken out, his eyes grazed a path over her arm where a grisly scar was left as evidence from the accident.

"Did it hurt to take them out?" he asked.

She shook her head. "It wasn't as bad as I thought it would be."

"You'll have a permanent scar." His voice was laced with concern.

She unconsciously rubbed her left hand over the ragged trail, trying to conceal it. "It's nothing," she mumbled and ducked her head.

It certainly looked ugly and she wouldn't blame him if he was repulsed by its appearance, but then what he did next startled her. Brows dipped into a serious line, he blazed the route of the scar with his thumb, raising goose bumps along her arm and setting off her pulse. His gentleness broke her. Eyes blurred behind tears, she watched as his head dipped closer to inspect it. From this angle she took the opportunity to study his face and noticed a small birthmark on the side of his cheek that she hadn't seen before. His lashes were dark fans against the rich tan of his skin, and his hair was growing out of its former shaved state. She couldn't help reaching out to touch the scar near his eye, feeling the pebbled skin under her fingertips. He looked up at her then and she rapidly blinked the moisture from her eyes.

The corner of his mouth tilted up into an empathetic smile. "Don't cry, Kiva. It's okay. I'll let you win this round for best scar story."

She let out an astounded laugh, even when her heart broke a little more. He was so beautiful. This imperfect, scarred boy with his crooked grin and calloused hands. Could he not tell what she felt for him? She swiped her eyes and settled down on the concrete floor next to him. "Are you looking forward to going back home?"

He let out a rough breath. "Yes and no. I'm a little worried about going back to my home town. Nothing would have changed, even if I have, and that's the scariest part. I don't want to return to the hollow shell that was my life."

"It takes a courageous person to admit what they fear."

"I'm not brave, Kiva. I won't be there long enough to face it. I'm going to apply to a few out-of-state colleges, see where I get accepted."

She picked up a wood chip and twirled it around her fingers. "America seems like such a world away. You're lucky to have so many opportunities. Sometimes I feel so isolated living here, that if I blink for one moment, my chance to leave will pass me by."

"Where do you want to go?"

She sighed. "Anywhere. Everywhere. When I was a child, we'd go to the airport to see relatives off to New Zealand or Australia, and as soon as we'd get there, I would race to the look-out area and press my face up against the glass window just waiting for the plane to arrive. I would see it come in and then watch as the people descended the steps. I noticed children clutching dolls and teddy bears close to themselves and believed that the plane was one big toy store with toys and candy. I remember hoping that one day I would also be allowed to go inside, but that day never came." She smiled and shook her head. "As I grew older of course, I realized that you could board a plane to fly to faraway places if you had the money. My one chance of ever boarding a plane is if I work really hard to earn a scholarship to an overseas university. I really want to go, and I really want to study fine arts."

"You could do it, Kiva," he stated. "I can see that you can achieve it all."

Her lips curved into a soft smile. "I'm going to try." She flung the wood chip away. "So tell me … What's it like where you're from?"

"Where I live gets pretty cold. We get some harsh winters that can go on for weeks. The town is a small, sleepy one, and not many people pass through it."

"There must be some things you've missed."

"Well … I've missed my mom." His cheeks flamed and he rubbed the back of his neck in such an endearing way that made Kiva smile. "I sound like such a sap, but it's true. She hasn't always had it easy because of me, and I want to make it better for her. I've seen the way kids here respect their elders, and it's a good thing. I've been in touch with her and my stepdad through the school, and I guess I didn't realize how much I'd miss the familiarity of home until I had to be away from it for a long time."

"What's your mom like?" she asked.

"She's a lot like Naomi. She loves flowers, and when she gets the time, she's out in her garden working on it. She's a homeopathist so she's good at listening to people's problems and coming up with homeopathic solutions to help combat their issues—me included."

She smiled before her thoughts turned serious. "Have you ever thought about finding your father?"

He nodded slowly. "Yeah, I've thought about it, but I don't know how to start looking. We've had no contact with him since he left the States, and when I asked my mom about it once, she became really sad afterward so I never raised it again." He sighed. "Half of me is this one big mystery, and I'm so curious to learn more. All I have is his name and the country he's from. What about you? Do you ever think about your own mother and father?"

"My mother, yes. I'm a phone call away from knowing more about her since she's Naomi's sister, but ever since I learned about her intentions for me, I'm apprehensive about ever facing her. She lives in London, so I guess I don't have to worry about that any time soon. As for my father? I have no idea who or where he is. I don't have a name. I don't even know what ethnicity he is."

"Hmm, let me see ..." He leaned back and studied her. "You're definitely part Polynesian, that much is evident, and I'm guessing the other part is Melanesian? Your skin is this creamy brown while your hair is straight when you let it out. In the shade it looks darker than it is, but when you're in the sun, you can make out a few golden strands." Kiva squirmed under his observation. Hearing him speak about her this way made her feel a jumble of emotions inside, while a big part of her was thrilled that he even noticed these minute details. "I can also tell when you're extremely uncomfortable because you do this funny little thing with your bottom lip," he added before attempting a mock imitation of her.

She laughed and flung a wood chip his way. She'd been gnawing on her lip and immediately released it from her teeth. He dodged sideways and smirked.

"Aren't we a couple of poster kids for the unconventional family," he remarked.

"I believe we create our own family, whatever that may look like, as long as it feels like home," she responded.

He looked at her contemplatively for a moment before returning to his work.

Later as Kiva joined her family around the dinner table, Mau brought Ry's departure to their attention as he sprinkled salt over his food. "It was sad saying goodbye to Ryler when I dropped him off today," he started. "He's a good kid. I'm going to miss having him around."

Kiva lowered her fork slowly. "He's not coming back?" she asked, her stomach clenching.

"No, he's not. It was his last day today."

She was quiet as Naomi passed her a plate of fried fish that she absently took.

She never got the chance to say goodbye. She never even exchanged addresses with him.

She caught Naomi's gentle gaze before flicking her eyes away.

How was she not aware of this? Why didn't he tell her? Did their friendship mean so little to him that he couldn't mention it was his last day? She knew he cared, so why didn't he say goodbye?

She ate in silence while Naomi and Mau talked about their plans for a future art show of their own.

"By the way, Kiva," Naomi said, breaking through her thoughts. "I got Dr. Vanu's contact information for you. It's good to have it for future reference."

"Why do you need her contact information?" Mau asked around a mouthful of taro, and Naomi informed him about their conversation at the art gallery.

He nodded with approval. "That's great. It's always good to have contacts in respectable places. Maybe she can help Hana, too."

"I'm not going back to school," Hana spoke up at the end of the table. She fidgeted in her seat and studied her half-empty plate.

Mau didn't spare her a glance when he said, "You will go back to school and complete your final year, Hana. I will not allow your pregnancy to be a reason to discontinue your education."

Kiva noticed her cousin purse her lips in an effort to keep it from quivering. "But the school kids will talk about me …" Her voice shook with emotion. "I can't go back."

"It's not going to be easy, you're right, but you will return after the holidays and face those classmates of yours whether you want to or not." Hana choked on a sob as he continued, "Don't cry, Hana. Chin up. There's nothing you can do now besides eating healthy and looking after yourself and your baby, and a large part of that is to also finish school. You only have a few months left so you show those kids that you can work hard and graduate regardless of your pregnancy, and if anyone gives you problems, then you come tell me."

Kiva wasn't surprised that students at the school already knew about Hana's situation. After all, it was a small place where everyone seemed to intimately know everybody else's business.

"I made an appointment to see the doctor tomorrow," Naomi said. "We'll leave at ten, and then we can have lunch in town afterward. Wouldn't that be nice? We haven't eaten out in a while."

Hana shuddered out a breath and wiped her eyes on her sleeve.

When they were done with dinner, Kiva stood to clear the table. With heavy steps, she carried the dirty dishes to the kitchen and scraped leftovers into a bowl for Masi. She reminded herself to keep moving, to keep her hands busy, because if she stopped for one moment, her thoughts would return to Ry. But washing the dishes afforded a quiet space for her mind to roam and she couldn't help thinking about him. She was crestfallen that she'd never see him again, that they'd never said goodbye, and she wouldn't have closure. As she rinsed the dishes and placed them on the rack, a sudden realization hit her. He never made an issue about her limp. It was never a topic of discussion for him. Was it because it never bothered him? Or was it because it had and he was just being polite about it? She had no way of finding out.

Carrying on the mundane tasks in the days that followed had a mechanical feel to it. Kiva's heart didn't pound rapidly as when he was around, and she didn't feel as if her chest was going to explode from anticipation from seeing him. Over time her right arm became strong enough for her to grip a pencil and draw in her art book where her sketches had one common subject: eyes, lips, neck, all belonging to him. She tried to capture his essence, his very spirit, the intensity of his eyes, and the teasing dip in his smile when there was nothing tangible of his to hold onto. Her heart wept when she realized the hardest part about loving someone was the idea that their love was never meant for her. Sitting in the *pulu* tree, she shaded in the edges of his face until the sun went down and she was bitten by mosquitos.

When Silei returned from her trip, she'd brought clothes and jasmine infused perfume, and a new sketchbook and art pencils for her. Kiva donned one of her new V-neck shirts as they went shopping at the flea market and ate fish and chips near the port. She welcomed the distraction which was a much needed break from her muddled thoughts and broken heart, but when Silei informed her that her parents had decided to enroll her in a girls' private boarding school in Auckland, Kiva imploded on the inside. Now she was going to lose two people in the same year.

Over the next several weeks, she threw herself into organizing the art show. She gathered together the kids' artwork and some of her own, including the artifacts and portraits hanging in the center, and cleaned and prepared the display tables and shelves.

She was serious about creating lapita pottery with her students and contacted Dr. Vanu in Hawaii about the process and materials needed. When the kids walked into the back yard on Saturday with wide-eyed curiosity, they were met with clumps of soil and clay on sacks. Kiva beckoned them over where they proceeded to stamp on the clay with their bare feet before beating it with wooden paddles. Shapes were molded and smoothed out with river stones and then placed in the sun to dry. When the children returned the following class, Kiva gathered kindling and rocks to build an open fire and placed the bowls on top for an hour. The fired pots that resulted were better than she'd imagined for a first attempt with only a few minor cracks here and there.

The show that resulted was smaller than they'd expected with mostly the children's families attending, and while they'd hoped to draw in the public to help boost the art center's popularity, the day turned out to be a stormy outside but had a cozy feel on the inside.

As weeks dragged into months and the season changed from dry to wet, Kiva busied herself by learning to carve from Mau. Her hands suffered splinters and calluses, but she was determined to learn. She also wanted to be reminded of Ry and his time with them. She continued to miss him daily.

When she wasn't in the art center, she was in the kitchen baking cupcakes and cinnamon buns, filling the house with a sweet aroma. She had a newfound interest in the kitchen and expanded her culinary skills to include pork buns and sweet and sour chicken much to the delight of Naomi who was only too happy to give up the responsibility of cooking to her.

As Hana's stomach started to protrude, she walked around the house with only a wraparound *lavalava* to stave off the humidity. In the last term of school, she squeezed into her uniform amidst the nasty rumors that floated around and committed herself to studying hard. She passed her exams with average grades and graduated with the rest of her class at town hall which was decorated with coconut fronds and frangipani.

Before the wet season ended, she gave birth to a healthy baby girl she named Talia, meaning to wait in anticipation for something spectacular. It was a befitting name since she had to wait a couple weeks past the due date to give birth. Both Naomi and Kiva had been in the hospital room when she went into active labor, and the whole process had been long and excruciating, albeit a miracle to witness. When they were discharged the next day, Mau and Naomi were overjoyed to welcome home a tired Hana and bundled-up Talia. Naomi prepared Hana's room for the baby where Hana could co-sleep with her on a simple mattress on the floor with a cozy mosquito net hanging over them.

As Talia grew, she filled the house with a warmth Kiva hadn't felt in a long time. Her gurgles and coos won her over immediately, and she relished the moments when she hitched her chubby legs over her hip and walked her outside to the *pulu* and bamboo trees. Born with a head full of hair, her dark brown eyes took in the faces around her with awe and delight, and Kiva found it intriguing how easy it was to be compelled by a little person and to quash the hurtful things her mother had said to her months earlier under the same bamboo. As Hana adjusted to motherhood, her temper abated as she took on her new role with a serious commitment that surprised even Mau and Naomi. They doted on their granddaughter, and it seemed there was more laughter floating across the house and more light in their eyes when she was around.

One day when Kiva was hanging the laundry on the line and Talia played by her feet, Hana came out of the back door and stood hesitating on the stoop.

"'Iva!" Talia cried, drawing her attention away. "Wock!"

Kiva smiled down at her. "That's right, a rock, but don't put it in your mouth, sweetie. It's dirty."

Talia flung it away, barely missing Kiva's ankles, before picking up another to inspect.

Hana strode toward them. She paused by the laundry basket and reached for a damp shirt of Talia's and a couple pegs. Without a word, she hung it on the line and proceeded to help with the rest of the laundry. She had never done that before, and Kiva's heart kicked into double time as they worked side by side. The silence was straining, festering the atmosphere with unspoken words when there were many important words that needed to be said. Kiva's chest tightened with the need to say something while the wind became a barrier to be heard, flapping the towels and bed sheets between them.

"Mama!" Talia broke through the tension.

Hana smiled tenderly and picked her up. Kissing her on the forehead, she looked away from Kiva when she said two words she wasn't expecting to hear, the weight of them bearing years of hurt caused.

"I'm sorry."

"Sowwy," Talia repeated.

Kiva looked between mother and daughter, their resemblance uncanny, and wondered about Talia's future. What kind of woman would she grow up to be? What challenges would she face? How would she rise to meet those challenges? What qualities would she possess? With every new life, one could break the cycle of hurt that would potentially pass from one generation to the next. Kiva didn't want Talia to live in the shadow of her mother's pain. She looked at her cousin and nodded once, acknowledging her apology, but it wasn't easy. In fact, it was singularly the most simple and difficult thing she did.

Hana expelled a long breath and turned to leave, but Kiva couldn't let her go.

"You really hurt me," she said to her retreating back and her cousin paused.

When she faced Kiva, her face was full of regret. "I know. I'm truly sorry. I've always been envious of you …" She sniffed. "Will you forgive me?"

Four powerful little words that asked for so much more than its measly five syllables.

Kiva swallowed hard. She acknowledged at that moment that she had experienced two types of hurt in her life—the kind where she was being treated badly, and the other where she *allowed* people to treat her badly. For too long, she had been living with Hana's cruelty, and while she understood her own suffering over the past few years, she could control how she responded to it now. "I want to," she finally said. "But it'll take some time."

"Alright," Hana responded. "I don't deserve it, but I'll take what you can give me."

Kiva nodded and Hana walked away with Talia blowing kisses over her shoulder.

The year Kiva turned eighteen, she had the potential of graduating with a high rank among her class and a chance of receiving a scholarship to a university overseas. Everything was falling into place and she hoped she could finally board that plane. She imagined Ry studying somewhere at a college with tall, neo-gothic buildings, lush green lawns and trees, and a river flowing nearby. She regularly heard from Silei who was going to move into a flat with a cousin in Wellington and attend Victoria

University, and she really didn't want to be left behind. It was now a waiting game—waiting to hear whether she was going to be awarded a scholarship, waiting to see if her dreams were going to come true.

Mau's carvings began to generate popularity after a journalist from one of the region's top travel magazines visited the art center and interviewed him. The publicity that resulted earned him the opportunity to display his work at Auckland museum as part of a week-long exhibit of Maori and Pacific Island heritage and art. When he returned from that trip, he received a call from a museum in Brisbane expressing their interest in his work as well. That evening Mau took them to an island buffet to celebrate.

As Kiva sipped on a pineapple drink and watched the fire knife dancers whirl around on stage, she leaned back in her seat and relaxed. Gazing around the table, she watched Talia bouncing on Hana's lap and clapping her little hands to the beat of the drums. Hana's head rested atop hers, and Kiva imagined it smelling like coconut. She smiled contentedly to herself as she noticed Naomi and Mau locking hands above the armrests, their attention on the performers. To an observer such as herself, she could see that they were finally happy, as if nothing had ever been amiss.

The next morning she was called into the school administrative office for a meeting. It was there that she was given the news she had been granted a full scholarship to the University of Canterbury in Christchurch as part of an aid program New Zealand offered developing countries in the South Pacific. Kiva could count on her left hand the number of times she'd felt deliriously happy, and this was one of those moments.

A middle-aged woman sat formally across from her and clucked about the forms she needed to fill out to begin her visa application process. Kiva tried to control her racing heart but she couldn't believe she was finally going to leave, and to Christchurch too! While researching universities out of interest, she had read that Christchurch was considered the garden city of New Zealand, its landscape flat, surrounded by distant snowcapped mountains to the west with the Pacific lapping its shores to the east. The university itself was established in 1873 and its fine arts alumni included major New Zealand artists such as Rita Angus and Louise Henderson. As her head filled excitedly with images of the campus, the woman suddenly glanced up and told her something she hadn't been expecting.

"You'll be studying a Bachelor of Arts, since that was your main field in high school, and you may choose your subject of focus—English,

History—but I can see here that you received high grades in English, so I recommend you concentrate on that. You can then combine it with education and return to Samoa to be an English teacher."

"Uh …" Kiva stammered, her brows pulled together in confusion. "I'm sorry … are you saying that I won't be able to apply to the fine arts program?"

The lady's eyebrows rose above the rims of her glasses and she replied with an air of dissidence. "Certainly not. This scholarship is only offered for specific subjects—priority subjects, I should add, that are relevant to the development of Samoa's economic and employment needs. These include engineering science, business management, and human development to name but a few. I'm afraid fine arts is not recognized as a tenable subject area. Now, you only have a couple of months to prepare before you leave for New Zealand, and you need to apply for a passport as soon as possible," she continued on in a professional tone as if Kiva's whole world hadn't started to crumble around her. The woman presented a check list and she tried really hard to concentrate on the neatly typed document in front of her, but her brain had halted when she learned that a fine arts program wasn't going to be an option of study.

"Is there a problem?" the woman glanced up, tapping her pen impatiently on the table.

Kiva shifted in her seat. "I'm just trying to understand something … so the only way I can receive this scholarship is if I choose one of these subject areas?"

The woman pursed her lips and answered as if she was speaking to a child, "That's correct."

Kiva swallowed hard. "What if I don't want to study any of these courses?"

The woman looked at her incredulously. Recovering quickly she said, "Let me remind you that this is a once in a lifetime opportunity that shouldn't be missed. Do you know how lucky you are to receive a scholarship? Do you realize how many students would die to be in your position? Everything will be provided for—the full payment of tuition fees, accommodation in the halls of residence, a generous allowance— and when you've finally graduated, you'll be able to return and contribute to the development of Samoa. What more could you possibly want?"

Kiva released her bottom lip and twisted her fingers in her lap. "I know, and I appreciate it. I really do. There's no other student that could possibly value this opportunity more, but I just … I need to think about it." She hadn't imagined studying anything other than fine arts. Painting. Sculpture. Photography. She could see it slipping away like wet ink.

"What is there to think about?"

"To be honest I was planning to study fine arts."

The woman laughed unkindly. "If you want to do that, then you might as well enroll in our local school of arts. This country needs teachers, doctors, engineers—not artists. It's a waste of finances sending you all the way to New Zealand just for that."

Just for that? Kiva tried to tamp down her shock, but it was the hurt that clung to her first and wouldn't let go. She swallowed the tightness around her throat while the woman leaned back in her chair, studying her.

"Think very seriously about this, Mativa. An opportunity like this doesn't come around often. In fact, it probably won't happen again in your lifetime. You're going to need to inform me as soon as possible what your decision is; otherwise, the scholarship goes to somebody else. I'll give you two days to decide." She turned to collect the papers off her desk, effectively dismissing her, and Kiva imagined what was churning over in her head: ungrateful, unworthy little girl.

She scraped back her chair and stood to leave. She knew she should have been thankful, relieved even, but she couldn't help the prominent swell of disappointment instead. Two days. She had two days to make a life-altering decision between studying an unwilling subject abroad or remain where she was instead and apply to the local art school. Plucking her bag off the floor, she made her way to the main road to catch the bus home, her mind swirling with numbers. Forty eight hours. She had only forty eight hours. She joined a few other people under the shade of a breadfruit tree and used her palm to wipe the sweat from her brow. How could she decide?

She had no way of knowing at the time, however, that it would only take her twenty-four.

CHAPTER TWENTY-TWO

She was in the *pulu* tree when it happened.

Armed with a pencil and art book in her hands, Kiva had been sketching a portrait of Talia when she heard a crashing sound emanating from the direction of the art center. Squinting through the spaces in the leaves, she tried to make out the cause of the noise. Was it a burglar? Or had Masi knocked something off a shelf? A further crash followed by a hard thump set her heart pounding and she scrambled out of the tree and limped quickly toward the steps.

She found Mau slumped on the floor, facedown and unmoving, surrounded by broken pieces of pottery.

"Mau!" she cried, rushing to his side.

With great difficulty, she rolled him onto his back and noticed that his face drooped significantly to the side, his eyes unfocused, appearing disoriented and confused. Pressing her fingers to his neck, she felt a rapid pulse. Her movements suddenly became sluggish, her mind fogged with panic.

"Mau," she cried out. "Can you hear me?" He groaned incoherently as Kiva's shaky hands hovered over his face and chest, unsure of what was happening. She had to call for help. "I'm going to get Naomi, okay? Just hold on!"

Pushing herself to her feet, she darted toward the house, slipping on the incline where the ferns grew, and yelled for Naomi across the yard.

Naomi appeared at the back door wiping her hands on a dish towel. "What? What is it?" When she saw Kiva's panic-stricken face, her tone changed to dread. "What's going on?"

"It's Mau!" Kiva exclaimed. "Something's happened to him. Come quick!"

Naomi dropped the towel and took off running past her and Kiva hobbled to catch up.

Her aunt was crouched low over Mau when she entered the center. "Kiva," she said in a voice that bordered between calm and panic. "Call Tui's father to come. We need to move him to the truck and take him to the hospital. Quickly, now!"

Hana appeared at the door with Talia by her side, terror crossing her features.

"Hana," Naomi called out. "Come help me."

Kiva turned her back to them and fled to the house.

With trembling hands she dialed the neighbor's house and spoke to Tui. They turned up a few minutes later and helped lift Mau to the bed of the truck. Tui's father got behind the wheel while Naomi and Kiva clambered at the back. Hana stood a short distance away with a crying Talia at her hip.

"I'll call you when we learn anything," Naomi said to her before they drove off.

It was like déjà vu, Kiva thought, as she remembered a time two years ago when she was being comforted by Ry in the same truck. She remembered the words spoken by him that made her feel infinitely better. Lowering to Mau's ear, she whispered, "You're going to be alright. Just hang on ... *please*." She straightened and noticed Naomi watching her. "He's going to be okay," she reiterated. "He has to be."

Naomi's eyes flashed with uncertainty. "I don't know, Kiva. We have to pray."

Kiva did for the rest of the ride. Holding his hand within her own, she implored and pleaded in her heart for her uncle to recover until she felt light-headed and exhausted.

Upon reaching the ER, she was pushed to the side as a doctor and nurse tended to her uncle behind closed curtains. Stunned, they made their way to a rickety, old bench to wait. Naomi clamped her hands over her mouth as lines of worry crinkled her forehead. Kiva gripped the edge of the seat, and her fingernails dug into the wood like she was holding on for dear life. How did this happen? There was no warning earlier that day that he was feeling unwell. She knew he wasn't the fittest person, and besides the little weight around his midriff and his tendency to overeat, he'd never experienced health problems before. Would he be okay? His position in the art center had terrified her. *Please God, let him be okay.* She would do anything to ensure that he would be alright. It was all too surreal and terrifying and she felt as if a heavy weight was pressing on her chest.

Minutes passed excruciatingly before a doctor emerged behind the curtains and strode toward them. She offered a sympathetic smile and informed them that Mau had suffered a stroke. The damage to his brain was significant and he experienced paralysis to his right side as a result. Movement in his right leg and arm would take weeks, maybe months to recover, she added, including memory loss and changes in perception and judgment, and that there was a strong possibility that his speech was impaired.

"Oh my God," Naomi cried, and Kiva gripped her arm to comfort them both. "Is he going to be alright?" she asked, desperation in her voice.

"We'll send him to the physiotherapist as soon as we can," the doctor answered. "The sooner he can receive treatment, the better the chances of him recovering are, and the less chance there is of permanent disability. Was your husband under any stress lately?"

Naomi touched her throat when she spoke. "My husband's an artist, a wood carver. He's been traveling overseas for work and was preparing to leave for another exhibition next week."

"I'm afraid he'll have to postpone that trip."

As she droned on about running a test for diabetes and something about obesity and high cholesterol levels, Kiva stepped away to gather her thoughts. Overcome with emotion, tears pricked her eyes as she tried to calm her breathing and process everything. "He's not out of the woods yet and will need to be monitored closely," the doctor continued. "A change in diet and lifestyle will be necessary to prevent another attack in the future." Kiva wiped her eyes. Poor Mau, she thought sadly. She hadn't realized how much stress his body was under with his new projects.

"When can we see him?" she asked.

"You can see him now before we move him out of the ER."

Kiva seized Naomi's hand as they followed the doctor behind the curtain. Mau lay limp on the bed. He offered a regretful smile that sagged in the corner of his mouth, and Kiva reached for his hand, squeezing it gently. When he tried to speak, Naomi smoothed back his hair to calm him. "Shh, it's okay, Mau. We're here now. We're going to take care of you."

Kiva glanced down at his face sadly and felt like her heart was breaking in two. She remembered a strong and determined face but was now struck with the fact that his once able body was failing before her. And it hit her. Seeing her dear aunt and uncle together like this made her realize that there was no way she could leave them. How could she? She needed to stay with Naomi and help take care of Mau like they had taken care of her for eighteen years. With a heavy heart, she decided that she couldn't bring herself to board that plane to Christchurch. Instead, she would probably be boarding it for another reason—to take Mau's carvings to Brisbane. She would do it for him. For as long as he needed her. She squeezed his hand again and tried to offer a comforting smile. "It's going to be alright," she said.

The days that followed were a whirlwind of trips to and from the hospital. The challenges that soon followed pressed on her from all sides where night and day rolled into one and she rarely slept. She was so tired. Physically. Mentally. Emotionally. When she wasn't at home looking after the center and carrying out the chores so Naomi could be with Mau, she was at the hospital overlooking his care. When her forty-eight hours had passed and she had forgotten to inform the woman at the scholarship desk about her decision, she received a brisk call from her on the third day. Kiva informed her politely that due to familial obligations she could not accept the scholarship and the lady wished her good luck in her future endeavors and hung up.

Kiva had stared at the receiver long after they'd disconnected. Emotions warred inside of her, cutting her up with regret and guilt and the overwhelming sensation that she'd just given up on something monumental she could never get back.

Later that evening she'd cried into her pillow and despised herself for it. Now that she'd made her decision, she mourned the loss of this one chance to attend university. Perhaps she could have made it work, she thought with remorse. She could see herself as a teacher. After all, she enjoyed teaching the kids every Saturday. She could have even become an art teacher. A professional one. An educated one. The pillow was moistened with salty tears, but when she thought about Mau lying paralyzed at the hospital, guilt engulfed her and she gave herself a mental kick. With a shuddering sigh, she decided she needed to get over Christchurch and the University of Canterbury, and she knew that the only way she could do that is if she threw herself into a project. She didn't want to be stuck in a monotonous routine every day. She needed to do something different, something more for the art center, which would take them in a new direction. Sitting up in bed, she grabbed her sketchbook and willed an idea to come to her. When nothing spectacular came to mind, she blew out a rough breath and found herself sketching absently. What could she do? She could certainly bake and cook extravagant meals now. Perhaps that was why Mau had high blood pressure and cholesterol levels, she thought with alarm. He was always indulging in her desserts and pastries, which weren't very healthy to begin with. What if she changed that? What if she opened a small café next to the art center and made health conscious food to serve? Would the public be interested? They were in a rural spot situated near the main stretch of road that connected the town and beaches. It could serve as a pit stop for tourists and locals searching for a place away from the bustle of urban life. They could expand the balcony to include a deck until it touched the cluster of bamboo trees. She imagined its culms and leaves surrounding the deck and providing shade from the glare of the sun. She would name it Café Bamboo and Art Center. Kiva's pulse started to race with excitement at the thought. She could do it. She could see it coming together in her mind as visually as if she'd sketched it. She would need to consult with Naomi first, of course, and they would need to apply for a bank loan. She would concentrate on tweaking her recipes and substituting sugar in her desserts for local honey, adding tropical fruit flavors to make smoothies and cold drinks, and using whole wheat bread instead of white for vegetable sandwiches. Hand shaking with anticipation, she brought her pencil down to her art book and brought her vision to life on the page.

CHAPTER TWENTY-THREE

Four Years Later

Ry scanned the airport terminal with tired interest before finding a chair to plop down onto. The cold metal bars bit into his elbows, but he was too exhausted to protest. The twelve-hour flight from LAX had been a taxing one. He hadn't gotten much sleep because he hadn't been granted the exit row like he requested, and his knees and legs were now sore from being pressed against the seat that was in front of him. He desperately wanted to shut his eyes and sleep away the transit time in Auckland before they had to board the next flight.

Glancing around at the other members of his Peace Corps group, he wondered briefly how they were going to react to a country he thought he'd never return to. They had no idea what was coming. That what they were about to embark on would magnify every one of life's tests and set them on a journey that had the potential to tear down their barriers. That their capacity for change and their levels of comfort would be stretched taut like a rubber band, and everything they'd thought to be true in life would be challenged and questioned. He remembered six years ago when his world first collided with Samoa's soil. He was informed by the Academy that it would initially be difficult to stay, but ultimately difficult to leave when he graduated. At the time he hadn't believed a word of it because he didn't want to be there in the first place, but with time he'd begun to see that it was true. He discovered that the collision he experienced was exactly what he needed to break him out of his stupor. He'd slowly accepted his fate as a result, and let go of his anger and ego to make room for humility that would allow the land and its people to tame him.

After he'd left, the months that followed had been formidable as he tried to assimilate back into his old life. He'd applied to several colleges soon after and was relieved when he got accepted to the architect program at Iowa State University. He'd worked hard and graduated among the top of his class and was consequently offered several jobs which boasted generous salaries which would have secured his future, but he'd turned them all down, choosing instead to join the Peace Corps as a volunteer. His mother and stepfather had initially thought he was crazy, but they'd slowly relented to his plans. What those plans were, he had no idea and was still trying to figure out, but what he knew with a certainty was that he was returning to give back to a country that had already given him so much.

The group numbered seventeen in total and was sprawled around on the carpet, leaning against their backpacks, listening to music through their iPods. Some slouched next to him rereading the information kits they'd received about Samoa. Blowing air out roughly, he scrubbed a hand over his ragged jaw, rough from a day's lack of shaving, and willed the time to pass so he could board the flight, find his seat, and go to sleep. He flicked the hood of his sweatshirt over his head, lowering it so it covered his eyebrows, and imagined it would be the last time he'd be wearing warm clothes for the next two years. He pictured their final destination and remembered the oppressive heat, the tongue-tied language that took him weeks to grasp, the wood carving and bamboo gun, and a certain gentle smile he couldn't seem to forget after all these years. Would she even be in Samoa? Or would she be someplace abroad studying like she had planned? It shouldn't have mattered if she was there or not, he thought with equal parts trepidation and elation, and he was quick to remind himself that he was returning to serve and to expect nothing more, but he couldn't help feeling a surge of anticipation that there was a slim chance she could be. Would she even remember him? Six years was a long time, and he couldn't blame her if she'd forgotten all about him. After all, he'd left without saying goodbye, without leaving any form of address to keep in touch, and the remorse and guilt had gnawed away in his gut for a long time after. He'd tried to erase her from his memory, but there were some kindnesses that just couldn't be forgotten. He remembered her dark brown eyes because they hid little emotion. They were a welcome reprieve from the crap he'd had to put up with most of his life. Hers were open and honest, and it was the little details that he remembered. The way they lit up even when her lips were sealed. The tiny crinkles around the corners when she laughed. The way they used to read him and all of his demons. They were a window to her spirit, and he considered himself fortunate to get a glimpse into hers years ago. He hadn't been worthy enough for her then, and that was why he'd decided to let her go. *But isn't that why you're going back now?* It wasn't that he considered himself worthy now, but if he could just see her one more time, he could move on, concentrate on his two-year mission, and then leave. He didn't expect anything from her, and if she simply nodded and never spoke to him again, he would have to be content with that. As much as it anguished him, he would have to finally let her go for good.

Ry tamped down his rattled thoughts and dug out a bottle of water from his backpack. He'd met a couple of guys in the group from the Midwest, fresh out of college with a little work experience who he thought he could become friends with. Taking a sip, he focused on the weeks ahead. They'd been briefed informally about the areas they would be serving in, and he'd understood some of the roles included developing English literacy resources in rural schools. They would firstly spend ten weeks in orientation to acclimatize themselves with the culture before being divided up and sent to various villages. He had no idea where he was going to be placed—whether he was going to remain on the island of Upolu or moved to Savaii—and the anticipation built in his chest like a balloon. That balloon swelled significantly when a woman's voice suddenly crackled over the intercom, informing passengers that they were welcome to board.

Ry watched as people filed into lines behind the counter and picked up his bag to follow.

"You ready for this?" A volunteer by the name of Adé asked as they joined the line.

"As ready as I'll ever be," he answered honestly.

"I heard you lived in Samoa before."

"That's right. I did my last year of high school there."

Adé whistled low. "That's awesome, man."

Ry handed over his boarding pass to airline personnel. As he made his way down the tunnel that led onto the aircraft, he couldn't help thinking he was about to experience the adventure of a lifetime. Six years ago he had no idea what he was in for and held himself back as a result. He erected barriers, kept an emotional distance. This time he was ready to give everything he had.

CHAPTER TWENTY-FOUR

Kiva inhaled the warm scent of honey and vanilla as she poked a toothpick into one of the cupcakes. The toothpick came out dry and she covered her hands with a dish towel to remove the tray. She hissed when her thumb came into contact with the pan and dropped it on the counter. Waving her hand in the air to quench the pain, she heard the back door slam as Naomi stepped in carrying a tray of dirty glasses. "You were right. Your hibiscus and ginger drinks are a hit." She piled the cups into the sink as Kiva leaned around her to run her thumb under the water. "Did you burn yourself again?"

"Hazards of the job," Kiva answered through gritted teeth. She had been distracted lately, and it was starting to affect her performance.

"Let me see," Naomi said, pulling her hand toward her for inspection. Kiva tried not to flinch when it was removed from the soothing water. Naomi's brows furrowed at the red welt. "Where's your mind these days?" Kiva didn't know how to answer that. "Rub some aloe on it and wrap it with gauze."

"It's fine," Kiva assuaged, putting it under the tap again. There was too much to be done in the kitchen for her to step away. Saturday mornings were always their busiest at the café, and she'd had to move her art classes to Friday afternoons as a result.

"Go," Naomi demanded. "Take a break. Hana and I can handle the customers."

Kiva sighed, took off her apron, and deposited it on the counter. "Alright. I'll be back soon." At that moment, Talia whizzed past her, bumping into her hip. "Whoa, slow down."

"Sorry!" came her tinny reply.

"Talia! Come here!" Naomi called out. "Help your nana with these cupcakes."

"Oh yummy!" Talia replied enthusiastically. "Can I decorate them with sprinkles? Please?" she stretched the last word.

"You can decorate one."

"For me?"

"Yes, for you."

Kiva smiled to herself as she opened the screen door and stepped out into the fresh air. She'd been cooped up in the kitchen since before dawn and didn't realize how much she needed a break. Rubbing the stiffness from her neck, she looked toward the café which was bustling with people. She noticed Hana bending over taking orders. She'd been instrumental in helping Kiva build the café from the ground up. It hadn't been easy in those first few months, or the first year for that matter, but as word of mouth spread, their little café under the bamboos became a popular eatery for offering healthy alternative. She watched as her cousin laughed at something a customer said, her face radiant. Motherhood had been good to her. Over the years, Kiva noticed a softness she'd never witnessed before, and while they all had a hand in raising Talia, Hana's transformation had not gone unnoticed. She loved her little girl with a fierce tenderness, and her outer beauty was made more evident by her enchanting smile and cheerful disposition, which in turn attracted many guys to the café. She'd been aloof to their attention, however, and Kiva imagined it had everything to do with Talia's father. The last Kiva heard of him was that he was living with a girlfriend and helping her family with their mechanical business. His abandonment and distance over the years left Hana apprehensive about having a relationship, so while she appeared friendly on the outside, Kiva knew she guarded her heart.

Kiva swept her gaze around the back yard where they took better care of the garden. Tropical plants and flowers now lined the pathway that led to the art center, and the wooden deck stretched around the center where bamboo limbs hung gracefully and provided shade. Naomi made sure that every table in the café was topped with colorful arrangements of flowers, and produce from the herb and vegetable garden was used daily in the dishes.

"Hello, Kiva!" an older woman waved from the deck.

Kiva beamed and waved in return. This was one of her favorite parts of running a café. Meeting people and learning about their travels. Recently she had hosted a couple from Egypt and a family from Norway. She was greeted more often than she could recall when she was out running errands from regular local customers.

Making her way to the side of the house where the aloe plant grew, she plucked a stem and pressed the sap onto her thumb. It helped soothe the burn a little and she kept it in place with her index finger.

With the café garnering more interest, Kiva was pleased to note that sales from their artwork had steadily risen. Her canvas of the girl with the black birds and quote from Rumi always drew interest, and while she had been offered generous amounts of money for its purchase, she refused to part with it. As if it called to her now, she limped across the yard, descended the steps to the art center, and was greeted with smiles as she passed customers munching on chicken and watercress wraps before she crossed the threshold.

Mau sat alone at the back of the room staring at a piece of *siapo* cloth. He didn't look up when she neared. While he had recovered from the first stroke, the second one that occurred a year later set him back and he'd experienced extensive muscle damage to his right arm and hand as a result. He now walked with the assistance of a cane, while his hand never fully recovered and he wasn't able to carve like he used to. Kiva sat across from him and took his hand in hers. He looked up, the right side of his face sagging low, and gave her a smile that came across as a grimace. She glanced over at the *siapo* and recognized it immediately as the one Ry created years ago. Inhaling sharply she asked, "Where did you find that?" Kiva thought she had hidden it away and buried the strong emotions that rose at the sight of it. She hadn't allowed herself to think about him for a long time, and she had been doing well not to dwell on him until now. Swallowing the tight knot in her throat, she took it from her uncle and read the script that had faded over the years. Before she could torture herself with thoughts that he ever cared or that she had been imagining his feelings for her, Talia bounded into the art center.

"Papa!" she raced and propped herself on Mau's lap.

"How's my little one?" he slurred.

"Good." She nestled her head into his chest and murmured, "I invited my teacher to come for lunch tomorrow. She's really nice. She's from America. We're going to pick her up after church." Kiva had forgotten about that. Talia had been singing praises about her *palagi* teacher for weeks, and they were finally going to meet her.

"Kiva, we need your help," Hana's head popped through the French doors.

"I'll be right there." Kiva rose and tucked the *siapo* under her arm. "Be good to your papa," she said playfully to Talia before she limped

171

outside.

Kiva helped clear the dishes from the tables, made a couple of vegetable sandwiches, and blended a few smoothies before the last of the customers left. Since they were open for breakfast and lunch only, she looked forward to the evenings when they locked up the art café and she could escape to her tree to sketch. This evening her heart was heavy with longing. Pushing her feelings down, she pulled the pencil from her hair and drew up some new ideas for the menu.

Later that night when she was preparing to read a bedtime story to Talia, she decided to recite poetry instead. Pulling one of her old art books from the shelf, they nestled together on her bed and flicked through sketches of the universe.

Talia stared with wide-eyed wonder. "Did you really draw these planets and stars?" she asked and Kiva nodded. "They're amazing."

Kiva's heart blossomed at her statement, and she proceeded to read the lyrical words translated from the thirteenth century poet from Persia. The words were like a balm for her spirit, providing unconditional strength and comfort, and she realized she'd needed this. To be reminded. To reconnect with her soul. Talia absently traced the jagged scar on her arm as Kiva read aloud each poem, enunciating each line and syllable with care as if they had been spun from the sun's gold.

"Do you want to know something?" she asked when they'd reached the end of the book. "You're the first person to see this."

"Your art book?"

"Yes."

Talia was silent for a moment, and Kiva relaxed into the comfortable space on her bed before she heard a whisper, "Can I sleep in your bed tonight, Kiva?"

Kiva tucked her closer to her side under the sheet. "Of course you can."

When she awoke the next morning, Talia was gone and Kiva suspected she'd woken up in the middle of the night and joined Hana in their room. Stretching, she checked the time on her bedside table and was surprised to see that it was almost ten. Pushing herself out of bed, she padded to the bathroom to wash up and then headed downstairs to find it deserted. Through the kitchen window she could see that Mau's truck was missing in the driveway and this confirmed her suspicions that they'd left for church, which meant she was in charge of preparing the *to'anai*. She looked out toward the art center and noticed the French doors wide open and concluded Mau was probably in there. Since they were having a guest over for lunch, she decided to prepare something a little more elaborate than their usual meal of breadfruit and baked fish. Kiva took out ingredients for a chicken curry, rice, and a chilled fish salad and set to work on the kitchen counter. She also planned to bake banana muffins, which she knew Talia loved.

Later in the morning she heard a soft knock at the back door. Peering over her shoulder through the screen, she saw Tui standing with a basket of baked taro and banana in his hands. "My mother sent these for your family," he said when she opened the door. At seventeen, he now towered over her.

Kiva accepted the basket with gratitude. "Come in," she said, waving him in. "I want to send something back with you." She poured some curry into a glass bowl and gathered several hot muffins onto a plate. For years their families had exchanged food like this every Sunday, and as she handed the bag over to him, she heard the truck's tires crunch along the gravel and rumble to a stop. Wiping her hands on a dish towel, she limped quickly to her bedroom to change out of her pajamas, which were really a baggy, old T-shirt and *lavalava*. Pulling on a cleaner shirt and wrapping a stain-free *lavalava* around her legs, she ran her fingers through her long hair, twirling it high into a bun before poking a pencil through. Stepping out into the hallway, she heard voices drifting up the stairs and she hobbled down to greet them. She listened as a young woman laughed at something Talia said and replied with equal enthusiasm in an American accent.

Kiva entered the living room with a smile, ready to meet this revered teacher, and froze. The woman was perched on the edge of the couch, bent over a coloring book with Talia, her long, fair locks tumbling over her shoulder, but it was the person sitting beside her that made her heart slam against her ribs. It was unmistakable. She would know him anywhere. Ry was leaning forward, arms braced on his thighs, watching her intently. His brown eyes met hers and burned with a magnitude she had become all too familiar with years ago, and while his eyes were still the same, she observed quickly that the rest of him was not. Although sitting, she could see that he had matured in a rugged way, his jawline defined and sculpted with a shadowy hint of stubble, and his shoulders had broadened and occupied most of the couch space. Dressed in a blue button-down and tan shorts, Kiva's eyes perused him quickly from top to bottom and noticed that his hair was longer, tied back to showcase a masculine forehead. Her heart continued its drum beat, once, twice, in rapid staccato. Blinking, it took her a moment to grasp the fact that he was in her house.

"Kiva," Naomi called to her as she entered the living room carrying a tray. "Isn't this a wonderful surprise?" She put the tray of cold drinks on the table beside the couch. "Please help yourselves," she said to Ry and the woman next to him. "Lunch will be ready in a minute." Straightening, she exchanged a potent look with Kiva that was laced with concern before she returned to the kitchen.

Kiva swallowed hard and took a step forward just as Ry stood, rounded the coffee table, and approached her. Pausing, her immediate thought was that he was several inches taller than she'd remembered. When she'd hugged him at the art gallery, she'd measured her height against his chin. Now she was eye level with his wide chest. Heart pounding, she sought familiarity in his face and recognized the scar near his eye.

His lips tilted into a half smile. "Hi," he said.

Even his voice had changed, she observed. Gone was his seventeen-year-old voice, replaced now with a deep timber that made her breath stutter. Overwhelmed, she took a step back until her legs bumped into the banister.

"I don't understand …" she started. "What are you doing here?" She felt a tugging on her *lavalava* that drew her attention away.

"Kiva, come meet my teacher," Talia said.

The woman who was sitting on the couch suddenly approached them, her mouth turned into a radiant smile. "Hi, I'm Claire Newman." She offered her hand and Kiva shook it. "Talia's told me so much about you. She informed me that you're an artist. I'm a painter myself. I'd love to see some of your work later."

Kiva smiled weakly, admiring her pretty face which was tanned from the sun. Her olive green eyes were ringed with dark lashes and brows, her small button nose smattered with freckles. She was beautiful. Her long blonde hair was pulled into a ponytail that hung over one shoulder.

"Thank you," Kiva replied amiably. "She's talked about you, too. She's been excited to have you over for the longest time. It's good to finally meet you." Claire stood in close proximity to Ry, and Kiva looked between them, picking up on their easy familiarity, and wondered when someone was going to explain his presence there, or rather his presence with her. "How do you two know each other?"

Claire smiled up at Ry. "Ry and I are from the same Peace Corps group. We work together at Talia's school."

"You're in the Peace Corps?" she turned to him and asked.

"Yes," came his reply. "I teach English to the middle school grades." His eyes perused her face and she couldn't help staring back. He taught at Talia's school? For how long? How did she not know about this?

Recovering quickly, she cleared her throat and swept her hand toward the living room. "Please ... take a seat. Have a drink. I'll go see if Naomi needs help." Facing the kitchen, she limped away as fast as she could. Her chest was coiled tight and she expelled the breath she hadn't realized she was holding.

Naomi looked up from her chopping board when she rounded the counter. She didn't say anything, and Kiva was grateful for the small reprieve. She needed a quiet moment to process her frayed thoughts. She couldn't believe that he was here, that he had returned. Picking up a few tomatoes and cucumbers, she washed them under the tap and placed them on the counter. Her hands trembled a little, and she took a few steady breaths to calm down. She felt as if her equilibrium had been knocked off balance, and she needed to hold onto something familiar, to do something with her hands, to ground herself. She retrieved a knife and board and set about dicing the cucumbers into a bowl. Her back to the living room, she could hear Claire talking animatedly in Samoan with Hana and Talia, telling them about her family back in the States and the farm she'd grown up on. Her pronunciation was a little painful to listen to, but from what she could hear, Kiva learned that Claire was a recent graduate from college where she'd studied English literature. She spoke eloquently and Kiva could tell by her voice that she was smiling. Her innate joy was contagious, and she understood now why Talia was captivated by her. Was Ry? Her throat constricted when her thoughts collided with that prospect, and she tried hard to push them away. She was kidding with herself if she thought she could ever forget him. His very presence in her home made her heart do things it hadn't done in years. Beat. Feel. Hurt. Vulnerable. Rapture. Attraction. She couldn't compartmentalize them, but they were inside of her all the same, battling for some form of release.

"Can I help?" he suddenly asked from behind her. He circled around and came to stand beside her. His nearness made her toes curl, his warmth and big hands just a step away, and she glanced up, giving him a faint smile.

"I'm just making a salad. Nothing fancy."

"Here, let me." He took the cutting board and knife from her and slid it toward himself. Kiva watched as his deft hands chopped the vegetables with precision. She had loved those hands. She loved them still. From this angle, she could clearly see the tattoo on the inside of his forearm, and its familiar curly script built a surge of nostalgia inside her chest.

Naomi turned and scraped a plate of chopped chives into the salad.

"It's good to have you back, Ryler," she said with a warm smile. "I'm glad Claire invited you. We would not have known you were here if she hadn't, and now we can finally host you in our home."

"Thank you, Naomi. How's Mau? I haven't seen him yet."

"He's in the art center," she replied. "He had a couple of strokes a few years ago and he never fully recovered. He likes to spend his days in the art center even though he can't carve anymore. It's his sanctuary."

Ry pulled back slightly in shock, and a frown line appeared between his brows. "I'm sorry to hear that."

Naomi smiled softly. "He'll be happy to see you. I'll tell Talia to run out and get him. Lunch is almost ready. Kiva, can you set the table?"

When the final bowl of food was placed on the dining table, Kiva took a seat across from Ry and bowed her head as Mau said grace. She kept her eyes averted from him when her uncle was done. Lifting a fan, she chased away the flies and helped pass the food around.

"So, Ryler, I hear you've returned as a Peace Corps volunteer," Mau stated as he lifted a spoonful of curry onto his plate. His words were slurred and Kiva noticed Ry had to concentrate hard on understanding him.

"That's right, sir," he replied politely.

"For how long?"

"Two years."

Kiva gripped the fan tighter.

"That's a long time."

"Twenty-seven months is the typical length of time for Peace Corps."

"How are you finding your stay in Samoa, Claire?" Naomi asked, passing her the bowl of salad.

"It's been an adjustment," she answered honestly with a sigh. "I don't live on the school property like Ry does. I stay with a host family in the same village. They prepared a corner in their main *fale* for me with a mattress and mosquito net so I don't get a lot of privacy, but they've been extremely generous and helpful. I've learned so much since we arrived three months ago. Plus, I love my kids." She smiled across the table at Talia.

They'd been in Samoa for three months? Why hadn't Ry visited sooner? She felt his eyes on her now as hurt speared her from the inside. She was a fool to believe that her family mattered to him. That she mattered. Ducking her head to avoid his watchful gaze, she accepted the bowl of curry from Mau and dished some onto her plate. Without looking up, she knew everyone had begun eating by the clatter of cutlery and grunts of approval. Glancing around briefly, she noticed however that Ry hadn't started. Only when she had piled everything she wanted onto her plate and bit into a piece of taro did she notice him pick up his fork to stab a piece of chicken. Taken aback, she swallowed hard and turned her attention away, concentrating on trying to finish the rest of the food on her plate. Her stomach was suddenly tied into knots, and she simultaneously wanted the afternoon to speed up as well as slow down.

CHAPTER TWENTY-FIVE

"Kiva is a wonderful cook. She bakes, too," Mau exclaimed proudly after the table was cleared and she came around serving muffins and tea. "She's taken good care of me these past years. The café really saved us."

Kiva's cheeks blazed from the attention, but mostly because her uncle had been so open about their tribulations over the last four years. He'd spoken at length during lunch about his strokes and the consequences that followed. How his physiotherapy had helped to some extent but that his hand still shook when he tried to carve. How Kiva had to fly to Brisbane to take his carvings to the exhibition after his first attack.

How she had turned down her scholarship.

"Would you like some tea?" she offered Claire, hoping to divert the topic onto something else.

"I'd love some." She lifted her cup and Kiva tipped the teapot, watching as the white porcelain changed to lemon grass green. "So good." Claire sighed when she took a sip.

Kiva moved onto Ry, who remained stoic during the entire exchange at lunch, only answering questions when asked. She learned that he had graduated with an architect's degree and had been volunteering as a firefighter most weekends. That explained his athletic build, she concluded to herself. She learned that his family had plans to visit him in Samoa during the Christmas break. It had almost been too much to hear.

Bending near his shoulder, she asked if he wanted tea and prayed her hands didn't shake, or heaven forbid let it spill all over him. "Thanks," he replied and raised his mug. Avoiding his eyes, she concentrated on pouring and was relieved when Naomi spoke from the head of the table.

"When you're done with your dessert, we'll take you for a tour of the art café."

Without its relaxed music chiming in the background, or patrons speaking and laughing among themselves, the café was a quiet place, almost desolate with its empty chairs. The flowers had been removed from their vases and dried bamboo leaves brushed over the wooden tables in its place. Kiva was the last to follow the group down the fern path, listening as Naomi explained to Claire her experience with acrylics. Talia bounded ahead with Hana in tow while Mau hobbled with a cane by Ry's side. Something moved in Kiva's heart at seeing them together, and she buried it within the folds of her emotions. Claire laughed, a melodious sound, and her attention snapped to her. She studied her from a distance and felt unease settle in the pit of her stomach. While she was overly pretty and generally nice, it was her intelligence, education, and worldliness that somehow intimidated her.

Moving into the art center, she stood hesitantly under the framed French doors and watched with one foot in and one foot out.

She waited in anticipation, her breath caught in her chest, and knew the moment he saw it. Her canvas. *Their* canvas. His eyes flickered with surprise, his brows pulled together to form a crease, before Mau asked him something and his face closed off and became as smooth as the pile of blank canvases behind him. A heavy weight pressed down on her as she conjured the memory of them working on it together. Her dreams. His hands. *Scar of the Bamboo Leaf.* Hanging now between paintings depicting village life and a woman weaving a fine mat, it could easily be missed among the burst of activity and flurry of color, its meaning lost between the creases of everyday life. And in a way it had, she thought sadly.

"This is beautiful," Claire murmured softly as she approached and stood beside him. She tilted her head to read the quote, her face squinting with mesmerized concentration, and Kiva suddenly felt very exposed. Hundreds of people had perused these portraits since the art gallery, and not once had she been affected by their critiques as much as she was now with Ry standing two feet away from her. He knew. He knew what this meant to her, what she had endured to complete it, and here they were—him living out his dreams while her own were lost and blown away with the wind that fanned the bamboo leaves outside. It suddenly hurt to see it illustrated all over his face when he turned to gaze at her. She felt vulnerable, caught with longing and hollowness and heartache. He witnessed it all before she schooled her features to blankness. His eyes beheld a question, and she didn't know how to answer him when she had many questions of her own. She silently begged for someone to speak, to deter his attention away and break the magnetic pull she felt from across the room. When Naomi began explaining some of the portraits, and Ry politely turned toward her, Kiva pivoted away from the portrayal of her past and limped back to the house and into the kitchen where she had found solitude, cooking and baking her woes away.

The mess that greeted her did little to soften the tightness in her chest. The kitchen counters were strewn with dirty pots and dishes. Blowing out a rough breath, she began to calculate the best way to tackle it.

Filling a bowl with water, she gathered the used utensils and dumped them inside. She moved onto the dishes next, scraping off the leftovers and stacking the plates onto a pile next to the sink. Squirting dishwashing soap onto a sponge, she scrubbed a cup until it was squeaky clean and then absently reached for another. Through the window screen she noticed Masi curled atop Mau's truck, her stomach round and ready to deliver kittens soon. Talia had a few names picked out already: Bongo, Tigger, and Popo. Kiva smiled at the thought. Her mind wandered as it often did when she was washing the dishes. Some of the stories for her sketches were born in this very place, standing in front of a sink full of dishes. Some of her recipes, too. Today though she tormented herself with thoughts of the *what-ifs* in her life—what if Mau hadn't suffered those strokes? His renowned carvings wouldn't have suddenly ceased like they had at the height of his career. What if she'd accepted that scholarship? She would have been graduating together with Silei. What if she'd graduated a teacher? She wouldn't have felt insignificant around Claire. Her thoughts churned over and over like a whirlpool, until they contoured around Ry. She had so many questions. How was he? How had he been? Why had he returned? As if his very presence in her mind conjured him to life, she heard the back screen door open and close and his voice that followed, deep and steady.

"Kiva."

She stilled, her back to him, hands poised over a bowl, disguised in soap suds. She heard his footsteps approach until he was beside her. All warmth and nearness and the scent of clean linen, as if they'd been baked in the sun. He paused and she couldn't look at him, but then he did something that surprised her. Without another word he took over, sliding his hand until it grasped the bowl in her own, and started to rinse it. Kiva looked up at his profile then, and the corner of his mouth curved into a half smile—an indent in the corner of his mouth, the same one that had made her heart do cartwheels many years ago. But this smile was different from the ones she remembered because it held a trace of sadness. She reached for a mug and hid a sad smile in return. They worked quietly side by side, her washing and him rinsing, the atmosphere growing thicker than the short distance between them when their hands accidently brushed against each other. They worked faster together, the pile disappearing on her right and growing on her left. She wanted to say something before someone returned to the house, but her words were tangled in her throat. When the dishes had been thoroughly rinsed, and Ry reached for a towel to start drying them, she finally found her voice.

"So ... three months." Her tone was not meant to be accusatory but he locked eyes with her, searching them, and nodded once.

"Ten weeks of orientation before we got our placements," he explained, reaching for a platter. "I walked here a couple times, but each time it had gotten late and the art center was closed. I didn't want to impose." He'd walked? She swallowed hard. He'd been placed in Talia's school—the chances of which still amazed her—close to the shore but miles away from where she was. It must have taken him over an hour at least to walk the steep incline. The road was a narrow, windy one, with nothing but stretches of dense bush and cattle on either side. It took thirty minutes alone by bus when she traveled to pick up Talia from school.

"You could have still come in, said hello. We wouldn't have minded. We've gotten used to random people stopping by the café." *She* wouldn't have minded, she added internally. Kiva imagined how that surprise reunion would have played out. The shock of it would have still been the same, the impact hitting her square in the chest.

"Your café is really something," he noted, and she didn't miss the admiration in his voice.

"Thank you." She half shrugged. "Something needed to be done." She didn't elaborate on the *why* because they both knew the reason.

"I'm sorry to hear about Mau." His voice softened.

Kiva retrieved another dish towel. "He's improved now, but the first year was tough. He couldn't really move, and he had difficulty remembering some things. He wouldn't speak because his words would come out all slurred. At times we thought we'd lost him. It was really hard on Naomi. But what breaks my heart the most is his inability to pick up the carving knife again." Her voice teetered with emotion. "He's in that art center every day hoping things could go back to the way they were. He won't admit it aloud, but it's obvious to everyone in the family. I couldn't leave him. I couldn't leave any of them." She pushed down the thick lump that formed in her throat and picked up a plate, absently running circular motions with the towel.

"I get it," Ry said gently, and she turned her head to see that he really meant it, that he understood, and in that moment felt a piece of herself fall for him all over again.

Straightening, she coaxed her heart to slow. She reminded herself that he was only a friend, and his sincerity was a natural consequence of that, nothing more, but his kindness was almost her undoing with him being here with her, helping clean the kitchen as if it was the most normal thing in the world. It felt natural, almost domestic-like, as if they were equals, *partners*, carrying out a regular task at the end of the day, conversing without barriers. But there were barriers now that prevented her from saying the most important things. Fear. Uncertainty. Confusion. Each one rioted inside of her like badly mixed paint.

She offered a half smile and shrugged. "God laughs at our plans." And yet Kiva tried to see the humor in it. Swallowing thickly, she buried her emotions and allowed the joy of having him there show.

"So, you just couldn't get enough of Samoa, huh? The heat, the mosquito bites, centipedes?"

He laughed then, an infectious sound that made her smile wider.

"At least this time I know what I'm doing and am sure this is the place I want to be."

His sentence hung in the air like a promise.

"And what have you been doing?"

"Well, so far I've continued to butcher the Samoan language much to my students' delight. Sometimes I feel like *they're* schooling me whenever they correct my pronunciation." Kiva's smile broadened even more and he smirked. "In the three months that I've been here, I've caught an eel and cooked and eaten it. I've learned to play rugby from the guys in the village and almost got my ass pummeled. I've jumped off a waterfall. I let a kid beat me in arm wrestling and managed to crack up the old ladies when I tried climbing a coconut tree. And I really love my job. It has its challenges, but it's all part of the experience. There's this one boy in my class who's just started to read. Eleven years old and he's never read a single word or sentence in his life because his parents would send him to sell match boxes and combs in town instead of enrolling him in school. When I first met him he was reluctant and awkward, and I know some of the other kids gave him a hard time. I guess I recognized myself in him, and I immediately wanted to help." He shook his head and a corner of his mouth tilted into a half smile. "And no. Mosquitos have never bothered me, nor have I been bitten by a centipede. It'll take more than that to chase me away."

"Never say never." She smiled and picked up a plate to dry. "So you're living by yourself? You don't have a host family?"

"I have one, which I visit on the weekends, but I generally stay in a house on the school property. It's nothing fancy, just four walls and a roof, but I like the solitude it gives me, especially when I feel as if I'm living in a fishbowl and everyone knows my business. There are people everywhere, all of the time, and they're always asking where you're going and what you're doing."

Kiva laughed. "There's village life for you."

He smiled and shook his head. "As much as I love my service, at the end of the day I like to get time to myself to regroup."

"I get that. The *pulu* tree in the back yard used to be mine."

"Used to be?"

"It was where I used to sketch. I climbed it every day. I never told you that?" He shook his head and she couldn't believe she'd never mentioned it to him before. "Now I just don't have the time. The café keeps me busy most mornings, and then I teach art classes in the afternoons. By the time the evenings come around I'm too tired."

"So where do you go?"

She raised her shoulders in response. "I stay here in this kitchen and bake. It's actually quite calming when I don't have a ton of orders to fulfill. Or I'm in the art center, but my time there is usually limited. And besides, it's not really mine. It's become Mau's, so I leave him to it. He needs it more than me. When he's not there, he's wallowing in front of the TV watching rugby games. He doesn't like to talk about it, but we all know he's been having a hard time."

They were quiet a moment, the silence broken by the clatter of plates being lifted and the utensils being put away in drawers.

"On Saturday morning, the primary school is organizing a clean-up event where the kids are going to be collecting garbage along the village road," he started. "You should come along with Talia. Afterward, there's going to be a fundraiser BBQ."

"That sounds great, but I don't think I'll be able to make it. Saturdays are our busiest mornings here. I'll let Hana know though."

He was pensive for a moment before he spoke. "It's weird. I never met Hana until today. She wasn't around when the students from the Academy came for lessons. She's Mau and Naomi's daughter?"

Kiva nodded. "She was rarely home back then."

"Talia's a smart kid. Claire adores her, talks about her all the time."

She bristled at the mention of Claire. "Yes, she is. A very sweet child. We all love her." She stretched her arms up high to place a platter on the top shelf and felt his presence behind her.

"I've got it," he said.

He took the platter from her and slid it in place with ease. Even with her back to him, she knew that he towered over her, and if she leaned back just a little she would be engulfed by his warmth. She felt him watching her now, the small space between her back and his chest charged with tension.

"We have a lot to talk about, Kiva," he murmured.

The effect of his words chased goose bumps along her bare neck. Her hair was pulled up high and she wanted nothing more than to release the bun and let it fall as a veil between them.

"We have been talking," she answered softly.

"About your canvas out there. Your dreams. About studying abroad."

"I already told you I can't leave."

A tense pause followed. "Are you happy staying here? Truly?"

She turned around then and peered up at his serious face. "What kind of question is that? Of course I am. I run a business now. People rely on me. And besides, it's not like I have a choice."

"But you do have a choice, Kiva. You've established the café and it's successful. Mau is in safe hands. You can leave."

She shook her head. "I lost my scholarship. I can't get that back."

"There are other scholarships, plenty offered from the universities themselves to international students. It's just a matter of looking for a few and applying to them."

"It's not that simple, Ry. This is my life. I can't just leave. I'm needed here. And I'm happy here." Her voice rose on the word *happy*, as if to prove her point.

A sigh escaped his lips. "I saw your face in the art center, Kiva. I know how much that canvas meant to you, what it still means to you. I know what you've sacrificed by staying."

She shook her head again, more vehemently. "Don't. Please don't. This is my family, and I will do anything for them. I owe it to them. This is *my* service to them."

His brows crinkled together. "I'm not trying to upset you, and I definitely don't question your loyalty to your family. I know how much they mean to you and what you mean to them. I just want you to see that you can still achieve everything you've ever wanted. That it's not too late."

She turned her head away. How could she explain that by leaving she would feel as if she was jeopardizing her family's happiness for her own? That she would feel selfish? They were finally in a good place and she didn't want to upset that balance. Plus, despite what Ry claimed, she was content with where her life was. She had to be.

"The choice doesn't have to be them or nothing."

She looked up at him and swallowed thickly. "It's not that easy." Pain in her lower back made her flinch and she bent her arm around to grab it.

"What's wrong?"

She waved her other hand in dismissal. "Don't worry. It's just back ache. It comes and goes."

His brows furrowed. "It's from your limp, isn't it?"

She nodded.

"You should be sitting and resting."

She smiled faintly at the concern in his voice and then tensed when she heard the door slam and Claire stepped into the kitchen.

"Oh, there you are," she said as Talia and Naomi followed her in. "I was wondering where you were." Kiva pulled away from Ry as Claire sidled up next to him. "I'm ready to go now. I need to get started on a lesson plan for tomorrow's class." She turned her attention to Kiva and smiled. "I had an amazing time today. Thank you for having us." She faced Naomi and thanked her in the same manner.

"Well, you must come back when the café is open," Naomi responded in kind, "and bring your Peace Corps friends as well." Addressing Kiva, she instructed her to pack the leftovers for them to take.

"Oh no, you don't have to do that, it's not necessary," Claire said politely and Naomi waved her hand dismissively.

"It's fine. Consider us your second host family. Hana's outside and will drop you both off."

"Can I go, too?" Talia asked excitedly.

"Yes, you can," Naomi replied.

Talia's face broke into a big smile as she grabbed Claire's hand. "I want to sit next to you."

Kiva turned away from the scene playing out in front of her and started scooping the leftovers into plastic containers. She wrapped a couple muffins and placed them into two separate bags. "Here you go," she said when she was done and handed one each to Ry and Claire.

"Thanks, Kiva," Ry said.

She looked up at his face, which didn't have the same intensity as it had before everyone arrived into the kitchen. Instead, his eyes had softened with concern and there was a message behind their brown depths, something potent, but she looked away before she could interpret it. Or dare to hope.

Stepping outside, she and Naomi watched as they climbed into the truck and Hana revved it to life. Kiva watched also as Ry lifted his arm and waved goodbye, flashing the tattoo along his forearm. When the truck backed away and disappeared from view, she released a tightly held breath and turned to see Naomi gazing at her with an odd expression on her face.

"What is it?" she asked.

"He came back." Naomi's lips curved into a knowing smile as she returned to the kitchen, leaving Kiva to muse over the weight of her words.

CHAPTER TWENTY-SIX

Kiva felt the first stirrings of nervousness in the pit of her stomach as she descended the bus and crossed the road to the village school. The tar seal was cracked in places and burned her feet where they slipped from the edges of her sandals and touched the surface. The afternoon sun beat down on her face as she squinted against its glare. Her anxiety amplified as the school bell rang and the children were hustled outside by their teachers to await their parents. She'd picked Talia up countless times before when Hana had taken the truck to run errands in town, but this time was significantly different because she was now aware that Ry would be somewhere in the vicinity. She glanced around briefly and didn't immediately see him. Disappointed, she turned her focus on the children and searched for Talia. She spotted her sitting on the grass chatting enthusiastically with a friend, her side pony tail bobbing up and down. She'd insisted on styling it this way after changing her mind several times in the morning, much to Hana's exasperation.

"She's five going on fifteen!" Hana had grumbled to Naomi over the breakfast table.

Naomi had simply put down her mug and responded with a sardonic grin, "Is that so? Reminds me of someone I know. Besides, I don't know many teenage girls who wear their hair in a sideways ponytail anyway."

Kiva called out her name and Talia whipped her head up and beamed. "Kiva!" Scrambling off the ground, she launched herself into her arms, and Kiva couldn't help laughing. She loved this part of her day, being greeted just like this. She felt a part of her heart soar and squeezed her in return.

"Did you have a good day at school?"

"Uh huh."

She put Talia back down on the ground and took her little hand as they prepared to cross the yard to catch the bus home. "What was your favorite part?"

"Claire cut up letters made from cardboard paper and then placed them inside a bowl of *lopa*, and then we all had to dig around to find them to make up words."

"That sounds like fun. What word did you create?"

"I came up with 'sun.' Claire asked me to form it into a sentence and I wrote, 'The sun is hot.'"

Kiva hid a smile as she struggled to pronounce the words in English. "That's great, Talia. Well done." With English being Talia's second language, Kiva was impressed, and while she read bedtime stories to her in English, she never really knew if she wholly grasped the concepts, but now she could see that it was helping.

"Hey, Kiva!" she heard Claire call out.

Turning around, Kiva saw her step out from the shade of the school building and head toward them. Dressed in a two-piece *puletasi*, the material a bold red, Kiva couldn't help but admire just how elegant she looked. Her curves were accentuated in all the right places, something the design of the traditional attire was prone to do. Without a lick of makeup on, the hibiscus flower she wore over her ear was enough to enhance her natural beauty.

"I'm glad I found you." She smiled warmly. "I wanted to return these." She held out the bag with the plastic containers inside. Kiva reached out and grasped the handle and her arm tugged downwards from the weight of it.

"Whoa. What's in here?"

"Just a little surprise. Ry and I wanted to show our appreciation for your hospitality yesterday, so we made dessert for your family. Well, I actually made them." She laughed heartily. "Ry just napped throughout most of the process." Kiva's stomach clenched. "It was my first time attempting *pani keke*," Claire continued. "Of course it's nothing compared to those amazing muffins you made yesterday, which we already finished, but I hope you'll like them anyway."

Moved by her thoughtfulness, Kiva's emotions wrestled inside of her. Her heart lurched at the mention of Ry's name and then sunk just as quickly at the thought of them together. She could certainly understand his attraction to her. Not only was Claire beautiful and intelligent, she was sincere and considerate. Swallowing thickly, Kiva thanked her and said goodbye. As she twisted away to leave, a familiar throaty laugh reached her from across the field. Whipping her head around, she squinted against the glint of the sun and saw Ry in the far distance, coaching a group of school boys in what looked like a couple of elaborate soccer drills. He had taken off his shirt, and she didn't miss the expanse of broad muscle flexing in the sun as he dribbled the ball back and forth between his feet before smoothly shooting it through an imaginary goal line. The young boys roared with laughter and excitement, and Ry turned with a breathless smile on his rugged face and gave them each a high five. Her heart sped up just by watching him interact with the students, but she felt Talia tug impatiently on her hand, pulling her attention away. "Come on, Kiva. Let's go. I'm hungry," she whined.

"Would you like to have one of the *pani keke* now?"

Talia nodded. Reaching into the bag, Kiva popped the lid of the container open and withdrew one of the fried pancakes out. Talia bit into it greedily and Kiva grabbed her hand as they prepared to walk to the main road. Glancing back over her shoulder, she couldn't see Ry anymore and was instantly sorry she didn't get the chance to talk with him.

Later that evening as the sky was tainted in vibrant hues and the crickets churned to life, Kiva found herself in a rare occurrence alone in the art center. Earlier she'd taught a lesson on textured collage and was now taking a moment's reprieve by herself. Naomi had taken Mau, Hana, and Talia to visit their extended family in the village, and Kiva was relieved to have the place to herself for a little while. Sighing aloud, she pulled a piece of paper out of the cupboard and placed it squarely on the table. It had been a while since she'd created anything new for herself, and she promptly decided to start something now. Dragging the pencil from her hair, she sharpened it and then positioned the tip in the center of the blank page. Her hand immediately became a graceful dancer, the ivory parchment a stage where movement transformed into delicate lines and spheres and music translated into the scratch of her palm as it shifted across the paper. Looming shadows with blurs and smudges were choreographed with precision and purpose as she imagined peering through a window sprinkled with rain drops, their descent slow and unintentional, the direction spontaneous, only picking up speed when it joined with another. The background beyond was obscured, the focus entirely on the drops and their journey. She imagined pressing her hands against the cool glass, imprinting herself with the breath of life as it fogged the pane and momentarily shrouded the rain. The sketch was soft but raw, and vastly different from anything she'd ever drawn before. It represented a part of her reality, the part where she was an observer, always watching from a distance on the fringes of life. Suddenly feeling exhausted, she signed her initials at the bottom and blew away the leftover charcoal before they smudged. Leaning away from the table, she put down the pencil and released a breath.

The sound of footsteps bearing down on the stairs was the first sign that someone was approaching. She hadn't heard the truck pull into the driveway and knew it couldn't have been her family. They weren't back yet. Her body tensed. Alarmed, straightening in her chair, she glanced toward the doors just as Ry strode in.

"What—" she was rendered speechless from relief and surprise as she gaped at his disheveled hair and sweat-drenched T-shirt. "Did you just walk here?"

He shook his head as his lips tugged upwards into a tired smile. "This time I jogged."

He disappeared from view as he collapsed on the floor. Kiva jumped out of her seat and peered over the edge of the table. Sprawled out with his eyes closed, his chest rose in harsh, rapid succession.

She frowned in concern. "Are you alright?"

He held up a hand. "Just give me a minute."

She stared unblinking at his outstretched body on the floor. Even lying down, his height dominated the floor space and exuded a rugged masculinity that made her stomach flutter. Her mouth went dry.

"Okay, w-well," she stammered. "You must be really thirsty." His lips twitched at her obvious unease, even when his eyes were closed. Rolling her own eyes, she cleared her throat. "Have you eaten?" When he shook his head she added, "I'll go get something from the house. When you're ready, you can take a seat out on the deck. I'll be right back."

Sidestepping around him, she hurried to the kitchen and prepared a chicken salad wrap before pouring ice water from the fridge into a tall glass. With the food in one hand and the beverage in the other, she limped down the pathway and stopped in her tracks when she noticed him leaning against the wooden rail, arms crossed over his chest. He'd taken off his T-shirt and slung it over his shoulder. Ry didn't notice her yet, and she quietly watched him as he studied the floorboards like they were a piece of art. The man was devastatingly handsome, his body cut and toned to physical perfection, hair pulled away from his forehead and tied back. But Kiva knew where his scars were, both within and external.

The rustle of the bamboo leaves brought her out of her reverie, and she took a step forward. Her soft treading alerted him to her arrival, and he jerked his head up in time to see her ascend the stairs. He smiled warmly as he accepted the food and water, and she drew a couple chairs next to a small table and gestured for him to sit down. He did so, opposite her, and bit into the wrap. His groan of satisfaction put a soft smile on her face. "How long did it take you to jog here?"

He swallowed and scrubbed a hand across his mouth. "Just under an hour. I left before the village curfew. I didn't want to get stuck on the road when the evening prayers started."

Kiva nodded in acknowledgment. "How did you know someone was home?"

"When I saw the truck missing from the driveway, I was about to turn around and head back. But I noticed the lights were on in the art center and figured I'd see Mau here. I thought I'd come in and say hi to him." Biting the inside of her cheek, she hid her disappointment. "But I'm glad you were here instead," he added. She raised her eyes to his and saw that he was serious. "Kiva, I'm sorry if I upset you last time, in the kitchen. I have no right telling you what you should do with your life. You've achieved so much already." He gestured around them. "I mean, look at this place. It's incredible."

Kiva smiled tenderly and glanced around. "It hasn't always been easy, but I've come to love it. I love the people that walk down that path and order pumpkin soup and sip on papaya smoothies. I love that Talia's life is enriched by the activity that takes place around here. I also just love being around Mau, to make sure he's comfortable."

"Always looking out for others. You've done great, Kiva."

They sat in silence for a moment while he finished his food. She leaned back in her seat and inhaled the evening's breeze. She couldn't believe Ry had jogged all that distance and was now sitting across from her. Her eyes wandered to him and explored the edges of his face and jawline, shadowed with a light dusking of scruff. She shifted her eyes downwards and they landed on the tattoo across his ribs. Kiva followed their pathway as it curved and straightened, the elegant script broken into four separate parts, and she wondered about its significance.

"What does your tattoo mean? The one on your stomach?"

"When translated it says 'I am unbreakable.' I was fifteen when I got it, and at the time I was such a rowdy kid, always getting into fights, smug and cocky as hell." He grimaced and shook his head. "I thought I was such a badass, that no one could touch me. Anyway, you know the story. When I had it done, it meant something very different back then.

Now"—he half shrugged—"it's been stripped of its arrogance." Kiva couldn't help smiling and he returned it with one of his own lopsided ones.

"So what you're saying is that you've been effectively humbled."

"How do I say this without sounding arrogant? Yup."

She laughed then. "I've always seen tattoos as a form of art, but unlike conventional art, they're unchanging. You have to be a certain kind of person to want something so permanent."

He nodded contemplatively and didn't say anything. She felt something in the atmosphere shift.

Ry looked into the distance when he finally spoke, "There's something I wanted to tell you before. A year ago, I tracked down and met my father."

Kiva leaned forward. "How did you find him?"

"When my grandfather died two years ago, we went over to help my grandma pack up some of his belongings. She found a letter from my father addressed to my mother, which had an old mailing address from Egypt stamped on the envelope. Turns out he'd been writing to my mother for years, but my grandparents had thrown them away before she ever got the chance to see them. Somehow they overlooked this one, and it brought things to the surface. A lot of buried pain. As you can imagine my mom was upset, but she was more apprehensive about me contacting him. After all, he had no idea I existed. I did some online research and found out he was living in Dubai, that he was a successful architect and had designed some of the most impressive hotels there. I couldn't believe the coincidence and figured if we shared that connection, then it wouldn't be so bad meeting him. After a few months of convincing, my mom finally relented, and I contacted him."

"What did you say?"

"I introduced myself. Told him who my mother was. To be honest, I had no idea what his reaction was going to be, whether he would simply ignore me or tell me never to contact him again, but after a month I heard back, and he invited me to visit him in Dubai."

Kiva released a long breath. "Did you go?"

He nodded. "I did. And it was the most amazing experience. My father is one of those men who radiate confidence without appearing arrogant. He commands respect from those around him and is well-liked in return. I don't understand why my grandparents couldn't like him. I found out that he was a widower before he moved to the States and met my mother, and he never remarried after that. He has a couple sons from his previous marriage, and he wanted a better life for them. So he left them in the care of his mother in Egypt while he went abroad to further his education. They're much older than me and move around for business, so I only got the chance to meet one. The three of us traveled to Cairo together and it was like a whole new world was opened to me. The people, the hospitality, the warmth. The busy streets, markets, just the whole vibe of the country was something to marvel at. The Arab culture is similar to Samoa's in that people will take you into their home and treat you like you're part of the family. The reunion went better than I anticipated. There was no weirdness about me being there at all. At least, I didn't feel any. I think they were just surprised that I could speak Arabic."

Kiva smiled tenderly. "That's incredible, Ry. I'm so happy for you." And she meant it. After everything he had been through, she was pleased he connected with the part of him that had brought him so much torment. "Cairo and Dubai. Wow." She breathed. "I can't imagine traveling so far. I went to Brisbane a few years ago and didn't really enjoy the experience."

"Why not?"

"The idea of being packed inside a steel cylinder for hours while it flies at however many feet above the ground is just plain scary. Don't get me wrong, I'd love to go places and see things, but the getting there part is just not very appealing. All that turbulence and the up and the down." She shook her head and noticed him trying to stifle a smile. "It's not funny," she tried to smother her own grin. "It's actually pretty terrifying."

"Yes," he tried to say seriously. "You're right. Very scary."

She flung a piece of a napkin she had in her hands at him. Ry laughed.

"So are you still in touch with your dad?" she asked.

"I am. He wants to visit me here at some point."

"He wants to come to Samoa?"

He nodded and his eyes searched hers. "I'd like you to meet him."

Kiva's mouth opened slightly and she blinked in surprise. "Really? I'd love to."

He smiled before he picked up his water and finished it off with a few gulps. "That wrap was delicious. Thank you."

She bloomed with pleasure. "I'm glad you enjoyed it." The wind whipped her hair around her face and she wished she had a pencil at hand to put it up. She noticed him watching her battle with the strands. "I came by the school today to pick up Talia. I saw you out on the field with the kids playing soccer."

"We turned a volleyball into a soccer ball. I'm on a mission to convert those boys from rugby to soccer."

Kiva snorted. "Good luck with that. Rugby is like a religion in this country. I'm sorry to be the one to tell you this, but it's not going to happen."

He smiled smugly. "We'll see about that."

"Aren't Peace Corps volunteers supposed to support their host country, not try to make monumental changes that will cause a riot?"

"Whoa, whoa." He held up his palms and laughed. "It wouldn't go that far. Maybe a small protest at most."

She smiled. "I don't know … you better watch your back from now on or you might have stones thrown at your house."

He grinned before his face smoothed and became somber. He suddenly took on a more serious tone when he spoke. "God, I've missed you." His eyes never wavered from her face as he said those four words.

Kiva sucked in a breath and stared back. "What did you just say?" she whispered.

"You heard me." His voice was low, gravelly.

Glancing away, her heart wouldn't stop quickening. She had long ago given up hope that he felt anything besides friendship toward her and now here he was saying something that had the potential to send her right back on that precipice. She faced him again. "But … you just left, without saying goodbye."

A conflicted expression flitted across his features. "I know, and I'm sorry. For everything. For hurting you. For leaving like that. It was inconsiderate of me. But I'm here now, and I'm not going anywhere."

Her emotions were a maelstrom inside. What did he want from her? A part of her was afraid to find out.

"What about Claire?" she blurted out and felt her cheeks flame as a result.

He cocked his head to the side and studied her in silence. "Claire is a part of my Peace Corps group. There's seventeen of us in total, and we consider each other like family. The fact that she and I ended up in the same school just means that we look out for each other. I know she's a big girl and can handle herself, but I can't help keeping an eye on her. She didn't always have it easy growing up, and I recognized something in her past that reminded me of my own. In a way, we're both here for the same reasons—to give back. When she asked me to join her for lunch on Sunday, I had no idea it would be here of all places, but I'm glad that it was."

"She's really beautiful and smart."

He nodded slowly. "Yes, she is. And she could really use a friend. Someone like you." He held her gaze and his eyes gentled. Kiva didn't know how to respond. The idea that he knew intimately what Claire needed sent a jolt through her and she tried to quash it down. She'd noticed recently that she and Hana were starting to become good friends and some part of her was happy that her cousin could have someone to confide in.

Where did that leave her and Ry?

Scraping his chair across the floor, he stood and shoved his hands inside his shorts' pockets. She peered up at his handsome face in confusion. "I have to head back before it gets too dark."

She stood and came around the table. Together they walked in silence toward the front of the house, the crunch of stones beneath their feet the only sound that could be heard. She wanted to tell him that she'd missed him too, that she never forgot about him, but how could she articulate it in syllables and sentences? She'd never been particularly good with words, and she had little experience when it came to matters of the heart. She expressed herself best through art and to this day still kept the sketches of his hands and profile with her.

"Wait," she said. "There's something I want to give you."

Without waiting for his response, she turned around and limped back to the art center. Her heart drummed in her ears as she approached the table in the center of the room and reached for her sketch. With shaky hands she clutched it tightly and turned to leave. Suddenly feeling hot with perspiration, she pivoted around and grabbed the pencil on the table to wrap her hair up.

Ry was standing patiently in the driveway when she returned. "I wanted to give this to you." She held out the drawing of the window and raindrops and watched his face closely for his reaction. His expression became incredulous as he took it from her.

"You did this?" When she nodded, his gaze returned to the drawing, and Kiva wanted very much to know what he was thinking at that moment. "This is exquisite work, Kiva. Who's the woman looking through the window?" he asked.

"That's me."

He was silent as his gaze lingered on her hands pressed against the glass, her longing and sadness evident in the way her fingers curled slightly in yearning, telling a story beyond any words she could muster.

"You were right about everything," she started. "From the other day in the kitchen. There are still things I want more than anything. Unfulfilled dreams and goals. But you see … how can I trade my dream for my family's wellbeing? I couldn't do that. I can't leave them. Not until I know they'll be okay—when Mau comes out of his stupor and when I know Talia's future will be taken care of."

"I know, Kiva. I know." He took a step closer and reached out to tuck a strand of hair behind her ear. "But there must be some small part of your dream that can be fulfilled right now."

She stilled as the implication of his words slammed into her. Did she dare to hope? Gazing up at his face, she searched his eyes to see if she was mistaken and discovered with disbelief that she wasn't. His expression was intense but bare to her, and so very honest. His eyes were sincere and warm, their brown depths reflected with longing, and she wanted to step into his arms and weep with joy. But fear and uncertainty held her back. Questions filled her head as she tried to process everything that had led them to this moment. Distance. Change. Responsibilities. And while she was the same girl she was six years ago, he certainly wasn't the same boy.

The rumble of the truck as it neared the house cut through her thoughts. She looked up at Ry to gauge his reaction, but his face became impassive to the interruption. She watched as the pickup pulled into the driveway and Naomi cut the engine.

"Ryler!" Mau boomed through the passenger window. "Have you come back for more food?"

Ry drew his attention away from Kiva and smiled at her uncle. "I was just leaving."

"Hop in, I can give you a lift down," Naomi offered.

"Thanks, but I enjoy the walk."

He turned to Kiva and gave her one last look before he said goodbye to everyone else and strode away in the darkness.

CHAPTER TWENTY-SEVEN

Kiva's heart felt heavy as she watched him disappear from view. She'd never told him how she secretly longed for the kind of love that inspired most of her sketches, and yet he instinctively knew. It had become a far-fetched fantasy and had taken a backseat to everything else in her life. Since Mau's stroke, she simply didn't have the time to pursue a relationship, not that any of the guys that came round the café interested her, but now that Ry had returned, he awakened feelings within her that she'd long suppressed.

"Kiva, I need your help," she heard Hana's muffled voice from inside the truck. Kiva stepped forward and opened the back door. Talia was asleep across her lap. "She's burning up with a fever," Hana explained. "Can you lift her into the house?"

Kiva tucked her arms under her little body and came into contact with her scorched skin. "Oh my God, she's really sick. What happened?"

"I don't know. She started feeling unwell as soon as we arrived at Grandma's, and I put her in one of the rooms to sleep. I tried waking her up to eat, but she refused and went back to bed. I need to give her something to reduce the fever."

Naomi circled around to them, touched Talia's forehead and neck, and immediately barked instructions for Kiva to take her inside, lay her down, and prepare wet cloths to place over her head. Kiva adjusted Talia in her arms and limped upstairs to Hana's room. She laid her over the mattress on the floor and brushed the curls from her face.

Talia stirred in her sleep. "Kiva?" her voice mumbled. "My head is sore."

"I know, honey," she said soothingly. "I'm sorry you're not feeling well. Your mama is going to bring some medicine to make you feel better, okay?"

She nodded and curled onto her side, closing her eyes.

When an hour passed and her fever still hadn't come down, they started to worry. Hana and Naomi wasted no time taking her to the hospital while Kiva remained with Mau. She paced back and forth in the living room until he told her to stop distracting him from watching a rugby game on TV. After some time, she heard the truck pull into the driveway and immediately rushed outside to hear the news. Hana's face was lined with exhaustion as she lifted Talia onto her shoulder and walked toward the house. "They suspect she has the chicken pox," she said tiredly. "They told us to go home and let her rest. It just has to run its course, but she should be fine."

Kiva sighed in relief and gently rubbed Talia's back. "She scared me." She breathed.

"It's all part of growing up," Naomi said as she bustled past them into the kitchen. "Kids will get sick and then bounce right back just as quickly. But the worry"—she clicked her tongue—"the worry will never go away." Placing a kettle over the stove she exclaimed, "It's going to be a long night. Who wants *koko*?"

***

Talia was kept from attending school for two weeks, which meant Kiva didn't get the opportunity to see Ry. He hadn't come round the art center either, which made her ponder his last words to her. Had he meant them? Where was he? Why wasn't he jogging over? She was driving herself crazy with anticipation. She missed him and wished she knew what kept him away.

As the days dragged on, however, she received an unexpected visitor which took her by complete surprise. Pulling into the driveway in a government-marked vehicle, Silei shut the engine off and hopped out. Sporting a glamorous outfit and sunglasses perched atop her head, she looked stunning. Kiva's eyes widened through the kitchen window. She quickly dried her hands and hurried out to greet her.

"What are you doing here?" she cried in delight when the door slammed behind her.

"Surprise!" Silei laughed as Kiva launched herself in her arms. "I arrived last night," Silei explained, pulling away.

"Look at you!" Kiva admired her short, dyed hair as her friend twirled around playfully.

"Do you like my hair?" she asked eagerly. Her hair was boy short with a prominent blue streak on the top. She reminded Kiva of a peacock.

"It's … wow … definitely something."

Silei laughed at her reaction. "I just had it done as a graduation present to myself, much to the horror of my parents."

"I'm sure they were beside themselves."

"They're hoping the dye will have worn out by the time I walk up on that stage and receive my diploma, which, lucky for them, is still months away."

Kiva swallowed thickly at the thought of her best friend graduating. "I'm so proud of you, Si. Hot shot accountant that you are."

Silei didn't miss the sadness behind her smile. "Oh, Kiva." She looped her arm through hers as they headed inside. "How have you been?"

"Well, the café is going great, and Mau is much better."

"I'm not asking about that. I'm asking about *you*."

Kiva smiled faintly. "I really can't complain, Si. The more I'm here, the more I feel confirmation that I'm right where I need to be."

Silei cocked an eyebrow. "Okay, but that's about to change because I'm here to take you out."

"Right now?" Kiva glanced outside as dusk settled over the yard and then down at her stained apron.

"Yes, right now. It's Friday after all and we need a ladies night out." She smiled excitedly. "Plus, I have something cute for you to wear. Let me run to the car and grab it."

***

The restaurant was packed when they entered through a canopy of fuchsia bougainvillea and jasmine, the design boasting both Mediterranean and Pacific influences after the owners moved from the south of Italy to Samoa eleven years ago. Arched windows and high wooden beams embraced a dimly lit space that was part restaurant and part bar. Kiva admired the black and white striped table cloths with tropical centerpieces and the menu that was printed on chalkboard in modern penmanship. Since running her own café, she appreciated the little details that added to the ambience of a place and was eager to experience this eatery for the first time. Between Silei's hair and her pronounced limp, they drew a few incredulous stares as they were led to the balcony that overlooked a lush valley. Beyond that, the town's lights flickered like fireflies in the distance. "Aren't we a sight to behold?" Silei scoffed as they took their seats.

Kiva glanced around briefly and noticed a few people pointing indiscreetly and whispering. Her stomach fluttered violently from the unwelcome attention.

"Ignore them," she said, trying to sound convincing.

Earlier when she was getting ready, Silei had surprised her with a maxi dress that flaunted her curves, while still modestly covering her shoulders, and dropped elegantly to her ankles. The color was a vibrant coral and made her feel spirited and beautiful all at once. She'd decided to wear her hair down with a frangipani behind one ear, and her face was softly made up thanks to Silei's dexterous skills with the eyeliner and mascara.

A waitress approached and gave them each a menu. After they placed their order for avocado salad and seafood pasta, Silei turned to Kiva and asked, "Do you remember when I said that I wanted to get a *malu* when I finished university?"

Kiva nodded. "You drew about it in art class."

"Well"—she blew out a rough breath—"I'm not so sure anymore."

Kiva furrowed her brows. "Why the change of heart? You've wanted that tattoo since we were kids. You even asked me to design an imaginary pattern for you when we were twelve, remember?"

Silei half smiled at the memory before her shoulders lifted in a shrug. "I don't feel worthy of it. It's traditionally supposed to symbolize courage, responsibility, honor, modesty, a connection to the land. I don't feel like I represent any of those things anymore."

"What do you mean?"

"I've changed. University changed me. Look at me. My hair is this silly blue and not long and thick like a beauty queen's."

"And?"

"And I'm wearing black nail polish and have body piercings."

Kiva's eyes widened slightly. "You mean the first one wasn't torture enough? Where did you get your new one done?"

Silei gave an impish grin. "Plural. More than one. And trust me, you don't want to know." Her face sobered. "The truth is, regardless of what I look like on the outside—and I certainly don't look like the typical *tamaitai* Samoa—I definitely don't feel like one on the inside. I don't feel like a Samoan girl is supposed to feel. Obedient. Respectful. Dutiful."

"Obedience and respect are human qualities, Si. They don't just belong to women." She paused to think of an example. "Take traffic lights, for instance. Can you imagine if men ran through red lights and women didn't? That'll be a little ridiculous, not to mention chaotic." Silei smiled faintly. "And as for being dutiful, you're going to be contributing to the economic growth of this country by using that articulate brain of yours. Companies will be squabbling after you to tally their books, and then the Ministry of Finance will demand your services because they'll know you'll be cutthroat with your honesty." She took a sip of her drink. "Or maybe they won't."

Silei laughed. She shook her head and picked up her own drink. She was quietly contemplative before she spoke. "I'm not like you, Kiva. You're the embodiment of goodness. You're here, supporting your family, caring for them. You've stayed while I don't want to come back. Not after I've been exposed to freedom and knowledge. My parents think I'm a *fia poko*, a know-it-all who needs to be reminded of where I've come from. They look at me and see a wannabe *palagi* with my short shorts and tank tops. They were the ones that told me I was unworthy of the *malu*. That hurt me more than anything. After all, the *malu* should never be exposed once it's imprinted on the thighs, right? Keep it covered, they say, like a good, humble girl should, but if I'm walking around in little shorts, what does that say about me?" Her voice wavered and she coughed into her hand to clear it. "Am I only worth the clothes that I choose to wear? Or the dark makeup on my face? I like the way I dress, but it doesn't mean that I've forgotten God and country." She shook her head in confusion. "Sometimes I feel like I'm floundering, that I'm neither here nor there, and it'll just be easier if I remained in Wellington because at least over there I can be alone. No one can affect you when you're alone. I've applied to the Masters' program at Victoria. I haven't heard back yet, but I'm hoping it'll come through."

"That's great, Si. I'm so proud of you for choosing to further your studies. But are you doing it because you want to or because you're running away?" Silei glanced away as if she'd touched a nerve. "I'm sorry about your parents," Kiva continued more gently. "They should not have said that about your worth. You are a strong, independent Samoan woman, and in my opinion that's more than enough to bear the markings of one."

"I don't know," Silei sounded dejected. "I'm kind of all over the place. I don't know where I belong anymore."

"Your sense of belonging doesn't have to be tethered to just one place but can encompass a diversity of places, stories, and qualities that you hold to be true. It shouldn't be about choosing between cultures or putting one down in favor of another, but choosing instead to embrace the good in all of them. And the goodness that you do find will become your core values, your true self. Your blueprint for life. Sometimes there's so much going on that you lose perspective of what really matters, but if you peel away those confusing layers, you're still just Silei.

A good person underneath. I know it and I know your parents know it, too. In their eyes, you went away a child and came back an adult—an adult with funky hair." Her lips curved into a smile. "You've returned a different person than when you left—worldlier, more knowledgeable, but with more questions about life and identity than when you were living under their roof and knew exactly who you were and where your place was. They probably don't know how to respond to that. Just give them time. What you're feeling is normal. Just take it easy on yourself, and be true, always."

Silei blew out an unsteady breath. "Thanks, Kiva." She smiled softly. "I knew I could talk to you about this."

"Of course." Kiva reached over and squeezed her hand. "Now I just have to follow my own advice," she added dryly.

Silei laughed as the waitress brought their food and placed it in front of them. Kiva inhaled the creamy aroma and stabbed a shrimp with her fork. As they ate, Silei spoke at length about her life in Wellington, the shopping that she couldn't seem to get enough of, which made her constantly broke as a result, and the night life that dominated her weekends. They talked about her studies and her professors and how she'd had a secret crush for the longest time on one of her young tutors. The topic slid easily onto guys and Silei wasted no time probing Kiva.

"So, tell me," she began as the waitress returned to clear their plates. "How's the male department around here? Are you seeing anyone?" The girl didn't beat around the bush. Earlier she'd informed Kiva that she'd had a boyfriend who was a student from Malaysia, but that it didn't work out after six months. "I didn't want to be with him anymore," she'd said. "The guy was an impulsive, obsessive gamer. All he wanted to do was sit around in his dorm room and play video games all day long." She'd shrugged. "I got bored."

Kiva leaned back in her seat and contemplated telling her about Ry. What could she say? She wasn't even sure what was happening there herself. Silei narrowed her eyes in suspicion. "There is someone, I can tell," she pointed out. "Who is he? Do I know him?"

Kiva tried to hide the smile that flitted across her lips. "Maybe." And her best friend wasn't going to believe who *he* was. Kiva proceeded to tell her about Ry, from his lessons with Mau at the art center to his return as a Peace Corps volunteer, and as Silei listened intently her eyes became round saucers on her face.

"He's back?" she asked in disbelief. "I remember him. The bad boy with the tattoo on his arm. What's he like now?"

"He's different, in a good way." Kiva half shrugged. "Nothing's happened, so, I don't know …" She shrugged again.

"Has he come around?"

"Yes … once. He jogged from the school."

"He *jogged* to come see you? Up that windy, steep hill?"

"Well … I don't know if it was just to see me. And it only happened once. It probably discouraged him from doing it again."

Silei shook her head. "No, Kiva. It's very clear that he did it for you. I mean, who in their right mind chooses to *jog* up impossible hills for fun?"

Kiva fidgeted in her seat. "Well … lots of people do. Marathon trainers. Health conscious people."

Silei waved her arm dismissively. "Do you want my advice?"

"That's a rhetorical question. You're going to give it anyway."

"You're right. Let him work for it because when a man wants something, there's nothing that'll hold him back from going after it. And this jogging business, my dear friend, is a classic example of that."

"Si …" Kiva's voice was patient as she tried to still her riotous heart. "I wouldn't jump to conclusions just yet."

"Do you like him?"

Well, yes. She loved him. She always had. She just wasn't sure how *he* felt and if those words he'd spoken the last time she saw him were in fact what she thought they meant, or if she'd completely misinterpreted them.

"Never mind, I can tell by your face."

Kiva startled. "You can?"

"Yes. You've always worn your emotions on your face, and right now it's doing this little, sappy, he loves me-he loves me not expression."

"Is not." She guffawed as she felt her cheeks warm.

Silei's grin was hidden when she lifted her drink to her lips. "Is too."

They stayed another thirty minutes and talked some more about their future plans. They shared a passion fruit cheesecake for dessert and when it was getting late, they paid the bill, and stood from their seats.

"That was fun," Kiva acknowledged with a satisfied grin and full stomach. "Thanks, Si. I needed that."

"It was great fun," Silei agreed. "But right now I need a wheelbarrow to carry me to the parking lot."

"I need to use the bathroom quickly," Kiva said as they stepped inside the dimly lit restaurant.

"Okay, I'll wait for you in the car." Silei strode toward the exit and disappeared under the floral canopy.

Kiva scanned the area for the restrooms and couldn't immediately see one. She bypassed the bar area as scores of people clustered around low tables and plush couches. She finally found the sign for the bathroom under an archway and limped toward it with relief. When she came back out, the room seemed more packed than when she'd left it. Edging her way through and hoping no one stepped on her toes, she strained her neck to find the way out. Someone bumped her from the back and another grazed her by the shoulder. *Where had all these people come from?* When she finally spotted the exit, a familiar, deep laugh reached her ears and made her pulse trip.

Pulling back, she couldn't immediately see him but knew that he was there somewhere among the crowd. What was he doing here? How long had been there? And how had she not noticed before? His laugh returned, joined by others, and they were *loud*. Glancing around, she noticed for the first time the people she'd been trying to avoid since she came out of the bathroom. They were all foreigners, and not the tourist kind. Peace Corps volunteers. She picked up on their accents quickly by their animated chatter as they clustered around in small groups. It looked like a reunion of some sort, a celebration perhaps, and Kiva guessed they were all part of Ry's group. Her eyes parted the crowd in search of him and found him sitting on one of the couches. Even dressed in a simple white T-shirt and shorts, he was as handsome as ever. With one of his long legs bent at the knee and braced over the other, he was speaking to a guy opposite him, but she couldn't hear what he was saying amidst the clamorous clatter in the room. Her eyes lingered on him for a moment, and she noticed that he seemed more relaxed, his mouth breaking out into a crooked grin that ignited a response inside her. When the crowd shifted, she noticed a woman perched on the arm of the couch, her shapely legs stretched out in front of her. Her long, pale hair was lose around her shoulders and obscured her face where her profile was fixated on Ry as he spoke. When she threw her head back in laughter at something he said, like beautiful women did in shampoo commercials, Kiva realized that it was Claire. Her chest tightened painfully as the air squeezed in and out of her lungs. She sensed her inadequacy build as it became apparent that she'd been spying on an exchange she was obviously not a part of. She suddenly felt very much out of place. She took a step back, and then another, before she stumbled on someone's foot and felt herself falling helplessly backwards, powerless to stop herself. The sensation was one of complete horror as she anticipated hitting the ground with dread and the humiliating aftermath that would result.

Her heart thudded as the room tilted, and she met the floor with a crash. She wanted to close her eyes and will the ground to open and devour her and her shame.

"Whoa, easy there. I got you."

Twisting, she peered up into a pair of warm brown eyes. "I-I'm sorry," she stammered, feeling her face flush.

"Are you okay?" he asked in concern. "Here, let me help you up." He offered his hand and she took it. Straightening, he pulled her up and let her go, but not before they drew attention. She glanced over to where Ry sat and caught his eye. His expression flickered between surprise and worry as he started to rise out of his seat. Heart slamming against her ribs, Kiva turned quickly, feeling a hundred pairs of eyes watching as she limped away awkwardly. *Clumsy, disabled girl*, she chanted to herself as she hurried toward the exit. She was so embarrassed with her sprawling in front of everyone—and especially since Ry and Claire most likely witnessed it—that she felt the threat of tears. She needed to get away before someone noticed. She needed to find Silei.

She spotted her friend waiting in the vehicle as soon as she stepped outside, her face lined with tired impatience. Kiva started toward her when she felt someone's hand wrap around her upper arm, halting her.

"Kiva, wait."

CHAPTER TWENTY-EIGHT

He spun her around until she was almost flush against his chest. "Are you okay? I saw what happened back there."

She clenched her teeth and refused to meet his gaze. Ry lifted her chin until she had no choice but to look at him. His expression was troubled as he explored her face, knowing somehow that she wasn't alright. The pad of his thumb caressed her jaw tenderly and her chin quivered. The tears came unbidden, and his face abruptly blurred before her.

"Ah, Kiva," he said roughly. "Your tears are like stab wounds inside my chest."

"I'm sorry," her voice broke. She sniffed sharply, wiping at her cheeks. "I really don't want to cry. It's just that I didn't want that kind of attention back there."

He nodded perceptively and reached out to grasp her arm in comfort. "How are you getting home?"

"My friend," she pointed to where Silei sat idly in the car, staring at them curiously. "I better go. She's waiting for me."

He looked reluctant to let her leave.

A flare of flaxen hair and limbs distracted her, and she peered around Ry's shoulder to see Claire step outside.

"Kiva, are you okay?" She came toward them as Ry stepped back. "I didn't know you were here until I saw you trip over Adé. Are you alright?" she repeated.

The guy she tripped over followed closely behind, smoothing a hand over his cornrows and flashing her a knowing smile. He was medium height and bulky and wore a floral button-down. "Hey, I'm Adé," he held out his hand to shake hers. A dimple appeared on his cheek.

"Kiva," she responded with a faint smile as his hand engulfed hers.

"Well, Kiva, now that we've been properly introduced, do you want to join us? We're having a little get together for my birthday and we're about to have cake." His voice was like honey, smooth and warm.

She opened her mouth in surprise and blurted, "Happy birthday."

"Thanks," he said with a charming smile. "Will you come in?"

"That's nice of you to ask, but I really shouldn't. I have to get up early for work tomorrow."

"Work on a Saturday?" He raised a brow.

"She runs a café," Ry cut in.

"Well, that's cool," Adé said. "Maybe we can stop by sometime, check it out."

"It's pretty amazing," Claire jumped in. "It's located in the middle of nowhere and there's this adorable little art place next to it. What's the name of it again? Bamboo something."

"Café Bamboo," she and Ry said together. Kiva looked over at him and smiled softly. He returned one of his uneven grins.

"That's right," Claire said. "We should definitely go." Turning to Adé she added, "She makes the most *incredible* muffins."

"Sweet," he responded.

Somehow Claire's praise didn't sit well with Kiva, and she shifted uncomfortably on her feet. Here she was standing in front of a few college graduates and they were talking about her muffins as if it were a worthy accomplishment.

"How's Talia feeling?" Claire asked with concern. "I miss her at school."

"Better." Kiva smiled politely at her sincerity. "The spots have mostly faded. She should be returning soon."

She heard Silei toot the horn as unobtrusively as one could toot a Land Cruiser, and Kiva smiled apologetically at the three of them. "I have to go. My ride's getting impatient. It was nice meeting you, Adé, and thanks … for helping me out earlier."

"No problem. I'm just sorry I didn't catch you."

Her face heated at his bold statement, and she risked a glance at Ry. His jaw was locked in tension and her stomach did a little flip. "Well … bye." She gave a halfhearted wave and turned to leave.

The whole exchange felt awkward, and she just wanted to get home to her sketchbooks, to familiarity. She knew instinctively that Ry was watching her, and she wished for nothing more in that moment than to have a normal, graceful walk, instead of an inelegant limp.

Kiva reached the car and opened the passenger side door. Sliding in, she sensed without looking at Silei that her brows were raised to her hairline. "Just drive, please." She sighed. "I'll explain later."

***

The next morning she couldn't get out of bed. Her body felt as if a whale had been sitting on her while she attempted to sleep. She'd awakened with a killer headache in the dead of night and was restless and in pain ever since. Exhausted, she tried to close her eyes and succumb to the pull of slumber that crept along the edges of her consciousness, but she ached everywhere and it wasn't going away. When dawn's first light slithered through the curtains, she tried to roll out of bed but couldn't even muster the energy to do that. When Naomi came into her room to see why she hadn't started in the kitchen yet, she checked her temperature with the back of her hand and frowned. "Hmm ... You have a really high fever. You may be coming down with the chicken pox as well." Kiva groaned as she closed her. Her throat was sore and she swallowed thickly to ease it. "I'm going to get some Paracetamol and water," Naomi said. "You're staying in here for the rest of the day. No more baking for you for a while."

"But ... the café." Her voice was gravelly and she winced at the effort to speak.

"Don't worry about that, Kiva. We'll handle it. Just concentrate on getting better." She pulled her hair away from her face. "Besides, we don't want to serve a side order of pox with your cupcakes, do we? Now rest. I'll be back soon." She stood from the bed and padded down the hallway.

Kiva stared up at the ceiling in misery. She followed the path of mildew that grew and dotted the wall and thought that it might look like someone riding a bicycle. Or was she starting to imagine things? God, she hurt all over. She shut her eyes and felt generally sorry for herself. How long was this going to last?

Naomi returned shortly with the medicine and glass of water in her hands. Kiva grimaced as she sat up and took them from her, swallowing the pills down painfully. The effort made her listless and she fell back on her pillow and closed her eyes.

The day dragged on as she wavered in and out of sleep. Sometimes the fever hauled her out of her dream-like state and she needed to take a pain reliever, at other times the ache pounded into her head like a chisel and mallet and she couldn't do anything but simply take it. She was aware of voices floating through the open louvers from customers coming and going along the pathway below; at another she heard Talia running up and down the stairs and had a sudden thought that she seemed to have recovered well enough.

By the time evening arrived, she was bone weary and weak and wanted desperately to crawl out of her body to give herself a break. The door to her bedroom nudged open and Naomi entered carrying a tray. "I brought you some soup. Are you hungry?"

"Not really," Kiva croaked. Her voice was starting to go.

"Try eating something. It's vegetable soup. Very delicious. " The bed dipped from her weight as she shifted the tray carefully on her lap. "Sit up," she instructed, and Kiva complied. Her head spun and she took a few even breaths. Taking the spoon from Naomi, she dipped it into the warm broth and brought it to her lips. Her aunt was right, it was delicious, but she couldn't take any more than a couple spoonfuls before she started to reel.

"Better?"

Kiva tried to smile but failed. She lay back down again. "How did it go today?"

"Very well. Since there were no fresh muffins to serve, we made mango smoothies instead."

"Did many people come?"

"The usual." She rattled off a list of people Kiva recognized. "And some of your Peace Corps friends stopped by for lunch," she added. "They're a good group of people. Very friendly. They asked about you."

Kiva's pulse picked up. "They did?"

"Mmm hmm."

Kiva wondered who they were and if Ry was a part of the group. She wrung her fingers together on her stomach.

"I told them you weren't feeling well."

"Oh." She studied the patterns on her sheet while Naomi moved the tray aside.

"Ryler stayed back when everyone else left."

Her eyes shot to her face. "He did?"

Naomi nodded. "He's been here all afternoon, helping out with the café. He's the one that made the soup." Kiva's heart accelerated as she absorbed this information. "He's downstairs now with Mau watching rugby." Speechless, she could only stare at her aunt. Naomi brushed aside a strand of hair from her forehead. "You still feel warm. I'll let you sleep now." Kiva stared after her as she stood and walked toward her bedroom door. She didn't want to sleep now, she couldn't.

"Naomi?"

She half turned.

"Can you tell him thank you for me?"

Naomi smiled tenderly in response. "Of course."

She shut the door behind her, and Kiva listened to the soft treading of Naomi's footsteps as they moved further away. She wanted to follow them downstairs to where he was. Or rather, for him to come upstairs since she couldn't really move. But Kiva knew that he wouldn't, that by staying back and helping her family, and making her *soup*, he was letting her know in his own quiet and strong way that he was there. Her heart blossomed at his thoughtfulness, and she wished she could send gentle messages of her own. Turning her head, she groaned from the motion and closed her eyes.

The spots started making their grand appearance the following day. Firstly on her face and scalp before they spread everywhere else, and the itchiness was unparalleled to anything she'd experienced before. She would react to one before another erupted somewhere else on her skin. There were simply too many blisters, and they were in the most hard to reach places such as her lower back and in between her toes.

Late in the afternoon she was sick of being cooped up in her room and ventured out for the first time in what felt like days. Tucking a sketchbook under her arm, she walked down the stairs and into the living room. It was deserted save for a pile of unfolded laundry on the couch and a stack of children's books on another. She heard Naomi tinker away in the kitchen and made her way there.

"Where is everyone?" she asked when her feet touched the cool tiles.

Naomi twisted her neck around from where she was washing her hands in the sink. "Oh, Kiva! Good to see you're up and about. Hana took Mau and Talia to the beach for a swim. Do you want something to eat?" Kiva shook her head. Her appetite hadn't returned and her throat was still scratchy. "Well, you know you shouldn't be in here." She proceeded to shoo her out of the kitchen with the tea towel she grabbed to dry her hands. "Why don't you go outside? Get some fresh air?"

Kiva lifted a *lavalava* from the laundry pile and wrapped it around her shoulders. When she stepped outside, a cool breeze touched her face and made her inhale deeply. She limped gingerly down the path to her favorite tree and sat resting against the base. It wasn't the most comfortable seat with its roots jutting above the ground snakelike, but she found solace in the tranquility it instilled in her while its leaves rustled high above her like kites. She knew she was too weak to climb its branches but was within reach of the tree's vibrant pulse, and for now that was enough for what she wanted to do. She stretched her hand to the pencil in her hair but stilled when she heard footsteps ambling down the pathway. Ry came into view and stalled when he saw her. Kiva gathered the *lavalava* close around her shoulders and had a fleeting thought that she wished she could throw it over her blister riddled head as well, but there was no point. He'd seen her and was cutting a path in her direction at that moment.

He came within a few feet, and Kiva peered up at his face. "Hey," he said. "May I?" He pointed to a spot next to her and she nodded in assent. He dropped down beside her with one leg stretched out languidly and the other bent at the knee. He rested his elbow on it. "Naomi said I'd find you here. This is nice." He glanced around at the wild flowers and vegetable garden. With his back against the tree and his profile to her, Kiva was keenly aware of his every move. He leaned forward, bending both of his legs at the knees and resting his elbows on them. The new position afforded her a better view of his profile, and she noticed his hair was damp and he smelled of sea salt, as if he'd taken a swim in the ocean before he came. She watched from the corner of her eye as he picked a blade of grass and twirled it between his fingers.

"Did you jog here?" she finally asked.

"I hitchhiked."

Silence grew between them as she practiced her next words in her mind. "I heard what you did yesterday. With the café. And the soup. Thank you."

He dipped his head in silent acknowledgment. "How are you feeling today? Your voice sounds pretty awful."

"I feel as bad as anyone can be under the circumstances," she said hoarsely. He cocked his head and looked at her then and she felt her face heat. "Please"—she raised a hand to block his view—"don't look at me."

"It's not that bad."

"You've just admitted there's a degree of badness there," she responded flatly. She groaned and covered her face with her hands. She knew she looked hideous, that the red spots spread from her cheeks to her neck and behind her ears.

"Hey." His voice had a touch of amusement in it. He grabbed one of her hands and tugged it free.

She glared at him. "You shouldn't be here, Ry. You might get sick."

"I've already had the chicken pox when I was a kid. I think that pretty much makes me immune for life." He held his elbow up for her to see. "See right here?" A couple tiny scars peppered the bone area.

She blew out a defeated breath. "It really sucks."

He nodded. "I hear its worse in adults."

"I'm so itchy everywhere and I know if I scratch them, they'll scar. I just hope I don't scar too badly." She gestured to the one on her arm from the bus accident. The deep crease was still there, and it looked as if her skin had been pinched together. "This has been more than enough to get me all sorts of interesting looks."

"You don't like it," he stated. "The attention. The other night …" He trailed off and Kiva was reminded of her embarrassing fall at the restaurant.

She looked over at him and almost laughed humorlessly. "Well, no. Not when people stare and gawk and feel sorry for me. For someone that already draws so much of that kind of attention, the last thing I want is to have even more opportunities to be shamefaced." She felt her annoyance rise and her voice changed to scorn. *"There goes the girl with the funny walk. Oh and look, she fell down. She really can't walk properly."*

"Kiva." His voice became stern but she ignored him.

"Poor little disabled girl," she mocked. *"What is she doing out late anyway? She should be home where she belongs."*

"Enough." He sounded mad, and Kiva swallowed back the tension that rose in her throat. A strained silence hovered between them as her heart pounded in her chest from her outburst.

"Tell me something, Ry," she finally said, her voice shaky with emotion, but there was something she needed to know. "Has my limp ever bothered you?" There. She'd asked it. The one question that had been secretly plaguing her for the longest time.

His dark brows slashed downwards. "Is that what this is about?"

"You tell me. You come here and then you leave for years and I don't hear one word from you. Not one. What was I supposed to think? And then you're suddenly back and you've become a different person while I've remained exactly the same. You've lived the kind of life I can only dream of, while I have no hope of budging from this place." Her throat squeezed.

She'd said too much and still nothing at all, but she mostly loathed herself for feeling so small. She was at her lowest point right now and she couldn't snap out of it. She attributed her self-pity to the fact that she was tired, her body sore, and throat scratchy, but she knew that wasn't all. Her heart bled with unspoken words and unanswered questions. With the feeling of being incompetent. Her fingers reacted by curling around the worn binding in her lap. It was an older book, one that held sketches of galaxies and stars. Of yearning and hope. And of him and his hands. Pulling the pencil from her hair, she flipped to a new page, which was no small task since most of the pages were almost full, and started tracing patterns and swirls. It was an absent-minded sketch, one that her heart wasn't into at all, but helped calm her a little.

"Kiva." His voice was gentle.

She was still raw, and the sensitive part of her that was connected to her heart was afraid of appearing vulnerable. Closing the book suddenly, she wound her hair up and jabbed the pencil through it. She was shutting herself up before he had the chance to say something she might question as being *too* sincere or *too* forced just to make her feel better. She stood quickly and felt her head swirl.

"Look, Ry. You've been a good friend." Her voice teetered on emotion as she swallowed to keep them from spilling over.

He suddenly sprang to his feet and towered over her. "I've been a good friend?" he echoed incredulously. His eyes roved her face, trying to find something, and her heart skipped a beat.

She moistened her lips. "I don't want you to think I'm the kind of person that allows this"— she motioned to her uneven leg—"to get in the way of living my life. But everyone has a limit, Ry. Even me. Every girl at some point in her life worries about her imperfections, and even though I know I should be above it, I still feel. I still hurt." She summoned her courage and added, "I've never wanted you to see the sides of me that are weak."

"Ah, Kiva." He blew out a rough breath and stepped forward, bridging the gap between them. They weren't quite touching, but she could feel his warmth, inhale his saltiness. "I don't think worse of you for having a bad day, and that's all this is. One crappy day. I know that even the most capable of people have a limit, but I also don't think your limp or scar or illness is the real issue here. You're hiding behind them." She felt the air squeeze out of her chest. "True, they're the most obvious physical weakness and everyone gets to see and judge you for them. And, yes, it hurts like hell when they do. But they're also a front for the side of you that you keep almost hidden. The side of you that I've only seen in the canvas that's hanging in the art center, where you're almost afraid to *want*, let alone reach out and take. I see in you what you choose to hide from the rest of the world. I see it so clearly. The part that you're so hesitant to let someone in because the risk of getting hurt would be far worse than anything your limp or scar would have ever caused you."

She was back on that precipice again, her stomach coiling round and round. "What are you saying?"

"I'm saying it doesn't have to be that way with me. You can let go because you're safe. I'm not the type of person whose ever been bothered by your limp—not now, not ever. I want you to erase those doubts from your mind because they've never been further from the truth." He looked almost as upset as she felt a few moments ago. She suddenly became light-headed as she felt the ache return to her body. How could she tell him that of all the people that came in and out of her life, he was the one person she feared letting go with the most? That she felt her heart was most vulnerable around him? That, because she loved him so much, she wanted to be her best self around him? And right then and there she certainly did not feel or look her best.

Something in her face must have relayed some of her physical discomfort because he appeared concerned. "You don't look so good, Kiva. Why don't I take you back up to the house?" She nodded gratefully, and he grasped her hand, careful not to agitate the blisters that appeared between her fingers.

"Thank you," she rasped as they walked together, her voice almost completely gone. "Thank you for making today better." He squeezed her hand gently in response. His hand was a warm comfort and Kiva wanted to bottle the steady strength radiating from it. With one hand laced through his and the other gripping her sketchbook, she realized she was sandwiched between the two things she loved the most. And she never wanted to let go.

CHAPTER TWENTY-NINE

Weeks crawled into months and Kiva kept busy with orders for the café. They'd started to close the restaurant to the public on Fridays and Saturdays to host private events, birthdays, and engagements, but no matter how small or intimate these parties initially intended to be, there ended up being so much work going on in the background anyway. She was thankful with the approach of school holidays and the numbers in her art class began to drop as more and more of the kids she taught prepared for their end of term exams. She'd decided to cancel the classes altogether until after the break.

Ry had been jogging to see her every other day. It wasn't planned and Kiva never knew when he would show up, but when he did, their time together would slip into a familiar routine. After he'd appear all sweaty and exhausted, she would prepare a cool drink and sandwich for him. Together they'd sit out on the deck and talk for hours. Sometimes he would tell her an amusing incident that occurred with one of his students that day; other times he would mention the challenges he faced with some of the teachers. She would then regale him with a story or two about one of her customers or that she'd botched up an order when it'd accidently burned in the oven. When Mau would join them, the conversation would switch to rugby or some new legislation. Sometimes Talia and Naomi sat with them under the shade of the bamboo, and Talia would entertain them with skits and songs from Pacific legends and mythologies, giving them a performance worthy of Broadway.

On the weekends Claire would occasionally join them for Sunday lunch, and Kiva started to warm up to her. She quelled her sense of inadequacy when she began to spend time with her and quickly learned that she'd moved from foster home to foster home until the age of ten when she was adopted by an older couple that owned a berry farm. They took care of Claire and treated her as their beloved child when they couldn't have any children of their own. Claire admitted it was rough to begin with, but that they had been patient with her throughout her transition. Something in her story touched Kiva when she started to draw comparisons with her own life. Like her, Claire didn't know her real parents, but she nevertheless lived her life with a cheery disposition appreciating the gift she had been given: a home and loving guardians who wanted her. She'd decided to join the Peace Corps as a volunteer in a genuine effort to help people, particularly children, since she had been helped as a child.

One time Tui stopped by to drop off food from his family. He and Ry hit it off right away and they went to the backyard to blast the bamboo gun together.

Adé came around for lunch a few times, and Kiva learned that he and Ry were planning a trip to New Zealand during the school holidays to go bungee jumping in Queenstown. She wasn't too thrilled about the idea of Ry propelling himself off a bridge, but his excitement made her quash her worry. For the time being.

Kiva savored the moments when it would just be her and Ry. Her days became instantly brighter when he would arrive, their conversations easy and light. As they spent time together, she started to learn more about him, picking up on his mannerisms and habits. When he was amused by something, his eyes would take on a teasing glint. When he was embarrassed, he'd rub the back of his neck, and when he was upset, his eyebrows would furrow together as he gazed absently in the distance trying to calm down.

She became aware that he was an avid reader, too, absorbing everything he could get his hands on in the house from the local newspaper and biographies to Naomi's how-to guides and subscription to Reader's Digest. He would take the books away with him, promising to return them the following week. He explained that reading helped pass the time in the village when nothing else was happening.

While it was obvious they were spending a lot of time together, Kiva was grateful when Naomi didn't raise the question. When Ry would leave after one of his visits, her aunt would simply join her in the kitchen and they'd plan for the following day. When Kiva mentioned she'd like to have someone—she didn't specify who—over for dinner, Naomi didn't miss a beat. She simply arched a brow. "Is this someone a-roast-the-pig over the fire kind of someone or crack-open-a-can of tuna someone?"

216

Kiva couldn't contain her smile. "Definitely roast-the-pig kind of someone."

They didn't end up roasting a pig in the end, since they didn't have any running around their yard like most families, but the spread she and Naomi prepared more than made up for the lack of it. Kiva was concerned Ry wasn't getting enough to eat when she noticed he began to lose weight. He appeared leaner to her. Because he lived on a modest volunteer allowance, and the small village shop nearest to him didn't stock a lot of variety, she knew that his meals were simple. When she asked him about it once, he told her a typical dinner mainly consisted of ramen noodles, spaghetti, or even cereal. So she planned a hearty feast that included a meaty stew, rice, and roasted vegetables with lots of leftovers for him to last a few days.

Sometimes she would catch him watching her, causing her heart to pound, and her attraction to him would grow even more. Love swelled at the oddest moments, and Kiva discovered the more she gave, the more her heart flourished with joy.

He came over to her once and said, "You've been sketching." He lifted his hand and rubbed away a smudge with the pad of his thumb. "I can always tell by this." That simple act alone set fireworks off in her stomach.

One late afternoon, he caught a lift up the hill and came into the yard slinging a bag over his shoulder. Kiva noticed he wasn't his usual disheveled state but freshly showered and dressed in a clean T-shirt and shorts.

"What do you have there?" she asked, puzzled. She closed her art book and tucked it under her arm.

"You'll see." He snatched her hand and continued walking, slowing down so she could keep up. They crossed the garden until they came beside the water tank. "Give me your foot, I'll boost you up."

"Up where?"

He tilted his head toward the tank. She looked between the moss-covered cylinder and back at him and shook her head. "No way. I'm not going up there."

"Why not? It'll be fun."

"I—" she gulped as perspiration broke over her.

"Are you afraid of heights? I figured since you climb that tree over there"—he nodded toward the *pulu*— "you'd be okay with this."

"No, it's not that."

He raised his brows. "Then what is it?" he asked patiently.

"I …" Her pulse thundered in her ears. She was immediately self-conscious but thought miserably that she might as well come out and say it. "I don't want you touching my legs."

Ry was silent. Kiva chanced a glance at him and squirmed under his gaze. He took a step forward, coming toe to toe with her, and dipped his head. "Kiva." His voice was low and thick. "You are a desirable woman." She sucked in a breath as he continued, "Do you know what I want? I want to take that damn pencil out of your hair and bury my hands in there instead. I want to press my lips to your neck to feel your pulse there. I want to map the shape of your beautiful body with my hands." He closed his eyes in frustration, as if to gain control over himself, before opening them again. "There are many things I want with you, Kiva, and touching your legs is the least of them." If she had been left speechless before, she was even more so now. Her heart thudded again and again as she tried to catch her breath. Aware of her riotous inner reaction but choosing to ignore it, he instructed gruffly, "Now give me your foot."

She complied but not without pinching her lips tightly to smother a smile. *Ry just called her a desirable woman! Her. Mativa Mau. The girl with the awkward limp.* Gripping his shoulders, he took hold of her and lifted. "Don't laugh," he grumbled without humor as he hoisted her over the edge.

"I wouldn't dare," she breathed out, trying to sound serious but failing poorly. She landed on her stomach and rolled away from the perimeter. Ry threw the bag over and used the stool she kept for washing the laundry to pull himself up, and before she had a chance to sit upright, he was over her in an instant, pressing her gently back against the concrete. She squeaked in surprise and all traces of humor fled from her mind as she peered up at his dark features. Her heart beat rapidly at the seriousness on his face. He touched the side of her neck, using the pad of his thumb to trace her cheek. Silence stretched between them. Her eyes sought his, seeking an answer to a question she'd been pondering on for so long, an opportunity for the truth.

"Do you know what else I want, Kiva?" he asked hoarsely, gently taking the pencil out of her hair.

"What?" she whispered.

"I want your heart. Not all of it because I know that it also belongs to your art and your family, to your dreams." He touched her jaw gently. "But I want the part that deserves to love and be loved in return. And I would take care of it, Kiva. I would. You just have to let me." He swallowed hard and she watched his Adam's apple rise and fall. "I remember when you mentioned once that everyone's worthy of that kind of love. I went away because I wanted to be worthy of you." She was speechless again, caught between incredulity and affection, as her heart swelled at his proclamation.

"It's always been yours, Ry. Always."

And in that moment when his hand wrapped around the back of her neck and he lowered his head, the space in between was lost and answers were found. His lips captured hers with a drawn breath, where years of yearning and uncertainty were inhaled and exhaled and doubts were chased away, replaced now with a longing spoken only through demanding lips and hands and tears. It was an urgent kiss, one that communicated his love and desire and one where Kiva chanted her own devotion in return, her heart taking flight and soaring like the birds in her canvas, connecting with his heartbeat and impressing onto him her own passion and love before it slowed infinitesimally to a whisper of tender promises that he would cherish and love and take care of her. His gentleness melted through her skin and took her breath away, filling her with a beauty she had never felt before. He pressed his mouth along her jaw, stopping only to catch a tear when it slipped along her cheek, before he whispered words near her ear in a language she had never heard spoken aloud until then. She peered up at the darkening sky through moist eyes and thanked the heavens over and over for this gift, this perfect moment. When Ry lifted his head and met her gaze, his face transformed slowly, from the serious, hard edges she was so used to, to the casual curve of his mouth as it turned upwards into a crooked grin.

"I love you," she whispered.

"I know. I said it in Arabic to you."

She breathed in. "I want to hear it again."

He spoke the lilting words she requested. And then in English and Samoan, before he repeated the process all over again.

Kiva giggled at his poor Samoan pronunciation.

"God, you're so beautiful," Ry responded seriously.

Kiva stopped laughing and looked intently into eyes that held such warmth and love. She smiled softly up at him.

"Are you hungry?" he asked.

"Not really," she breathed.

He grinned. "Come on." He kissed her once on the forehead before moving away. "I intend on keeping my promise to Mau all those years ago about not touching you even though it's really difficult for me not to."

Kiva's cheeks heated at his meaning. She sighed and sat up slowly.

"I respect you, Kiva," he added seriously. "And for now, I'll attempt to show my love to you in other ways." He unzipped the bag and pulled out a *lavalava*. He spread it on the tank's surface and took out a few more items, placing them down on the material.

"What's all this?" she asked, pushing a lose strand behind her ear.

"Since you're always cooking for me, I decided to cook something for you." He took out a small container and popped open the lid. "It's simple but delicious."

She smiled and joined him on the navy sarong, the hue mirroring the darkening sky above.

"This is hummus." He pointed to a thick paste the color of sand. "I found some ingredients from a shop in town and made it last night." He broke off a piece of sliced bread and dipped it in before offering it to her. "Try it."

She accepted the bread and took a bite. The flavors burst in her mouth. "What is this made from?"

"Mostly ground chickpeas, garlic, and lemon. It needs tahini and olive oil as well, but I couldn't find any tahini and olive oil is too expensive."

She licked her fingers. "It's delicious."

He smiled triumphantly and she reached for another piece. "I should try making some for the café. Where did you learn to do this?"

"It's something I picked up when I traveled to Cairo. It's very easy to do. I could teach you."

"Okay." She smiled. "Tell me more about your trip. I love to hear about it."

"What do you want to know?"

"Where you went, what you saw. I want to live vicariously through you."

He smiled. "The entire trip was overwhelming to say the least, but there were some quiet moments when it would just be me. Cairo is an extraordinary, bustling city with over twenty million people. The streets are busy and loud and there are skyscrapers everywhere. I used to visit a place where you could get away from it all. A hill called Mokattam Mountain. They call it a mountain, but it's really only a cliff overlooking the city where you can see the sunset above the smog and buildings. I would purchase coffee from a local vendor and just sit and watch and think. I realized for the first time I was in a place where I looked like the people around me, where there was no animosity, no suspicion, and I was completely at ease.

"In Dubai, my father took me to all the tourist sights. We went to grand hotels and restaurants, and tried camel riding. We ate out in the desert with oriental rugs under our legs and the stars above us. I even tried smoking the hookah, which was delicious and addictive and very hard to put down." He turned his head and faced her. "And everywhere I went, Kiva, you were with me. I imagined looking at things through your artist eyes. You would have seen beauty in everything. People's faces, their sunbaked skin, the wrinkles. The colors and flavors. All of it would have come alive under your hands."

Kiva imagined him in aviator sunglasses among dusty sand dunes, his neck wrapped in a red and white scarf with dark stubble on his jaw, hair mussed from the wind. He was an incredibly attractive man and he wanted her. *Her.* He'd kissed her with both fervor and tenderness and spoke words she had only imagined hearing. She'd never known a joy so incredible until this moment and it made her heart sing. How could it be possible that someone could feel so happy? She beamed until her cheeks hurt. She suddenly wanted everyone to have what she had. Certainly the world would be a better place if they experienced a fraction of this indescribable elation. Everything was heightened ... her senses, her emotions, her vulnerability, all of it was both thrilling and frightening at the same time.

"I want to show you something." She picked up her sketchbook from where it landed on the water tank and handed it to him.

He angled his head. "Is this what I think it is?"

"Open it and find out."

His mouth tugged upwards. "You're always carrying this around. I was beginning to think it was attached to one of your limbs."

She laughed. "In many ways it has been."

Ry opened her art book. He leafed through the pages, pausing now and then to admire a sketch or to read a poem, until he came upon the drawing of his hand.

He stilled and looked up at her. "Is this ...?"

Kiva nodded and her heart skipped a beat. "I did that when I was trying to figure you out." She told him about her dream and about the pearl. "You were such a mystery and I couldn't help it. Hands tell a story, and I knew there must have been an interesting one behind yours."

"They're what got me here in the first place," he said without emotion.

She reached over and very slowly touched his hand. She explored the raised veins and knuckles before she threaded her fingers through his own. It was a perfect fit, her small hands melding together with his large ones, his hand wrapping around hers protectively.

"I've always wanted to do that," she spoke softly. It felt incredible to have his hand engulfing hers. She felt loved, cherished.

He brought her hand to his mouth and kissed the back of it. "Me, too." His breath feathered across her skin and her heart bloomed.

They ate the hummus with diced salad and pickles under the dusky sky and talked about his college experience. He told her about the never-ending study hours where night became day and day became night, and how he had been challenged beyond anything else he'd ever done before. How he witnessed students darting across campus in their pajamas after pulling an all-nighter to hand in an assignment. Kiva laughed when he told her stories of some the pranks he'd pulled on some of his dorm friends.

When she quieted, she looked off into the distance, imagining herself on a campus somewhere.

"You could still go, you know," he said softly, interpreting the reason for her silence.

She turned to him. "I know ... but I'm afraid it'll change me."

He furrowed his brows. "What do you mean?"

"My best friend's recently returned from university and she's struggling to find herself between two countries and two very different cultures. Her parents are having a hard time accepting who she's become. What if the same thing happens to me?"

"Kiva, of course change is inevitable when you take yourself out of your comfort zone and enter a new environment. It'll happen because you'll adapt and grow as a person with both knowledge and awareness of the world around you."

"But ... what if I come back a different person and I'm not what you want?"

"Is that what scares you?"

"What scares me is the thought of losing you ... losing my heart to you all over again and then you leave."

He took her hand. "I don't know where the future will take us, Kiva, but I know without a doubt that I want us in it together."

"I want that, too."

"Good." He smirked. "Then we'll adapt to whatever comes." He drew her closer. "But for now let's not talk about leaving. No one's going anywhere. I've just got you, and I'm not letting you go anytime soon."

She smiled and leaned into him. She had no intention of going anywhere either, and every intention of spending her evenings just like this.

CHAPTER THIRTY

A letter arrived inconspicuously the following day in an ivory-hued envelope with her aunt's name scrawled elegantly on the front. Kiva knew something wasn't right when she stepped into the house and saw Naomi's face. She looked up from the dining room table, her skin pale.

"What is it?" Kiva asked, moving forward with her art book in her hands. She'd just been outside sketching in the *pulu*.

Naomi tried to smile but Kiva didn't miss the strain around her eyes. "It's a letter from Viola. Your mother."

Her mother? What did she want? Kiva furrowed her brows and dropped into the chair next to her. "What does the letter say?"

"She sent a plane ticket. She wants you to visit her in London."

Kiva reeled back. "What? Why?"

"I don't know why."

Kiva reached for the letter at the same time Naomi slid it across the table to her. Her hands shook as she scanned the text first, noting the neat, cursive handwriting. It wasn't very long, and she got a whiff of something sweet and musky, before she started to read.

Dear Naomi,

I know this letter will come as a surprise to you since I have never been good at keeping in touch all these years. Nevertheless, I feel compelled to write and request that Mativa visit me here in London. I would very much like to spend time with her. You will find enclosed plane tickets and a check to assist with the necessary visas and for her safe travels. You can rest assured that Leon and I will take care of her once she has reached our home. I will await your response.

Your sister, Viola

Kiva's heart was pounding. The letter sounded almost cold and business-like. Who was this woman? She read and reread the letter several times over, trying to decipher its meaning and came up with nothing. Viola had signed it off with a phone number for Naomi to reach her.

"I don't understand," she finally said, looking over at Naomi.

"You don't have to go if you don't want to, Kiva."

"I don't know what I want." She was so confused. "Why does she want to see me? And why didn't she just call first?"

"Letters are more dramatic. She knew we would need time to think about it."

Kiva glanced at the ticket and the check with the generous amount typed in bold. The ticket dates were open, which meant she could decide on her own when and if she wanted to go. "She's your sister, Naomi. But you're my mother," she said, trying to sound reassuring for Naomi but more for herself.

Naomi smiled and reached for her hand. "I know that, Kiva. I've never doubted that for a second."

"Will you tell me what happened? Who was my father?"

Naomi considered her quietly. "You want to talk about this now?"

Kiva nodded. "I don't want any more secrets."

"How much do you know?"

Kiva fidgeted slightly. "I know that they had an affair and it ended badly."

"Did Hana tell you that?"

She nodded. "It was a long time ago."

Naomi sighed. "She should not have told you. I have a feeling that whatever Viola wants to say to you will include all of this."

Kiva leaned back and released a tightly held breath. "I don't know if I feel comfortable going. I don't even know her." She felt her stomach knot with anxiety.

"I'll tell you this. If you decide to stay, then I can tell you what I know. But if you choose to go, Viola will disclose a lot more than I ever could, especially since she's requested to see you."

Kiva's brows puckered. "But why did she leave in the first place? Why all of this awkward secrecy? And why didn't the two of you remain in touch?"

Naomi peered at her tiredly. "I tried. For years I tried. I sent her letters and photographs, but she never responded. Viola was always in search of something more. She was never content as a child growing up and even more so as an adult. She had a wild spirit in her and combined with her beauty, it was a lethal combination. She was more beautiful than anyone in the whole district. Men wanted her while women envied her, and she became isolated as a result. Her beauty was intimidating and kept the people she needed the most away, while the people who desired her were drawn closer and closer until that's all she had left. Beautiful or not, people judged her harshly. She suffered because of her face, and then later on because of her actions.

"I tried talking to her, getting close to her, but she always pushed me away.

"This affair with your father … when he left and she found out she was pregnant, it was the final straw.

"I don't know what to say other than perhaps I failed her as a sister, or that the entire extended family failed her as well. We didn't want to stir gossip, but that's exactly what happened anyway. The whole village knew."

"You didn't fail her, Naomi. You did more—much more—when you took me." Kiva held her gaze to emphasize her point. She gripped the letter in her hand. "But what should I do now?" she asked.

"Whatever you want to do, Kiva. You're an adult now and you have the right to questions and answers that pertain to your life."

Kiva smoothed the letter back on the table. "I need to think about this."

"Alright. You do that. In the meantime I need a drink." She started to rise. "I just wish I had something stronger than tea since we're all out of *koko*."

Kiva gathered the contents of the letter and shoved them inside the envelope. She placed it carefully inside the folds of her sketchbook and walked to the kitchen. Naomi stared absently out the window. The kettle hadn't yet been put on and there was no mug on the countertop.

"Are you alright?" Kiva asked.

Naomi turned and smiled sadly. "I was just thinking." She reached for the pot and filled it with water. "Whatever happens, Kiva, I want you to know that you will always have a home here with us. Never forget that."

Kiva stilled. "You think I should go."

"I think it's time, yes. Time to open that chapter and close it once and for all."

Kiva expelled a breath. She needed time to think, to talk. She needed to see Ry.

She left Naomi with assurances that she'd think it over seriously, and stepped out of the house. Limping toward the main road, she hoped to meet him. The road was quiet without a vehicle in sight, and the thick brush on either side swayed with the wind. The sketchbook was tucked under her arm, the letter from Viola inserted safely inside. She saw Ry approach from the distance and her heart picked up. He was walking but as soon as he saw her, he started to jog. She limped faster to reach him.

"What is it? What's wrong?" he asked with concern when they finally met and he saw her face.

"I needed to see you."

He immediately pulled her into his arms and tucked her head under his chin. "Better?" he asked. She smiled against his neck and nodded. He smelled of sea salt, sweat, and deodorant, and she instantly calmed.

Taking a few steady breaths, she finally spoke, her words muffled against his chest. "I got something in the mail." Kiva took a step back and pulled the envelope out of the art book.

Ry glanced up when he was done reading the letter. They'd moved under the shade of a tree, not far from the side of the road.

"What do you want to do?" he asked. "Do you want to go see her?"

"I think I should." Kiva nervously wrung her hands together. "She'll tell me things if I go. But what if it's too painful to hear?"

"Then you call on the part of you that makes you strong and resilient, the part that knows exactly who you are and where you've come from. The girl from the canvas."

She swallowed thickly. "Were you afraid when you went to Dubai?"

"Of course I was. I had no idea what to expect from my father, if he would even like me or just simply tolerate me until I left. The fact that Viola's requested to see you means that she wants to do this."

"Yes … I suppose you're right." Her voice was hesitant.

"Do you want me to come with you?"

She was taken aback. "What—to London?"

"Sure."

"No, you couldn't. You have school and then you have plans to go to Queenstown with Adé."

Ry was quiet as he looked out toward the thick pasture that surrounded them and stretched for miles. "Will you come back?"

She almost laughed. "Of course I will. This is my home. And you're here." Her forehead crinkled in question. "Why do you ask?"

He took a deep breath and let it go. "It's just that … it's London. City of art and history, of opportunity. You might like it there a lot more than you realize." He gestured to the envelope. "And by the looks of it, Viola has no problem supporting you."

Kiva took a step forward and peered up at him. "Ry, I'm coming back. Whatever happens between now and then, I promise you that."

He nodded seriously, contemplatively. "I don't like to be selfish, but I can't help it when it comes to you." He glanced up and pinned her with a conflicted look. "If she offers you the chance to go to art school, though, I want you to take it."

"Ry—"

"Kiva, promise me."

"She's not going to—"

"She might."

"Why are you doing this?"

"Because as much as it'll kill me if you chose to remain there, it would kill me even more if I prevented your dreams from coming true … if I was somehow responsible for holding you back."

She sucked in a breath. "You're my dream, too, Ry."

He touched her cheek gently, his smile sad and wistful.

Kiva let out an audible breath. "This is silly. Why are we even talking about this? This whole scenario is crazy with no basis whatsoever, so let's just forget about the what-ifs, okay? You're here. I'm here. That's all that matters. I'm going to go see her and come back, okay?"

"Okay," he said unconvincingly.

Her voice softened. "We'll adapt to whatever comes, remember?"

Ry gathered her in his arms. "I remember." He bent down and kissed her tenderly on the lips, gathering his willpower to communicate to her everything he didn't say aloud in words … *I love you … We'll get through this … We're going to be okay.*

She sighed and melted into him and for one breathtaking moment forgot about everything around them. She forgot about the letter and Viola. She forgot about the impending trip. She forgot, too, about her anxiety and simply clung onto the love emanating from Ry, drawing strength from him.

Her bravado lasted all of four and a half hours.

Later that night, as she lay in bed glancing up at the shadows that played on the ceiling, she didn't feel so confident anymore. A knot of worry settled in the pit of her stomach, preventing her from falling asleep. Questions plagued her mind. Questions about Viola. About what she wanted. About what she would say. About her own reaction. What were they even going to do together? She didn't know this person at all except that she was an estranged family member.

When she knew she wasn't going to be getting any sleep, Kiva threw off the sheet and went downstairs into the kitchen. A quick glance at the clock on the wall told her it was three-twenty in the morning. Sighing aloud, she decided she might as well start baking for the café.

When an hour and a half passed and she'd managed to complete two trays of cupcakes, baked a dozen banana muffins, and rolled several butter croissants, Kiva collapsed on the couch and closed her eyes. She listened to the sounds of the house waking up and the distant crowing of a rooster. She knew Naomi would be up soon, and she waited patiently for her to come down, rehearsing the lines in her head over and over. She decided she would go to London—and the sooner the better—to apprise herself of this whole mystery and to hopefully bring closure for herself and Naomi.

It wasn't Naomi that came down the stairs, but Hana. Kiva peered up at her in surprise when she plopped herself on the couch opposite her. Her hair was in a messy bun on the top of her head and her clothes were wrinkled from sleep.

"Hey," she said quietly, so as not to wake anyone, her voice groggy. "You look like you got attacked by a spatula."

"Thanks." Kiva's lips curved. "And you look like you just stepped out of a magazine."

Hana snorted and lay back on the couch. She stretched and groaned. "I didn't sleep well. Talia kept kicking me in the back. My poor kidneys got a beating."

"Is she still asleep?"

"Out like a light."

"I couldn't sleep either." Kiva sighed.

Hana turned her head. "I heard about the letter from Viola. Are you going to see her?"

"Yeah ... I think I should."

Hana glanced up at the ceiling and was quiet a moment before she finally spoke in a soft voice. "I couldn't imagine giving up Talia. I know that the support I've received from all of you has made the difference, but I believe that even if it weren't there, it would still be incredibly difficult to give her away. If I absolutely had to though, for whatever reason beyond my control, I would probably give her to someone I grew up with. Someone I could trust." Kiva's heart raced at her insinuation. "That's what Viola did," she continued. "She did what so many women do in this country with their children. They give them to their sisters, their aunts, and grandmothers to raise. An entire extended family will look after a child and it's perfectly acceptable. The only difference here is that your mother stayed away from hers."

"I don't think I can bring her back, Hana, if that's what you're thinking. She has a life there, a partner, and I'm only going to be a part of it for a short period of time."

"I know. It's just that … I feel like I understand a part of her."

Kiva glanced at her cousin and realized there were many sides of her she would probably never know. Dawn's light crept into the room, basking everything in warmth, and she closed her eyes against the approaching trip and the unnerving reunion that would result.

CHAPTER THIRTY-ONE

Kiva clenched and unclenched her fists nervously in her lap as she gazed out the window of the plane. After her trip to Brisbane, she decided with a hundred percent certainty that she didn't like flying. She was so cold. She shivered from the air-conditioning above and rearranged the blanket on her lap, tucking the corners more snugly around her legs. They hadn't taken off yet, and she was already dreading the experience. Now she was going to be spending the next thirty hours traveling to London. What had she been thinking? She was seated next to a burly man whose hairless arm spooned her own along the armrest. Kiva was thankful she had the wall to lean into, but when it brought her flush against the window and she began to think of the layers of glass that separated her from the atmosphere outside, she started to panic a little on the inside. Resting her head against the seat, she closed her eyes and took slow, even breaths.

Her thoughts immediately flew to Ry.

They'd said goodbye to each other earlier that day and she already missed him. He and Adé were flying out the next day, the school holidays already upon them, and she made him promise to be careful when they went bungee jumping. She later learned that Claire would be joining them on their trip and the thought of them altogether on vacation made her stomach clench. She couldn't help it.

She and Ry would be apart for three weeks. Twenty-one days. How was she going to endure that time without him?

"Is this your first time flying?" the man next to her interrupted.

Kiva opened her eyes and turned her head only. "No," she answered politely. "It's my second."

"You don't look well."

"I'm fine … I'm just a little nervous."

He patted her arm comfortingly. "Don't worry. It's only four hours to Auckland. Go to sleep and the time will pass quickly."

Kiva heaved a sigh and looked out the window. She could make out some of the runway lights and beyond that the glimmer of the ocean as it sparkled in the moonlight. It was nearing midnight, and the flight had been delayed over an hour. She thought ahead to her journey, which would take her from Auckland to Hong Kong, and then finally to London, and she prayed everything would go smoothly without further delays.

Several weeks earlier, Naomi had contacted Viola to inform her that Kiva would be coming to see her. Kiva wasn't privy to that conversation and wasn't aware of what passed between them, but when Naomi hung up the phone, she seemed more at ease with the idea, which made her a little more calm as well.

She packed light for the trip—there weren't many shops in town that stocked for cool weather—and she took a few art pieces as gifts. She felt awkward at first. After all, what did one gift the woman who gave birth to her and then gave her up? But Naomi insisted on taking something from the art center, a few wooden artifacts and printed *siapo*, out of politeness. The woman was too kindhearted.

The captain crackled over the intercom and informed the passengers they were going to be taking off shortly. Kiva fumbled for her seatbelt, checking to make sure it was buckled, before she gripped the armrest closest to the window. The man beside her was already dozing, his snorts and snores, pricking her nerves.

A flight attendant passed by carrying out a final check before the lights were dimmed and they were taxing down the runway. The plane picked up speed and Kiva's pounding heart was muted against the roar of the engines. Her stomach dropped as it lifted off and cleared the ground. Her head swooned, and she closed her eyes again, counting to ten. The aircraft shook and she sucked in a breath. *Oh God. Oh God. Oh God.* When it leveled out and the lights came back on, she felt like throwing up. The man beside her woke with a grunt. He unbuckled his belt and rushed to the bathroom. Kiva turned toward the window again and watched the clouds drift by like eerie ghosts. She grasped the armrest in an attempt to ground herself to something solid. Her hands and body were so cold. Doubts invaded her mind and she started to question her decision to travel. What was she thinking? What was Viola going to be like? Would she like her? Could her heart take another hit?

How was she going to survive two long-distance flights? How much longer until they landed? She heard movement beside her. The muffle of people's voices. Someone's laughter. The thrum of the engine. She inhaled sharply, her heart banging wildly against her ribs, when she felt a firm hand on hers and a familiar voice saying, "Just breathe, Kiva."

She turned and gasped. "Ry—what? How?"

"Jesus, your hands are freezing." He took both of her hands between his own and rubbed warmth into them.

"What are you doing here?" she finally managed out.

"I asked the gentleman sitting next to you to swap seats with me. I figured he'd appreciate the exit seat more."

Kiva blinked and glanced down at his long legs, which were squished up against the seat in front of him. What was he *doing* here? Sitting next to her, *on the same plane?* "How are you here? And where's Adé and Claire?"

"They'll fly out tomorrow. I just moved my flight one day forward to be with you."

Her breath caught. "You really did that?"

He gave her a slow, steady grin. "Surprise."

She threw herself into his arms and buried her head into his neck. He smelled incredible. Like a mixture of soap and roasted cocoa. Of everything familiar. Of home.

She felt his chest rumble with soft laughter. "So I guess you're happy to see me."

She pulled back. "More than happy." She swallowed hard. "This was a bad idea, Ry. I can't do this anymore."

He squeezed her hand reassuringly. "What are you afraid of? The flying part or what awaits you in London?"

"Both. But right now, mostly the flying. I've been having heart palpitations every time the plane shakes." Ry smothered a smile.

The plane suddenly dipped and Kiva inhaled sharply. She dug her fingernails into his arm and held on tight.

Ry winced slightly. "Okay, Kiva, before you claw me to death, I'm going to explain a few things to you." He very gently removed her hand and grasped it within his own. With his free hand, he withdrew a pen from his shirt pocket and asked a passing flight attendant for a napkin.

"What are you doing?" Kiva asked, curious.

"You'll see."

The flight attendant returned with a napkin, and Ry took it from him, unlatching the tray in the seat in front of him. Placing the napkin on the surface, he started to draw a bird's-eye view of an aircraft. "Let's imagine this is our plane," he started. "Air flows horizontally in what's called a jet stream." He drew lines in what Kiva imagined was the air stream. "Imagine air like a river. If we wanted to save energy, we'd try to flow with the current, not against it. It's the same with flying. Pilots will align the jet with the flow of wind that's heading in the direction of their destination to save time and fuel costs. However, like a river if it suddenly merged with another stream and caused the boat to rock a little, the jet stream would likewise cause turbulence on a plane if it suddenly mixed with slower-moving air. It's just air not getting along very well."

Kiva tilted her head in disbelief. "That's it?"

"That's all there is to it."

"And it's normal?"

"It's perfectly normal."

She felt the tension in her body give way to relief. "And all this time I thought it was a sign we were going to crash."

He shook his head. "Not going to happen. Pilots will try to maneuver their way out of it for the comfort and safety of passengers, in the same way a bus driver will avoid pot holes on the road, but a degree of turbulence is always expected on flights."

She sighed and leaned into him. "You make it sound so normal when all along I've been in a little panic." His posture caught her attention, his long legs braced apart and bent at an awkward angle to fit into the crammed space. "You don't look very comfortable," she said in concern. "I'm sorry you had to give up your exit seat."

"A little discomfort is a small price to pay when I get to sit next to you."

She smiled against his shoulder. "I'm glad you're here."

"Me, too. Go to sleep if you're tired."

She shook her head. "No way. I don't want to waste what little time I have with you." He moved his mouth to her forehead and pressed his lips to it.

"About your other fear in London"—he said against her skin and she tensed slightly—"if you want me to come with you, just say the words, and I'll change my flight in Auckland. You don't have to do this alone."

Her breath hitched, forming a tight knot in her throat. She was incredibly moved by his sincere offer and wanted nothing more than for him to join her, but she knew that it wasn't possible. That it would be too much of a sacrifice for him, since he lived on a humble allowance. But the biggest reason, she realized, was that she needed to face this challenge on her own. She wanted to prove that she could handle it alone, that she was a strong enough person who could keep it together. She knew she had the unwavering love and support of Ry and Naomi to strengthen her along the way, and she bottled this inside of her where the imminent truth of her past could not affect it. It would be sufficient because they were the most important people in her life. But that didn't mean she wasn't wary of what lies ahead. She was about to meet her mother. The woman whose body carried and prepared her for this life. And what a life it turned out to be. Kiva reflected on the nature of motherhood and how a child's first human connection was with her mother. That connection transcended the physical into something noble, spiritual, and it was unmistakable that she had that with Naomi. She could forgive Viola for severing that tie. After all, the life Kiva traded for would not have been as enriching. She would not have had her art or café or met Ry. She would not have known his tender, protective love. She knew he would try to shelter her from every anticipated difficulty if he could, like he was trying to do now, but she recognized that she couldn't be saved from the truth.

She peered up at him and his brown eyes were questioning, expecting a response from her. "Ry, I think I need to go alone. I just need to face this and then I can move on. I'll be fine, really."

He searched her eyes to make certain she spoke the truth before finally drawing her close. He didn't say anything but held her tight, and Kiva relaxed in his embrace, closing her eyes. Exhaustion quickly overtook her and she slipped into a dreamless sleep.

She awoke to a dim cabin and the sounds of people snoring around her. She shifted in Ry's arms and he stirred awake. "Sorry. I didn't mean to fall asleep," she rasped.

"It's okay. You needed the rest." His voice was rough from sleep also.

"How long was I out?"

"Over two hours." He checked his watch. "We're going to land in an hour. Are you hungry? They served dinner while you were sleeping, and I asked them to hold onto it for you."

She shook her head. "I'm okay, thanks. I just need to use the bathroom." She straightened in her chair, feeling the muscles in her back protest from leaning over. Unbuckling her belt, she stood and started to climb over Ry to get to the aisle. He leaned as far back as he could in his seat, the corner of his mouth twitching in amusement. "You know, it'd be easier if you just got out so I could too," she said, trying not to smile.

"Why?" He smirked. "This is way more fun."

She shook her head, chuckling. Bracing her arms on his shoulders, she attempted to maneuver her way over. With very little effort, he helped lift her onto the aisle, and Kiva stood unsteadily on her feet before she was able to find her balance. She hobbled toward the rear end of the plane where the washroom was thankfully available. After she washed up, she glanced at her reflection in the mirror and noticed her hair was a frightful mess. She pulled the pencil out and used her fingers to comb out the tangles. Choosing to wear it down, she unlatched the door and headed back up the aisle.

When she returned, Ry had moved over to the window seat. He'd ordered her a fruit juice and she took it from him, finishing it in a few gulps. Leaning against the headrest, she allowed her thoughts to wander to Viola and her stomach once again clenched in anxiety. Ry gripped her hand comfortingly and she gave him a wan smile.

In no time at all, the cabin crew were preparing them for landing and Kiva peered around Ry's shoulder to catch a glimpse of Auckland city through the window. The clouds drifted away to reveal clusters of homes and roads. The early morning sun broke out on the horizon, casting long shadows across the ground.

"We don't have a lot of time left," he murmured quietly.

She tried to put on a brave face. "You sound as if we won't be seeing each other in about a month."

"It'll be the longest month of my life."

"When is your next flight to Queenstown?"

Ry shook his head. "I'm spending the night in the city at some backpackers I found online until Adé and Claire arrive tomorrow. We'll rent a car and drive down south together."

"You're *driving* to Queenstown?" He nodded in response. "That's a long trip."

"We have time, and we'll stop in some towns along the way, take in the sights."

Kiva sighed. "Well, my next flight to Hong Kong isn't for a few hours. We have at least that time to spend together."

The plane landed smoothly and they deplaned hand in hand, passing departure gates and duty-free shops, scurrying passengers and crying children. Her limp drew a few stares from some people, and when Ry noticed them gawking, he bent down and kissed her tenderly on the forehead. After they cleared customs and immigration, he led her to a café in the arrivals' area, which was bustling with people for the early hour. They ordered coffee and sandwiches and sat side by side overlooking the busy terminal. They were quiet as they watched families colliding in hugs, the helium balloons they carried bobbing above their heads. One young couple embraced as tears streamed down the woman's face. The man held her close, burying his head into the curve of her shoulder. Ry was pensive as he gazed at them.

Kiva touched his arm and asked, "What are you thinking about?"

His brows dipped in thought. "There are three things I know to be true," he rasped in a low voice. "One, I will never acquire the taste of slimy banana soup—*suafa'i*—no matter how many times it's shoved in my face in the staffroom and I politely end up eating it anyway." Kiva's mouth tilted into a smile. "Two, my life would have taken a very different path if I hadn't been sent to Samoa six years ago. I recognize now that it means nothing if I don't live it for others, which brings me to number three." He glanced up, pinning her with a serious look. "You have been the one constant in my life. Through all of the crap and bullshit that goes on in this world, you've shown me what it means to love and let go and be in control of my decisions. When we were apart, there was only you. I know that I bring my faults and flaws and ego into this relationship, but I love you, Kiva, with what little good I have in me, I love you so much." His eyes wrestled with emotion: despair, uncertainty, hope. "I realize that we'll be apart for three weeks, but I can't shake this ominous feeling that it might be more. I don't want to propose like this …" Her pulse jumped and he took her trembling hand within his own, rubbing them gently to make them warm. "I don't want you to feel that I'm pressuring you, especially because we're about to say goodbye, but I also don't want you to leave without knowing how I feel. I have nothing to offer you, I don't even have a ring, but I want to be there for you and with you every day of our lives, Kiva. I see you so clearly in my future. I know that we've come from broken homes and unconventional families, but together we can create a happy one of our own. When I walk away from you today, I want to know that we have this to look forward to. That we have something real to work toward." He swallowed hard and looked at her with raw, honest emotion.

Kiva inched forward and framed his strong jaw with her delicate hands, feeling the overnight growth of stubble under her fingertips. She pressed her lips to his cheek and closed her eyes, feeling as if her heart was simultaneously breaking and filling up with hope again. She whispered, "I have the same dream, Ry."

They said goodbye to each other at the entrance to international departures under a billboard that wished passengers a safe journey. Kiva wrapped her arms around Ry's waist and rested her head on his chest until she memorized his scent. She felt his heart beat strong and steady through his shirt, and it calmed her instantly. They'd spent hours planning out their lives on little white napkins the café provided. Ambitious ideas came to life under his architect's hand, and she was more than happy to relinquish the sketching for once to him. They planned to travel to exotic destinations together and build a home that he would design from natural resources. The words *art studio*, *marriage*, and *babies* were exchanged in the early morning light in a place where new beginnings formed and people reunited around them. The blueprint for a life together with Ry made Kiva's heart leap with excitement, and it didn't escape her notice that she was opening a new chapter at a moment in her life when she was on a journey to close one from her past.

Ry cupped her face with his hands and everything else disappeared around them. The corners of his mouth tipped up into a crooked grin and his brown eyes softened with affection. "I'll see you soon, bamboo girl." His simple statement was a promise of great things to come and Kiva couldn't wait to experience them all with him.

She left him standing with his hands shoved in his jeans' pockets as she limped toward the area that separated the passengers from loved ones left behind. She turned around once to see that he was still watching her with a rueful expression on his face until she disappeared from view.

CHAPTER THIRTY-TWO

Kiva saw her first.

Dressed impeccably in a silk blouse, ivory pants, and high heels, she took in the sight of her mother through the shifting crowd in the airport. Her hair was cropped to her shoulders and blow-dried to perfection, the curls on the ends bouncing when she turned her head, no doubt scanning the arrivals' terminal for her. She'd dyed it blonde and looked nothing like the picture Naomi had shown Kiva before she left. Of course the woman before her now was years older, her body more round, her expression smooth and guarded. She stood next to a tall, lanky man she guessed was Leon from the letter. He had a friendly face with laugh lines carved around his mouth, and hair that was graying along the sides. Kiva liked him immediately.

With a shuddering breath, she pushed the trolley toward them and watched when Viola finally noticed her. Viola froze for a moment, and Kiva didn't miss the slight widening of her eyes and the sudden rise and fall of her chest. She was as nervous as Kiva felt. Leon's face, however, broke out into a smile.

"You must be Mativa," he said warmly when she stopped in front of them.

"Please, call me Kiva," she answered. Her throat was clogged with tension, and she was amazed she could even speak.

Leon then did something that took her by complete surprise. Drawing her into his arms, he gave her a heartfelt bear hug. His hands patted her on the back comfortingly and Kiva imagined this was probably what a father's embrace was like. Mau had never been affectionate in that way, but then he never had to be.

"It's good to finally meet you, Kiva," he said when he pulled away. She couldn't place his accent, a mixture between American and British, and she smiled warmly in response.

She glanced nervously toward Viola and her stomach twisted in knots.

Viola took a tentative step forward and bent down to peck her on the cheek. It wasn't the same depth of warmth Kiva felt from Leon, but it was enough so as not to be overwhelming. "I'm glad you accepted the invitation to visit us." Viola's voice was low and throaty. "We have a lot to catch up on, but you must be tired after your long trip. Let's go to the house and you can have a rest."

Kiva nodded jerkily. Moving was good. Her nerves could manage walking because her body probably couldn't handle standing steady in one place. Leon took the trolley from her as they led the way toward the exit and underground car park. He unlocked the doors to a black Audi, and Kiva slid into the backset, admiring the cream leather interior. She clasped her hands in her lap for fear of touching anything by mistake and getting it dirty. She felt filthy after traveling for two days.

The house was really an estate in the rural outskirts of the city. A gravel road lined with impressive trees snaked its way from the imposing iron gate and helped prepare Kiva for the grandiose two-story building that came into view. Her eyes drifted from the red brick exterior to the arched glass windows, until she glanced up at the slanted roof and counted five chimneys. She realized that she had very little knowledge about what Viola and Leon did for a living, but whatever it was, it was obvious that they were more than comfortable.

The car rolled to a stop beside the front steps and Viola got out first, ushering her into the house. The inside was modern in comparison to the exterior and tastefully decorated. An ornate silver mirror the length of Kiva hung in the hallway where a white potted orchid sat atop a glass console table below it. The wallpaper behind the furniture was of a blue filigree design, and Kiva traced the patterns with her eyes. She had taken her shoes off by the door out of habit, and the plush white carpet was soft beneath her grimy feet. She felt like an intruder in such an extravagant setting and was instantly reminded that she desperately needed a shower.

Viola came beside her and spoke kindly, "Welcome to our home, Kiva. While you are here, consider this your home, too. I'll take you to the room you'll be staying in. There's an en suite so you can freshen up before dinner. You must be hungry. Leon will prepare the meal. You will soon learn that he is the cook around here." Kiva wasn't really hungry, her stomach coiled tight from a combination of nerves and jet lag, but she wasn't about to say that out loud. "Follow me," Viola instructed.

Kiva plucked her suitcase from where it was deposited on the floor and trailed behind Viola as she climbed the windy staircase that led to the second floor.

Her room was down a wide corridor, and Viola pointed to a door they passed on the left. "That's the spare office. You're free to use the laptop in there whenever you'd like. The house has Wi-Fi and the password is written beside the keyboard." That was good, Kiva thought with relief. She couldn't wait to send an email to Ry to inform him that she'd arrived safe. She missed him and wanted to know that he was okay and the road trip was going well. "This will be your room," Viola opened the door to reveal a room twice the size of hers back home. "I call it the Blue Room because it reminds me of the ocean." The colors were muted grays and blues like the name suggested, and Kiva stepped over the threshold, taking in the queen-sized bed and matching furniture. "I hope you'll be comfortable in here," Viola added.

"I really like it," Kiva murmured, turning in a full circle. The room exuded a quiet serenity and stillness, things she had not been feeling since she left Ry. An image on the wall caught her attention, and she walked over to it. It was a portrait of a woman's face and she was partially covered by wind-tossed hair. "Who sketched this?" she asked in awe.

Viola came to stand beside her. "A friend of mine. When Naomi called to tell me you were coming, she informed me that you are also a sketch artist and that you love art. If you'd like, we can visit some art galleries in the city."

Kiva swallowed. Viola really had no idea who she was or what she loved to do. What her dreams and aspirations were and how she chose to spend her time. She was acutely aware that they were alone for the first time since she arrived, and anxiety spiked in her stomach. Kiva looked at Viola expectantly ... expecting *what*, she wasn't sure. There was no guidebook about how to behave in these situations and she couldn't help feeling lost. Naomi had told her to simply be herself and to help wherever she could in the house. She shifted awkwardly on her feet, and Viola's eyes flew to her uneven legs. Now *that* was something she knew. Kiva inhaled sharply and felt for the first time since she left Auckland like she was being scrutinized. She shoved her insecurities deep down and willed her heart to slow.

"I'd like that," she finally responded to her suggestion, a little shakier than she expected.

Viola's eyes roved the scar on her arm. "What happened there?"

Kiva's hand touched the disfigured skin, squeezing the flesh unconsciously. "It was from a bus accident years ago. I'm fine now."

Viola gave a curt nod. "Well then"—she cleared her throat—"I'll leave you to freshen up. There are clean towels in the bathroom and shampoo and conditioner under the sink. I'll go downstairs to see how Leon is doing. Is there anything you can't eat?" Kiva shook her head. Viola gave her a wan smile. "Take your time. We'll eat when you come down." She walked to the door and closed it behind her.

Kiva let out a shuddering breath and felt her eyes sting with tears. She dashed them away with trembling hands and bit her bottom lip. *Keep it together,* she tried telling herself, but the overwhelming sense of loneliness, confusion, and exhaustion—coupled with the fact that she missed Ry and everything familiar back home—became too much for her control. She broke down in the middle of the room, stifling her sobs with the palms of her hands. What was she doing here? What was the purpose? It was all so … *weird* and confusing. She didn't know these people, and they certainly didn't know her. She was suddenly counting down the days until she could leave. Maybe she could cut the trip short. Her cries turned into hiccups. Ten minutes, she told herself. She would allow herself to cry for ten minutes and then she was going to pick herself up off the floor and take a shower. She wondered what time it was in New Zealand and Samoa. She wanted to use the laptop in the office to write to Naomi and Ry separately, but only after she was clean and showered. That gave her the incentive to stand up and walk toward the bathroom.

Twenty minutes later she was sitting in the office typing an email to Ry. She tried to be strong, but she couldn't help breaking down and telling him of her apprehension about this whole trip and the feeling of utter loss she was experiencing. She wished now he was there with her, and she told him so. She wrote to Naomi next, but not with so much angst. She didn't want her to worry.

Feeling a little better now that she was dressed in clean clothes and her skin and hair smelled like roses, she logged out and headed downstairs. She followed the sound of cutlery clattering and found her way into the kitchen. Leon stood behind a granite kitchen island shredding cheese into a large bowl of pasta.

"Kiva." He beamed. "You're just in time. Are you hungry?" She was, and she was feeling especially tired now that she had purged her emotions out to Ry. Her stomach grumbled loudly in response and she covered it. Her cheeks heated and Leon laughed. It was a sincere, hearty laugh, not one meant to embarrass her, and she instantly relaxed. "I'll take that as a yes," he said with a smile.

She rounded the island. "Can I help?" she offered.

"Sure. You can help set the table."

Kiva sighed in relief. She didn't want to be treated as an awkward guest and jumped at the opportunity to keep busy.

Viola entered the kitchen when she'd placed the last bowl of food on the table. Kiva stiffened immediately and offered a smile she hoped didn't come out too wobbly. Viola simply nodded in response. "You look refreshed, but tired. After we eat, you can go to sleep." She turned to Leon and stretched her neck to peck him on the cheek. "It smells divine."

They ate on a banquet table that could easily seat sixteen. The conversation went from stifled to small talk until Kiva finally asked them what they did for a living. Leon told her they owned a textile company that supplied to big brands in the clothing industry, and most recently they'd branched out to include hotels and home furnishings. "Simply put," Leon added, "Viola creates the designs while I fly out to our factories in Dubai to oversee the work."

Kiva turned to Viola. "So you're an artist, too."

Viola gave a tight-lipped smiled above the rim of her wine glass. She took a small sip before placing it down on the table. "I guess you could say that. We used to hire designers until I decided to study graphic design myself."

"The wallpaper in the hallway—is that your work?"

She nodded.

"It's beautiful. Naomi does *siapo* printing and tie-dyeing. She would be so impressed with your designs. Have you ever infused Samoan patterns into your work?"

Viola twisted the stem of her glass between her fingers. "No. I don't think there's a market for it here."

Kiva furrowed her brows. "It'll be different from what's already available out there. You should consider it."

Viola lifted one shoulder in a nonchalant shrug and didn't say anything. Kiva felt she touched a nerve and backed off. Raising the glass to her lips, she took a long swig and felt the liquid burn a path down her throat.

"What would you like to do tomorrow?" Viola asked. "Shall we go to an art gallery?"

"Okay," she replied.

They finished dinner soon after, and Kiva wandered back upstairs after she'd helped clear the table and wash the dishes. She sat down at the office desk and logged onto her email, hoping there'd be something from Ry. To her joy, she saw a message from him and clicked on it immediately.

Dear Kiva,

I'm so relieved you've arrived safely, although I'm sorry to hear that you're having a difficult time. I know that everything will be new and unfamiliar to you, but give it some time. You have one of the most beautiful hearts of anyone I know, and if anything can influence a challenging situation, it's your heart and your goodness and your ability to navigate through difficulties with your feminine insight and wisdom. Be strong, bamboo girl, and know that I love you and think about you every minute of the day.

Ry

He'd enclosed a picture and Kiva clicked on it to reveal him standing with a picturesque view of a river and mountain in the background. Her breath caught as she gazed at his handsome face, his mouth tilted up into a soft grin. He was wearing dark shorts and a gray sweatshirt, the hood pulled over his head and his hands shoved inside the deep pockets. Her eyes roved his features with the familiar deep scar, dark brown eyes, and sculpted jaw bristled with stubble. She stared at the picture for a long moment until her chin trembled. Swallowing back her rising emotions, she typed a quick reply, pushed send, and logged out.

She padded back to her room where she changed into her pajamas, brushed her teeth, and climbed under the soft covers of the queen-sized bed. Staring up at the ceiling with its intricate light fixture, she couldn't help noticing how vastly different it was to her mold spotted one back home. Even the bed felt and smelled differently.

She closed her eyes and pictured Ry's face until exhaustion claimed her.

CHAPTER THIRTY-THREE

The following morning, Kiva sat in the passenger side of a luxury car, different from the one she'd been picked up in at the airport, as Viola drove them toward the city. The narrow country road wasn't paved but lined instead with lush hedges and trees. They sat in silence until they turned off onto the highway, cutting across lanes and shooting past slower-moving vehicles. Viola's platinum bracelets jingled against the steering wheel and the whiff of her expensive perfume surrounded the interior of the car.

"This art gallery we're going to is owned by a friend of mine," she started. "It's small in comparison to most galleries in the city, but I believe the exhibition that's on display at the moment will be something you'd enjoy more."

Despite her nerves, Kiva's heart spiked with excitement. Earlier after breakfast, Leon had shown her some of their latest design work for a boutique hotel they were working on in the south of France, and the artist in her came alive. Dressed in the same outfit she wore to dinner with Silei, Viola had purchased her an ivory cardigan to stave off the autumn chill.

"Leon didn't want to join us today?" she asked. She admitted to feeling a little claustrophobic in the car with just herself and Viola. Leon's presence seemed to help ease the tension.

"He had to work," Viola answered. "And besides, he thought we could use some time together by ourselves." She was silent for a moment before she spoke again. "You must have a lot of questions for me."

Questions? Kiva had plenty. She started with one. "Are we really going to talk about this now?"

Viola's lips curled into a smile. "I like that you're forward. You remind me of myself when I was younger."

Kiva's pulse rattled inside, and she tried really hard to be brave for the conversation that would come. She pulled the cardigan tight around her abdomen and stared ahead of the windscreen.

Viola sighed. "I've made many mistakes in my life, Kiva, but giving you up was not one of them." Kiva swallowed hard. "I knew my sister would take care of you in ways that I couldn't, and now look at you. You're all grown-up."

"What happened?" she finally managed. "Why did you leave?"

"I left because of a broken heart. It's selfish, I know, but I saw no other choice. Your father …" She blinked several times before continuing. "I loved him. I did. I loved him the only way I knew how to love … passionately and with all the expectations and dreams of a young woman. He was from New Caledonia and came to Samoa for an agricultural conference. I was part of the lineup to greet the visitors with floral garlands and that's when we met. He was attentive and charming and everything happened so quickly after that." She took a deep breath. "When I found out I was pregnant, I was terrified. But then he would look at me and I was happy for a while because I thought that I would have a loving family of my own." She heaved a sigh. "When I found out your father was married, however, everything stopped."

"You didn't know?"

"I swear I didn't know. There were rumors flying around among some of the conference volunteers and when they snowballed, they reached me."

"What happened?"

"I confronted him, of course, and he denied it right away. I think he was afraid, maybe a little shaken up, but when he finally admitted it, he told me he'd been married for seven years and his wife had recently given birth to their second child. He told me I made him forget about his life, his responsibilities, that he felt young and free with me. But when the other conference participants found out and his reputation was affected, he cut me off. I remember thinking how foolish I had been, how blind. I was angry. I was hurt. My heart was broken, and when he left, he never came back, and I never heard from him again. Everyone knew what had happened by the time my pregnancy started to show. Those months were the most difficult, and when you were born with a leg length deficiency, everyone blamed me, saying it was my fault my baby was imperfect. There's nothing worse for a young mother than to have accusations thrown at her when she's at her most vulnerable. And so I put the blame on you."

Kiva tried to digest all of this information. "Did you try to abort me when he left?"

Viola inhaled deeply before she answered. "Yes." No pretense or embellishment of words.

Kiva stared absently out the windscreen. She felt numb. It began to rain, the drops sprinkling on the glass and forming rivulets, and she was suddenly reminded of a sketch she did months ago that almost mirrored this exact same scene—gazing out a rain-splattered window and feeling disconnected from the world. So Hana had been right, she thought dejectedly. She couldn't define just how heartbreaking it was to hear this detail confirmed by her mother. There was simply no way to mask the hurt except to take it.

Swallowing hard, she mustered her courage to speak. "So why did you invite me to come? Especially when we haven't heard a single word from you all these years. Why now?"

"This may come across as insincere to you, especially after what you've just learned from me, but I truly want to get to know you, Kiva. I realize I can never replace Naomi as your mother, but I'd like to be your friend."

Her friend? The idea almost seemed unbelievable. Kiva's brows pinched together in confusion. Beyond this reunion, she hadn't thought about where their relationship would go from here. She had plans, future plans that included Ry and art school and the café. She never pictured Viola in it.

"It was Leon that encouraged me to write," Viola continued. "He's always wanted children when I didn't. He's been very patient with me over the years, and despite everything I've put him through, he still loves me, flaws and all. I have had every luxury at my fingertips, but my life is far from content. I realize happiness cannot be provided by things or by people, even by the people you love, and so I knew what I had to do."

"I'm not responsible for your happiness," Kiva said.

"I'm not asking for your forgiveness in order to make me happy. I know that I don't deserve it, that I don't deserve you, but I don't regret my decision to give you away either because you would have turned out a very different person from what you are now. If I stayed, I would have looked at you and seen *him*. I would have seen my mistakes all over your face. I would have looked at your leg and perceived ugliness, and then I would have taught you to hate yourself because of it."

Kiva's breath caught on a shudder. "So that's why you left?"

"I left to protect you. And then I stayed away to protect myself."

"Then why?" Kiva's voice almost broke. "Why all of this?"

Viola was quiet as she gripped the steering wheel, her knuckles stretched taut. When she finally answered, her voice battled between remorse and uncertainty. "I needed to make sure, Kiva. I wanted"—she swallowed hard as she looked out at the stretch of highway—"I wanted to make sure that I made the right decision. I needed confirmation, to see for myself that you're okay."

Kiva's eyes prickled with tears. "Naomi wrote to you. She sent letters and photos."

"I know. I never opened them."

Kiva's mouth opened and closed in shock. "You never read her letters?"

"No. I couldn't. I always sent them back, until she got the message and stopped writing."

"Why?"

"You have to understand, Kiva, I was in a very bad place. Those letters were too painful a reminder of the kind of person I was. Motherhood will sometimes bring out the best in some women, but it brought out the worst in me."

"I think you were just lost. You were so young." Kiva's voice gentled. "Why don't you come back now? This is more than about you and me. Your family is there, and Naomi would love to see you. I just know she would." She then told Viola about their art café and how Naomi was now a grandmother to a beautiful little girl.

Viola smiled sadly into the distance. "My bigger sister was always the motherly kind. She always had her heart set in the right place." She shook her head. "But no. When I left Samoa, I vowed I would never return. That's not my life anymore. Naomi understands."

"Understanding or not, she's had her fair share of hardship." She then told her about Mau's strokes.

Viola sniffed and lowered her designer sunglasses over her eyes, effectively creating a barrier between her and the conversation. "We're almost there," she said, merging into a lane that connected to an upcoming exit.

They didn't speak for the rest of the ride. They passed upscale shops and restaurants, busy intersections and historical landmarks, until Viola turned into an underground parking lot. Easing the car into a space, they got out and walked onto the street. The art gallery was in a central part of the city and had been converted from an old Victorian-style building. Climbing the steps, they emerged into a spacious room with wooden floors and stark white walls. Breaking up each wall were black and white portraits illustrating every kind of facial expression imaginable. Kiva immediately moved forward. Her breath caught at the exquisite detail, raw emotion, and almost lifelike quality of each feature. One woman's face in particular made her pause. Eyes downcast, her profile was tipped to the side and lowered as if she were meditating. Faint freckles speckled her nose, and her long black hair fell across her bare shoulders like a stream.

"This is beautiful," Kiva mused aloud. "She looks so real."

The artist had captured the tranquility on her face perfectly, and the shadows that played softly across her cheeks gave her an almost ethereal quality, as if her spirit was being elevated.

Surrounded by a dozen similar images, Kiva wanted to learn to sketch just like this, where reality and art blurred into one and made the observer question whether the work was in fact a photograph of a real person instead. Her heart pounded at the thought and whether or not she could actually do it.

"It's very beautiful work," Viola agreed beside her.

"I would love to sketch like this," Kiva murmured almost to herself.

Viola angled her head, studying her quietly. "Have you ever considered going to art school?"

Kiva chuckled under her breath. "Many times, but it's never worked out."

"Why not?"

Kiva half shrugged, not in the mood to tell her how she'd lost her scholarship and how Mau's strokes had prevented her from leaving.

Viola led the way into the next room where landscape paintings occupied the walls. They spent the next hour roaming each exhibition until a garden café caught Viola's attention. The rain had stopped and they decided to order tea and sit around a table under the open sky. It reminded Kiva of Café Bamboo. She proceeded to tell Viola about the café back home and the humble art center beside it. Viola listened with interest until their cups of tea and scones arrived. They talked about art and design and never revisited the topic of Viola's past again.

Later when they returned to the house, Kiva logged onto the lap top to find a message from Ry. He informed her they were about to cross from the north island to the south on the ferry. He enclosed a picture of the three of them standing beside a red car she assumed was their rental, in the order of Claire, Adé, and Ry. Ry's face was tipped into a grin and he was wearing dark sunglasses. Kiva pressed reply and typed out a message that included the tense conversation she'd had earlier with

Viola. She still didn't know where her place was in Viola's life or where they would go next. She pressed send and read the next message she'd received from Naomi. When she clicked away, she saw another new message pop up from Ry. This one simply read: *Can I call you?* Kiva was grateful Naomi had given her Viola's number in the event of an emergency and she'd passed it onto Ry before they parted. She typed out an enthusiastic *YES!* and pressed send.

Fifteen minutes later, the phone in the office rang, and Kiva could hear the ring echo in several places in the house.

She snatched it up before anyone else could and answered breathlessly, "Hello?"

"Kiva," his deep, strong voice came through the line. "It's me."

Kiva inhaled a shuddering breath and let it go on a sigh. "It's so good to hear your voice."

She heard him chuckle quietly.

"You sound a little sleepy," she said. She peered over at the clock on one of the shelves. "What time is it over there?"

"It's"—his voice trailed off as she imagined him checking his watch—"past three in the morning."

Kiva gasped. "It's so late!"

"It's fine. We have to get up soon anyway to catch the ferry. We're staying at a backpackers', and I left to find a payphone. I wanted to talk to you. I just read your email and wanted to check on you. You had a big day today."

Kiva sighed. "You could say that. It was … interesting, but nothing I wasn't expecting."

"How are you doing?"

"I'm okay now. I miss you."

"I miss you too, *habibty*."

Kiva's heart warmed at the endearment. "Tell me how your road trip is going. How are Claire and Adé?"

"They're fine. Enjoying the comforts here. New Zealand is a beautiful place. We've stopped along the way to check out some sights, and Adé's been reading *Lord of the Rings* and wants to visit the areas the movie was filmed." Kiva smiled at the image of Adé being caught up in a world of hobbits and wizards. "How was the art gallery?" Ry asked.

"It was incredible." She sighed. "Something happened to me there." She continued to tell him about the portraits she had become enamored with. "Ry, I want to learn how to sketch like that," she added. "They were amazing—each one meticulous and so very real. Now that I've seen this quality of work, I want to go to art school to polish my own skills." She sighed. "But I know I have a long way to go."

"You can do it, Kiva." She smiled at his encouragement. "We can add it to our list on the napkins from the airport café," he said.

"Do you have those napkins? I wondered where we'd put them."

"Of course I have them." She heard the smile in his voice. "They're tucked with my passport and wallet. I'll just write 'Kiva goes to art school and becomes a world famous artist' next to 'Ry designs award-winning turbulent-free aircraft."

She beamed down into the receiver. "You're an architect, not an engineer."

"I know…but I'd do anything to make my girl happy."

They talked for another hour until he had to leave to get ready for the ferry trip across the strait. Kiva hung up with a soft smile on her face and headed downstairs.

She found Viola sitting at the dining room table with a lap top open in front of her. "Kiva, what do you think of this?" She waved for her to come over.

Kiva approached the table and bent down to see the image on the screen. The design was a simple blue bloom against a white backdrop. "It's beautiful," she said. "What is it for?"

"It's for the bedspread for this hotel we're working on in Cannes. The flower will go on the bottom right hand corner of the comforter in each room." Her voice rose with excitement. "Let me show you the rest."

Kiva sat in a chair beside Viola as she clicked through a folder of her designs. She was in awe of her creativity and commented on each one until she stopped looking at the designs and stole glances at her mother instead. Viola's face lit with satisfaction and pride, and Kiva recognized the feeling. She realized the connection Viola was trying to make through their shared passion of art, and Kiva was more than happy to oblige. Art was safe. It was freeing. One could simultaneously get lost and then found again within its depths. An understanding could be reached, and Kiva and Viola found theirs in that quiet dining room. They were never going to be mother and daughter—not in the conventional way—but together they could share this.

Dinner was more comfortable than the evening before. Leon had made a pot roast in the slow cooker and served it with rustic vegetables and gravy, and then he and Viola regaled Kiva with stories of their adventures as a young couple traveling across Europe, taking three months off to explore the major cities and countryside. Leon told her how they'd accidentally gotten separated at a train station in Prague and he was forced to file a missing person's report when he couldn't find Viola after several hours had passed.

"It was one of the most terrifying moments of my life," Leon said. "I was desperate. I thought she'd gone off and left me." Viola threw her head back and laughed loudly. "Why are you laughing?" he asked her, trying not to smile. "The policemen were giving me a hard time. They were adamant that that was the reason, especially since you had all the money and passports in your hand bag."

Viola swiped her eyes from her laughing tears and leaned over to kiss him on the cheek. "I would never leave you," she said with a soft expression on her face. "Not for anything."

Kiva had been smiling at their stories, and she swallowed thickly then looked away.

The days that followed passed quickly. Viola took her to the national gallery in Trafalgar Square where Kiva felt as if she was in paradise. They went shopping at Harrods where she received a new wardrobe of clothes, and then attended a soul-stirring concert at the Royal Albert Hall.

It was when they were in Harrods that the topic of her deficient leg came up. Kiva pulled on a new pair of jeans and walked out of the dressing room. Viola eyed her up and down before her focus zeroed in on her uneven legs. She frowned. "Have you had a specialist look at your leg recently?"

Kiva shook her head. "No. Any chance to surgically lengthen my leg would have had to take place in my growing years as a child. But there was no such procedure available in Samoa, and we couldn't afford to fly overseas." She shrugged as if to say, *that's just the way it was.*

Viola pointed a finger at her feet. "What about wearing special shoes so you're not always slouching?"

Kiva's cheeks flamed at her bluntness. "I don't think those will work because of the seven centimeter height discrepancy between my legs."

"But have you ever tried?"

"No," she answered dryly. "Samoa doesn't sell many *se'evae kosokosos* with a heel lift, unfortunately."

Viola's mouth twitched in amusement. "At least you have a sense of humor about it."

Kiva's expression smoothed as she sighed. "I've had to learn to accept the way I am, especially when there was no opportunity for treatment available growing up."

Viola pursed her lips as she looked her over again. "We'll see about that now."

Kiva frowned. "What do you mean?"

Viola placed her hands on her hips. "What I mean is that I'm going to order you some special shoes with a heel lift, like you said. Sandals, too, so you can wear them in Samoa. Even though I haven't been there in years, I know it gets hot as Hell. You'll only need the lift for one shoe, so it shouldn't be too difficult to get."

Kiva's mouth popped open in surprise. "Viola that's not what—"

Viola raised her palm to cut her off. "Let me do this, Kiva. Alright?"

Something in her sharp tone made Kiva pause in her protest, as if Viola needed to do this for her own peace of mind. She slowly nodded. "Alright," she agreed.

When she mentioned this to Ry over the phone that afternoon, he was quiet for a moment.

"How do you feel about it?" he finally asked.

Kiva beamed brightly. "I know it's just a shoe, but I can't help feeling excited to try it out, especially if it has the potential to alter the way I walk for the better." She bit her lip to contain her joy. "I kind of feel like Cinderella."

Ry laughed. "It's good to hear you're happy, Kiva, and if this is what it'll take to achieve an ounce of that, then I'm happy for you."

Kiva went quiet.

"What's wrong?" he asked.

"I don't want my happiness tethered to something so ... cosmetic."

"This is more than cosmetic, Kiva. You've lived your entire life with a limp, and now you finally get the chance to receive treatment for it. It won't change the person you are—you'll always be my bamboo girl—but it will make your life a little easier, and it's okay to want that. It'll probably help alleviate some of your back pain, too."

That was true, she thought. Her lower back was always aching from the stress placed on it by her crooked pelvis. "You're right," she said. "So tell me, what did you do today?"

"We finally went bungee jumping," he said, and she could tell he was smiling.

"You did it! How did it go?"

"It was exhilarating and terrifying rolled into one."

Kiva laughed. "Well, I'm glad to hear you survived to tell the tale. When do you head back to the North Island?"

"We're going to stay here for a few days and start driving up next week."

She sighed into the receiver. "I can't wait to see you."

"Me too, love."

That night when she went to bed, she couldn't stop the smile that spread across her lips.

CHAPTER THIRTY-FOUR

The shoes arrived the following week in the mail. They were strappy sandals—like Viola had promised—that crisscrossed on the front of Kiva's feet and ankles with one heel significantly higher than the other. When she walked in them, her limp didn't completely disappear, but it was less noticeable, and her heavy gait wasn't as obvious as before. It took some time getting used to them and when she had, she wore them for the rest of her visit. Viola was beside herself with joy. She had clapped her hands together and announced they were going out to dinner to celebrate.

The remainder of Kiva's visit flew by quickly. When she wasn't in the kitchen learning new recipes from Leon, she was spending time with Viola either in her spacious design office or at a coffee shop and live show. On her last day, she decided to take the underground tube to explore the city by herself. She walked for hours along busy streets and small alleyways, some paved and some cobblestoned, until she came by a park lined with trees turning orange and wooden benches. She sat in one and pulled out her art book from her bag. It was a rare, beautiful day and Kiva took the pencil from her hair and started to sketch. She remembered the portraits from the art gallery and tried to emulate them, but when it became clear that her drawing looked nothing like the woman meditating, she blew out a frustrated breath and put her book away. She watched people walk by. Joggers passed with their ears plugged into music, and mothers pushed strollers with sleeping children inside. She began to reflect on the past two and a half weeks with Viola and Leon. A part of her admitted it had been an enjoyable trip overall, but she missed Ry and she missed home, and she looked forward to getting back. She had plans now, and a life with Ry she couldn't wait to begin.

Later when she returned to the house, Viola stopped her from going up to her room. "A young man called you this afternoon," she said.

Kiva pivoted round to face her. "Ry?"

"Yes, that's him. He introduced himself to me." She arched a perfectly prim eyebrow. "I didn't know you were seeing someone."

Kiva smiled sheepishly. "I am. It kind of just started. Well, officially anyway. It's a long story."

"I like him. He was very polite on the phone. I told him I'd let you know he called and that you'll probably email him when you got back."

"Okay, thanks." She turned and hurried up the steps to the office. She logged on and an unexpected new message from him brought a smile to her face.

Dear Kiva,

I don't have much time, but I wanted to let you know that I'm thinking of you and can't wait to see you soon. We're in Taupo at the moment and will probably stay overnight before we drive to Auckland tomorrow. If I don't get the chance to talk to you before your flight, be safe and remember what I said about turbulence—look for the nearest exit and brace yourself. I'm kidding. I'll be there waiting at the airport for you when you arrive in New Zealand.

I love you,

Ry

Kiva smiled to herself then typed a quick response before she went into her room to start packing. Since her flight to Hong Kong was in the early morning and was most likely going to be cold, she laid out her new jeans and warm cardigan to wear to the airport.

Leon and Viola drove her to Heathrow in the same car they picked her up in. This time when she sat in the backseat, however, her nerves were replaced with anticipation and excitement. She was finally going home, and she was finally going to see Ry.

After she checked in, Leon gave her a big, warm hug and told her to visit them again soon, and then Viola stepped in front of her, pulling her into an embrace. Kiva's eyes widened slightly in surprise as she returned the hug. When Viola stepped away, she withdrew an envelope from her purse and placed it in Kiva's hand.

"What's this?" she asked, puzzled.

"Open it when you get to Samoa," Viola instructed.

Kiva thanked her.

She said goodbye to them again and walked to the departure lounge, her mind already occupied with what awaited her ahead.

The flight to Hong Kong was long and uncomfortable and she was relieved when the plane finally landed and she could stand up and stretch her legs. She had several hours in transit until her next flight to Auckland, and she went looking around the terminal for a desktop computer to type a quick email to Ry and Naomi. When she finally found one, she logged on, and discovered there were no new messages from him. She composed an email anyway, informing Ry that she had arrived safely, and pressed send. Her stomach grumbled from hunger, and she got up to search for a place to eat. She found a busy eatery that served Asian cuisine and slurped down noodle soup and steamed spring rolls. She then walked aimlessly around the shops for an hour until she found herself back at the computer kiosk once again to see whether Ry had responded. He hadn't, and Kiva logged off disappointed. She found a bookstore and perused the shelves for something she thought he might like. Choosing a historical novel set in ancient Egypt, she paid for it, and then exited the shop. She spotted a toy store next and decided to get something for Talia. Twenty minutes later, with her purchases swinging from her hands in plastic bags, she decided to head to her gate.

She slept for most of the flight to Auckland and awoke to the flight crew preparing them for landing. Her stomach spiked with excitement at the thought of seeing Ry on the other side of arrivals. They planned to fly back together to Samoa with Adé and Claire.

She disembarked from the plane and tried to rush ahead to get in line early for customs and immigration. With her limp, she was unsuccessful.

Forty minutes later, she was pushing the trolley into the arrivals' area and searching the crowd for his face. Kiva's heart pounded as she imagined him smiling his crooked grin at her. Someone accidently bumped her from behind and she was forced to move her trolley out of the way. She cleared out from the crowd and looked around. She couldn't immediately see him. She went and stood near an information desk. Craning her neck, she looked around for any sign of Ry but couldn't find him. She then searched the area for Adé and Claire and discovered that they weren't there either. Where were they? Had they arrived in Auckland yet or were they still driving from Taupo?

Kiva turned to the information desk behind her and asked where she could check her emails. She assumed Ry had sent a message telling her they would be late. A middle-aged man dressed in a royal blue coat informed her there were internet kiosks available for public use. She followed his instructions to where one was located and headed there. When she logged on, there were still no new messages from Ry. Kiva's face crumpled in disappointment. What was she going to do now? She decided to return to the arrivals' area just in case they were running late. She thought quickly and calculated how much time she had until their flight to Samoa. They still had a few hours. She would give them thirty minutes, she decided. If they didn't show within that time, she would go to the international departures' area and search for them there.

Thirty minutes passed. Forty. Forty-five. Fifty. With each passing minute, Kiva held out hope and gave them more time. But soon worry started to build inside her, and she tried really hard to tamp down her rising alarm. They were coming, she told herself. Ry said he'd be there.

"Can I help you, miss?" the same man from the information desk asked her.

Kiva turned and gave him a faint smile. "I'm waiting for some friends of mine. They were supposed to pick me up by now, but they haven't arrived yet."

"You've been waiting an awful long time. Do you have a number you can call them? There are pay phones nearby that you can use."

Kiva shook her head. "I don't have a telephone number." Ry had always used public phones. A sickly feeling rose from the pit of her stomach and formed a tight knot in her throat.

The man gestured outside. "There are taxis available outside that can take you to your friends. Do you have an address for them?"

Again, Kiva shook her head. "I'm flying out in a few hours. My friends are on the same flight as me."

"Maybe they're already checking in." His face was friendly, and Kiva was touched by his sincerity to help. "I can direct you to the departures' area if you'd like."

"Alright," she nodded.

The directions were pretty straightforward, and Kiva pushed her trolley in the direction he pointed. She tried not to break out in a run. If they weren't there, she decided she would quickly turn around and come back. Worry that she might miss them if they'd suddenly arrived while she was gone raced in her mind.

She passed the international flight board and noticed that their flight was on time, but that no one was checking in yet. She scanned the area quickly and didn't see Ry or the others. She started over, searching more carefully until she realized they really weren't there. Feeling defeated, she pushed the trolley back to the arrivals' area and took a seat that gave her an open view of the terminal. When fifty minutes passed and there was still no sign of them, she went to the little café she and Ry had spent hours in and ordered a hot drink. When she was handed the coffee on a napkin and saucer, an overwhelming sense of nostalgia hit her in the chest and she felt tears prick her eyes. *Where were they?* she thought desperately, swallowing the hard knot in her throat. *Where was Ry?* If they didn't come soon, they'd miss their flight. Kiva sniffed and wiped the moisture from her eyes. She finished her coffee and got up and headed back to the departures' area.

Samoans and tourists alike converged around the check-in zone, signaling to Kiva that the counters were open. She got in line behind a family of six and glanced around the roped-off area. When she didn't see Ry, her heart sank, and hope that he would show started to dissipate.

Her legs carried her forward through check-in and security, past duty-free stores and restaurants, until she was standing in line to board the plane. She looked around the emptying gate and found there was still no sign of Ry. Dread settled over her like a thick cloud, and it took every bone and muscle in her body to keep from turning around and going back to search for him.

Once she was aboard the aircraft, she found her seat near the back. The seat was next to a window and she stared out into the distance without any coherent thought. She was a puddle of emotions: confusion, unease, concern. Perhaps she had misunderstood their plans? Maybe he'd gotten the dates mixed up. Maybe they were actually flying out the next day. Kiva settled back in her seat and decided that was what it was. A clear misunderstanding. Once she arrived in Samoa and learned all of this from him, everything would be fine. They would laugh it off and she'd be so relieved.

But something gnawed at the back of her mind and she couldn't shake it. Her chest rose and fell until she was gulping back air through her mouth. Her eyes searched each passenger that came down the aisle until there was nobody left and the captain announced they were departing soon.

The plane disengaged from the gate and taxied down the tarmac. It shook as it turned into position on the runway and started its momentum, picking up speed, the engines roaring in Kiva's ears as it tilted up into the sky. She gripped onto the armrests and closed her eyes. Her anxiety spiked as the plane finally lifted off the ground, and then remained that way as high as the clouds they were flying through. She couldn't bring herself to eat or sleep the entire four hours. She fidgeted in her seat and stared out at the darkening sky, half hoping and half expecting Ry would suddenly surprise her like he had before. But he never did. She was emotionally and physically drained by the time the aircraft started its decent into Faleolo airport.

After the plane landed and came to a stop, Kiva unbuckled her seatbelt and followed the passengers out into the inky night. She made her way carefully down the stairs into the wet tarmac. A drop of rain fell on her cheek and she brushed it aside, anxious to get to Naomi and Mau.

After clearing through customs and immigration, she rolled her trolley to the arrivals' area and immediately spotted Naomi in the crowd. Kiva navigated her way to her while Naomi did the same. They met halfway and crushed in an embrace. She instantly relaxed.

"It's so good to be home," Kiva murmured into her shoulder. Pulling back, she noticed Naomi's face fall as sadness swept through her features.

"What is it?" Kiva frowned. "Is Mau okay?" She glanced quickly around for him.

"Mau's fine," Naomi said in a quiet voice. "He's at home with Hana and Talia."

Kiva returned her gaze to Naomi and searched her features.

Naomi swallowed thickly as her eyes conveyed sympathy.

Kiva's heart stopped. "No," she exhaled on a whisper, taking a step back and clasping her hands over her mouth.

Naomi tugged on her arms, drawing her close as Kiva started to struggle, shaking her head in disbelief. "Where is he?" her voice broke.

"Kiva." Naomi's voice mimicked her own, fractured and heartbroken and at a complete loss. She pulled her in and held her tight, and then murmured words close to her ear that would forever tear her apart.

"What? No, no, no, Naomi, no, that can't be true," Kiva cried as she absorbed the news, fighting for release. "No, please, God, no!" Tears formed and spilled over her cheeks. She tried to wrestle out of Naomi's grip, but she was too strong and Kiva was too weak, and she succumbed and collapsed into her shoulder sobbing. "Please … tell me … it's not true."

Naomi released a shuddering breath, and Kiva realized she was crying, too. "It was in the news, Kiva. They released his name this afternoon. The Peace Corps office confirmed it and went to Talia's school to inform them. The whole village knows."

Kiva's heart broke over and over. *No,* she wailed on the inside. *Not Ry. Not her Ry.* She cried and cried as the hurt spread everywhere … her heart, her head, her very soul. The pain was like thick lava, burning and scorching her skin and burying her alive all at the same time, and there was no stopping it. It rolled over her in folds and waves, a heavy weight pressing her down until she gasped aloud.

They were drawing attention to themselves, but Kiva didn't notice.

Everything else fell away as the news that Ry was gone consumed her. All that time she'd spent worrying in the airport … when she'd believed he'd been running late when he hadn't. She gasped in pain and smashed her fingers against her mouth to stifle her sobs.

Naomi ushered her to the truck and helped her into the seat on the passenger side. The rain had stopped then started up again, as if the skies, too, were mourning. It trickled over the hood and down the side of her window, leaving tear tracks in its wake. Kiva stared out of it without really seeing anything as Naomi rounded the driver's side and got in. She started the engine and drove out of the airport parking lot onto the main road. The roads were slick with oil and water, and she drove slowly like she was part of a funeral procession.

Silence hovered in the cab until reality hit Kiva in the chest again and she broke down in tears. Her quiet sobs filled the empty space, a heartrending sound that combined with the rain outside. Naomi kept silent, allowing her to let go while her own tears fell unchecked over her cheeks.

"How?" Kiva finally choked out. "How did it happen?"

"The news report said there was a fight. It sounded like he was attacked in self-defense." Naomi's voice cracked. "I don't know any other details."

Kiva closed her eyes in agony. Her heart cried out for Ry, for a promising life cut short, and for the pain he must have suffered. There was no escaping her anguish as she imagined his final moments. What had he been thinking? Where was he when he was attacked? What prompted it? And where were Claire and Adé? She was desperate for answers.

"What about Claire and Adé?" she asked. "They were traveling together."

"The news mentioned he was with two fellow Peace Corps volunteers. It must be them."

Kiva gazed out the windscreen at the passing villages. "It's my fault," she choked out. "He wanted to come to London with me. If I'd only let him, this wouldn't have happened. He'd still be alive." Her voice broke on the last word.

Naomi reached over and touched her hand. "Kiva, honey, you can't think like that. That's a dangerous way to believe and it won't gain anything except more heartache."

"He knew," she cried. "He knew something was going to happen. He'd felt it." Her throat squeezed as she remembered the concern he had over their three-week separation and how he was worried they'd be apart for longer. He'd been right.

Kiva closed her fists, digging her nails into her skin, leaving sharp indents. Any pain was better than the pain she was experiencing now. How could one bear this much hurt and suffering? How could one's body remain intact when the heart and spirit were broken? Everything was gone. Her love, his vision, their plans.

Kiva leaned into the window and let her tears mirror those of the rain outside.

She simply didn't know what else to do.

CHAPTER THIRTY-FIVE

Ry never saw them coming. It was dark in the parking lot, and Claire and Adé's constant talking masked their stealthy approach.

They'd just ordered fish and chips for takeaway and were heading to their car. They'd booked themselves a room at a backpacker's for the night and were going to set off for the long drive to Auckland the following morning. Ry's heart banged against his chest when he thought about seeing Kiva again. God, he'd missed her. He couldn't wait to bury himself in her neck and inhale the sweet fragrance that was uniquely hers—vanilla from baking cupcakes, salt from her sweat, and the combination of lead and wood from the countless pencils she used for sketching. He looked forward to the life they'd planned together and the memories they would soon be creating. His thoughts were pulled away suddenly when Claire snorted at something Adé said. She choked and spluttered on the soda she was drinking until Adé thumped her none too gently on the back. "You alright there?" he asked.

"Ouch!" she protested. "Easy there, big boy, I'm not dying."

Ry looked over at his two travel companions and smiled to himself. It had been one amazing trip filled with adventures that included hiking in Fiordland and jet boating in Queenstown. Ry hadn't had many buddies growing up, and he considered himself fortunate now to call these two his close friends. But he quickly realized over time that they'd become more than friends, they were family—his Peace Corps family. They recognized in each other the challenges faced when rendering their services, the vision that went into helping build communities, and the hope they carried that they were making a real difference in people's lives. Ry looked over at them and realized he wouldn't exchange the experience for anything. When four guys in black ski masks converged on them in the parking lot, he stiffened in alarm. One of them crept up behind Claire, startling her, before Ry saw the glint of a knife raised to her throat.

"Whoa, whoa." He raised his palms up in surrender. "Take it easy."

"Shut up and get down on the ground!" The guy with the knife instructed.

Ry looked over at Adé whose eyes were starting to fill with a mixture of uncertainty and dread. His mouth went dry. "Look, we'll do what you say, alright? Just don't hurt her." His eyes darted over to Claire whose breaths were coming in sharp, rapid bursts, the knife inches from her neck. Together he and Adé lowered themselves slowly to the ground, their arms outstretched.

"Hands over your heads. Do it now!"

Ry and Adé complied and one of the guys stalked behind them and started to pat them down. He found their wallets and took out the cash, tossing the rest on the ground.

"Now your purse, bitch," the guy behind Claire demanded. Her hands shook over the handle of the bag that slung diagonally over her shoulder.

"It's going to be alright, Claire," Adé said, trying to comfort her. "Just do what he says."

"Shut up, you!" One of the guys punched Adé in the face, knocking him to the dirt. He remained motionless. Ry clenched and unclenched his jaw. He peered over at Claire, whose face turned deathly pale as she stared down at Adé.

The guy behind her started to smile. "Ah, Claire. Is that your name, love? We're going to have a bit of fun, you and I." The other guys started to snicker.

"Just take my purse and leave," she said, her voice trembling.

He tsked. "Patience, patience … What's the rush?" With one hand holding the knife, he moved his free hand to the front of her stomach, lowering it to her crotch. He cupped her roughly and Claire froze, her face stunned.

Ry fisted his hands and started to rise. "Take. Your. Hands. Off. Her." His voice was low, menacing.

The guy who held Claire faced him. "Look who we have here—a terrorist. You know, my cousin was in the Australian army and died in Afghanistan. You should be shot for what your people did."

Ry blinked, stalling for a moment. He hadn't been associated with 9/11 for years, and to hear it now was like a physical punch to his gut.

"Look man," he finally managed, swallowing hard. "We're not asking for trouble. You've got what you came for—the money—now leave her alone."

"Not everything," the guy said suggestively before he cast Ry a hateful glance and started to move further into the dark, tugging Claire with him.

She whimpered in fear, and Ry watched as her eyes rounded with terror, begging for help. Something in him cracked. There was no way in hell he was going to let that asshole hurt her. He needed to do something fast.

He started to move.

The other guys straightened and came toward him, but before they could reach him, Ry lunged forward, knocking one out of the way with an elbow to the face, the tell-tale *crack* of his nose reverberating through the still night. The guy shrieked and fell down, clutching his face in agony. Ry turned swiftly and punched one of the attackers as he ran toward him. *Boom! Boom!* Ry hit him twice with his fist—one in the face and the other in his abdomen—and he slid to the ground groaning. The guy with the knife stumbled back, taking Claire with him, and she suddenly cried out when her skin was cut open, the blood trickling down her neck staining her blouse. Ry thrust forward, shoving her out of the way, and grabbed the guy with the knife. His face contorted in anger as he reached for him, his judgment momentarily clouded as he forgot about the fourth attacker. The guy tackled him from behind, the full force of the momentum taking the three of them down on the rough gravel. The air was punched from Ry's lungs as he felt something enter his chest. Claire screamed. His eyes widened in shock. The two attackers cursed loudly and shoved him away. They stood quickly and hesitated for a moment before they panicked and took off running in the dark.

Claire crawled over to Ry. She noticed the blood first, a dark pool spreading on the ground. He was facedown, his body limp, and she pushed him onto his back. "Oh, God! Oh my God!" she cried out in shock. The knife was buried deep in his chest, the wooden hilt the only part visible. "Ry! Oh, God. Can you hear me?" She cradled his head in her lap and looked around desperately for help. "Somebody help us! Please!"

Ry stared straight up at the sky, his eyes unfocused. He had difficulty breathing with blood bubbling from his mouth and nose and running down his face. There was no opportunity to speak, no chance to form words, his body already failing. There were only thoughts and emotions and a realization that this was it. His mother came fleetingly to mind, and his father in Dubai. Guilt. Regret. Fear and pain. Each one of his demons from the past wrestled inside of him, until he was left with one question: had he done enough to redeem himself? It didn't escape him that he had come full circle and what started with a fight six years ago that landed him in Samoa was now ending with one. And then there was Kiva, his bamboo girl with all of her love and kindness and purity of heart. He clung onto each one of her qualities tightly, channeling them deep inside, as if they alone could save him. His heart broke for her and for what she would endure when he was gone, and so he did the only thing he could think of. With what little energy he had left, he looked at the stars above and gathered all of the love and strength he could and sent them out into the universe, the same universe Kiva had sketched in her art books among Rumi's poetry, and hoped she would feel it. He wished he could have seen her one more time, but with that final act complete, he closed his eyes and exhaled.

CHAPTER THIRTY-SIX

Peace Corps Press Release

WASHINGTON, D.C., Sept. 17, 2009—Peace Corps Acting Director Elizabeth Haliburton is saddened to announce the death of Peace Corps volunteer Taaraz Ryler "Ry" Cade in Taupo, New Zealand. Ry, 23, was on vacation and died as a result of a knife wound sustained from an attempted robbery on September 12. The investigation is currently ongoing by the authorities in Taupo.

Ry was a primary school teacher in the village of Siumu, Samoa. A graduate from Iowa State University, he arrived in Samoa at the beginning of April 2009 for pre-service training and was sworn in as a Peace Corps volunteer by the end of May. He was a committed and dedicated volunteer who served as an English teacher, soccer coach, and literacy and math tutor. Ry was an active member of his local community and worked tirelessly to combat inter-school violence and bullying. He will be remembered for his dedication to his students and the faculty he served.

Grief counseling and support are being provided to Peace Corps volunteers and staff.

Ry is survived by his mother, Anna Cade, father, Youssef Taaraz Naser, half-brothers, Hassan and Omar, stepfather, Thomas Cade, and stepsister, Skye. The Peace Corps offers its sincere condolences to his family and friends during this difficult time.

CHAPTER THIRTY-SEVEN

Kiva stared vacantly at the blank page. Her back was pressed against the headboard of the bed and her legs were tucked under the covers. Light rain fell outside and moisture flew in through the open louvers, sprinkling her art book. She swiped them away with her thumb. It had been weeks since Ry's passing, and she couldn't bring herself to do the one thing that had always saved her from anguish—sketch. She was numb on the inside with a hollowness that couldn't be filled with mere drawing or baking or climbing trees.

She had learned through the local paper that Ry's family traveled to New Zealand to claim his body before they returned to the States and to the little town they were from for his funeral. Kiva's initial thought was that Ry hated that town. He'd tried to escape it numerous times, and now he was being returned there to be buried. The picture the paper had printed was one of him surrounded by his students, his smile wide. Kiva had stared at it for a long moment until his face blurred behind her tears. Her second thought was that she would never get to see him one final time. She would never have the chance to stroke his hand or kiss his cheek, to get the closure she needed. He felt so far away and her heart broke because of it. She'd cried into her pillow late that night.

Claire had come by the house to see her. A bandage covered her neck from where the knife grazed her throat. She'd been lucky, the paramedics had told her. Her eyes glazed over with pain as they sat close together on the dining room table. Naomi had prepared tea and set the steaming mug in front of her. They began talking, and Claire told her everything—how their attackers crept up to them in the dark parking lot, how they'd been immobilized, and how Ry had tried to save her.

Kiva looked up and saw the same hurt reflected on her face. "I'm so sorry, Kiva," she'd rasped in a broken voice. "It all happened so quickly."

Kiva reached over and grasped her hand. "It wasn't your fault, Claire. Not yours or Ry's or Adé's." Her voice cracked when she said his name and she looked away, blinking quickly.

Adé visited her next. She was in the art center and turned to see him framing the door. They met in the middle, his long strides reaching her quickly before he pulled her into an embrace. No words were exchanged, just tears and a need to find comfort in the space between them. When Adé pulled away, he reached for something in his pocket and Kiva immediately recognized the napkins before he had a chance to explain. "I found this in Ry's bag," he said. "I think he would have wanted you to have them." Her hands shook as she took them from him. She glanced down at Ry's familiar handwriting where words jumped out at her, conveying everything they'd hoped and lost. "There wasn't a single day that went by on that trip where he didn't mention you," Adé added, his voice hoarse. "I know what you meant to him."

Her chin trembled. "Thank you for bringing me these."

Later that week, Silei had driven to the house to pick her up and take her to the memorial service the primary school was commemorating in his honor. Floral wreathes hung from the ceiling as the pastor of the village led the service in prayer. A framed photograph of Ry draped with a fragrant lei stood prominently in the front of the school hall where hundreds of people had gathered to pay their respects. Kiva had sat near the back like the observer she was and listened as volunteers and faculty alike stood and shared their memories about him. When it had become too much to bear, she'd left quietly, retracing the same route he would have taken to her house every day, until Silei caught up with her in the car.

In her bedroom, lightning flashed and rain fell harder on the iron roof, the noise deafening. The sky dimmed, throwing a shadow across her room. Kiva didn't turn on the light. She stared at a thread coming loose on her bedspread and beyond that to the pile of dirty clothes left on the floor near her door. Her attention caught on the bag she'd used to travel to London and Viola's letter stuck out from one of its pockets. She hadn't read it yet and had no desire to do so now. A clap of thunder resonated in the distance, and Talia was suddenly at her door, eyes wide with fear.

"Hey," Kiva said faintly. "Come here."

Talia rushed over, climbing under the sheet. Her tiny arms went around Kiva as she burrowed her head into her side. They slept like that into the late night when Kiva got up to use the bathroom. She slipped quietly from the bed so she wouldn't wake Talia and fumbled her way in the dark to the door. Reaching for the handle, she tripped over the bag on the floor and went sprawling head first, arms outstretched. Her knee scratched something sharp and she hissed in pain. She clutched it close to stifle the ache and then stood, her legs wobbly, and continued down the hall to the bathroom. She washed up quickly and returned to her room. Her foot caught on something when she crossed over the threshold and she squinted in the dark to see what it was. She recognized the outline of Viola's letter and bent down to retrieve it.

Kiva stared at it for a long moment, her name scrawled neatly on the front, before she turned around and went down the stairs. She retrieved the key from the kitchen counter and was out the back door, brushing past the ferns, her bare feet treading the wet grass to the art center. The rain had stopped, replaced by a chilly wind, and Kiva shivered as she ascended the steps and unlocked the doors. Swinging them open, she turned on the light, blinking rapidly, and let her eyes adjust to the brightness. She looked around then, and her eyes paused at the rectangular table in the center of the room. She moved to it, raising her hand to run her fingers over the scratches and stains where years of memories had been created on its surface. She sank into the stool beside it and started to open the envelope. Two letters slid out and the familiar whiff of Viola's perfume drifted upwards to her. Kiva picked up the one with her name and unfolded the crease.

Dear Kiva,

The purpose of this letter is to share with you things I don't have the courage to say aloud. I know at times I came across as cold to you, but it's because I was protecting myself, hence the reason for this letter now.

I want to begin by thanking you. Thank you for coming to visit me. I know that I had no right to ask this of you, that I wasn't entitled to it, but I had no idea that when I sent the request and then you actually came, that your visit would bring a certain kind of peace I never knew I would gain, and for that I want to apologize. I'm sorry I wasn't there for you. I'm sorry for all of the years I missed when you were growing up. I'm sorry, too, that I couldn't love you the way a mother should. But here's the thing I've learned about love. It doesn't become real until you've suffered and sacrificed yourself in its path, and I know that you and I have both suffered in our own ways. I admitted to you that I tried to have you aborted, but I never told you the reason that made me stop. It's because I knew the exact moment you were conceived. I felt you, your fiery little spirit, and it was the most overwhelming experience of my life. It was both beautiful and spiritual and took me by complete surprise. Your soul connected with mine in a way that I didn't completely understand at the time. And then I became terrified because there were so many overpowering voices surrounding yours that it got lost in my pain and betrayal. I gave you up as a result, not because I never loved you—I did and I do—but because I didn't love myself enough to deserve you. I severed you and everyone else around you from my life, but I realize now with the glimpse your visit gave me that I want that to change. I know that I'm not ready to visit you there, but I'm going to try to work hard on that and to work on myself. I know that I have a lot of buried pain to let go, but in the meantime—and if you agree—then perhaps we can begin by meeting halfway in the world somewhere. It'll be a start. What do you say?

With love and gratitude,

Viola

Enclosed is a letter for Naomi and a check to help with your application for art school. I see wonderful accomplishments in your future.

Kiva released a trembling breath and stood up from the table, leaving the letters behind. She walked over to the French doors and flicked off the light. Stepping outside, she sank down to the steps of the deck and tucked her arms under her knees. She peered out at the dark yard until her eyes could make out the silhouettes of bamboo stalks, the *pulu* tree, and beyond that the water tank. The memory of her and Ry atop the tank came to mind, and she closed her eyes in anguish as the tears gathered and slipped under her lashes. She held onto the image of his face with his piercing brown eyes and slashed scar, crooked grin and dark stubble, and hoped she would never, ever forget. Leaning against the deck rail, she cried into the quiet night until her body became listless and she eventually fell asleep. It was here where Naomi found her at dawn, curled into herself on the wooden floor. Kiva slowly blinked and opened her eyes as Naomi gently stroked the hair away from her face.

"Hey," Naomi spoke softly. "You're shivering."

Kiva rose and launched herself in her arms, burying her head in her chest. Naomi held her tightly as the sky turned pastel. She moved her head and together they watched the sun peak over the trees.

Her voice quivered with emotion when she spoke. "I didn't know it was possible to hurt this much."

"The hurt we feel when we lose someone is a measure of how much we love them," Naomi answered softly.

"I keep going over the same questions in my head, but I can't find any answers," Kiva murmured. "Why him? Why this way? Claire told me it started off as a robbery but then they began to taunt Ry because of his Arab ethnicity." A tear slipped down her cheek. "My heart breaks to know that hate-filled words were the last thing he heard. We had plans.

We had dreams. We wanted to get married. We wanted to travel. But now he's gone."

"Ry's not gone, Kiva. He's closer to you now than he ever was before."

Kiva shook her head. "I can't feel him though."

"That's because your heart is broken. Where he is, there's no pain and there's no heartbreak, only love. And I know without a doubt that he's loving you right now."

Kiva's throat tightened. "Do you really believe that?"

"I do, and someday you will, too. Someday you will feel it and you will know. This physical life and the life in the spiritual realms are closer than we can ever imagine. I believe his death emulated the kind of life he was trying so hard to lead, a life lived for others in a world where people will pull you down and try to crush you. He died so Claire could live. It's as simple and as painful as that."

Kiva heaved a shuddering sigh and watched in silence as the sun rose, radiating the bamboo trees that surrounded her.

CHAPTER THIRTY-EIGHT

Kiva leaned away from the sketch she had just completed and released a deep breath. Her lips tipped up into a soft smile. She'd done it. It had taken her six months to create a portrait that conveyed the kind of raw emotion she'd perceived at the exhibition in London, but she'd finally accomplished it. Sadness. Serenity. Hope. She'd captured each one delicately. Lifting the art work gently, she placed it together with her portfolio and application form, and sealed them inside an envelope. A gentle breeze blew in through the windows of the art center, bringing with it the sounds from the café, a child's raucous laughter, and the stirrings of the birthday song. A family was celebrating a first birthday and Kiva knew Hana and Naomi were running around tending to them. She stood and grabbed the envelope and headed outside.

Entering the house, she looked around for the keys to the truck. When she found them on the kitchen counter, she limped to the driveway.

She called out to Naomi as she was walking back up the pathway, her hands full. "I'll be back, Naomi!"

"Where are you going?"

"I need to mail something in town. I'll be quick."

"Alright then, drive safe."

"I will."

Kiva adjusted the seat of the truck and cranked the engine. She rolled the window down and backed up. The wind whipped the hair around her face as she traveled down the dirt path before she eased the truck onto the main road. As she began to pick up speed, she inhaled deeply and gripped the steering wheel. Her palms were damp with perspiration and her stomach cramped with nervousness when she contemplated what she was about to do.

Reaching the town's main post office, she parked the vehicle along the street and hopped out. Climbing the steps to the main door, she let herself in, and stood in line. Once she reached the front of the queue, she placed the envelope on the counter, paid for registered mail, and watched as the young man took her parcel away. Kiva hesitated for a moment before she turned to leave, hoping with everything she had that she'd done enough.

CHAPTER THIRTY-NINE

**The University of Hawai'i,
Hilo**

May 01, 2010
Mativa Mau
P.O. Box 8104
Apia, Samoa

Dear Ms. Mau,
We are pleased to inform you of your admission in the Art (B.A.) program at the University of Hawai'i's Art Department at Hilo for the 2010 fall semester. We congratulate you on your achievement and look forward to welcoming you to our community.

Enclosed herewith, you will find documents pertaining to the university and the next steps of the admission process. Enclosed also is information regarding international students, orientation, and application for student housing.

Again, we congratulate you and wish you all the best for your continued success.

Sincerely,
Maryann Kahale
Director of Admissions

EPILOGUE

The ocean felt cool against her ankles. Warm sand trickled between Kiva's toes, and the salty breeze tossed her hair around as she treaded the water's edge. She glanced down and saw a galaxy before her, stretching for miles on end. Pieces of coral and broken shells dotted the shoreline, shimmering like stars in the moonlight. It looked like a universe, reflecting the one above her, and she was suddenly reminded of the sketches she'd drawn years ago, depicting a star system very similar to this, where words had been strung into poems, and the poems had brought her comfort. A wave came unbidden and changed the pattern, and Kiva was worried for a moment. She didn't want anything to disappear, but then when the wave retreated, the brightness came back, winking as if to tease her. She smiled in relief. Something caught her eye in the distance, something that didn't fit. She walked to it and her breath caught when she recognized what it was. Bending down, she picked up the shell and turned it over in her hands. Her fingers went immediately to its lips as she tried to pry it open. The clam cracked, revealing the dark pearl inside.

Kiva came awake on an inhale of breath. Her heart pounded in her chest as she gazed up at the ceiling of her old room. Her mouth was dry and she swallowed to relieve it. Rising from her bed, she grabbed her art book and limped downstairs.

Her pulse calmed as soon as she entered the art center and dragged in its familiar scent. A noise drew her attention outside where she could hear Naomi talking with someone. She ignored them and started to sketch. She drew galaxies with stars and planets until her eyes tired and her hand shook. Finally, she blew out a rough breath and closed her eyes. When she opened them a few minutes later, a young man stood braced at the front door. "Hey," Tui said, a faint smile on his lips.

"You're back," Kiva said, startled.

"Yup. I arrived a couple days ago."

She stood and walked toward him. "I hear congratulations are in order. Your parents must be so happy."

Tui hid a shy smile. "Thanks. They are. I heard you graduated from university as well."

Kiva waved her hand dismissively in the air. "That was months ago. It's old news now."

"Naomi doesn't seem to think so. She kept talking about it outside."

She laughed softly. "So what are your plans now that you've earned a degree in business?"

"Sleep," he huffed out a laugh. "All I want to do is sleep. And then when I wake up"—he shrugged—"who knows?"

She smiled up at him. "I'm so proud of you, Tui. And I can't believe how much you've grown!"

His eyes locked onto hers, their brown depths softening. "I'm not the little boy you used to know, Kiva." He studied her for a moment before he tipped his head in the direction of the doors. "I'm going to walk out to the main road to catch the bus to the beach. Would you like to join me? I promise this time you can sit on my lap."

His mouth tilted up into a crooked grin that was so endearing it reminded her of one just like it from a long time ago. Kiva inhaled sharply at the memory. He waited for her, and she looked up at his face, which had matured into hard edges and dark stubble, his shoulders now broadened. She knew what he was asking, and if she went with him, everything would change.

"Do you want me to wait for you while you get ready?" he asked patiently.

He had no idea how weighted that question was.

She finally nodded.

He beamed. "Sweet. I'll go find Mau and say hello. I haven't seen him since I got back." He backed up a few steps before he turned and jogged down the stairs.

Kiva stared after him. What had she just agreed to? Her eyes darted around desperately until they landed on a canvas hanging on the far wall. She walked to it and raised her hand, tracing each letter and word until they clouded behind tears. Kiva touched one of the fluttering bamboo leaves, and then she took a deep breath to compose herself, and walked outside.

Do you know what you are?
You are a manuscript of a divine letter.
You are a mirror reflecting a noble face.
This universe is not outside of you.
Look inside yourself;
everything that you want,
you are already that.
Rumi

The end.

ACKNOWLEDGMENTS

Special thanks go to a myriad of people who helped bring this story to life, and for those who supported this endeavor on the sidelines so that it could be possible.

Max Dobson of The Polished Pen. My editor and second-, third-, and fourth eye. You are the best safety net any writer could ask for.

Galumalemana Steven Percival. Thank you for your artistic knowledge and for responding to all of my hounding questions. Your answers breathed life into Kiva and Mau. Any mistakes or elaborations are my own.

Ryan Kivitz. Thank you for providing me a glimpse into your life prior to and during Samoa. You are an example of transformation and are an inspiration for youth everywhere.

Tautala Asaua-Pesa. Sincere thanks for sharing your expert knowledge on Lapita pottery in the South Pacific.

Siuomatautu Tapelu. My go-to nurse for all things medical. Thankyou for patiently responding to all my questions.

Selvi Adaikkalam. Thank you for your piercing insight and advice.

Mojan Sami. I'm in awe of your talent. Thank you for designing the beautiful cover.

Sahar Sabati-Safai. Your encouragement raises me up, and from one sister-writer to another, thank you for your never-ending support. I love knowing that I can always turn to you because you *totally get it*.

To the CafeCafe group/soul sisters. Thank you for listening, for embracing, and encouraging, always.

To my wonderful family. Thank you. Toda raba. Merci. Thank you for your love, laughter, and understanding.

And finally but certainly not the least—to my readers. A tremendous *fa'afetai lava* for your personal messages, reviews, and overall support on social media. It is my hope that Kiva and Ry's story inspires faith, strength, and hope even in the most challenging situations.

With warmest gratitude,
Sieni

ABOUT THE AUTHOR

Sieni A.M. is a world traveler, avid reader, and aspiring writer. She was born and raised in the South Pacific, graduated from the University of Canterbury, and is currently living in Australia with her husband and two daughters.

CPSIA information can be obtained
at www.ICGtesting.com
Printed in the USA
LVHW052311111219
640173LV00006B/1109/P